T. R. Wilson was born and brought up in [illegible] on the edge of the Fens. He attended the University of East Anglia, and his love of East Anglia – its landscape, people and history – has always been central to his life and work. He submitted his first novel, MASTER OF MORHOLM, for publication at the age of twenty-three, at which time he was a student on the University of East Anglia MA Course in Creative Writing, under Malcolm Bradbury and Angela Carter. His MA submission was part of the novel which was later published in 1989 as TREADING ON SHADOWS. His five most recent historical sagas, A GREEN HILL FAR AWAY, HEARTSEASE ('a beautifully written new novel' *Fife Free Press*), HESTER VERNEY ('a lovely book' Reay Tannahill), ROSES IN DECEMBER ('a spellbinding summer read' *Peterborough Evening Telegraph*) and JOHN TWOPENNY ('filled to bursting with memorable characters' *Peterborough Evening Telegraph*) are all available from Headline, as are his three thrillers, PURGATORY, CLOSE TO YOU and FREEZING POINT. He was shortlisted for *The Sunday Times* Young Writer of the Year Award for 1992. He and his partner Mary-Anne live in Peterborough with two cats.

*Also by T. R. Wilson*

A Green Hill Far Away
Heartsease
Hester Verney
Roses in December
John Twopenny

# The Strawberry Sky

T. R. Wilson

KNIGHT

First published in 1996
by HEADLINE BOOK PUBLISHING

First published in paperback in 1996
by HEADLINE BOOK PUBLISHING

This edition published 2000 by
Knight an imprint of Caxton Publishing Group

10 9 8 7 6 5 4 3 2 1



ISBN 1 84067 190 4

Typeset by CBS, Felixstowe, Suffolk

Printed and bound in Great Britain by
Mackays of Chatham PLC, Chatham, Kent

Caxton Publishing Group
20 Bloomsbury Street
London
WC1B 3QA

For Beryl and Cyril

# Part One

*July 1938*

# ONE

## 1

One disadvantage of falling for the boy next door, Stella Tranter thought, was that he didn't disappear from your life when you fell out with him. He stayed right next door.

This was something that was never mentioned in the films; those folksy American films where the boy next door was a sort of modern equivalent of a knight in shining armour. But then in those films the heroine usually ended up marrying him and living happily ever after, and Stella wouldn't have married Harry Fisk if you'd held her under water until she did it. And that wasn't the pettish resentment of a still-burning flame. Stella was rather good at lying to herself, but not in this case. The plain truth was that she couldn't stand him.

Of course it was easier for those Hollywood moonshiners, even if they did fall out, because they all lived in enormous houses about half a mile apart and you probably couldn't even see who was sitting on next door's front porch without a pair of binoculars. Whereas in Corbett Street next door's front doorstep was a mere matter of inches from your own and when, as on this stifling summer evening, you were standing at the street door hoping that the last breath of fresh air in London might waft your way, your chances of avoiding the boy next door were pretty slim.

Especially when the boy next door couldn't or wouldn't get the message. When you'd made it clear that you didn't expect to be jumped like an all-in wrestler on the strength of one trip to the

Gaumont to see *Snow White and the Seven Dwarfs*, when you'd made it even clearer that you didn't find the prospect of watching him play dominoes in the Cat and Fiddle irresistibly appealing, when you'd made it clearest of all that you could just about put up with him examining his handkerchief after he had blown his nose but that being invited to have a look for yourself was beyond the limit – well, after all that, surely most men would have called it quits, and tried to keep out of your way. It could be done, with a will. Even in a place like Corbett Street, where the only privacy was in your own head – and not always there. They could have timed their entrances and exits so as not to coincide and so on: made the best of a bad job, until time softened the awkwardness.

But no. Not Harry Fisk. One of the many things about him she hadn't bargained for was his monumental obtuseness. Wooden head, brass neck, thick skin, that was Harry. And nice eyes, unfortunately, even though there was nothing behind them: it was on account of the eyes that she had gone out with him in the first place. That was the trouble with men, a lot of them did have nice eyes. Nice eyes were pretty much standard issue. She ought to remember that next time.

If there ever was a next time. Just now Stella couldn't have been less interested.

But not so Harry Fisk, who wouldn't leave her alone. Plainly he thought that being told to get lost, jump in the lake and go boil his head were signs that he was still in with a chance. But he didn't press it: he seemed to be relying on his sheer presence to work its mysterious magic on her. If she went out to the back yard, there he was on the other side of the gas-tarred fence, pretending to hammer something. Anything would do. He hammered the water-butt. He would have hammered Pop Fisk's pigeons if they'd let him. If she went out to the street to call her little siblings in for tea, out he popped too: he didn't have any little brothers or sisters, but that didn't stop him. He haunted her like a persistent, daft ghost.

And as she stood at the open street door this evening, leaning against the jamb and longing for a breeze, Stella became aware at the periphery of her vision that Harry Fisk was standing at *his* open street door.

He was being subtle about it so far: she could just see his nose peeking past the wall and the toes of his boots on the step. Now, the question was whether it was worth staying here in hope of a breeze, and running the risk of fresh approaches from Harry. There certainly didn't seem to be any air this evening, and just as certainly there was nothing much to see on the other side of the street. Corbett Street, in fact, didn't really have another side. They had demolished a lot of the houses there when their tendency to fall down had become chronic, and the rest of the space was taken up by Dicky Dixon's scrapyard, which made the view a touch monotonous at best. She couldn't turn her head to the left because that was where bits of Harry were protruding, and to the right there was only the turning into identical Gordon Street where a few women were sitting out on the pavement on bentwood chairs, fanning themselves with their aprons and looking out for tattle. You could go mad looking at this view day after day, Stella thought without rancour. Normally she didn't mind: it was life, and you took what pleasure you could; there were a lot of people worse off than themselves. Her father had worked hard to bring them here to this reasonably decent part of Hackney from the much grimmer streets of Docklands, and she remembered well what they had been like. But there were times when counting your blessings just didn't help and this was one of them. Not only was there Happy Harry next door to contend with, Stella was out of work. The draper's shop where for a year she had enjoyed that rarest of luxuries, regular employment, had closed down last month when the owner had added fiddling the books to drinking the profits. Since then she had found nothing but a little casual laundry work – a morning here and there filling in for women who were having their annual baby; and though her father would never reproach her for bringing so little money into the house, as he blamed international capitalism for it anyway, Stella herself felt it keenly. She wanted desperately to help the family's permanently stretched budget; and if she wanted only a little less desperately to have a few bob for herself, well, she was not yet twenty, and only human.

No, this was definitely not one of the high points of Stella Tranter's life; and the dusty street with its roof of overheated cloud that refused to break into a thunderstorm was not much of a reviver of the spirits. All you could say for it was that it was preferable just now to the sweltering house behind her, where her father and a couple of his cronies were setting the world to rights over a bottle of Bass. For weeks now all the talk had been of Czechoslovakia, and whether there would be a war over that unpronounceable place. The trenches being dug in the London parks suggested there might well be: Jack Tranter thought otherwise. It would be a capitalist war, he said, and the workers would only have to down tools to end it. For her part, Stella had had a bellyful of Mr Chamberlain and Herr Hitler and all their doings. Her home was like a small kiln full of earnest dispute and she was bored with the whole business.

And now there were developments on the Harry front. The nose and the boots were inching forward and at the same time Harry let out something that she supposed was meant to be a lovelorn sigh.

Stella began to shuffle backwards into the doorway, and then it occurred to her that the pair of them must look like the little figures on one of those decorative barometers. Mr Rain and Mrs Shine . . . Oh, the whole thing was ridiculous. She came to a decision, and stepped outside.

'Harry . . .'

Clearly this was the last thing he had been expecting: he jumped like a nervous kitten. Stella saw that he was in a high state of Brylcreem. The comb had left marks like tramlines on his head.

She steeled herself.

'Harry, can't you and me be friends?' she said.

'Well . . . we are, aren't we?' he said, after gaping a minute.

'You know what I mean. It's awkward living next door to each other, after what's happened, but let's just make the best of it, eh?'

'How do you mean?' Probably he couldn't help it, but it was awful the way he wouldn't look you full in the face. He talked to you as if he was trying to sell you something shady.

'I mean . . . you don't have to keep hanging around like this. You know. You should go out with other girls. It's a waste. There's plenty of other girls who'd like to go out with you, I know.'

'Yeh. I might just do that.'

'Good.'

'Make you jealous, would it?'

She looked at him to see if he was serious.

He *was* serious.

'I just think it'd be best,' she said, persevering. 'Because it's silly, going on like this.'

'I bet you wouldn't really like it if I went out with somebody else,' Harry said, in his most smirking sideways fashion. 'Would yer?' He winked.

This wasn't going at all to plan. 'Look – Harry – I like you, but we ain't suited to one another—'

'I like you too.' He winked again.

'Oh, for crying out loud, can't you get it into your head I don't want to go out with you?'

Harry looked knowing. 'Well, you would say that, wouldn't you?' He produced a cigarette and lit it, smoking it between his teeth rather than his lips. That was another thing, she thought.

'Harry—'

'How about the flicks, Friday night?'

'No, thank you.' She summoned up her last reserves of self-control. 'And please don't ask me again.'

'Not till next week, you mean,' Harry said, and winked again.

With a despairing groan she fled from him, into the house, leaving him smoking gangster-style and looking highly pleased with himself.

* * *

# 2

The bottles of Bass had been drunk and the ills of the world satisfactorily discussed, and now her father's friends made ready to leave. For a lot of men in the neighbourhood this would merely have been the prelude to making a night of it, but Jack Tranter was a sober man – sometimes, Stella thought, a little too sober. Kind and gentle-handed, he seldom smiled or laughed outright. He said goodbye to his comrades at the door with a serious handshake and a few last words about the struggle, and then returned to his chair and his newspaper. Stella, clearing away the bottles and glasses, wondered briefly whether she should say something to him about Harry Fisk and what an unbearable bind he was becoming. But experience had made her wary of going to her father with any problem that was not actually life-threatening. Not that he was careless or dismissive. He would listen with great patience and attention, his blue eyes, young and fresh in his narrow lined face, dwelling thoughtfully on you; and then in the kindest, softest manner possible he would demonstrate to you that your difficulty, troublesome as it no doubt seemed, was really very small beer compared with all the dreadful things that were happening in the world. If he did not go so far as to make you feel guilty for having a problem, he made you chary of ever mentioning it.

So she left it, and helped her mother get the tea – which consisted of tea, bread, Echo margarine, a few radishes, and a couple of penny slices of corned beef which Stella was painfully conscious would have been more if she had been in regular work. As a matter of course they went on her father's plate.

'Ain't you having a bit of that, Mum?'

'Oh, I'm not all that hungry.' Connie Tranter was so used to setting aside her own wants that the reply came automatically. She was a small, worn, pretty woman, with a sort of quiet grace about her: as a small child Stella had heard her grandfather call her mother 'princess' and had immediately fastened on to an idea that that was exactly what she was – a genuine blue-blooded princess who had somehow ended up marrying an East End cabinet-maker. 'Princess Muck,' her mother would laugh, 'I left me crown down the pop shop,' and sometimes to amuse Stella and the other children she would parade with a blanket round her shoulders and a pastry cutter on her head, waving loftily. The fun and liveliness were still there, lurking at the corners of her mother's eyes and mouth, but they were seldom given free rein. Jack Tranter had grown more solemn as he grew older and though he did not frown on frivolity, that regretful look would come over his face as if you were dancing on the graves of the oppressed.

'Are you all right, love?' her mother said now, with a quick look at Stella.

'Why shouldn't I be?'

'You just seem a bit on the quiet side, that's all.'

Stella was instantly contrite. That was the trouble with those who gave you unconditional love: you could take out your temper on them with no fear of consequences.

'Oh, it's only . . . I've just been telling that daft Harry Fisk where to go, and he won't.'

'Is he bothering you?'

'Oh, nothing like that. Not really. He's just so thick-headed . . . What is it about some men? Do they really reckon they're God's gift? What do you have to do to convince 'em you ain't interested? I think if I pushed Happy Harry under a steamroller he'd still come up smiling and saying I was only teasing.'

'Dear. Talk about turning him down flat.' Her mother's chuckle came bubbling up. It was infectious and for some minutes they giggled together in the little scullery like schoolgirls.

Then Stella's mood, not untypically, took an abrupt plunge again and she burst out, 'Oh, God, perhaps it would save trouble if I just gave in and said I'd marry him.'

'Marry Harry?' her mother said, and nearly started them off again.

'No,' Stella said, laughing distressfully, 'I mean yes, maybe. A lot of girls would, I suppose. Perhaps it's my fault. Perhaps I set me sights too high.'

'Well, Harry Fisk is all right. But I wouldn't call him much of a catch.'

'Not just him. I mean, look at Edie. She met Fred and they went courting and then they got married and had a kid, chop, chop, no fuss. I envy 'em that in a way.' Stella omitted to mention her opinion of her elder sister's husband whom she would have jumped into the river to avoid: she was feeling heartsore and restless, and she could argue black was white when this mood was on her. 'So perhaps I'm going about it all wrong.'

'Going about what all wrong, love?'

'Oh, I don't know – life,' Stella said vaguely, wrapping a towel round the base of the teapot where it leaked: it had leaked for so long that she thought of this as part of the natural process of making tea. 'I mean, perhaps people don't have to be suited to get married. D'you think?'

'Perhaps not,' her mother said after a moment. 'I think they've got to love each other to start with, though. There's got to be *something* there . . . Anyway, what's put this in your head? Is it because you're not bringing in so much money now?'

'It doesn't help. We are skint, aren't we?'

'We manage. God almighty, don't go marrying Harry Fisk just because of a bit of corned beef! I'd never be able to face the stuff again!'

'No,' Stella said, laughing. 'No, I know. Sorry, Mum. Got the mulligrubs, that's all.'

'Something'll turn up soon. You'll see.'

Would it? Stella thought. Normally she was a firm believer that it would. But suddenly it struck her, from the unthinking way her mother said those words, that she must have been saying them for years and years. Perhaps you went on saying it even when you had stopped believing it?

A terrible thought. Stella dismissed it. She tried to dismiss too the thought of Happy Harry and the dismal attentions she would have to endure until – until when? Until he simply got tired of it? It might be months.

They sat down to tea: Stella, her parents, her fifteen-year-old sister Dot – as gigantic as her name was diminutive – at the table, the two younger children, Archie and Lennie, taking their tea on their laps. The street door stood open, as it did in all but the coldest weather; and according to custom likewise, when there was a knock on the jamb and a cry of 'Coo-oo?' the children hollered out 'We've having our tea!' The folk of Corbett Street were always in and out of one another's houses, but mealtimes were universally agreed to be sacrosanct.

Where most people, however, would have called out 'Sorry!' and beat a retreat, these visitors waltzed straight in. They were like that. When it came to being thick-skinned, Auntie Bea and Uncle Will made Happy Harry look like a model of subtlety.

'You get on with yer tea! Don't let us stop yer!' screeched out Auntie Bea, a long cawing crane of a woman with a scraggy neck and feet like a policeman's.

'Come in, why don't you?' muttered Stella's father, bent over his plate. The milk of human kindness ran a little thin in him when it came to his brother Will, who lived with his chaotic wife and brood two streets away. Jack Tranter took life seriously: it was – his favourite word – a struggle. Uncle Will and Auntie Bea, who careered across the surface of life, bouncing innocently back from every obstacle, were a standing affront to his view of the world.

'Don't mind us – we'll sit quiet till you've done,' said Auntie Bea. She propped herself on the sill of the open window, snatching up Stella's mother's knitting and busily applying herself to it. Stella intercepted an unhappy look from her mother. Bea would have that in a hopeless snarl in two minutes flat. As a child several home-made gifts from Auntie Bea had come Stella's way, and she had particularly vivid memories of a pullover that clung round her armpits like a hairy lifebelt. Her mother said Bea was the only woman she knew who could do needlework with a hammer and chisel.

'What yer got there then? Eh?' Uncle Will, his horn-rims glinting and his spectacularly ill-fitting false teeth juggling round his smiling mouth, advanced on little Lennie. 'What you got, eh?'

'Radishes,' answered Lennie.

'*Have* yer? Eh? You got radishes, have yer? Eh?' Though addressed to a child, this was a fair sample of Uncle Will's conversational style. It was all at booming volume too, bass to Bea's treble. When the two of them talked in unison, as they frequently did, it was enough to rattle the teacups.

'We're off early tomorrow morning so we thought we'd come and say ta-ta to you,' Auntie Bea hollered, knitting needles flailing. 'The kids wanted to come but we packed 'em off to bed 'cos I said to 'em, you've got to be up at the crack of sparrows tomorrow. All excited they are, can't do nothing with 'em, can you, Will?'

'Can't do anything with 'em, little beggars,' bellowed Uncle Will; then, presenting his protruding smile to Archie, 'Are you a little beggar, eh? Are you a little beggar? Are yer?'

'No,' murmured Archie.

'*Ain't* yer? *Ain't* yer?'

'We shall be gone till September-time, depending on the apples,' Auntie Bea said. 'Flo Carberry next door, she's keeping an eye on the house for us and feeding Mopsy.'

'Looks like the weather'll be nice for you, anyway,' Stella's mother said.

'Ooh, we always get beautiful weather up there,' Uncle Will said. 'Get stripped, and you come back brown all over.'

Stella suffered a loss of appetite at this image. Uncle Will, a stubby leathery little man like a run-to-seed jockey, was nobody's Adonis.

'Ah, beautiful sunburn you get,' Auntie Bea agreed. 'Beautiful sunburn. D'you remember the summer before last, Will?'

The pair of them embarked on some deafening reminiscences of the summers they had spent fruit-picking in the fens. Everyone had heard them before, but that didn't bother Auntie Bea and Uncle Will, who were self-appointed ambassadors for this seasonal work which had become more and more popular in the district in recent years. Formerly they had spent the summers hop-picking in Kent, but there was too much competition for that sort of work nowadays, they said – gyppos and what have you. But up in the fenland, around the town of Wisbech, there were miles and miles of strawberry fields and orchards, and the fruit-growers needed all the labour they could get. The picking season lasted longer too: when the strawberries and cherries were over there were the plums and then the apples, and sometimes there was work till October if you wanted it.

This was no small consideration for Uncle Will. Unlike Stella's father, he had no regular employment: a week's building work here, a few days at the docks there, was his way of getting by. The annual trip to the fenland, in fact, was probably the most secure time of the family's year. They came back each autumn nut brown, temporarily flush, and full of praise for the experience. It was really a working holiday, they said: healthy exercise and clean air and communal sing-songs under the summer sun, with money in your pockets at the end of it. And the fen fruit-growers were fair dealers, they said, not like that Kentish lot who would skin you alive as soon as look at you.

The idea had never much appealed to Stella. She had no high opinion of the country, even when it was within reasonable reach of the city; and as for East Anglia, or wherever the fens were, she thought it sounded like the ends of the earth. But today, though she had heard it all before, she found herself half-listening, and then wholly listening, to Bea and Will's glowing stories of their orchard summers. And when tea was over and the cloth cleared away and the children turfed out to play, she found herself to her own surprise saying, 'Uncle Will, whereabouts do you stay up there? D'you have to camp out?'

'Some do, gel. Some rent rooms in the villages. But they've got a ready-made place now. A lot of the growers all clubbed together and had it built. Just like that Butlin's place it is. Cabins, right in the middle of the orchards.'

'Huts, you mean,' Stella's father said frowning. 'They make you live in a lot of wooden huts while you do their work for them.' He was always a little sour on the subject of Bea and Will's fruit-picking, for obscure reasons to do with the obstacle to the revolution presented by the peasantry.

'Smashing they are. Standpipe and washing-lines and everything,' went on Uncle Will, taking no notice. 'Place called Monks Bridge. Now the camp's just outside the village, as you take the Wisbech road, only it's not the first turning because that's a farm track and if you go wrong there . . .' Uncle Will was off, waving his arms about. He loved giving long detailed descriptions of how to get somewhere.

'And the kids,' Auntie Bea cut in, outshouting him, 'you should see 'em! They have the time of their lives! Like little Red Indians!'

'You want to mind they don't go and fall in the river,' Stella's father said, filling his pipe.

'Ooh, no, they're looked after,' Auntie Bea said with satisfaction. 'While you're doing the picking, all the kids are looked after so you don't have to worry about 'em. Last year it was these young fellas from Cambridge. Lovely boys, all in shorts.'

'University fellas,' Uncle Will said. 'Not stuck up, though. Not lah-di-dah.'

'Why on earth would they do a job like that?' Stella asked.

'Class guilt,' said her father.

'It's a voluntary thing,' Uncle Will said. 'They don't get no money for it. They come and look after the nippers just to help out.'

'Soothing their consciences,' Stella's father said. 'Give the workers a pat on the head and maybe the day won't come. They're the worst sort.'

'And I'll tell you what,' said Uncle Will, who merely smiled vacantly through his brother's political pronouncements as if he were talking Dutch, 'if they do have a war, it's a lot safer up there. We shall make sure our little 'uns are out of London if it comes, don't you worry.'

'Will the children really be safer if they send them away, do you reckon?' Stella's mother said anxiously. 'I don't know whether I could bear to part with 'em.'

'Nowhere'll be safe,' her father said. 'Look at Spain.'

'Oh, it won't happen anyway. Who wants another war?' Stella said. Sometimes lately she felt that people enjoyed making each other's flesh creep with awful prophecies of war, and her own position on the subject was somewhere between optimism and fatalism; but she knew that this kind of talk greatly distressed her mother. Connie Tranter was cursed with a powerful imagination: sometimes as a child Stella had woken in the middle of the night to find herself being wordlessly embraced by her mother, and only when she was grown did she learn that these pleasant visitations were caused by nightmares of maternal danger and loss.

Besides, she wanted to know more about the fruit-picking. And Uncle Will and Auntie Bea were happy to tell her: they spoke – or shouted – of the acres of orchards, the scent of the strawberry fields, the camaraderie at the end of the day when the pickers, Londoners all or nearly all, gathered with jugs of beer for a knees-up under the starlight. They made it sound attractive. To someone who had no regular work, who felt herself to be just another mouth to feed in a crowded, sweltering, nerve-taxing household, and who was living next door to a pixilated chump who thought he was Ronald Colman, it sounded very attractive indeed.

Stella had never been the sort to think long and hard. It only needed the merest prod to tip her over the brink of decision, and soon it came. Uncle Will peered at her through his horn-rims, struck no doubt by the fact that someone was expressing an interest rather than trying to shut him up, and said, 'You fancy coming along, do you, gel?'

'Well – I don't know – I wouldn't mind,' Stella said; and then the whole force of the notion leaped out at her. To be away from Happy Harry! To be away from the dusty heat and war talk! To fend for herself for a while and not feel like a burden! To jump on a train and be whisked out of the city to something completely new!

The train.

Stella had given her mother her last sixpence this morning. She plummeted.

'It's a nice idea,' she said, 'but I ain't got the fare.'

'Ah, you don't want to worry about that, gel,' Uncle Will said. 'I got a win on the gee-gees this week. We can get your ticket.'

'We'll have no charity, thank you very much,' her father said. 'If Stella did want to go, we'd pay her fare ourselves.'

'Naow, it ain't charity,' Uncle Will said. 'Just call it a sub. You'll have earned your fare and more in your first week o' picking, gel. You come along, you'll love it! There'll be plenty of room in our cabin. I wrote off to the farmer who does the letting and bespoke the same cabin what we had last year.' This word seemed to please Uncle Will. 'Bespoke it. All ready for us.'

'It ain't as if she'll be on her own, Connie,' Auntie Bea said. 'She'll be with us, you know.'

Stella's mother did not seem to find this as reassuring as she might have, but she looked at Stella with a small smile and said, 'Should you like to go, love?'

There was so much of her mother in that look and that smile. The strong love that said she would miss her if she went: the strong love likewise that said she wanted her to be happy and would be on her side whatever she chose to do.

And Stella did want to go: for her the suddenness of the proposal was a point in its favour; a long-matured plan would not have captured her as this out-of-the-blue prospect had. And the more she thought about it, the more she could see in its favour, as is often the case with something we have already decided to do. There was nothing against it, indeed, except the fact of having to leave her mother. Her father too, and the rest; but the relationship with her mother was special. Stella was closer to her than anyone. And though she had seen a man killed in a pub knife fight, though she had gained her first insight into sex at nine years old when a sailor with his tart had given her sixpence to keep watch outside the doorway where they were at it, though she had eaten quite a raw and salty diet of experience from an early age, Stella had never spent a night away from home. The Tranter family was close-knit; and if she had lately begun to feel it as stiflingly, oppressively so, she was hardly aware of it.

No, if her mother had really wanted her not to go, Stella would have stayed. But her mother, sensitive to Stella's itch of frustration, was staunch. 'It would do you a power of good,' she said. 'You've been looking a mite peaky. And there doesn't seem to be any work going round here at the moment. I think it's a good idea.'

Of course there was no question of Connie Tranter going herself. Jack Tranter might be a man of advanced views, but they had not advanced as far as learning to make his own dinner. He was a radical of a dour, manly, puritanical sort: he tolerated but did not approve of the smothered gaiety in Connie that sometimes broke out in unwifely frivolities, dinners burnt while she entertained kids in the street with games of her own devising, fits of uncontrollable giggles when the union representative who looked like a surprised walrus came to tea. It was clear that he thought her a less-than-perfect helpmate as it was: for his wife to have gone away for the summer and left him to look after himself would have been a revolution indeed, and not the sort he favoured.

It was the matter of her father's consent, in fact, that was the chief obstacle to Stella's going. Plainly he did not think much of the idea. The fruit-picking sounded to him like gang labour, and he muttered about Tolpuddle. But then something happened. And afterwards Stella would remember that, in the end, it was her father who practically insisted that she should go to the orchards that summer.

It was the matter of charity, or what her father called charity. Uncle Will and Auntie Bea stuck cheerfully to their notion of lending Stella the train fare until she got her first wage from the fruit-picking, but Stella's father wouldn't have it. Perhaps his motives were not entirely pure – his dislike of Uncle Will probably got mixed up with his principles – but the end result was the same. Stella would have her train fare all right, but he would supply it from his club money: never let it be said that a member of his family took handouts. From disapproving of her going at all, Jack Tranter painted himself into a proud corner where it was a point of honour that she would go whether she liked it or not.

So it was decided, except for a brief wavering on the part of

Stella's sister Dot, who came out of her customary torpor long enough to wonder whether she wanted to go too. But Dot was in a situation rather like Stella's in reverse: she had a yen for a boy down the street, and taking her presence away from him for a whole summer might be more than he could bear. Dot would stay.

'It was in me tea leaves!' Auntie Bea shrilled before they left, with a promise to call for Stella in the morning. 'It was in me tea leaves that you'd be coming with us, gel!' The accuracy of Auntie Bea's tea leaves was uncanny. Whenever something occurred, Auntie Bea would suddenly remember that her tea leaves had forecast it.

'Well, at least it wasn't a dark stranger this time,' Stella's mother said, as they chipped a bit of the muck off Archie and Lennie before sending them to bed.

'Happy Harry's dark,' Stella said. 'And they don't come much stranger than him.' They laughed together, avoiding the subject of Stella's departure as long as they could.

'Ain't it daft?' her mother said at last, beginning to polish her father's boots for the morning. 'You're only going to the country and you'll be back at the end of the summer, and here I am feeling like . . .'

'I might be back before that,' Stella said, trying for lightness. 'If the local yokels don't like the look of me they might put me on the first train home.'

'It's funny, posh people don't seem to think anything of it. Send their kids away to boarding schools and what have you. Like they haven't got any feelings at all . . . You'll send us a letter when you get time, won't you?'

''Course I will, Mum. And a big basket of strawberries.'

Connie Tranter scrubbed at her cheeks for a moment; and then the mischievous smile dawned on her face. 'And if Happy Harry asks where you've gone,' she said, 'I'll tell him you've gone away to try and forget him, shall I?'

'To a monastery.'

'Nunnery, you mean.'

'No. A monastery. Now there you *would* be sure of a warm welcome.'

And they laughed again, like conspirators, and could only shake their heads when Jack Tranter wanted to know what was so funny.

## 3

The train that left King's Cross for Peterborough early the next morning was full of Londoners heading for the orchards, but Stella was very nearly not amongst them. She had managed to drag herself out of bed at the required unearthly hour: it was the journey from Hackney to King's Cross that had brought them within an ace of missing the train. Uncle Will and Auntie Bea were the sort of people who hurried slowly. Burdened with a medley of battered luggage and a trio of children who could scarcely have been kept in check with leads and muzzles, they showed signs of never getting there at all. There was a long hiatus at the bus stop when Auntie Bea found a pair of her vast drawers leaking from one of the suitcases: Bea had fits and demanded a comprehensive redistribution of the luggage whilst bus after bus passed them by. Even when they finally came struggling on to the platform with the guard's whistle blowing and the train on the point of jerking into motion, Auntie Bea had a sudden thought and stopped dead.

'Here! Did you bring a straw hat?' she squawked, dropping a bag or two in her abstraction. 'I never thought to remind you! You'll get sunstroke without a straw hat!'

Hasty as her packing had been, Stella had thought to include a straw hat. 'Half a dozen of 'em, now get on!' she cried, and scooping up the dropped bags she propelled the flapping figure of Auntie Bea on to the train by main force, hustled the rest of the family after her, and jumped aboard with seconds to spare.

Well, here she was, and it was hard to believe she was not still in bed and dreaming. No regrets, though: the moonlike face of

Happy Harry watching her from next door's top window as she left this morning made sure of that. There was no space for reflection, anyway, because getting themselves settled in the carriage was for Uncle Will and Auntie Bea a complex operation that involved everybody changing seats at least twice; and then Auntie Bea's drawers escaped again and Uncle Will, in holiday mood, scandalized her to shrieking point by waving them out of the window like a great beige flag. Meanwhile the two younger children, Cecil and Ivy, played as much merry hell as was possible in the confined space. Only nine-year-old Geoffrey was quiet: he was always quiet. Chin in hand he gazed out of the window at the suburbs of London slipping smokily by; and when the ticket collector braved the riotous carriage, he cast a wistful glance at Geoffrey, as if wishing all children were as good.

But Geoffrey was not especially good, not in Auntie Bea and Uncle Will's eyes. He was beloved, but disappointing. Where the Tranters came from, children were admired not for quietness and self-containment but for being full of beans. 'Cheeky' was a reprimand but also a tribute, and no one could call Geoffrey cheeky. 'I wish mine were as quiet!' neighbours would say, nodding at Geoffrey with narrowed eyes, not meaning it. His parents drew the blunter conclusion, apparently supported by discouraging reports from school, that he was backward. Stella was no shrinking violet herself, but she sometimes felt there was more to Geoffrey than met the eye, and that there was more intelligence behind his air of dull withdrawal than they gave him credit for. Auntie Bea's topsy-turvy household, where even the canary screamed at the top of its voice, was not after all a place for the naturally unassertive.

'Are you excited, Geoffrey?' she asked him.

He turned and nodded gravely, then returned his attention to the window.

'I've never been before. You'll have to show me where things are and what to do and everything.'

'Gawd, it's no good asking him, bless him!' crowed Auntie Bea. 'He doesn't even remember he's been before, do you, chicken?

'Course he doesn't. Here, gel, you want an 'ard-boiled?' With an improbable amount of rustling she produced provisions from a brown paper bag. Stella contented herself with a sandwich, but Uncle Will, spreading his handkerchief on his lap, made his way through a whole meal, starting with eggs and finishing with celery, his hypnotic dentures performing strenuously. The celery was a particular challenge: you saw it three times before it finally disappeared.

Accustomed only to day trips as far as Southend or Margate, Stella was surprised and then a little dismayed at the sight of so much country. Her father had once dragged her along to one of those films about the development of the Soviet Union that got him so excited, and now as the wheat fields grew larger and flatter she began to feel she had somehow strayed into one. Would they ever get there, or would this empty landscape just go on and on for ever like Russia? Her impatience was probably as much to do with the company of Cecil and Ivy, who for some reason had started a loud monotonous chant of 'Salvation Army, all gone barmy, all gone to heaven in a corned beef tin', as with the length of the journey; and it was little Geoffrey who pointed something out to her that lifted her spirits again.

'Look,' he whispered, tugging at her sleeve, 'nice clouds.'

And they *were* nice clouds: wonderful clouds, in fact, clouds such as she had never seen, or never noticed, at home. Massive, white and extravagant, they sailed slowly across a blue ocean of sky. They cast no shadow over the beauty of the summer day: they made it more beautiful. An absurd gladness filled her. She felt she was going to like it there.

The feeling continued after they had changed at Peterborough – Auntie Bea turning the comfortable five minutes between trains into a hair's-breadth affair by getting herself locked in the ladies' and having hysterics when the attendant shoulder-charged the door – and were on their way to Wisbech, the centre of the orchard country. Yes, Uncle Will said in answer to Stella's query, these *were* the fens; and she thought it best to conceal her surprise. Somehow she had pictured tracts of splashy bog with, at best, fruit trees ingeniously growing out of them like giant water lilies. Instead the flat wheatland gave way to a country that seemed to be one great orchard. Soft crowns of foliage melted away to the horizon in layer upon layer of rich colour, and here and there the trees would open up to reveal vistas of roses – roses only, growing in long gorgeously tinted rows as far as the eye could see and giving Stella a momentary, lightheaded impression that the people here lived on them, as lesser mortals might live on potatoes.

'Ah! Nearly there. I can smell the strawbug fields,' Uncle Will said. 'There's no smell like strawberries ripe for pickin'. You ain't *seen* strawberries till you've seen how they grow 'em out here. I remember last year one of the growers came up with two dozen strawberries weighing two pound. They were like . . .' Uncle Will's descriptive powers failed him. 'They were like the biggest strawberries you ever saw. Weren't they, Bea?'

'How should I know?' Auntie Bea said sharply. She occasionally had these acid moments, regardless of whether her husband had offended or not. It was as if she suddenly decided she didn't like the look of him.

'It's a lovely smell,' Stella said. Another surprise: when she thought of country smells she thought of pig manure and rotting hay. She was coming to a garden, it seemed; a garden of fruit and flowers. From other carriages came the sound of singing in lusty holiday voices: the whole of the little branch-line train, it seemed, was taken up by the fruit-pickers. She put her arm round Geoffrey's shoulders. 'A lovely smell, ain't it, duck?'

He did not answer, and at first she thought it was because he had sunk into himself again; and then she saw that he was pointing. In a paddock full of buttercups a chestnut horse was romping and galloping as if it would outrace the trundling train for the fun of it. She laughed, and Geoffrey laughed; and Uncle Will, smiling on them with all his impossible teeth on show, said, 'I told you you'd like it, didn't I?'

It was late morning, warm and dazzlingly bright, when they disembarked at Wisbech station, and it seemed the arrival of the trainload of work-hungry Londoners was expected. A bus bearing the name 'Walsoken' was waiting outside the station, and a good number of the travellers piled on to it; some of the farmers had come down in their trucks too, and were offering lifts out to the various villages.

'Monks Bridge! Anybody for Monks Bridge?'

A wiry sun-dried man with a pepper-and-salt moustache was perching jauntily on the back of his truck and using a rolled-up newspaper as a megaphone.

'Who's for Monks Bridge? Speak up now or for ever hold your peace.'

'Here! That's us.' Auntie Bea screeched it out so piercingly that the farmer nearly leapt off his perch. 'That's where we're going!'

They were not the only ones, and by the time Auntie Bea had finished flapping and dropping her bags and counting her children the others had already scrambled up on to the bed of the truck. The farmer waited with genial patience by the tailboard, where the words W. LUTTON, FRUIT & VEGETABLES were painted, and when Bea was finally ready extended a courtly hand to help her climb up.

'All aboard the jolly old Skylark,' he said in a droll, dry, soothing accent. 'Hold on tight once we're gooing. Don't want nobody rolling in the road, now do we?'

'You might remember us,' Uncle Will said eagerly. 'We've been before. Tranter's the name. You're in charge of the cabins, ain't you? I wrote off to you. I bespoke a cabin. I bespoke it already.'

'Oh, ah!' the farmer said vaguely. 'I think I remember.'

'Here,' called out a fat husky woman from the truck, 'how do we get one of these cabins then? We didn't know nuffink about that. We thought you just turned up. First come, first served—'

'All right everybody, hold your hosses,' the farmer said, as there was an indignant clamour from the truck. 'There's no need to worry, you'll all git accommodated. There's room for fifty at Long Lane End, and if there's any left ovver I know plenty of folks who'll put you up. So keep your hair on and hold on tight.'

Uncle Will clambered up, muttering about bespeaking, and Stella, following suit, caught a gleam of humour in the farmer's eye. And then he closed the tailboard and trotted back to the cab and in a moment the whole motley truckload, jammed in cheek by jowl and clinging on to whatever came to hand, was on its way with cheers and guffaws and cries from overtired children and an almighty rattle of dangling pots and pans.

It didn't take long to get to Monks Bridge – just long enough for Cecil and Ivy to be symmetrically sick over the sides of the truck – and all Stella saw of the village was a huddle of low roofs before they turned down a tree-lined lane that led to the camp. Well, Butlin's had been rather an exaggeration on Uncle Will's part: her father had been nearer the mark when he said huts; but they looked solid and airy enough, with felt roofs and glazed windows, and duckboard paths running between the quadrangles, and a row of latrines. As for the setting, it was almost idyllic. There were trees on all sides of them. The only comparison Stella could think of, as she jumped down from the truck, was the dwarfs' cottage in *Snow White*.

Uncle Will stepped down beside her, beaming, and gave his braces a hitch of satisfaction. 'There,' he said again, 'I told you you'd like it, didn't I? Eh? I told you, didn't I? Eh?'

I do believe, Stella thought, I do believe I will.

# TWO

## 1

Kate Lutton rose early to perform a task which she both enjoyed and feared.

Yesterday the first batch of seasonal fruit-pickers from London had arrived, and Kate's father, one of the leading fruit-farmers of the district, had been busy most of the day with settling them into their quarters and agreeing hiring terms with them. It was a job that the other growers willingly let him take responsibility for; they needed the labour, but not all of them got along with what they called 'them there Cockneys', whereas Walter Lutton was a man who took as he found and could backchat with the best of them.

Kate usually rubbed along well with them too: for as long as she could remember the horde of needy Londoners had descended on the orchard country every summer to gather in the fruit crop that needed so few hands in the growing and so many in the harvesting. It was her father, indeed, who had first suggested having the hutted camp built at Monks Bridge, to the benefit not only of the village but of the whole orchard country, for growers from miles around could draw on such a well of labour. The yearly immigration added interest to life at Monks Bridge – which not even its warmest admirer could call full of variety – and Kate looked forward to it. She had got into the habit of going to see the new arrivals at the camp once they were settled, to make sure they had everything they needed. Usually a rough communality established itself at once, led by the regulars who knew the ropes:

someone could always be relied upon to have brought an oil stove, at least. But she had found from experience that taking along such items as a basket of eggs, a jar of ointment and a bundle of old newspapers helped greatly on the first morning.

And this was her task this morning – the task that, though she performed it of her own volition, made her stomach flutter too. For though there might well be faces she knew amongst the pickers at the camp, in essence Kate Lutton was going to meet a crowd of strangers, and that was not easy for her. It was so difficult that she forced herself to do it, as one must exercise a weak limb.

Kate's curse was shyness. As with most people who are genuinely shy rather than merely self-absorbed, it was not an obvious affliction: she kept it on too tight a rein for that. It was the constant struggle to conquer it that made her feel it as disabling. She had nothing else of the mouse about her. Her twentieth year found her clear skinned and strong boned, never having known a toothache or a sleep of less than eight hours in her life. She was only five foot two in her stockings, but her body was well developed: her features though small were regular, and she had thick black hair of an almost Mediterranean lustre. Country living had given her few physical inhibitions, and she had been accustomed to leading elephantine carthorses since she was barely higher than their fetlocks. In fact, she would far rather have entered a loosebox with a bad-tempered colt than walked into a room full of laughing people.

But come what may she would go to the camp. In the cool morning kitchen she packed her baskets, whilst her brother Pip, a dry comical youth who could imitate every film star you ever heard of, munched his bacon and remarked that a jar of gin would probably go down best with the Cockneys as a breakfast beverage. Her father was already out inspecting his strawberry fields and, Kate guessed, agonizing over whether to begin picking today or leave them for one more day's ripening: the exact moment of perfection was so easily missed. Her mother was making a dreamy, humming inventory of the pantry; today was the big baking day, when the old bread-oven would blaze till dusk, with the laundry going in to be aired at the end of it. The three cats were moulding their sinuous bodies to fit various patches of sun that fell on the brick floor. It was precisely the sort of day that tempted Kate to stay home, and that was precisely the temptation she wanted to avoid.

She hefted her baskets and left the house, calling her goodbyes, treading carefully down the steps from the front door, where the hens had got into the habit of sunning themselves against the risers.

It was a brilliant day and would soon be a hot one: according to several weather-wise codgers of the village, the rest of the summer would be scorching. The fruit-pickers would have to start shedding some clothing, which she knew did not always come easily to them. They could be startlingly salty in their language, but most had a peculiar physical modesty. She had seen men who could swear for five minutes without repeating a word, sweat and suffer in cotton shirts that they were too embarrassed to take off.

Kate's home was at the end of a drove, a quarter of a mile from the village proper, and surrounded on all sides by fruit trees: in spring and early summer the volume of blossom was such that on a moonlit night Kate's bedroom was filled with a soft glare, as if from a snowscape. Life here was basic and in many ways inconvenient. All their lighting was by paraffin lamp, and in winter the only really warm place was the kitchen hearth. Washing clothes and bodies meant filling the dolly-tub and the zinc bath, and there was no piped water. The drove that she now walked down with such ease could be in severe weather an almost impassable obstacle. And yet there was a certain unstressful amplitude here too. Land was cheap when the house was built, and she and Pip had always had a spacious bedroom each. There had been difficult years when her father had drooped and winced over each letter from the bank, but in the kitchen austerity was the exception and the rule was thumping portions, eggs and cream used with a liberal hand, and vegetables so large they made the average greengrocer's stock look like dwarf varieties.

The reason for this lay all around her. Monks Bridge was situated in the northern area of the fens known as the Marshland, which in spite of its name was a much kinder and more smiling landscape than the black fens to the south – as Kate's father often asserted. That was where he had been brought up, and it was in that windswept world of peat and wheat that he had first begun farming as a young man. It was said of the black fens that you could plant a walking stick in the ground and it would grow, but all Walter Lutton had ever reaped there was heartbreak. The best decision he had ever made, he said, was to cut his losses and move up to Marshland and try his hand at fruit-growing.

'I don't care if it ain't really farming,' he said. 'If watching your whole crop git torn up by the wind in five minutes flat's real farming, then I'll stick to me strawberries.'

The Marshland was a place of smallholdings, as diverse as the wheat-growing fens were monotonous. It was a place where everyone grew something, usually on their own account, and usually something that could be eaten as soon as it was picked. As a child Kate had thought this way of life was the norm: even the more conventional farmers of the district, like the Maxeys who went in for potatoes and barley, had small catty-cornered fields bordered by apple trees. Only when she visited those bare prairies to the south were her eyes opened; and then she was thankful that her father had made the move and brought her up in a flowering garden. She would have felt, she was sure, exposed in that world, and Kate hated feeling exposed. She relished safety as others relished adventure.

Perhaps in this she resembled her father, who took a Dickensian pleasure in cosiness, who loved Christmas and blazing fires, and who would often murmur, whether enjoying a convivial evening indoors or a summer evening on the porch, 'Good here, en't it? I like it here.' He was a bright, brisk man, tough and gnarled rather like the apple trees he tended. A friendly neighbour, generous with help and well liked, there was yet something about him that set him a little apart from his fellow growers in Marshland. They were deliberate people, and there was quicksilver in Walter

Lutton's temper. He delighted in local humour, both the intended kind, which was dry and tart as a plate of capers, and the unintended: he was quite a collector of country solecisms, such as the farm labourer's announcement that his wife had given birth to two twins. It was as if the blood flowed a little faster in his veins than that of his neighbours; and the reverse side of this was impatience.

Not when it came to his trade: with his strawberries and gooseberries, his cherries and damsons and plums and apples, he was a model husbandman, watching and nurturing his crop with maternal tenderness and forbearance. But when life showed itself recalcitrant he could be fiercely bitter, with none of the traditional phlegm of the countryman. When Kate was ten her father's favourite dog had died, choked by a freakish accident with its collar, and the blackness of his mood for weeks afterwards had been alarming. He was not violent: if he wanted to fight anyone it was God, or whoever was in charge. It was as if life mocked him, and he felt his helplessness before that enigmatic smile on the face of the heavens.

'It can't be helped,' Kate's mother would say at such times. 'It's just the way it is.' Which, of course, was exactly what he chafed at; but this was a divide between her father and her mother that there was no bridging. She adored him and he doted on her but they were chalk and cheese.

Maud Lutton was a plump, pretty, slow-moving woman with coal-black eyes and eyebrows and a look, at all times of day, of having not been long up. Careful and capable in all she did, she yet displayed at certain times a shattering clumsiness. Trays leapt rather than dropped from her hands: she took dreadful purlers and never missed a puddle. To someone as nimble and dapper as Kate's father these habits were agonizing, and he could only retort with rarefied sarcasm.

'Never mind, duck,' he would say when his wife, after working at one of her beloved jigsaw puzzles all evening, sent the whole lot flying with a jog of her elbow just as the end was in sight. 'I can see the appeal, in a way. It's a sort of challenge to your soul, en't it? Gitting a jigsaw nearly finished and then chucking it on the floor. Like those Indian blokes who stick pins in theirselves.'

Sometimes, too, when the black mood was on him, her father would salve his disappointment with life by bitter half-joking references to the 'fish man'. As far as Kate could gather, this was a fishmonger who had once courted her mother, before her father came on the scene. Whether there had ever been anything like an engagement, Kate could not tell – she thought probably not – but when her father had the blue devils he conjured up a showdown scenario in which the fish man was the unlucky loser and Kate's mother had made the wrong choice.

'Ah, to think you could have had the fish man! Probably got a chain of fish shops now. Wet fish and battered. Probably got a coat of arms with a haddock and a shrimp on it. That's the trouble with this life. It only teks one mistake and you're beggared till doomsday.'

'Whatever do you mean, Walter? I'm not complaining.'

'Ah, you're kind. That's the trouble, you're too kind. You won't even admit it to yourself. But I'm seen that look in your eyes when we have fisherman's pie.'

And his irony would go on, building fantastic structures on itself. It was too complex for Kate's literal-minded mother; but she was hurt and bewildered by it, Kate knew. 'Why, I don't mean anything by it,' he would say when Kate remonstrated with him: but he did, and when the fit left him he was desperately affectionate in his remorse.

For they loved each other; and the curious thing was, Kate had grown up in a home as peaceful and happy as if her parents had been suited to one another.

Kate came to the turning of the drove into the village high street, and waved as a farm truck rumbled past her with a toot on the horn; Ernie Delph, another fruit grower, his truck loaded with chip baskets ready for the strawberry picking. It was the only vehicle in sight: Monks Bridge was not a bustling place at any hour and, but for the swirling of the dust, the scene presented by the wide street was as still as a rural painting. The rich masses of the many trees took precedence over the houses, which were low-roofed and retiring: the only buildings not overshadowed by green leaf were the church, which because of subsidence of the foundations was leaning very much like an ancient tree itself, and a clocktower of brick and stucco that stood in the very middle of the street. It was modern and looked it: it had been erected as a memorial to the men of Monks Bridge who had died in the Great War.

Twenty-four of them, from this small village: Kate knew the names inscribed on the base of the clocktower by heart. The recent talk of a new war, together with a personal memory from her childhood that was as well hidden as it was harsh and painful, combined to give Kate a cold feeling as she passed the memorial. It was one of the few subjects that could rouse her placid temper to fire.

As she walked down Long Lane towards the camp, however, her chief sensation was the old familiar fluttering in her stomach at the prospect of meeting strangers. The two young men who waved cheerily to her from the grass meadow beside the lane, where they were breakfasting outside their tents, were not so bad: she knew them after a fashion. They were students from Cambridge, and for the last three summers they had come up to the orchard country to help with the fruit-picking season. Others had joined them from time to time, but these two were the mainstay: a hearty clean-cut pair of young men who spent the whole of the season under canvas and in shorts, except on Sundays when they could be seen striding early to the village church in neatly pressed flannels and old school ties. Their chosen job was to look after the fruit-pickers' children while they were at their work; and they did good service, for the pickers' children were many, and their parents needed all the work they could get. If there was a certain Sunday-school zeal about the way the young men tackled their task – the children could often be seen sitting in a circle in the meadow being led in uplifting song – no one thought much the worse of them for it.

Still, Kate was glad when the pair contented themselves with a

'Good morning' and then returned to their breakfast, which they were taking Boy-Scout style from a pan over a neat wood fire. They had a way of pumping your hand and staring into your eyes that was unnerving at best, and they had been known to hand out religious tracts; and Kate had inherited quite a flinty scepticism from her father, who dismissed all organized religion as 'hypocrisy in nightshirts'. Congratulating herself on her escape, she came to the entrance to the camp – a short drove screened on both sides by apple trees, which at this time of year was like a leafy tunnel. Turning into it, she almost collided with a young woman hurrying in the other direction.

'Oh! I'm sorry . . .' About to pass on, the young woman stopped and with a direct, anxious look said, 'Here, you ain't seen a little boy on your travels, have you? About nine. Stocky little fella. Ginger-nob. Geoffrey his name is.' And as Kate shook her head she went on, clapping a hand to the top of her head, 'Hell's bells, Aunt Bea'll go bleedin' spare. She'll go absolutely doolally. Oh, why did I have to have that drink last night? Me head's thumping, I can't think. Where's he gone?'

'When did you miss him?'

'First thing this morning. Like I say, we all let our hair down a bit last night, what with it being the first night and all. Most of 'em are still sleeping it off. I wakes up and finds the cabin door open and Uncle Will and Auntie Bea snoring their heads off and no sign of Geoffrey. He's their kid, see. Bit slow. He wanders off . . . Gawd, I shall have to find him before they wake up!'

'Shouldn't you tell them? Your aunt and uncle?'

'You don't know 'em.' The young woman's face, highly expressive, was doubly so as she said this. 'Aunt Bea goes up like a rocket if she can't find her hankie. If anything's happened to him . . .'

'I'm sure he's all right,' Kate said. 'You're sure he's not in the camp?'

'I've looked everywhere. Like I say, most of 'em are sleeping it off. He's always going AWOL at home, but at least he knows his way around there. Oh! Bloody hell fire—' She seized Kate's arm.

'What if he gets in a field with a bull?'

'It's all right, there aren't any bulls around here,' Kate said; but already this thought had set the young woman off on a trail of other terrors. 'Or fell in a pond,' she said, gripping Kate's arm, 'or got trampled by a horse, or stuck in a ditch—'

'Listen,' Kate said firmly. 'I'm sure he'll be quite safe, honestly. I used to play all round here on my own when I was little, and I never came to any harm.'

'Yes, but you ain't tuppence short of a shilling.' The young woman gave herself a cuff on the cheek in reproach, half-laughed, then looked ready to cry. She was a thin, vivid redhead with green eyes that were pale and yellow-flecked in the sunlight, a retroussé nose, and a humorous mouth that was as mobile as her speech was rapid: she was as vital and alive as a wild rabbit on open ground. And somehow, Kate, usually abashed by animated presences, warmed to her at once.

'Don't worry,' she said. 'He can't have gone far. If he's not in the camp he must have gone the village way. We'll find him. I'll come with you and we'll find him.'

'Would you? Oh, bless yer . . . It's the thought of Aunt Bea having kittens, you see. You think *I'm* in a tizzy. Aunt Bea would just go . . . no, don't think about it.' The girl took Kate's arm as they hurried back down Long Lane. 'We'll just find him, then she'll never know. Gawd, I wish I'd never come! No, I don't mean that. My first time here, see. Just got here yesterday. Thought I was in clover – now this happens. I dunno, it's like me mum says, sometimes it seems like the bluebird of happiness likes nothing better than to shit on your best hat. I'm Stella, by the way.'

'Kate Lutton.'

'Lutton, hang on, wasn't that the fella who brought us from the station yesterday?'

'That'd be my father.'

'Well, he seemed a nice bloke. Helped us get settled in and everything. I dunno, what have you done to deserve a crew like us landing on you every year? Here, I'm not stopping you going somewhere, am I?'

'No, no. I was just coming to the camp to – you know, bring a few things people might need.'

'Cor, you're a bad 'un, ain't you? Give us hold of one of them baskets, you'll bust a vessel. Kate, there's a nice name. Why'd I have to get stuck with a name like you'd give a steamboat? Oh, Geoffrey, Geoffrey, don't do this to me!'

'What's he wearing?'

'Oh, Lord knows. He ain't too hot at dressing hisself at the best of times. Aunt Bea's corset probably. Like I say, he's a bit slow. I mean he's been here before, Bea and Will come up here every summer, but whether he'd remember his way around . . . That's mean saying he's slow. I reckon he's more of a dreamer. In a world of his own most of the time.'

'Not such a bad place to be.'

'Here, you, Kate Lutton, don't go thoughtful on me, not with me head the way it is. Blimey, I swear I'll never touch it again. I'll drink it through a straw instead. No, I dunno why I'm laughing . . .'

## 2

Helen hoped that Richard wouldn't turn up without a tie.

It wasn't that she minded one way or the other. It was how the Hamblins would react that bothered her. She was fond of the enthusiastic professor and his even more enthusiastic wife, but she thought there was such a thing as being *too* open-minded. A little conventionality made life less wearing: the mind needed a few prejudices and received ideas as the body needed a comfortable bed. But the Hamblins were receptive to everything, and everything called for remark. If Richard turned up without a tie, Mrs Hamblin would start a discussion on freedom of dress as a reflection of freedom of the spirit, and Professor Hamblin, in all probability, would remark that the wearing of trousers by the Persians was seen by the ancient Greeks as a symbol of their barbarism . . .

No, unfair, Helen thought as she pinned on her hat before the mirror in her room. The Hamblins, relatives of her mother's, were enormously kind people who had made her very welcome here in their book-stuffed, cupola-crowned house in the Cambridge suburbs. She had long promised them a visit; and it had been intuitive of them to suggest that she come after she had graduated, a time when many students – female students especially – felt a sudden swoop of anticlimax at returning home after three years at university. This way the severance was more gradual.

'Or,' Richard had said mischievously yesterday, 'you could say that you're one of those students who clings on to the place long after term's over because they can't face the big wide world.'

'Like you, you mean?'

'Oh, very much so. It was me I was thinking of, in fact.' He had been amused, unabashed. 'But now I've found a perfect watertight excuse not to go home yet.' And that was when he had told her about the fruit-picking in the fens. He had driven up there the other day to see two Christian Union-sounding types who went there every year, and last night when the Hamblins had invited him to dinner he had been full of it.

Somewhat to her own surprise, Helen had agreed to go with him to the fens today. Partly it was because she welcomed a break from the endlessly vivacious Hamblins. Partly, no doubt, it was because Richard Marwood was the sort of person who wouldn't take no for an answer.

They had talked in their habitual bantering way, but there had been truth in what Richard said of himself. He had crowned his three years at King's with an indifferent second in history – Helen, at Newnham, had taken first-class honours – and now, with term over and the colleges empty, he was living in digs off Huntingdon Road. His money was nearly gone and all his friends, with one exception, had left Cambridge. He was treading water and he knew it but he didn't seem to care. Sometimes she wondered what was going on inside him.

Unusually, Helen found herself indecisive over the hat, and tried another. It had occurred to her, as they would be motoring, to tie a scarf round her head instead; but even leaving aside the exhaustive comment that would call forth from the Hamblins,

Helen Silverman was a smart and correct person, who disliked slovenliness as much as she disliked dowdiness. She examined her reflection in a sort of detached dissatisfaction, as one might look at an old school exercise performed without understanding. Her looks were of the kind that suggest the words 'English rose', which to her had connotations less pleasing than unfortunate – like English cooking or English music. As for her height, she gave it as bleak a recognition as if it had been a hump on her back. She was so used to deprecating it in herself that she made mental amendments whenever tall women were described approvingly. 'Lanky, you mean,' she would think if she found the heroine of a novel described as willowy or long-limbed or statuesque. But it was also part of Helen Silverman's nature to refuse any attempt to make less of her height as she had seen other tall women do – hunching and stooping and shrinking into themselves. It was a point of honour with her to walk upright.

From the street outside there came the familiar sound of Richard's car, an old Riley that he had bought at Cambridge market for twenty pounds and that rattled like a kettle-drum. Helen peeped out of the window and saw to her relief that he was wearing a tie. She watched him hop out of the car and hurry up the front path to the door, and she had a guilty illicit feeling. Observing someone when they were unaware of it was something that struck her as faintly distasteful. It wasn't the sort of thing she did at all.

She left the room and had reached the top of the stairs when a curious doubt afflicted her and made her hesitate. This fruit-picking business really didn't sound like her cup of tea: in fact normally she would have avoided such jolly do-gooding like the plague. She distrusted instinctive feelings and considered them likely to land you in deep trouble, but this seemed rather to be her rational mind that was posing the question. What on earth was she doing?

Richard's voice was audible in the hall. He was being fulsomely greeted by Mrs Hamblin. Helen listened a moment. Richard had a slow soft voice, tenor in timbre, at times oddly tentative as if he were about to stammer. She couldn't catch the words, but whatever he said made Mrs Hamblin laugh in excited toothy fizzings. A spiteful acquaintance had once said that Richard's universal friendliness reminded her of a man continually establishing an alibi: he spoke to waitresses and porters as if he wanted them to remember him. But establishing a rapport with Mrs Hamblin didn't require much effort: she adored all young people. Helen rather preferred the company of her elders.

She heard Richard speak her name, and began to walk down the stairs.

Well, she had promised to accompany him on his quixotic mission today, just out of curiosity; and she was a woman of her word.

'Ah! Here she comes!' cried Mrs Hamblin, a little stout woman in tailor-mades, an obsessive gardener who carried slug pellets in her pockets and sometimes sat down to dinner in leather gloves. 'I was just saying to Richard what a splendid thing it is, you young people giving your time to help these poor fruit-pickers, most of them quite Children of the Jago, so I understand and *how* strange the country must be to them! *Will* you beware of the sun, my dear? Only *I'm* just like a tough old boot from the gardening but you're not accustomed, besides being fair and your mother would never forgive me if I sent you home poorly.'

'I'll be careful, aunt.'

'Not that I approve of being careful as a hard-and-fast rule of life by any means because if no one ever took a risk then where would we be, using the wooden plough and sacrificing to the gods I dare say or at any rate being dreadfully hidebound all in all. I was just saying to Richard how refreshingly things have changed since my day when a young man and a young woman driving off in a motor car together unchaperoned would have been thought awfully fast and I dare say still would be in some quarters. The very idea of their being *friends* just wouldn't go into some people's heads and that just shows how dreadfully prurient their minds are if you ask me. I think your friendship's rather a beautiful thing. Richard, shall you come to us for dinner again? And I don't mean you have to hurry back to be on time because I've always disliked those sort of set hours extremely and so has Henry. But you know you're more than welcome, don't you?'

'I'm more than willing, Mrs Hamblin, thank you,' Richard said. 'Your only trouble will be getting rid of me.'

'Oh, pooh, I'd fill the whole house with young guests if I had my way. Well, well, off you go,' she said, flapping her hands and clucking with laughter as Richard aimed an impetuous kiss at her brown cheek. 'Don't let an old woman keep you. I must be mulching. Goodbye, dears, goodbye!'

'I did wonder whether you might have had second thoughts,' Richard said, cocking a smiling look at Helen as they went out to his car.

'I often do, but I never act on them,' Helen said. 'That's what you call being single-minded. Anyhow, I shall simply treat this as a day in the country. Which happens to have one of your hare-brained schemes attached.'

'Aha, you'll like it when you get there.'

He opened the car door for her with a prompt decorum. As their eyes met they both registered the inappropriateness of the gesture, and laughed.

'Training,' he said with a shrug. 'As a child I believe I formed an idea that women simply *couldn't* open doors. Not, of course, that they were ever referred to as women. "The Ladies",' he said in a mock bass, lifting an imaginary glass.

The usual lightness of Richard's tone became a little conscious when he spoke of his family background, though probably only someone who knew him as Helen did would have noticed it. It reminded her of someone balancing something shiny and sharp on their fingertips.

'That was nice of Mrs Hamblin to invite me to dinner again,' he said as the car rattled and shuddered out on to the road. 'I feel rather as if I'm using their place as a restaurant.'

'It's just as well. What *do* you get to eat at those digs of yours?' Since term had ended Richard had been living in a peculiar pair of rooms behind a locksmith's shop. The bedroom was separated from the sitting room by a staircase of such dizzying steepness that he took his life into his hands every time he got up in the morning.

'Oh, there's a gas ring, you know,' he said vaguely. 'By the way, the old fellow's shop was broken into the other night. I never heard a thing. I think it takes a certain flamboyance to break into a locksmith's shop. Wit, even. I'm not getting thin, am I?'

'No thinner than usual. Anyway, they love having you. Aunt Hamblin was talking just this morning about all the wonderful potential she sees bursting out of you.'

'Good Lord,' he laughed. 'Seeping more like. Thinly trickling.'

There was silence between them until they were out of Cambridge, the restful companionable silence that does not fear misinterpretation: it was evidence in itself of their friendship. His last words, though, seemed to cling about him a little, and several times Helen threw him a speculative glance, wondering what he was thinking.

He was not easy to read: she found that his heavy-lidded, wry, sensual face, with its full lips and intensely dark brown eyes, made quite as effective a mask as an icy hauteur; and a sort of lazy restlessness characterized his movements which could equally reflect tension or lassitude. When she had first met him she had been reminded of a rangy half-grown cat; that was part of the reason, indeed, why she had taken to him. In Helen's experience men as a whole, and Cambridge men in particular, more nearly resembled dogs in their boisterous, transparent, dismayingly straightforward personalities. That touch of the feline had first drawn her to Richard Marwood when other things about him would not have engaged her interest. For she had met many cleverer people at the university, many more fascinating and original and exceptional; and the position of a woman in a still overwhelmingly male institution, where you had to shine twice as brightly to be noticed at all, had given her a general disdain for the second-rate mind. Richard was not brilliant: he was an intelligent young man from a comfortable Home Counties family that had sent him to university because it was the proper thing to do. And in truth, that first impression of him as like a cat had also included a feeling that he was rather a spoiled one.

That feeling had been moderated by now, though she knew he could be irresponsible and careless, sometimes infuriatingly so. It didn't matter: the fact remained that in the last year she and Richard had become firm and close friends – and getting to know a member of the opposite sex at all was a difficult enough feat under the university's suspicious and antiquated 'chap rules'. Richard had once said, in his half-serious way, that the basis of true friendship was *disliking* the same things, and she thought there was some truth in that. The peculiar mixture of naivety, solemnity and heartiness that predominated at Cambridge was anathema to both of them – which made this new undertaking of his all the more inexplicable. She said as much, as they struck the Ely road.

'You'll like it when we get there,' he said smiling.

'You keep telling me that, Richard. You protest too much.'

'Only because you don't look at all convinced. Anyway, I thought you liked the country.'

'I like the country very much. And I'm all in favour of co-operation and philanthropy. It's just the prospect of open-air hymn singing I don't fancy.'

He laughed. 'Whoever said anything about hymn singing?'

'Well, really, Richard, isn't that what it's all about? Running a mission to the benighted heathens of Darkest England. All very earnest and muscular and Toynbee Hall. How on earth *you* came to be mixed up in such a thing I can't think. Have you been hiding your true self from me all this time?'

'Call it at act of contrition for three wasted years,' he said, still laughing. 'Besides, these fellows are very nice, you know. Rather too sober for me, but very nice. I ran into them on Parker's Piece when I was desperately trying to think up an excuse for still being up and hey presto, they supplied me with one. Come and join us, they said, and that was it.'

'It's only the beginning of July. You don't need an excuse for still being up.'

'You do with my family.' He spoke a little too quickly – almost curtly; then ran a hand through his fringe of thick dark hair. 'Anyway . . . when I drove up the other day they were still waiting for the fruit-pickers to arrive. So precisely how they go about the job, I don't know. All I know is they look after the pickers' children while they're at work. Now admittedly I did catch sight of a pile of hymn books in one of their tents . . . Oh, Helen, don't look like that! Surely a few hymns won't hurt a daughter of the clergy.'

'My father is a good old eighteenth-century sort of clergyman who thinks religion should be kept in its proper place and prefers a bottle of sherry to a prayerfest any day.'

'Hmm. He doesn't sound like Knatchbull and Neeve's type at all.'

'Oh Richard, those are not their names? Surely. Oh, surely not.' Helen began laughing. 'Tell me you're making this up . . .'

'Knatchbull and Neeve, I swear. No idea of their first names – they just address each other by the surname like school prefects. But they really are very nice people.'

'They sound like a firm of undertakers. No, I'm sorry, that's unfair.'

'Well, I told them you'd be coming with me today and they were highly delighted.'

'You told them? You didn't even know I'd be coming. I still can't quite believe I am.'

'Oh, I was confident of my powers of persuasion. As I say, they were all for it. No shudder of horror at the mention of Newnham. In the sight of the Lord even female undergraduates are equal, it seems.'

'Female graduate, thank you. I'm proud of my degree even if you're not.'

'Yours is better than mine. Anyhow, the men have it easy. The laziest fathead can get by at Cambridge as long as he's the right sex.'

'You needn't feel guilty.'

'No, no. Just stating a fact. Oh, I know things have improved. At least they allow women the title of degrees now. But it's still as if they're trying subtly to drive them all out of the place. I tried to give Mother and Father some idea of it last time I was home, but I might as well have been talking Chinese. When I mentioned that the women students at Cambridge were forbidden to wear trousers, my mother said in a very pained perplexed way that no respectable woman would wish to.' She noticed the constraint in his laughter. 'Do you mind if I have a cigarette?'

'Not at all. I take it you'll not be telling soapy stories about your university days in twenty years' time, then.'

'Oh, probably. Perhaps it's resentment because the old place is finished with me now. I can't hide under its skirts any more.'

Helen studied him a moment, then withheld the question that was on her lips. 'Well,' she said, 'curiously enough, I've loved it. You're right, of course, about the way women are treated there, but still I wouldn't have missed it for the world. I've learnt a lot: I've made good friends.'

'Even friends who drag you off to babysit for fruit-pickers in the fens? Of course,' he went on before she could reply, 'that's another thing the pig-headed authorities can't conceive of. That men and women can be friends.'

'It's pretty unusual.'

'Is it? I suppose it is. Dear brother Maurice couldn't grasp it at all whenever I mentioned you at home. "Do you mean this woman is an acquaintance?" "No," I'd say, "Helen is a friend, probably the best friend I have at the university. We met at the Union." Puzzlement. "Is she someone's sister, do you mean?" And so on.' Richard ground the gears a little savagely. 'Anyhow, Knatchbull and Neeve have given me an excuse not to go back to *that* just yet, so God bless their healthy bare knees, I say. Oh, I didn't tell you about the bare knees, did I? Mandatory.'

'If you break out in shorts, Richard, I shall refuse to speak to you.'

'Don't worry. I haven't got the legs for it.'

'You've told your parents, then? How you're going to be spending the summer?'

'Ah . . . not yet. The official line is that I'm still in Cambridge because I've a few bills to settle and my books to sort and so on

. . . Yes, I know, I shall have to tell them. Maurice, alas, is already making inquiries for me in the City. Beware of brothers making inquiries . . . You are lucky, Helen.'

'Am I?'

'You know what I mean. Your people don't think anything of you staying on in Cambridge for the summer.'

'That's because I'm staying with Aunt Hamblin. And women aren't really expected to do anything other than pay visits to relatives and be generally sociable. Even when they've just got a degree.'

'Except get married, of course.'

'Of course. Did I tell you I heard a Girton girl greet the news of her graduation with the words, "Oh, good, now I can get engaged"?'

Richard slowed to allow a farm cart to emerge from a side road. They were in pure country now, the wheat stiff and tawny in the fen fields, the sky a blazing blue: the cow parsley crowding the verges was higher than their heads.

'Not that I've got anything against marriage in theory,' Helen said as they moved on. 'But I simply can't see why a woman would go through three years of university just to be thrown on the marriage market at the end of it. Thank the Lord my parents feel the same.'

'No dropping heavy hints about all the girls you were at school with getting married?'

'They know me too well!'

'Ah, that's what I mean. You're lucky. I'm expected to do something and don't know what I want to do. You're not expected to do anything and know very well what you want to do.'

'Well . . . I know my goal. I don't entirely know how to go about reaching it. But I've made a start. I've written to Olive Kingswell. With luck she'll remember me.'

'Kingswell? Is she the *Manchester Guardian* one?'

'And *Time and Tide* and a lot of other papers, though she doesn't write so much nowadays. She gave a talk to the Newnham Arts Society last term and when I spoke to her about wanting to be a journalist she was actually encouraging instead of laughing in my face. She gave me her address and said to write when I'd graduated. I put it away thinking oh well, that's just politeness, but when I thought about it again I realized a busy woman like her must have meant *something* by it. So we'll see.'

Helen spoke casually, but she was excited. Olive Kingswell was a woman who over the years had assumed semi-legendary status in her mind. Hers had been a pioneering role in taking women's journalism out of the realm of hats and frocks and light literary reviews into the wider world. As a young woman she had even written reports from the front in France during the Great War; she had also interviewed Mussolini and covered Roosevelt's first election victory from Washington. Poor health had curtailed her rovings but had not dimmed her sparkle, and Helen had listened to her lecture at Newnham with something as close to hero worship as her own sceptical nature would permit. Olive Kingswell dressed for comfort and dismissed a foolish question with a brusque lack of ceremony, but to Helen she represented true sophistication. She had looked with a canny eye on the world as it really was and had set down what she saw in clear sharp prose: without holiness or axe-grinding she had devoted her life to truth.

It was what Helen wanted: she was absolutely sure of that. Her achievements at Cambridge – where the severest criticism she had come in for had been the comment 'Too journalistic' on one of her glibber essays – had added a firm belief in her abilities to fulfil her desire. It wouldn't be easy – Miss Kingswell had not pretended that it was easy – but Helen was used to that. Going to university was not easy: at Cambridge there were five hundred women students to six thousand men; even with the support of parents who respected her wishes, she had found life for a woman who wanted to do something other than marry and reproduce to be a constant battle against incomprehension and downright hostility. Her eyes were open and she saw the obstacles, and was not dismayed by them.

And for now she was at leisure, her degree achieved, her future before her. The Hamblins wanted her to stay for a month or more and her mother and father, who had come down at graduation full of pride, raised no objection: probably they felt the Lincolnshire vicarage would strike dull after three years at Cambridge. Everything was in place for Helen: the will, the capability, and now – if Miss Kingswell remembered her – the opening she needed.

Yet sometimes she lay awake at night adding up this auspicious sum and it didn't come out right.

'I suppose it'll be London?' Richard was saying. 'And, whatsit, a room of one's own . . . You *are* lucky.'

'Well . . . there's many a slip 'twixt cup and lip, as those infuriating old grannies would say.'

'Not for you. You'll do it.'

They passed Ely, the cathedral rearing above the insignificant town, a stately giant in Lilliputian clutches, and continued north. They were leaving Cambridge far behind now. The fens were more fenny, the place names more outlandish, the people fewer.

'I don't see any orchards yet,' Helen said.

'You will soon. They're all round Wisbech, miles of them. The handsomest little Georgian town you ever saw, by the way. Like a bit of Bath, and no one's heard of it. Here, what about working this up for your first piece? For one of the lighter magazines, say. A summer spent with the fenland fruit-pickers.'

'Who said anything about a summer? I'm only coming along today because you wouldn't take no for an answer.'

'Or give it a sociological slant for the heavy periodicals. Most of the pickers come up from London, the East End mainly – and then there's the idealistic young chaps from Cambridge spending the vac helping out by looking after their children. Perfect. Make it a two-nations sort of thing. Hopeful or bitter, depending on the editor's prejudices.'

'It's a possibility, I suppose. The two nations on the eve of war.'

Richard made a face. 'I can't see it happening. There isn't the will. Twenty-five years ago people could get worked up about plucky little Belgium, but plucky little Czechoslovakia's a different matter. It just sounds like something out of *The Prisoner of Zenda*.'

Helen was irritated when he spoke like this, though she had had ample time to get used to it. Their very first meeting, in the gallery of the Union, had set the tone. She had been reproved by the Chair for applauding a speaker – women were admitted only on condition that they listened in silence – whilst Richard had been reproved for snoring: he had fallen asleep across two chairs.

'Why flippancy in the face of peril is supposed to be a virtue I've never understood,' she said.

'It isn't. It's our national vice,' Richard said, not at all put out. 'I've just got it rather more badly. I say, it's rather a job lighting a cigarette like this – could you light one for me?'

Helen did so, conscious of a certain lack of poise in the action. At such times she felt herself to be very much a vicar's daughter from Lincolnshire. Olive Kingswell, she recalled, freely smoked Balkan cigarettes that smelt like a bonfire. She puffed and coughed and handed the lit cigarette over.

'Thanks. Sorry, could you put them in the breast pocket?'

She had been about to slip the cigarette pack into the side pocket of his sports jacket. 'You and your superstitious routines,' she said, switching the pack.

'Dickens couldn't write without certain ornaments arranged on his desk. Mark of the creative temperament or something.' He laughed, but he patted his breast pocket to be sure. He was, she thought, a strange mixture. Alongside the vast carelessness that had led him to mislay not just one but three bicycles by forgetting where he had parked them, there were these punctilious habits. Whenever she had gone for tea in his rooms at King's – door standing open for propriety – she had had to sit in a sort of grotto made up of shifting piles of gramophone records, clothes, magazines, shoes, newspapers, bottles, letters and books; but he would take fastidious pains to make sure there was a jug for the milk and flowers on the table.

'So you think there'll be a war?' he said.

'Sooner or later. I think it's practically inevitable, will or not.

Maybe these fruit-pickers have the right idea. The country will be the safest place for their children if it comes.'

'Dear God,' Richard said. 'Five thousand years of human history and here we are threatening each other with poison gas. D'you know, I loathe these politicians – all of them. Statesmen and great leaders and half-baked damned theorists of this and that. If I had my way I'd put them all in a boxing ring and let them slug it out.'

Helen looked at him with interest. The friendship between them had been very much a third-year friendship: they were linked by light cool chains of humour and sympathy, with no freshman soul baring; but here was a hint of deeper waters. And Helen, despite a good deal of poise and tact, was an inquisitive person, at times her curiosity of the sort that will discover how the machine works even if it means destroying it.

'Would you be a pacifist, Richard?' she said. 'A conscientious objector?'

He gave a shout of laughter into the warm blue air. 'Good God! I can just see how my family would react to *that* one!'

'But would you? If it came, would you fight?'

'Worth being a conchie just to see their faces,' he said, still chuckling; but then, unconcernedly, 'Oh, yes, I'd fight, of course.'

'For what?'

He thought for just a moment. 'For these children we're going to see.'

'But suppose fighting for these children meant dropping poison gas on children in Germany?'

'Ah, there's the rub. You'd have to listen to what your conscience told you, I suppose. Follow your inner light, as the Quakers say.'

'The Quakers are pacifists.'

'You argue like a barrister. Look there – plum trees. We're nearly there. No, I'm not trying to change the subject. You've just got me stumped. If and when war comes I'll fret about it then, how's that? Anyway what about you? What would you do? Would you be like one of those women in the last war who went around handing out white feathers?'

'You know me better than that, I hope.'

'Well, yes and no. I've known you as a fellow spirit at beefy jolly Cambridge, where I think we were the only two people who weren't either dons in the making or sporty oafs. But Cambridge is over now. We should be going further, shouldn't we? I know some of you, perhaps, but not all. Who *is* Helen, that all her swains commend her?'

Helen turned her face a little away from his look, as from a bright light. 'Just an ordinary person like anybody else,' she said.

'There's no such thing as an ordinary person.'

'Oh yes there is – thank heaven! Anyhow, I'm not one for confessionals, Richard. That's where I differ from Aunt Hamblin. She thinks *everything* should be out in the open – like a sort of psychological nudism. Not for me. There's a bit of Forster that I've always thought hit it exactly – about keeping a small corner secret even from people we love. "It is a human right: it is personality."'

'Sounds like the cynicism of the smothered romantic to me.'

'Anyhow,' she said, ignoring this, 'as you say, we met at university. University friendships are different. Everyone swears they'll keep in touch and everyone drifts away in time.'

'God, that's an awful thought. God, I hate that idea. Don't say it.'

His frown, which on his indolent, slightly raffish face appeared like actual pain, showed that he was serious. Helen was surprised, and then confused. She had an abominable schoolgirl habit, which all her self-command and coolness could not eradicate, of blushing deep red: she was afraid she was doing it now. And all at once she found herself on the edge of a dismal precipice of self-revelation – about to make the leap.

She was saved. They had just turned a bend in the tree-lined road, and Richard had to slam on the brakes to avoid running straight into a small boy.

'Christ!' Richard said as the car squealed to a halt. 'What is he playing at?'

The child was trudging along in the very middle of the road with a heavy-legged exhausted gait, his head drooping, like some miniature Beau Geste on a desert march. He was crying, not with infant fractiousness, but with a square-mouthed despair as old as the world. When the car stopped in front of him he simply stopped too, scrubbing his eyes with a dirty fist and seeming to resign himself to the will of the gods.

'Dear, dear,' Richard said, getting out of the car and crouching down beside the boy. 'Are you all right, old chap? Where's your ma?'

At any age there is nothing like a kind voice to make you feel worse. The boy howled.

'Shush, shush, old chap. You shouldn't walk along in the middle of the road, you know. Not even a quiet road like this one.' Richard squinted up ahead. A church tower, not quite perpendicular, was visible above the trees. 'Well, I think that's Monks Bridge . . . Is that where you live? Where are you from, old chap?'

The little boy stopped his wailing and said clearly, ''Ackney,' as if it were a question he was used to being asked.

'One of the fruit-pickers' children, surely,' said Helen, who had got out of the car and joined Richard. She felt her height, and crouched down. 'Perhaps he fled the hymn singing. What's your name, dear?'

The little boy stared.

'So much for my rapport with children,' she said. 'What now?'

'Well, there's a sort of camp at Monks Bridge. It's where a lot of the pickers lodge for the season, apparently. I wonder if—'

'I got lost,' the boy burst out, with a child's sudden informativeness, 'an' I can't find them 'uts.'

'The camp,' Richard said. He ruffled the boy's hair. 'Come on, old chap. We'll go and find your folks. You ever ridden in a motor car?'

The fact of the car, and of his actually getting into it, silenced the boy's cries and seemed to put him in a trance of wonder. But as they drove on towards the village he came out of it to murmur to Helen, as if his life had become filled with novelty almost beyond bearing, 'I went on a *train* yesterday an' all!'

'Did you?' said Helen. She was unsure how to talk to children: even as a child herself she had preferred the company of adults. 'Well . . . perhaps you'll go up in an aeroplane next.'

'I might do,' the boy said, non-committally.

After a moment's hesitation Helen got out her handkerchief and dabbed at the boy's tear-streaked face. He seemed used to this, only adding helpfully, 'Me mum spits in it.'

'Good heavens.' Helen looked at the handkerchief. Well, there was a picnic basket on the back seat, there might be some soda water or something . . .

'That's Stella!' the boy suddenly cried, bouncing in his seat and pointing. 'That's Stella over there!'

The spacious main street of the village was empty of people except for two young women who were just emerging from the churchyard. One of them, seeing the little boy, gave a squeal and, dropping the basket she was carrying, lit out towards the car like a frantic leggy deer. By the time Richard had brought the car to a halt the young woman, flame-haired and breathless, had half-climbed into it and was smothering the boy with kisses and hugs, at the same time gasping out, 'Oh, you little beggar! Don't do it to me, Geoffrey, for Gawd's sake! Oh, you little devil!'

'Well, that's all right then,' Richard said laughing.

The other young woman, a dark pretty tidy girl with shaded violet eyes, had gathered up the dropped basket and now stood at a little distance, smiling shyly. 'We found him a little way down the road,' Helen said, addressing her. 'He's quite all right, I think. Just lost his bearings.'

'What have you been told about wandering off?' the red-haired girl said, taking the boy's face in her hands. 'You had me worried sick!'

'Is Mum mad?' the boy said warily.

'She doesn't know,' the red-haired girl said, 'and with a bit of luck she never will, if we get you straight back. Come on.' She looked at Richard and Helen for the first time, with a vivid high-strung smile. 'Thanks ever so much. I was that worried, you see. His mum – well, she gets a bit worked up. You know.'

'I'm hungry,' Geoffrey moaned.

'Yes, well, this nice lady was just bringing us some grub, and you'd have had it if you'd stayed put. See – all nice eggs and— Oh!'

The dark girl, with a rueful gesture, held up the basket that had been dropped. It *had* been a basket of eggs.

'That was me!' the red-haired girl said, clapping a hand to her face. 'I didn't think – oh Gawd . . .'

'It doesn't matter,' the dark girl said. 'We've plenty more at home you can have. We . . .' With a sort of helpless bemusement she held the basket away from herself. It seeped and dripped grotesquely, the yolks and whites hissing as they fell on to the hot surface of the road.

'Well,' Richard said, 'you've got the makings of a ruddy big omelette, anyhow.'

It was hard to tell who began laughing first: but for a long time none of them could stop, and each lascivious plop and sizzle of the broken eggs on to the road made them laugh harder. Even the little boy's solemn tear-streaked face brightened, and he chuckled in a relieved way, as if he had fully expected the situation to produce a row.

'Well, look here,' Richard said at last, getting out of the car and propping himself on the bonnet, 'we were going to take him along to the fruit-pickers' camp. Is that right? That's where you're staying?'

'S'right. Just come up from London yesterday,' the red-haired girl said, answering his smile.

'Oh no! Not me,' the dark girl said, as Richard looked at her. 'I live local. I was just taking them some – eggs and things . . .'

That started them off again; and Richard proving completely incapable, it was Helen who took control, getting out of the car and saying, 'Perhaps we'd better introduce ourselves. I'm Helen. *That's* Richard. We were on our way here to . . . well . . .'

'To help,' Richard said, wiping his eyes. 'To look after the children when the picking starts. Lend a hand. So we've just made an early start really, haven't we?'

'I'm Stella,' said the red-haired girl cheerfully, 'and trouble here's me cousin Geoffrey. And this is Kate – first friend I've made up here. Well, I think she's me friend, even though I smashed her eggs to bu . . . to bits.'

Kate gave her shy smile. It struck Helen that the violet eyes and dark colouring gave the girl a look, even in this sun-bleached street, of standing a little in shadow.

'Looks like we'll all be seeing something of each other, then,' Richard said, with a mischievous glance at Helen as if defying her to back out. 'So come on then. On to the camp. Two in the front, two in the back, and Geoffrey wherever he likes.'

'Cor, would you?' Stella said eagerly. 'If we whizz him back his mum'll never know he went AWOL. No,' she said, as Geoffrey gave her an urgent look, 'I won't tell her, as long as you don't give me no more heart attacks.'

'All's well that ends well,' Richard said; and as they got into the car there was a sort of collective presentiment between the four of them, that their meeting was not the end but the beginning of something.

# *THREE*

## 1

Dark, dusty, and so awkwardly crowded with piled and dangling stock that you seldom came away without a bruise on your shins or a bump on your forehead, Gathergood's general store was still the indispensable hub of the commercial life of Monks Bridge.

It *was* the commercial life of Monks Bridge.

Outside the shop there stood a telephone box, and if anyone should wish to use it Mr Gathergood would step out to offer his advice, as if it were just as much part of his enterprise as the petrol pump on the forecourt. Behind the shop was a bakery, for Mr Gathergood was a baker too: he was also the sub-postmaster. And inside the shop he sold everything from motor oil to dog biscuits, from a sack of coal to a twist of aniseed balls. He sold cheese and carbolic soap and coffee and paraffin and, as he seemed to arrange his stock on the principle that no two similar goods should be on the same shelf, they all smelt of each other.

For a penny he also recharged wireless batteries, and this was Kate Lutton's errand one hot noonday, a week after the seasonal fruit-pickers had arrived at Monks Bridge. She expected Mr Gathergood to favour her with a few words on the subject and he did not disappoint. Transactions with his customers were for Mr Gathergood simply something to be got out of the way before he got down to the real business of expounding his views. He waited for Kate to place the recharged battery in her bag before leaning his arms on the counter and announcing in a meaningful tone, 'I see we've got them Cockneys again.'

'Yes,' Kate said, 'no shortage of hands this year.' A further trainload had arrived the other day: the camp at Long Lane End was full and every village for miles around had its complement of fruit-pickers lodging in spare rooms and attics or camping in the open. 'Dad's very pleased.'

'*Is* he?' Mr Gathergood took this, as he took every morsel of information, with a sort of eager, solemn relish. He was a tall bald long-faced man with protuberant eyes that gave him a fishlike look and he had a way of gasping and pouting at some particularly juicy piece of gossip that was very fishlike too. 'Well now. He's started on his strawberries, I suppose? With that lot? Oh, tomorrow, eh? Well now. 'Course, you've got to have the labour. I know that. But I'll tell you something about them Cockneys, shall I?'

Mr Gathergood lowered his head conspiratorially: Kate leaned forward obligingly, wondering what he would come up with this time. Mr Gathergood was an encyclopaedic repository of knowledge, all of it dubious. He took a friendly interest in every letter you sent or received, studying the address or the postmark and then treating you to a lecture on the place. As a result, one old lady of the village whose son had emigrated to Nova Scotia was under the hazy impression that her firstborn lived on a diet of raw fish, in an igloo.

'Now I'm not saying anything against 'em, mind,' Mr Gathergood said. 'But they're different, you know. The way they live down there in London, it meks 'em different. All the children are pickpockets, for a start off – they're brought up to it. They've got no idea that milk comes from cows. And they piddle in the cupboards.' Mr Gathergood, counting these charges off on his fingers, nodded gravely at her expression. 'That's a fact. It's second nature to 'em. When they need to go they go in the cupboard. What d'you reckon to that?'

Kate could only look suitably impressed, while Mr Gathergood poked his lugubrious face between the strings of onions and buckets and bootlaces and added as a clincher, 'Here's another thing that'll surprise you. *The women don't wear anything underneath.* Winter or summer. Don't think nothing of it in London. The way they live . . .'

Mr Gathergood tailed off. He had been so absorbed in enlightening Kate that he had not noticed the ping of the shop doorbell; and only now did he notice the young woman standing at the other end of the counter.

It was Stella Tranter.

Kate met her eyes, feeling dismayed and embarrassed. Stella, straight-faced, winked and then coughed.

'What can I get you?' Mr Gathergood said, making his way along the counter at a wary creep.

'Aaow, bless yer, just a couple o' slices o' that there 'am and a nice crusty loaf. Gorblimey, never et so well in me life, I ain't. Don't get nuffink like this in London. Jellied eels mornin' noon an' night, fair gives you the pip it does.' Stella drew the back of her hand noisily across her nose and fixed Mr Gathergood with a guttersnipe grin. 'How's yourself, me old china?'

'Not so bad, thank you,' Mr Gathergood said uncertainly, fumbling at the ham slicer. 'Hope you're the same.'

'Hark at 'im! Proper gent, 'e is! I'll bet you're a regular one with the lydies, ain't yer?'

Mr Gathergood muttered something into his moustache, and nearly added his finger to the slices of ham.

'Aow, 'ello 'ello, least said soonest mended, eh? Don't tell the old trouble-and-strife, eh? Don't you worry, guv. If I had a penny for every time my old man had a spot of how's-your-farver on the side, I'd be a bleedin' miwwionaire, so help me I would!' Stella gave a loud dirty laugh, her arms folded on her bosom.

'Will there be anything else?' Mr Gathergood said, in a subdued tone.

'Well, listen, me old darlin', I don't suppose you could slip me a bobsworth o' gin, could yer? Under the carnter, like. For the byby, it is. Bless him, yer can't get him off withaht it. Tykes after his dad, I suppose – wherever he is. Back in the nick I shouldn't wonder. No? Ah, well. I shall just 'ave to grin and bear it, as the Duchess said when her skirt blew over her 'ead. Toodle-oo.'

Stella spun her penny change on her thumb and exited with a trollopy wiggle, whistling.

Just keeping a straight face long enough to say goodbye to Mr Gathergood, who looked as if a very skilful taxidermist had stuffed him and propped him behind the counter, Kate made her escape.

Stella was waiting for her outside. They managed to look at each other straightfaced for several seconds before the collapse.

'Oh dear . . .' Kate said at last, wiping her eyes. 'I was afraid – when I turned round and saw you . . .'

'What, that I'd take it serious? Life's too short. But I did have to take him down a peg or two, cheeky beggar. Walk my way? We've been picking over Delph's this morning. I'm starved.' Stella plucked at the loaf and chewed briskly as they went along.

'We're not all like Mr Gathergood up here,' Kate said.

''Course you're not. Mind you, there are some rum old characters in your neck of the woods, ain't there? This Delph fella. Treats you very nice and all, but he can't look you in the eye. Talks into his collar like a little boy. Is it me?'

'No, no. Just a bit shy,' Kate said; but she could imagine the reaction of Ernie Delph, who though brawny as a bull was as modest as a lamb, when faced with Stella's startling green eyes and unbuttoned personality.

'And this place gets me as well. I mean why Monks Bridge? Where's the bridge?'

Kate laughed. 'I know. And there aren't any monks either. It could be worse. There's a village a few miles away called Three Holes.'

'Blimey. Three's enough for anybody,' Stella said with her ripe laugh; and then, lowering her voice, 'Oh, no, it's him. Don't look. Across the way. Keep talking to me. Don't give him a chance to muscle in else I'll never get rid of him. Blah blah rhubarb rhubarb . . .'

'Him' was a thick-necked fair young man with a sort of spurious good looks, like a portrait done with a high finish and no taste. He was sauntering along in shirt sleeves on the other side of the village street, and cocking a look at Stella that left no doubt as to its meaning. He stopped as they drew level, and stood regarding them with his pink lips pursed in a soundless whistle; but the presence of Kate seemed to discourage him, and after a moment he went on his way.

'Who's he?' Kate said.

'Oh, his name's Frankie Hope. Frankly Hopeless I call him. Thinks he's God's gift – trouble is, there's plenty of girls who think the same, and that makes him worse. He's in the cabin two doors down from ours, wouldn't you know it.' Stella made a face. 'I reckon he practises that smile of his in the mirror. Not my idea of talent at all. Here, what about you, anyway? Anybody got their eye on you or vice versa? Don't mind me asking, I'm just nosy.'

'No . . . well, not really.'

'Go on. *I'll* bet. I'll winkle it out of you in the end, don't you worry. Mind you, I'm out of that game for keeps, ta very much. Had enough of that back at home. There's a couple of silly beggars at the camp creeping in and out of each other's huts like Romeo and Whatshername, but I mean where do they get the energy? I go out like a light soon as I've had me supper. This strawberry picking does me in good and proper.'

'I know, it's hard on your back. It'll be better when you get to the top fruits. If you stay that long, I mean.'

'Oh, I reckon I will. I like it here. And it's nice to be earning a few bob, though I don't know how I shall get to spend it. Living like a Girl Guide so far. What do you do round here for entertainment?'

'Well now. Old Gaffer Giles, he do the broomstick dance if his rheumatism let him. Thass a treat to see. And then us watches the stagecoach come in, right exciting that be, and of course there be the maypole . . .'

'Here, here, you had me fooled for a minute there!' Stella said laugh-ing. 'Fair enough. I reckon we're even now. Broomstick dance . . .' She chuckled, then studied Kate a moment with friendly, amused eyes. 'You're a bit of a dark horse, you are, Kate

Lutton, ain't you? Definitely a dark horse.'

'Better than being a brown cow, I suppose.'

'Oho, now you're beating me . . .'

Kate suddenly suffered one of those cold flushes of misgiving that her shyness inflicted on her – a swift draining of confidence, an abrupt conviction that she was making a fool of herself. 'Anyway,' she said, with a dip of her chin that she recognized and detested and could not stop, 'we usually go into Wisbech. You know, for entertainment. The pictures and things like that.'

'Funnily enough, I haven't missed the pictures at all since I've been here, and I used to be a right film nut back at home. Never missed a programme.' If Stella noticed the sudden change in Kate, she did not show it. 'We'll go into Wisbech one night, you and me, what d'you say? You can show me the sights . . . Here – what? Is it me? Have I said something wrong?'

It was Kate's dread to have her awkwardness confronted in this way: the more someone rapped on the shell the more she shrank into it. Yet Stella looked genuinely bemused, even a little hurt. As a friend would.

'No, of course not,' Kate said with an effort. 'It's just . . . I'm afraid you'd find it ever so dull, going out with . . . going out like that, I mean there's nothing much . . .'

'Blimey, is that all? Coh, you've got me wrong, duck. Back where I come from some people's idea of a good time's drinking two pints of half and half over a game of dominoes. And then walking all of half a dozen yards home. We ain't the Monte Carlo set, you know. It's funny really. You hear folks at home saying you'd never catch them living in some little village where everybody knows everybody's business. Drive 'em mad, they say. And yet they've never been further than the Mile End Road in their lives and if a stranger walks down the street they give him such a stare like you never saw. Tell you the truth, they give me the pip sometimes. I mean, they'll never stand by and see you in trouble, they'll always help you out . . . it's just they want your soul in return, do you see what I mean?' Stella's smile had a trace of frown in it. 'Anyway, let's have no more of that, thank you very much. I shall drag you out for a beano whether you like it or not. Deal?'

'Deal.'

Kate was absurdly touched; but glad all the same when Stella changed the subject, saying, 'See our friends who found Geoffrey are still around? Been up here practically every day, helping out with the kids. Geoffrey's full of that Richard one – always talking about him. Come and see.'

The open-air nursery for the fruit-pickers' children had established itself, as usual, in the Long Lane meadow where the two beshorted young men pitched their tents; but Kate found the scene much changed by the presence of Richard and Helen. The children were not seated in circles chanting rhymes or playing decorous guessing games, and there was not a hymn book in sight. The children were all over the place. The meadow was a riot of children, and many of them were dressed in outlandish odds and ends of costume, including Geoffrey, who came running up to greet them in a large black hat and a crimson sash that drooped to his grubby knees.

'Oh my giddy aunt, who are you?' Stella cried.

'Captain Crook,' Geoffrey asserted, and then careered off again to engage in an imaginative swordfight with a miniature Amazon who was wearing a tinfoil crown and had her skirt tucked in her knickers.

'See?' Stella said. 'Aunt Bea practically has to tie him down at night.'

The chaotic game seemed to be a very free variation on the theme of Pirates, with bits of Peter Pan thrown in. One group was swarming over Richard's car, parked in a corner of the meadow, and Richard himself could be seen standing on the bonnet wearing an eye-patch and brandishing a toy sword. The two young men – Knatchbull and Neeve – were doggedly reading a story to a few tired infants outside their tents, but even they had been sufficiently infected by the general madness to add spotted neckerchiefs to the shorts and hiking boots. As for Helen, she was squatting very elegantly on her haunches in front of a tent pole, her arms behind her back and a motley collection of feathers stuck in her buttery hair.

'I'm the Red Indian princess, Tiger Lily,' she informed them in her cool dry way, as they approached her in fits of giggles. 'I've been captured by the bad pirates and I'm going to be rescued by the good pirates. Or I *was* going to be. I rather suspect they've forgotten all about me. How, I wonder, can one be a *good* pirate? Does one politely ask for the treasure?' She got to her feet gracefully, brushing grass from her pleated silk dress. 'Well, I'm still in one piece. Hard to believe. Hard to believe I'm here at all, in fact. Why on earth do I keep coming? I can only suppose that I actually enjoy it.'

'Where did all this stuff come from?' Stella said, as a small Bluebeard hurtled past her in a pink cloak.

'Richard's been ransacking Cambridge market,' Helen said. 'What poor old Knatchbull and Neeve think of it, I don't know. I think they feel a bit supplanted. But the children are so worn out by three that they're quite happy to listen to Bible stories till teatime, so it works out quite fairly all in all. Oh – thank you,' she said, as a little girl presented her with a daisy chain. She added it to the half-dozen already round her neck and smiled ruefully at Kate and Stella. 'There's a bottle of hock in the boot of the car. What say we splice the mainbrace?'

Kate was unused to wine, and the clear golden stuff that Helen produced from a hamper in the car boot – 'now this is what *I* call buried treasure' – seemed to her alarmingly heady, though Helen sipped at it as if it were tea, and Stella drank it down as if it were lemonade. Richard joined them, though only after he had died a suitably dramatic death by toppling off the car bonnet with the sword sticking out from under his arm, and only after promising one of his most clinging followers that he would play again in a while.

'What we need is a ship,' he said, mopping back his sweat-soaked fringe. 'Kate, Stella, how are you? A ship with a plank you can walk and everything.'

'What do you propose?' Helen said. 'Flooding the fens?'

'Scoffer. A pretend ship. Their imagination will do the rest. Just an old boat hull or something, and some timber for a mast. The children could help to build it.'

'George Maxey's got a lot of old timber in his yard,' Kate said. 'He's our neighbour. I could ask him if you like.' The wine loosened her tongue. 'And we've got some old black serge at home somewhere. I could make a Jolly Roger.'

'Could you? That'd be marvellous. I could paint up my old trunk as a treasure chest . . .' Richard caught Stella's look of amusement, and grinned. 'Or am I taking this a bit too seriously?'

'Squaw say-um nothing,' Helen said, perching on the boot and enjoying her wine.

'Well, you've certainly livened Geoffrey up,' Stella said. 'I've never known him chatter so much.'

'He's a nice kid, isn't he?' Richard said. 'I don't think he's as slow as they make out. I think he just needs bringing out of himself. Lord, I've got a thirst. I wish we had some more of this stuff.'

'Coh, good job you haven't. I've got to get back to me picking soon,' Stella said. 'Any more of this and Ernie Delph'll find me face down in the strawberries.'

'And *you've* got to fight Billy Bones over there,' Helen said. 'He's waiting for you like a faithful pup.'

'Oh, him, he's Tarzan,' Richard said, offering cigarettes.

'How did Tarzan ever get mixed up with pirates?'

'It's his second job,' Richard said, deadpan. 'There's no money in the apeman business, you know. Barely keeps him in bananas . . .'

How nice they are, Kate thought, looking at each of them through a haze of wine and laughter: how different from anyone I've known. The lowering of the screen of inhibition also revealed to her, fleetingly, something of herself: revealed a person flattered and a little alarmed that such people should like her, include her.

For she was fascinated by each of them. Helen, so poised and at ease in the world, as if there was nothing it contained that could possibly surprise or disconcert her: Stella so at ease within her own leggy body, her frank, ripely friendly personality like a round fresh apple fitting into your outstretched hand; and Richard.

Most of all he was unlike any man she had ever met. She knew very little about him except that he had been at Cambridge and that he was, accordingly, from a world that hardly impinged on the Marshland at all – the world that was summed up in the one word 'posh'. Out here there were a few big farmers who, mainly by miserly garnering, achieved something like wealth, but nobody knew it till the reading of their misspelt wills; and of 'county society' there was virtually nothing. There was a Hall at Monks Bridge, but it was empty and half-derelict. Even the clergy out here tended to be eccentrics who mounted the pulpit with their hands black from planting celery. Kate's whole life had been spent amongst people who were all on an equality: she had been raised in a commonwealth. But everything about Richard proclaimed his foreignness, his difference. Helen too: but her cool self-containment made it less noticeable. Richard was not cool. He had much less reserve than the average young man of Monks Bridge, for example, who was dour with children and would not have countenanced leading them in an anarchic game of pirates. Yet he had no scoutmaster jolliness either. He was lithe and nervy where the local young men were blockish – they would have sat stiffly on the running board of the car rather than coiling themselves on to it as he did now; and he often seemed on the verge of saying something extremely saucy, which would appear in his eyes even when he thought better of it. He was transparent and opaque: he did not appear to think, as most young men of her acquaintance did, that masculinity required him to conceal his every thought and feeling as stubbornly as if he were under torture – and yet what he was really like, who Richard Marwood really was, she could not guess.

All in all Kate could very easily have fallen in love with him – very easily. The mere fact that she realized this, suggested to her that she probably wouldn't; but she couldn't be sure of any of her responses any more. Living all her life in this small village, ensconced in a close family, Kate was used to people as known quantities; and the same applied to herself. She was Kate Lutton, Walter Lutton's girl, the quiet one – everyone knew that. What else was there to know? Yet here with these three people there was mystery and discovery, and it cut both ways. She too was an unread book. She felt it with a solemn sort of excitement. She was a little tipsy.

'Don't you think Kate looks rather like Jessie Matthews?' Richard said all of a sudden, startling her out of her reverie.

His eyes dwelt on her, friendly but perceptive. That page in the book, at least, was very clear to him: the shyness that made her dread such a singling out, such a focusing of attention, talk suspended and all eyes on her. And she saw that he was offering her a challenge. He was daring her to blush and shrink and stammer and make them change the subject so that she could fade into the background. It was a challenge and it was also an avowal of faith in her. He believed she could overcome it and he was giving her the opportunity.

'Here, you do an' all,' Stella said, studying her. 'Just how she looked in *Evergreen*.'

'Ooh, I don't know about Jessie Matthews,' Kate said. 'When I see myself in the mirror first thing in the morning I reckon I look more like Jack Buchanan!'

To someone who had lived with shyness as Kate had, the general shout of laughter that greeted this was like being handed an unexpected gift. She felt absurdly pleased with herself yet even now she had to guard against the instinct to clam up, to feel she had done her bit. 'I wish I did look like her though,' she went on. 'I wish I could dance like her.'

'I wish I could dance at all,' Richard said. 'You have to shove me round the floor like a tailor's dummy.'

'Not true,' Helen said. 'You're very good at dancing. Like most frivolous pursuits.'

'They're the best kind,' Stella said, winking at Richard.

If there was a little friction in the air, a little rubbing of emotional elbows, it hardly lasted long enough for Kate to be aware of it. But something brought out her deepest instinct, the thing that for all her diffidence she knew she was good at – being the peacemaker. 'Well,' she said, 'we have a dance at Monks Bridge on our village feast day. There's the fete in the day and then in the evening there's a formal dance in the schoolhouse. Third Sunday in August. We can all show off our dancing then. If – if you'd like to come, I mean.'

'It sounds lovely,' Helen said. 'But I don't know whether I shall still be around then. At some point I shall have to go home.'

'Home – why?' Richard said. 'Spend the summer here, Helen. The Hamblins love having you. And look at this place. How can you go?'

'We all have to go home sooner or later, Richard,' Helen said, gently.

'Oh, I know that.' Richard's hand went to the top button of his shirt, unfastening it and then fastening it again, a little consoling habit that Kate had just begun to notice in him. 'But not till we've had our days in the sun. And in any case – ' he threw back his head, and the gaze he threw on the pure and gigantic fen sky was almost worshipful – 'which ever way you look at it, there won't be another summer like this one. Will there?'

## 2

There would never be another summer like it, Richard had said; and from the talk of war that filtered through even to the sun-drowsed, fruit-heavy fens, it seemed that that might be literally true.

But Stella didn't believe it, or chose not to, which for her came to the same thing. Once or twice when she was strawberry picking she looked up to see a procession of dark official-looking trucks go rumbling along the country road, heading, it was said, for a new airfield being built in West Norfolk; but the dust of their passing soon settled, and the throbbing of the engines would give way to the song of larks and the drunken buzzing of wasps.

And these things, Stella felt, were far more real and truthful than the gloomy mutterings about air raids and conscription. Some of her fellow fruit-pickers hankered for London as the novelty of their situation wore off, but Stella was surprised to find herself quite an enthusiast for the country. You could breathe out here. She found her appetite keener, her sleep more satisfying, her senses more alert. She found herself very much alive.

The work was tiring and sometimes monotonous, but it was leavened by the spirit of friendly communality that prevailed in the fields, not just amongst the pickers but with the locals too. When you took your chip baskets up to the trestles where the farmer or one of his family was counting and weighing, there was always a bit of backchat; she even managed at last to bring a twinkle into the eyes of Ernie Delph, who seemed frightened to death of her at first. And when the working day was over, there was plenty of cheerful company back at the camp. If she had had to spend the whole summer exclusively with Uncle Will and Auntie Bea, she would have been climbing the walls in short order; but luckily in the atmosphere of the camp, where scarcely an evening went by without an impromptu party under the stars, friendships came as naturally as breathing.

Enmities too. There were several deep-drinking docklanders present who liked to while away their leisure hours by putting each other's heads through the hut windows, and marital screaming matches punctured the deep country quiet at least once a night. Stella was not immune. She had her *bête noir* in the smooth shape of Frankie Hope, alias Frankly Hopeless.

He was awful, because he was so very nearly nice. He had the looks, except that weak self-pitying mouth; he had an attentive, tell-me-everything way about him that could win you over if you didn't happen to see the glint of the main chance behind those melting eyes. Stella was willing to bet that in spite of that groomed hair he was wearing the dirtiest old pair of drawers and hadn't washed his feet since Christmas, but she had no intention of finding out if she was right. He had already made a conquest of a naive little Jewish girl from Poplar who was now following him with bewildered eyes and wondering why he didn't say those sweet things to her any more, and it was plain that he had Stella next on his list. He played the mouth organ and once or twice had serenaded her with it outside her hut. It would have been laughable except for the fact that some girls had fallen for it and still carried the grief. And added to that there was something too shifty about Frankly Hopeless which suggested that what he could not have he would soon hate.

Disliking someone was one thing: finding that someone disliked you was another. It was always a shock, no matter who the person or how indifferent you were to their opinion. So it was with a woman called Mona Bloss, who had arrived at the camp a few days after the Tranters and who took against Stella with a vengeance for no apparent reason. Perhaps it was simply the fact of Stella's being there first, because it was plain that Mona Bloss liked to be queen bee. She was a hard-faced woman of thirty with a mass of crow-coloured hair that she tossed a lot, a big mouth made larger by liberal application of Tangee lipstick, and bosoms like unruly coconuts. Stella thought she looked like a horse in a black wig but there was no accounting for taste and there was no doubt that there was something about Mona Bloss that set the men tail on end. No doubt, too, that that was just the way she liked it: in fact by the end of the first week you could be forgiven for wondering whether she had come there to pick fruit or to pick men. Curiously enough, she had a husband, a little smirking rabbit of a man who took no especial heed of her flagrant goings-on, and even seemed to look on in a spirit of mild appreciation. As for Stella, she didn't care either way about Mona Bloss's man-eating activities: as she'd told Kate, she was out of that game and well rid of it. But Mona Bloss took it into her head to see Stella as some sort of rival, and the result was such a lot of snide stupidities as Stella hadn't endured since the school playground. 'Madam' was Mona Bloss's preferred title for Stella, and there was no denying it got Stella's goat. 'Oh, better hurry up, Madam's waiting,' Mona would say, if Stella was next in line behind her at the camp standpipe; or, 'Put the flags out, Madam's with us,' if they were picking in the same strawberry field. And she would flick that unlikely hair, and train the mighty bosoms on Stella like a pair of six-shooters.

For her part Stella consoled herself by rechristening the woman as Moaning Bliss, and she found a powerful ally in Auntie Bea who, not a person to conceal her feelings under any circumstances, became quite ungovernable when it came to Mona Bloss.

'I know her game,' Auntie Bea would hiss. 'I've seen her looking at my Will. She'd have the trousers off him faster than you can blink. That's the trouble being married to him, bless him. He's the sort women want. He gets 'em going. Well, she ain't having him!' And though, as she told Stella, she had too much dignity to bandy words with that sort, sometimes the presence of Mona Bloss provoked her into letting slip a hint of her feelings, such as 'What d'you think you're gawping at, you filthy mucky trollop? You 'ad your fourpenn'orth?'

It didn't matter. Frankly Hopeless and Moaning Bliss were insignificant clouds in the blue sky of Stella's days. She was not the type to put more energy into a feud than a friendship, and there were people here she greatly liked. Not least among them were the three who had helped her track down the errant Geoffrey on that first day: Kate, Helen and Richard.

Stella hated it when people said 'It just goes to show' and 'You can never tell' – but nevertheless it just went to show that you could never tell, because none of the three was the sort of person she would have imagined herself making friends with. A quiet country girl who wouldn't say boo to a goose; a vicar's daughter who looked as if she was wearing cast-iron knickers; a young college rip who motored about in a Riley and wouldn't know a pawnshop from his elbow . . . Well, that was how some of the folks back home would have dismissed them, and Stella might have thought the same herself, once. Not now, though. There was change in her; and it was perhaps too simple to say that it was coming here that had caused it. The feeling that there was more to life than Corbett Street must have played a part in her decision to come here in the first place.

And it *did* just go to show. Kate Lutton was a quiet country girl all right, but there was more to her than met the eye, Stella was sure of that. She saw a good deal of her as the pickers moved on to Walter Lutton's strawberry fields, and everything she saw she liked. Cursed with a skyrocket temper, Stella admired people who had the gift of calmness, and Kate Lutton had it: whenever a squabble or dispute arose amongst the pickers, who could be a bumptious lot when they had the sun on their necks and last night's booze in their livers, it was Kate who gently smoothed things over: sometimes it seemed her mere presence was enough to shame them into reason.

And yet there was a spark in her too – something sharp and bright and uncompromising. When you said something she seriously disagreed with, that spark penetrated the shyness and let you know it. One of the pickers, a very young man with more spots than sense, found that out one day when they were taking their dinner break in the field. The usual war talk had started, and the young man offered his opinion that having another war would be a good thing.

'I'd go. I'd go like a shot. My dad was in the last lot and he says he had the time of his life.'

'Then either he's a fool or you are,' said Kate, who had brought them out a batch of fresh-baked biscuits, and who suddenly trembled so hard she nearly dropped the tray. 'How can you say such things? You ought to be ashamed.'

The young man looked startled; but went on with an awkward shrug, 'Well, soldiering's a good life. It's comradeship, ennit?'

'Seeing your comrades get blown to bits,' Kate said, 'that's what it is. When will you men ever learn? Not until you've all killed each other off, I'll bet.'

'You certainly took him down and dusted him,' Stella said to her afterwards.

Kate flushed; but said with a flickering of the same spark, 'I can't bear to hear a young man say such things. I know it's just ignorance and not thinking, but it still makes me wild.'

'I liked it. Here, you're not one of those Quakers, are you?'

'No, I'm not anything.'

'Not even C of E?'

'Well, I don't believe in God, if that's what you mean.'

'No kidding?' Stella was not exactly shocked, but it was not what she expected from a girl like Kate – which also showed that you could never tell. 'My dad's a bit like that, but that's to do with him being a Bolshie. Stalin doesn't have any truck with religion so he doesn't either. Mum sometimes says it'd be nice if Comrade Stalin suddenly took to ironing and washing dishes.'

Yes, there was a lot more to Kate Lutton than met the eye: she had formed some pretty firm ideas for herself out here in the fens. And one of them, unfortunately, was that she was a dull plain nobody who ought to feel grateful every time anyone spoke to her.

She didn't say this in so many words, of course; but Stella, who was quick to form a judgement on people, came rapidly to the conclusion that that was what the shyness and hesitancy boiled down to. The girl didn't value herself – perhaps didn't even like herself. Stella saw it in her reaction to George Maxey.

Stella's own thought, when she first saw the big farmer climb down from his truck and stride across to the field where they were working, was that he was a fair old bit of talent: not exactly her type, but certainly a figure to knock Frankly Hopeless into a cocked hat. He was all of six foot two, with a corresponding breadth of shoulder, and just the right side of thirty. There was something slightly bull-like in the set of his shoulders and the way he came at you with his great dark head a little lowered; but that was offset by the gentlest pair of brown eyes, with lashes long and curved as a baby's. All in all, Stella reckoned, he would have the local girls round him like ants round a sugar bowl; but it was Kate, who was weighing at the trestles that day, that he had come to see.

It was about the timber that Kate had asked him for: it was in the back of his truck and he wanted to know where to unload it. Stella, picking and eavesdropping nearby, thought that if it hadn't been about that it would have been about something else. Anybody with eyes could see that he would have brought Kate a truckload of pearls if she'd asked him. Good for her, Stella thought; and when he had gone away again, after a few remarks so revealingly gruff and short that he might as well have gone down on one knee there and then, she could hardly wait to hustle her chips up to the trestle and quiz Kate about him.

'So, that's the George Maxey I keep hearing about,' she said eagerly.

'Yes,' Kate said, 'that's him.'

'And he's not married or spoken for? And he's got his own farm?'

'Yes. Arable, mostly.'

'Well – you're a cool one and no mistake. I suppose you realize what a glad eye he was giving you?'

'No, no . . .' For a moment Kate actually looked distressed. 'We're friends, that's all.'

Stella just looked at her, one eyebrow raised.

'Really, he's just a sort of . . . friend of the family.'

'Sort of.'

Suddenly Kate put her hand on the top of her head – the nearest she ever came to a tizzy – and moaned, 'Oh, Stella, I don't know . . . I don't know what he sees in me, it's . . . I think he's just kind, that's all, he can't really mean it . . .'

'Come off it,' Stella said, 'all you've got to do is reel him in—' but she stopped, seeing that Kate wasn't making the usual disclaimers that any girl short of an outright swell-head would make. She genuinely didn't believe that she had made a conquest.

Stella dropped it, because Kate's eyes were begging her to; but she intended picking it up again, quite soon. Not just because she was curious but because she cared about the girl – and if Kate Lutton was going to go around thinking a man was doing her a great honour by liking her then she was heading for trouble one way or another.

This was something Stella felt sure Helen would agree with her about. Stella wouldn't have ventured to predict much about what she would think or feel, simply because Helen Silverman didn't keep the goods in the shop window: she had some quality that Stella couldn't quite place even as she envied it – a sort of confident reserve. But one thing Stella was sure of; Helen would never let a man lead her by the nose. Her first uncharitable thought on meeting Helen, in fact, had been that she was what her father called the 'tailor-made' type: dry and spinstery and more interested in golf than men. Getting to know Helen made her aware not only of how mistaken this estimate was but how crudely dismissive were the terms of reference she had half-consciously taken on board from her father and his kind. For one thing Helen wasn't the sporty sort: even participating in the undemanding games of tag or rounders that the children enjoyed in the nursery meadow betrayed in Helen a sort of graceful gaucheness. As she freely confessed, she preferred a stiff drink to a brisk walk any day. As for the unwomanly quality of wanting an independent life of her own, Stella had seen enough of Frankly Hopeless and his predatory kind to put that in an entirely comprehensible light, even if it had never fully occurred to her before. The glumly pregnant girls who were a familiar sight at home, creeping along beside their thin-lipped mothers, had always seemed to Stella an inescapable fact of existence, like rain or old age: it was only when she was struck by the contrast between Helen Silverman and the broken-hearted, broken-spirited little girl whose bewildered eyes followed Frankly Hopeless wherever he swaggered that she began to see that such disasters were as much man-made as natural.

Of course, it was easier for Helen because she had money: everything was. But once again, new experience was making a mess of old preconceptions. The rich were different all right, but they were also different from each other. Stella admired Helen for her smartness and coolness and her obvious determination never to be anybody's doormat, but sometimes she displayed exactly that aloofness and asperity that in Corbett Street formed the caricature of the stuck-up toff, and Stella found that off-putting: you had to drop a hairpin once in a while. But at the other end of the scale, and making nonsense of the caricature, was Richard.

When Auntie Bea and Uncle Will had first told her about the Cambridge students coming up to the orchards to look after the children, Stella had pictured earnest young chaps of the sort who ran missions to the worst slum districts back home, trying to uplift the local boys with a mixture of boxing and Christianity. Overgrown Boy Scouts, in fact – and Knatchbull and Neeve fitted her prejudice perfectly. Richard overturned it.

The timber that George Maxey brought was, of course, for Richard and his dotty notion of building a pirate ship in the meadow. When the pirate ship did actually begin to take shape, Stella was surprised and then unsurprised. She had caught several hints from Helen, who seemed to like him only so much, that Richard was the type to put a lot of effort into something footling – with the obvious corollary that the serious business of life he simply let slide. Stella could understand that. She had no high regard for the serious business of life herself, believing that it would get you in the end whatever you did. He was, she saw, a tinkerer: he could knock up a very convincing model ship out of bits of wood but he wouldn't be able to put up a straight fence. Money again, of course: he could afford to be frivolous.

But if he'd been no more than an aimless young buck amusing himself with good works, Stella wouldn't have given him the time of day. As it was, she had a lot of time for Richard Marwood, not least because he had no solemnity in him. He didn't pretend: he was doing what he was doing because he enjoyed it. Solemnity was Stella's bugbear, and her feelings about it were perhaps even stronger than she knew. She hated it when Corbett Street marked a funeral with drawn curtains and hushed children: she hated the po-faced political wranglings of her father and his cronies: she hated the tragic stares and gulping demands with which the likes of Happy Harry conducted a courtship. She could put up with a lot of irresponsibility, even foolishness, as long as it didn't take itself seriously.

And little as she knew of Richard as yet, she knew he could be irresponsible. Several times Helen had to lend him money for petrol to get the two of them back to Cambridge of an evening: he couldn't resist a drink and more than once he turned up at the orchards in the morning looking like a deathly scarecrow. But when it came to the children he was always careful, and he was much handier with grazed knees and tearful tantrums than Knatchbull and Neeve, who groped at philanthropy through a screen of inhibition. And he had formed a special bond with Geoffrey.

The change in the withdrawn little boy was already plain to see, and it was Richard's doing. Instead of assuming that he was a clot who would be happiest working raffia, Richard gently pushed him. In the rambling play-acting games in the meadow he always thrust Geoffrey into a prominent role: when the children collected mushrooms from the morning grass, he set Geoffrey the task of counting them; and having conceived the idea of the children presenting a little show for the village feast, he began preparing Geoffrey for a solo recitation.

Geoffrey doing a recitation! Stella must have shared a little of his parents' opinion of him, because her first thought was that the boy might not be up to it; and when she came to the meadow after work one day to collect him and Cecil and Ivy, and found a rehearsal going on, she was sure of it.

'"Come live with me and be my love, And we all – we all will . . ."'

'"We will all the pleasures prove,"' Richard prompted him.

'"That valleys, groves, hills and fields . . ."'

Stella sat down on the grass and listened as Geoffrey stumbled through an obstacle course of jaw-cracking verses. The beginning was fair enough, but the rest sounded like gobbledygook to her.

'That's such a hard poem!' Stella said, when Geoffrey had finished and run off to Richard's car to fetch something he called his 'bolker'. 'Couldn't he do something easier?'

'That's the point. The more people underestimate him, the less he's going to try. He'll have that poem word perfect come the village feast, I promise you.'

'I wish you were his teacher.'

'God, I couldn't teach to save my life.'

'Get out of it. You seem to know what you're doing with Geoffrey.'

'Well . . . let's just say I know what it's like not to shine.'

His smile at this was so enigmatic that it might not have been a smile at all. She would have asked him about it if Geoffrey had not at that moment come charging back and proudly thrust the 'bolker' into her hands.

It was something that Geoffrey had carved from an old piece of wood. Stella thought at first it was meant to be a bird; then, holding it at another angle, decided it must be a motor car. It was neither of these things, Geoffrey informed her impatiently, it was a bolker. Stella, exchanging a glance with Richard, said it was a very nice bolker and left it at that.

But that was not the end of her dealings with the bolker, because that evening back at the camp she had to rescue it from the dustbin where Uncle Will threw it.

'Oh, he's always bringing bits of old rubbish home,' Auntie Bea shrilled blithely, 'and then he's forgot about 'em by next morning'; and when Stella expressed her indignation, saying that Geoffrey had made it with his own hands, they chuckled as if to say she was getting as bad as him.

'Good God, they're so bloody pig ignorant,' Stella muttered as she slipped the bolker under the sleeping Geoffrey's pillow; and at once felt desperately ashamed, as if she had found herself stealing from her mother's purse.

# FOUR

## 1

If Kate's father had been a less careful and conscientious farmer it might never have happened.

It was late afternoon, hot and hazy, and she was with her father in the west apple orchard, checking over the early-maturing Gladstone and Worcester Pearmains. Some fruit had been dropping prematurely because of the unbroken hot weather. Walter Lutton insisted on gathering these early drops, which were a magnet for wasps, but it was a point of honour with him not to sell them even as cooking fruit. And it was in the same scrupulous spirit that he propped his ladder against one of the damson trees that surrounded the orchard and climbed up.

He had no high opinion of damsons – he sometimes said that the only thing you could do with them was make them into jam and then throw the jam away – and the market demand for them was limited; the chief reason why he grew them was that the damson trees, being hardy, made excellent windbreaks for the more vulnerable apples. So it was not strictly necessary for him to mount up into the top of that tough Merryweather damson to bend and tie a single branch that was growing a little too woody. It was just the way he was.

Kate was picking up the last of the early drops when she heard the crack and the shout and then, what seemed all of five seconds later, the heavy thud. And she seemed to feel the thud through the ground at her feet as much as hear it.

She ran through the trees to where she had left him and it was as if she were running through a long tunnel of dread. The fact that she could hear him cursing and groaning at the other end of the tunnel did not make it any better for Kate: not at all.

'Dad! Dad . . .'

He was lying at the foot of the tree grinning at her. Of course, Walter Lutton was known as a bit of a joker . . .

But the grin wasn't his, not the grin she knew. It was the grin of an animal in extremity. It was pain and injury and at the sight of it the panic blasted through Kate, blowing away almost all other feelings. It was only with a supreme effort that she was able to make herself kneel down and touch him and speak to him.

'Where is it . . .? Oh, Dad, what – where . . .?'

'Dunno.' He couldn't sit up, could only gasp the words out through clenched teeth and grip fiercely and passionately at his own right shoulder. 'Heard it . . . felt it . . Gah!'

She muttered something and ran. Such was her state of wild fugue that at first she ran in wild zig-zags like a corralled deer, and when at last she headed for the house it was as much from some childlike instinct as with any practical purpose.

Her mother was there, her brother too: somehow they made sense of her gabblings and ran back to the orchard with her.

'Oh! Walter, whatever have you done . . .?' Her mother, after the first shock, was all practicality. She mopped his streaming face and slipped her thick brown arm under his shoulders to try and sit him up. But though he struggled, even with Pip supporting him on the other side the pain was too much.

'No good, gel . . . can't git up . . .'

Kate hovered at a distance, a stifling balloon-like sensation in her chest, a taste that was both coppery and powdery in her mouth. It was the taste of worst fears being realized.

'What do we do?' Pip, boylike in his distress, turned to her. It was natural. Usually Kate was the one who quietly cleared messy things up.

Not this, though. They would have to excuse her on this one because she simply couldn't, couldn't do anything, wanted only to flee . . .

'We'll have to get you to the hospital, duck,' Kate's mother said, stroking his hair; and then all three looked their helplessness. The truck was standing outside the house, but only Walter Lutton could drive it.

'Richard.' Kate blurted the word as if invoking the name of a saint. 'Richard can take you.'

She was at the Long Lane meadow in a couple of minutes, and within a couple of seconds of her gasping out the story Richard had shucked off his pirate cloak and unceremoniously shooed a brace of children off the bonnet of his car.

'Come on – jump in. We'll get him to hospital.'

Helen, after a searching glance at Kate's face, came with them. It was a tricky business steering the car through the orchard and Richard maintained a silent concentration. Helen, seated in the back with Kate, patted her hand and said, 'I'm sure it'll be all right. Where's the nearest hospital?'

'Peterborough.'

'Well. That's not too far. It'll be all right.'

But it would not have been, Kate thought, if it were not for other people: her uselessness burned her and burned her still as she watched Richard and Pip carefully lifting her father into the Riley, laying him on the back seat, her mother slipping in beside him – no clumsiness now – to support his head in her lap. Her love for her father burned her too: she wanted to weep but something else was too strong. It was fear, and it overmastered her completely when Richard hopped back in the driver's seat and beckoned to her.

'Room for both, if you want to squeeze in, Kate,' he said; but already she was shaking her head. Pip, Pip could go. She couldn't go, not to the hospital.

'I'll . . . I'll wait here,' she said. 'I'll wait at home,' and through a haze of unshed tears and self-loathing she watched Pip get in beside Richard and then her father lifting a hand in a weak affectionate wave as the car carried him away.

Helen was standing beside her. Tactfully she waited a while before speaking.

'I'm no doctor,' she said, 'but I'm pretty well sure that your father hasn't hurt himself as badly as you might think. He's got movement and feeling in his limbs and he's talking. I think we should go up to the house and have a cup of tea and then later telephone the hospital and see how he's doing. If you don't mind me inviting myself in, that is. No, I don't expect a smile. Come along.'

Kate didn't realize it just then, because all she wanted to do was hide her head, but an uneffusive, self-contained presence like Helen's was just what she needed – indeed, was the only one that would have been tolerable. Like a sleepwalker she went up to the house, where Helen made her sit down while she made tea, quietly and unfussily finding her way about the kitchen and wholly refraining from intrusive consolation.

'Well! Entertaining as they are, it's nice to be free of children's voices for a little while,' Helen said, bringing the tea tray to the kitchen table. 'Messrs Knatchbull and Neeve were just getting ready to give them a dose of hymns anyway. Ancient and Modern, Richard calls them, not to their faces of course. Here. Sugar's supposed to be good for shock.'

'Oh – I'm all right. I'm not the one who's . . . been hurt.' Kate dipped her lips in the sweet tea, but could not swallow. 'All these years with the orchards and pruning and lopping and he's never had an accident before; well that's not true, once he slipped a bit and hurt himself with the saw but . . .'

Kate ran down exactly like an alarm clock. She stared at the tea things and into the silence.

'My dear,' Helen said gently, 'there's no sin in being squeamish.'

'Isn't there? Even when it's your own father lying there?'

Helen looked at her mildly.

'I'm just no good with illness. I go to pieces. I know it but I can't stop it.'

'I'm sure your father understands. And I'm sure he's going to be quite all right. We'll go down to the village and telephone to the hospital soon. Drink your tea.'

'This is very kind of you.'

'Not at all. Thank you for *your* company. I'm rather afraid you can't get rid of me till Richard gets back with the car.'

'Oh – I didn't think—'

'No, no. Aunt Hamblin never minds what hour I get in. D'you know, when her friends ask where I go all day she tells them I'm "helping with the harvest". Rather makes me feel like one of those German maidens with blonde plaits all bound up on their heads. Not that I think German maidens can do much any more except have babies for the master race. Absurd. Hitler looks about as Nordic as Disraeli and Goebbels isn't exactly prime breeding stock . . . Kate, I'm not *very* good with tears, but I can manage, honestly.'

They came and were noisy, though they did not last long. They were for her father but they were for something else too and it was the anguish of that which lingered after the honkings into the handkerchief and the stammering assurances that she was better now . . . better.

She was not better, because what had happened – and most of all her response to it – had raised a ghost that would not be laid. And all of a sudden she found she was talking about it. It was not because Helen asked her or even subtly invited confidences: she simply sat in an attitude of relaxed attention, as if prepared to wait any amount of time for anything or for nothing. It was a social skill but it was a skill of personality too and it had the effect on Kate of cutting through the tight grim knot that kept in the dreadful figure of Uncle Ralph.

The worst part of it was, he was such a nice man: a man with all the geniality of his brother, Kate's father, and rather more evenness of temper. It was the Great War that had thrust upon him the role of childhood demon. Kate had been born after the war had ended, and it had touched her life very little until the coming of Uncle Ralph. Her father had been spared service because of a chest defect, and only the slow raising of the clocktower memorial in the centre of the village gave her infant mind a glimmering notion that something vast and cruel had taken place beyond the edges of her quiet world.

Uncle Ralph had gone to the front as a corporal in 1917 and been brought back to England three months later, shattered and barely alive. Surgeons toiled long over him and at last released to the uninterested world a twenty-four-year-old man who had one leg, one usable arm, a face that had been cobbled together like a badly darned sock, and chronic breathing and skin conditions. It was hardly too much to say that there was not a single part of Uncle Ralph that gave him no pain.

He had a wife. She had married him when he was not only bearable to look at but handsome. She looked after the maimed imposter whom the war had returned to her for five years, and then one day couldn't take it any more and ran away.

Kate's mother and father took him in. It was about that time that the illustrated papers began to show a lot of inspiring pictures of disabled ex-soldiers taking up new trades and making new lives: gamely they fathered twins and shoed horses with three-fingered hands and learnt Braille. But Uncle Ralph was not like that. He was too ill: in fact his days were spent in a long slow process of dying. The agonies of a battlefield death were his, except that they lasted for seven years.

'Children are supposed to be good at these things, aren't they?' Kate said. 'It's supposed to be the grown-ups who are all awkward and revolted by it while the children are sort of innocent and don't mind touching Grandpa's funny thumb or whatever. I wasn't. I hated to look at Uncle Ralph, he was so ugly and frightening, and yet I think I hated myself for that because I knew he couldn't help it. Looking back, I think he knew: he tried to cover himself up and keep out of my way as much as he could. But he loved children. I think he would have loved it if I'd been . . . you know, a little friend to him instead of avoiding him. Isn't that a terrible thing? When I think of it . . .'

'I don't believe a five-year-old can be a very bad person, you know,' Helen said. 'Not in the way you think.'

Kate shrugged: she was not so sure about that. 'He didn't complain, not really. But he suffered such a lot of pain that sometimes he couldn't help groaning and crying out and weeping.

Sometimes he screamed. I've read about that somewhere: women scream in fear but men scream in pain. It's an awful sound . . . Mum and Dad were very good. The district nurse came round to help with some things but mostly it was them. He had a bedroom at the front of the house. I used to run past the door. It's awful I know but I thought of it like a . . . a torture chamber or something, it was where these sounds came from and where Uncle Ralph had to have things done to him and sometimes when the door was open you'd see his crutch leaning there and there was something about it, the leather pad all frayed and sweat-stained . . . Sorry. I don't know what I must sound like.'

Helen, chin on hand, made a gentle negative.

'Well, poor old Uncle Ralph was – set free of it at last. He used to have a nap in his room in the early afternoons, I think he tended to sleep better then, and one day . . .' Kate folded her hands in her lap: some people took that for quiet self-possession, though it was really to stop them trembling. 'One day he was up there, and Dad was out working in the glasshouses and Mum, she was carrying Pip at the time, she was having a sit down in the kitchen . . . and I went upstairs to my bedroom to fetch my dolls. I was going to hurry past Uncle Ralph's room as usual, but he – he called out to me. He must have heard my footsteps and he called out "Katie!" and then again "Katie!" in this voice that was like . . . Well. Even I couldn't be such a little beast as to ignore it, and so I pushed open the door; it was just slightly ajar and I pushed it open and found him lying on the floor. He'd tried to get to the door, I suppose, but he'd collapsed. He was naked – he preferred to go without clothes as much as he could because of his skin. He was just sort of floundering there and clutching at his stomach with his good hand. And he was wetting himself as he lay there, and the stump of his leg was wagging, that's the only word I can think of, so dreadfully red and sore it looked, just like meat—'

'Oh, my dear.' Helen reached out a hand. 'That must have been—'

'Oh, I was all right, I was a perfectly healthy little brat with my life ahead of me, I wasn't the one lying there like that . . . Well, he was kind even then. He said "Fetch Mum or Dad, quick, could you, duck?" God knows what it cost him to speak like that but he did, and he tried to get hold of the counterpane off the bed to cover himself up because he knew it frightened me so . . . Well, I ran and fetched Mum and Dad, and the doctor came out from Wisbech, and then they moved him to the infirmary at Peterborough, but he was dead by the next morning. It was something to do with his stomach – that was a mess too, he'd got shrapnel in his abdomen, and something ruptured at last, and that was the end.'

She had never spoken of this to anyone – even with her family she fell silent if the subject was mentioned – but there was no glad relief of unburdening: her feelings, as far as she could understand them, were more like those of a criminal finding a long-regretted misdeed exposed at last. 'Well,' she went on, as Helen still gravely regarded her, 'you'd think after something like that I would get a grip of myself, wouldn't you? But I've got worse over the years. When Pip got scarlet fever and needed a lot of nursing – I was simply useless. Couldn't even sit with him. Mum cut her finger at the sink once and I had to run half a mile and fetch Dad because I just couldn't put the bandage on for her. And now when Richard asked if I wanted to come to the hospital . . . Did that seem very bad?'

'No,' Helen said. 'I can see it makes you think you're bad, but it's not so. I'm sure you're not the only one who has those sort of feelings. I don't know how I'd manage myself if it came to it – my family have always been disgustingly healthy.'

'Richard must have thought I – I didn't care or something.'

'Richard doesn't judge. That's one thing I can definitely say for him. In fact I don't know what you'd have to do to earn Richard's disapproval.'

'Well, it was very kind of him to take Dad. I must make sure and thank him . . .' All of a sudden it was as if Kate became aware of her own voice, and how long it had gone on. She began falteringly to apologize, but Helen was firm.

'My dear, there is absolutely nothing wrong with talking. I

think it's the healthiest exercise there is. At Cambridge there are people who never do anything *but* talk, and no one thinks any the worse of them for it.'

'I feel a fool, going on—'

'Then you shouldn't. I feel honoured that you've told me. A confidence is like a gift and I appreciate this one.'

It seemed to Kate a nice way of putting it and very typical of Helen: for her, words were a useful tool instead of a snare. 'I do wish,' Kate said suddenly, 'that I was more like you.'

Helen laughed. 'Justify that extraordinary statement.'

'Oh, I don't know . . . It's something about being in control of your own life. It's like if we were boats – I'd be a sailing boat or something, at the mercy of the winds . . .' Suddenly they were both laughing. 'And you'd be a steamboat, ploughing straight ahead . . .'

'Oh, my dear . . .' Helen patted her face with a handkerchief, regarding Kate with bright amused eyes. 'I've been called some things in my time, but I have never been compared with a steamboat. Dear, dear. It's a tantalizing comparison though. I have a feeling I'm not going to be able to look at anybody now without wondering what sort of marine vessel they would make. Aunt Hamblin, now, would surely be a little tugboat. And Stella . . . perhaps a pleasure boat?'

'How about Richard?'

'Richard, let's see . . .' Helen's eyes fixed themselves on the distance, and the expression in them was unreadable. 'How about a gondola? Something charming and singular and not entirely real.' She put her handkerchief away. 'Well now. What do you say we walk down to the village and see if there's any news from the hospital.'

There was a certain change in her: she was quiet as they walked. Kate, whose laughter had had a certain hysteria of anxiety in it, wondered if she had offended.

'I didn't mean,' she offered, 'about the steamboat, you know – I didn't mean—'

'Hush, I take it as a compliment,' Helen said, coming out of her abstraction. 'But even steamboats can go off course, you know . . . Here we are. Would you like me to telephone?'

Kate gratefully said yes; and while she waited outside the telephone box gave a brief account of what had happened to Mr Gathergood, who popped out of his shop like a lugubrious jack-in-the-box, and would have stayed to hear the rest if the tiresome inconvenience of a customer had not called him back in. Kate chewed her fingers and stared at the clocktower and the two sparrows having a feathery squabble under its eaves and wondered if this was to be one of those moments that are imprinted on the mind with all their details nightmarishly intact . . .

Helen was touching her arm.

'Broken collarbone and two cracked ribs. Patient resting comfortably, as they call it. Sounds most uncomfortable to me, but there we are. My dear, he's going to be all right.'

'Is he – will he—?'

'Oh, it's horrid and painful and I'm sure he'll have to stay in hospital for a while, but he'll mend, Kate, I swear. Where I come from is, alas, hunting country and that frightful crew are always breaking their collarbones. They do it on an annual basis. Unfurrow the brow, my dear. Now I don't know how long it'll be before the others get back but I suggest we can't do better than wait at the house, if you can put up with my company for a while longer, that is. And if you were absolutely to force me to take a slice of that admirable ham I saw in your kitchen I dare say I'd accept. Yes, it's funny how relief makes you cry, isn't it? As a child I never used to cry when I had to visit the dentist but I would always cry after. Never mind, my dear, there's no one to see. Come along . . . Why, I wonder, do they say "stiff upper lip"? It's the lower lip that lets you down . . .'

## 2

It was as Helen had said: Walter Lutton would mend, but he had to remain in the hospital at Peterborough for the time being, and that meant the Lutton farm was without its guiding spirit right at the height of the picking season. And fruit, as he often said, had to be caught right: harvest a week early or late and your whole year's crop was so much mulch.

He could, of course, give instructions from his hospital bed, and did. Kate and her mother, from experience, could judge fruit almost as well as he; and there was no problem in getting labour for picking and packing. But soft and stone fruits could not be stored like grain in a barn. They had to be transported to the wholesalers, quickly.

That was where Richard came in. He had as good as said, when he brought Maud and Pip Lutton back home late on the evening of Walter's accident, that he was idle, willing, and entirely at their disposal; but Kate's mother was a little in awe of him, and would have fought shy of his offer if Richard had not presented them with a *fait accompli* by turning up early at the house a couple of days later dressed in rough corduroys and a workshirt and, absurdly, a hat with a piece of string dangling from it.

'This is what they used to do at the old hiring-fairs,' he told Kate. 'If you were a thatcher you had a piece of straw in your hat. If you were a carter – ' he flicked the string with his finger – 'you had a piece of whipcord. That's me. I'm offering you my services as a carter. Now you take the string off. That means I'm hired. Now throw the string on the ground. That means I want to do it for nothing and won't take no for an answer—'

'You're making this up as you go along,' Kate laughed.

'No, no, all authentic. Of course when I say carter I mean truck driver but, you know, I could hardly have a tyre or a, what, petrol cap on my hat, could I? I mean I would just look silly.'

So Richard took over the truck-driving duties, with Kate accompanying him to the wholesalers to navigate and to do the bargaining on her father's behalf. Formerly her shyness would have flinched like a touched snail at the thought of this; but she already felt that she had let her father down – she still could not bring herself to visit the hospital – and in compensation she made herself jump into the deep end, swapping gnarled fen witticisms with the buyers as they fingered the wax-papered samples and standing her ground when, eyeing her size and sex and nervous colour, they tried to do her down. In the end she drove some pretty tough bargains, and surprised herself in more ways than one.

The strawberries were over now and it was picking time for the cherries, plums and gages – the busiest part of the season. Richard's new role kept him well occupied, and though he tried to make time each day to be with the children and Helen kept the wild games going as best she could, they missed him. 'I rather fancy Ancient and Modern are glad I'm out of the way, though,' he said. 'I think they regret ever inviting me out here at all. They want to improve the kids, not turn 'em into hooligans. I dare say they're right.'

'Oh, I hate all that churchy stuff,' Kate said. 'It just makes hypocrites. I wouldn't let any child of mine be force-fed with that rubbish. I'd rather it grew up a heathen.'

'Good for you.' Richard relished it when she talked in this robust way. 'Would you like to have children, Kate?'

It was a curious question: if you were a woman it was naturally assumed that you wanted to, unless you were strange or wicked. In fact the prospect terrified her, though she had never said so. But it was typical of Richard to ask it, and typical that he should ask it as they were bowling along a fen causeway, amongst the smell of exhaust fumes and rattling of crates.

'Children perhaps,' she temporized. 'Not babies. I don't see the appeal of babies. I'd rather they came ready grown, walking and talking and showing a bit of personality.'

'I'd like six or seven. But Helen would tick me off for that, no doubt.'

'Why?'

'Well, on the grounds that this is no world to bring a child into just now. International tension. The gathering darkness and all that. I don't know. Isn't that just giving in to the darkness? My God, look at that – we've talked about religion and politics without arguing.'

She did not find this so surprising: in her home no one ever argued. 'Is that very unusual?'

'Let's just say I wouldn't try the experiment where I come from.'

'Where *do* you come from, Richard?'

'Oh, nowhere much.' His hand went to his shirt, buttoning and unbuttoning. 'Schloss Marwood is to be found at a place called Abbotsleigh. It's on the border between Hertfordshire and Essex – neither of them particularly want it, in effect. It was once a little country village where real things went on but then they built a railway station and some villas with cupolas and tennis courts and it became nowhere instead of somewhere. From there my father went to the City every day and from there I was sent away to school and from there my brother Maurice now goes to the City likewise, my father having sort of retired . . . Sorry, it's dreary, isn't it? Don't take any notice. They're splendid people. It's just different.' He was a great talker and could spin out a bright conversational thread from anything or nothing, but this subject shut him up like an oyster.

She avoided it, because she valued their talks. They sometimes made her wonder, again, whether she was falling in love with him; and again she concluded that she was not. The occasional flirtatiousness he displayed was so much a part of his general lightness of character that she could not imagine it narrowing into something more specific; and besides, within Kate the place for such feelings was already occupied – partly, confusingly.

She wasn't sure when it was that George Maxey had first begun to present himself to her in the light of a lover. His figure had always been part of her landscape; and though he was only eight or nine years her senior, he seemed to her always to have been a grown man. Perhaps it was because he had entered on his inheritance early, his parents both dying when he was barely twenty-one and leaving him sole master of the largest farm in the district; but it was something to do also with the massive assurance of his personality, which had always seemed to her to incarnate everything that she lacked. There had been a touch of equivocation in her response to Stella's quizzing that day in the strawberry field – she knew well enough that George's interest in her was more than that of a friend and neighbour; but her perplexity at this was real enough. Finding herself singled out by George Maxey felt, to Kate, like discovering she could conjure rain or heal with her bare hands – a singular and alarming concentration on her of a force of nature.

And George was no flirt. He went at everything with that head-on, bull-like determination that characterized his work on the farm, where he had been seen to mow a two-acre hayfield single-handed before breakfast, barely breaking into a sweat as he did so. His battles with the local Drainage Board were legendary: he beat them every time. George was a little short-sighted – his refusal to wear glasses was a curious twist of vanity in his ruggedly straightforward character – and there was something of this in the way he went about life, concentrating with narrow intensity on what he wanted and letting minor detail take care of itself.

And at some point he had fastened that potent attention on Kate. She was, undeniably, flattered; but her self-regard was so little developed that she had a feeling of being an imposter – that he would surely wake up soon and discover his mistake. Confusion came with the competing knowledge that George Maxey was the last man in the world to delude himself. He knew her very well, almost as well as her own brother: it didn't put him off.

Assessing the shape of her own feelings for him through such a fog of self-doubt was no easy matter, and Kate, with an impulse that she recognized as all too typical, preferred to take refuge in denial rather than make the attempt. One thing was for sure: in George's attitude to her there was a strong streak of protectiveness, if not possessiveness, as befitted a man who had an air of being prepared at any moment to take the weight of the world on his shoulders. As soon as he heard of her father's accident he was prompt with offers of help, despite it being the busiest time of year on his own farm: Kate had no doubt that he would have gone without sleep entirely if it had been required of him. He was plainly put out to find Richard stepping into the breach. Things and people that he did not like he tended to ignore, simply denying them the honour of his rather fierce attention; but his opinion of the Cambridge cuckoos in general and Richard in particular was obvious.

'Oh, yes, it's very good of the fellow, I suppose,' he said when he called at the house one evening to inquire after her father. 'But you'll have to take care, you know, that he doesn't leave you in the lurch.'

'Why should he do that?'

'Well, because it doesn't matter to him. These people come up here with these fine ideas about helping out, but they're only playing at it really. They can chuck it any time when they get fed up.'

'Oh, Richard likes doing it.'

'Precisely what I mean.' George registered a fleeting distaste at her use of Richard's name, but his gaze on her was as intent as ever: he never looked away. 'When he stops liking it, he'll pack it in. That's not a luxury we can afford. But don't worry if that happens. Just promise me you'll call on me as soon as it does.'

She didn't think it would happen. Whether or not Richard was using the orchard summer as an excuse for not facing up to the world, as Helen sometimes seemed to suggest, there was nothing half-hearted about his involvement there. Rather more surprising to Kate was the fact that Helen herself still came up with him practically every day. Something drew her, and Kate couldn't suppose it was simply the friendship they had formed. That was undoubtedly real, however – even Kate's habitual self-deprecation had to admit that; and what was more, Helen took the responsibilities of friendship seriously. She persuaded Kate to visit her father in the hospital.

She had several times given Kate's mother and brother a lift down to Peterborough in Richard's car, but had carefully refrained from pressing Kate on the matter. And it was with the same care and tact that she came upon Kate when she was alone in the glasshouses one afternoon and said, 'Well, the brats are all blessedly sleeping in the shade – Aunt Hamblin sent them down a very large hamper of cakes which did the impossible and actually made them quiet. So I thought I'd drive down to Peterborough. What do you say to coming with me?'

The guilt was burdensome: Helen was offering to help lift it. Kate looked into the face of her own fear, and found it monstrous still – but she was not alone with it.

'Thank you,' she said. 'I'd like to.'

That was how Helen did it: she maintained the helpful fiction that they were just going for a drive, and even when they were on the road to Peterborough she made no mention of Kate's father or the hospital. Instead she talked to Kate in her urbane way of some promising news she had had.

'You know I've got my heart set on having a fling at journalism. Well, I've had a reply to a letter I wrote to a marvellous woman called Olive Kingswell. The *grande dame* of women journalists. We met briefly at Cambridge and she was kind enough to encourage me in my notions and, well, the upshot is she's invited me down to London to have lunch with her on the twentieth and let's just say she's not a woman to give away her time lightly. Which doesn't mean, I have to keep reminding myself, that I'm instantly going to be the leader writer for *The Times*, nor even that she's going to do anything more than advise me to drop the whole idea. But it is exciting.'

'When did you decide that that was what you wanted to do?' Kate asked, interested in spite of the fear that was looming on the edge of her consciousness like the giant kilns on the horizon – the brick-kilns of Peterborough.

'Oh, years ago, I think,' Helen said. 'Probably back when I completely monopolized the school newspaper. Whoops, that's bad style. "Completely monopolize" is a tautology. Miss Kingswell would have my head. She writes so brilliantly. Clarity and precision, no muddled thinking, not a word too many. That's what I must aim at.' Kate saw Helen tilt her long-jawed profile, as if scenting a breeze from the future. 'That's what I shall always aim at.'

'It must be wonderful to know exactly what you want to do in life,' Kate said.

'Oh, my dear, you know me, the old steamboat,' Helen said with a brief laugh. 'But what about you, Kate? What do you want to do?'

Kate gazed at the road ahead a moment and then without knowing why said, 'I should like to be able to drive.'

'Yes? Well, it's not difficult to learn. Believe me, I have all the physical co-ordination of Laurel and Hardy, and I managed it. My father taught me. He has some idea that a woman who can drive is not so much at the mercy of cads.'

Kate felt an inward murmur of disloyalty: for, momentarily, her heart had reproved her own father. He had sometimes spoken of teaching Pip to drive – but not the women in his family. She perceived that his undoubted affection for her mother and herself fell some way short of respect, and that affection without respect was fitter for dolls and teddy-bears than for people; and the perception once made could not be unmade. She covered it up, but already it altered her. One curious by-product was that her fear of the hospital visit began to diminish a little. She would still rather have had several teeth pulled than enter that place of sick sounds and rubber-soled shoes and Lysol smell, but she no longer feared that she would explode in wild panic as soon as it came into view.

Nor did she. As they drove into the city past the cathedral Helen commented on the beauty of the Bishop's Gardens and suggested a walk there; but grateful as she was for the thought, Kate declined and said she would like to go straight to the hospital. And when they parked outside the building, a florid structure of burgher solidity built as a memorial to the city's fallen in the war, Kate was the first to get out of the car and approach the steps.

There were bad moments. The place seemed as big as a castle inside: the squeak of a wheelchair echoing round the high ceilings scraped on Kate's nerves like fingernails on slate; a glimpse of the mute face of a dreadfully ill child in a side ward nearly sent her running. But at last she stood beside her father's bed, Helen a tactful distance behind her.

And he was still her father. Despite the neck-brace and the plaster and the ghastly accoutrements of healing, it was her father's face that looked up in almost stunned surprise to see Kate standing over him. Not a sick person's face: not Uncle Ralph's face. Her father.

And the realization of the victory she had achieved, coupled with a renewed twinge at the disloyalty of her earlier thoughts, prompted Kate to an uncharacteristic gesture. The Luttons were not a hugging and kissing family, but she hugged and kissed – as far as she could without hurting him.

'Well, gel! Well, my old booty! This is a treat!' he gasped. And then, showing that he too could be tactful, he did not embarrass her with references to what she had done; instead giving her hand a speaking squeeze, and asking as if it had been the one thing on his mind, 'Now, how are the cherries a-doing?'

## 3

How Auntie Bea came to be perching on the roof of their hut clutching a frying pan and threatening to throw herself off was a difficult question to answer unless you knew her. And even when you knew her as Stella did it was a bit of a facer. You had to remind yourself that with Bea and Will's lot, a crisis was not something that was ominously built up to. It just fell out of the sky.

They had been plum-picking all that day for Ernie Delph: a balmy, peaceful day's work in the shade of the scented trees, with only a minor irritant for Stella in the top-heavy shape of Mona Bloss, alias Moaning Bliss, who could not mount a stepladder without a lot of pneumatic wiggling, and who made several loud asides about how sorry she felt for people with red hair and freckles. Auntie Bea and Uncle Will were, if anything, in lovebird mood, roguishly feeding each other with hard-boiled eggs at the dinner break and even nibbling at either end of the same sausage, a sight which Uncle Will's dentures rendered more trying than affecting. And when at the end of the day they elected to go down to the pub in the village 'for a swift half', leaving Stella to pick up the children and take them back to the camp, she thought nothing of it beyond mildly registering how nice it was to see an old married couple go off with their fingers intertwined like that.

She found the children in the meadow sleepy and quiescent from cakes sent down by Helen's aunt in Cambridge. Richard was there, and tired too. He had been helping out with packing and loading for the Luttons earlier, but he had made time to coach a not-very-responsive Geoffrey in his recitation. The pair of them, with Cecil and Ivy, were lying under a tree desultorily making daisy chains when Stella found them.

'Isn't Helen here?' Stella said.

'She borrowed the car to take Kate down to Peterborough to visit her father,' Richard yawned. 'Said she'd meet me back at the Luttons'. So I'm temporarily grounded. Not that I mind. Just lay my weary bones down. Soft living, Stella. Had it too easy.'

She looked at him lying there, flat out like a cat in a sun pool, lazy and humorous, his impenetrably dark brown eyes squinting up at her. Now as she had told Kate and as she had told herself, she was out of that game because it was more trouble than it was worth. Just her and the fruit and the ten-bob notes nicely accumulating. She had had a letter from her mother only yesterday informing her – amongst much impish and affectionate gossip that made the tears start to Stella's eyes – that Happy Harry asked after her on average three times a day and wished her to know that he would Wait For Her; and that should have been a sufficient reminder of what happened when you let yourself fall. They said a fool and his money were soon parted and the same surely applied to your heart. So this tantalized, magnetized, fascinated and downright attracted feeling she got when she was around Richard was not to be viewed as anything but a contemptible weakness, and certainly not to be acted on.

But as long as she knew – as long as she was forearmed, wise, not about to make a fool of herself – then there was no reason why she shouldn't be good friends with him. Enjoy his company. Why not?

'Why don't you . . .' She cleared her throat, which seemed to be full of sand. 'Why don't you come back to the hut with us, and have a bite to eat?'

He sprang up as if he were made of rubber. 'Could I really? I must admit I'm famished. Would your uncle and aunt mind?'

'Mind? I doubt it, last I saw of them they were headed for the boozer. It won't be a feast, you know, but we've got some nice potted beef in, and there's a pork-and-egg pie wants eating.'

'Food of the gods. I must say it's awfully kind of you.'

It tickled her when he talked like that: touched her also, somehow; she didn't know why.

She decided not to think about it.

Geoffrey, at any rate, was thrilled at the prospect of Richard's coming back with them, and claimed his hand at once, while Stella was tugged along by Cecil and Ivy. At the camp some of the fruit-pickers were already back, and some were enjoying the impromptu showerbaths that a couple of joiners from Stepney had rigged up in the quadrangles – wonderful contraptions, but the canvas screens barely covered your modesty and the sight always made the children fizz with laughter. A ludicrous sight of a less pleasant sort was Frankly Hopeless, lounging on a deckchair outside his hut like a poor man's Franchot Tone. He made it quite plain that he had seen her, and who she was with: she wasn't quite sure what the low soft whistle he let out was meant to signify. There was, at least, no sign of Moaning Bliss. Stella had a moment of panic as she opened the hut door – suppose, as was not unlikely, the place looked a disgrace, festooned with Uncle Will's gigantic combinations or something? But it didn't look too bad: they had partitioned it with curtains made out of old blankets, and luckily most of the unmentionables were hidden.

And besides, it was Richard who was coming in, not Lord Muck. If he'd had any trace of the snob she wouldn't have liked him. And his first action on entering was to throw down his jacket and roll up his sleeves and cry, 'Now, what can I do?'

'Well, you can light the oil stove if you like, and lay the table. No, what am I saying? You sit yourself down, you've been on the go all day.'

'So have you.'

'Well, I'm the host and you're the guest, so do as you're told.' She found him standing quite near her, his hands out in a willing gesture, and she suddenly slapped out at him with a sort of playful embarrassment.

The children didn't want much tea, after their picnic, and Cecil and Ivy soon ran out to play. Geoffrey stayed with them, though; and Stella was rather glad. Somehow Richard seemed bigger in here, darker, more vivid – altogether rather too much to be alone with. 'Remember,' she had to admonish herself, as they sat together at the little deal table, and again, 'Remember,' when Richard ran outside and came back with a little spray of wild poppies and placed them in a glass in the middle of the table, 'Remember – remember Happy Harry!'

Geoffrey, at any rate, felt no awkwardness, and regaled them with a garbled version of his recitation throughout the meal.

'Nearly there, old son,' Richard said, with no trace of impatience. 'We'll have you word perfect come the great day.'

'What is that poem all about then?' Stella said. 'Is it Shakespeare?'

'It's Marlowe. He lived about the same time as Shakespeare. A rum character, Marlowe. He worked as a spy and ended up being stabbed in a pub brawl. And he declared his favourite things to be tobacco and boys.'

'Blimey.' Stella was a little wide eyed: this was startling talk, for while she was used to colourful obscenities, they didn't really have reference to anything. 'Here, there's nothing saucy in that poem, is there? Aunt Bea'd have a fit.'

'No. Just pure romance. The shepherd invites his love to an idyllic life in the country. "And I will make thee beds of roses, And a thousand fragrant posies."'

'Beds of roses, eh?' Stella said. 'Just what they're always telling you life isn't.'

'That's what Sir Walter Raleigh thought. He wrote a reply to the poem, pouring cold water on it. "Thy gowns, thy shoes, thy beds of roses, Thy cap, thy kirtle, and thy posies, Soon break, soon wither, soon forgotten, In folly ripe, in reason rotten." In other words, forget it, because it isn't going to last. More realistic, of course. Or is it? Maybe they're lying when they say life can't be a bed of roses. Maybe it's just because they haven't found it so. What do you think?'

Stella thought. 'I'd be on the first chap's side. Nothing lasts for ever, does it? You'd never try anything if you thought like that. In fact, you wouldn't bother living at all.'

He gazed at her. 'I knew you'd understand.'

'It's not that hard,' she laughed.

'People don't, though,' he said with energy. 'They don't! You're supposed to be sensible. Now why?' He made an inquisitorial gesture with his butter-knife. 'Aha! See? No answer to it. Why be sensible? No reason. Whoever heard of a sensible dog? Or cat, or mouse? Nobody.'

'Maybe not a dog or a cat,' Stella said. 'But a mouse, like a fieldmouse or something, he has to be sensible in a way. He has to go round gathering seeds to eat or whatever, and making a nest to bring the baby mice up in, rather than just – just . . .'

'Going down to the Mouse's Arms and playing dominoes,' Richard said very seriously.

She looked at him a moment and then shrieked with laughter. 'What am I talking about? What on earth am I talking about?'

'The domestic life of a fieldmouse. Don't stop, it was interesting. I don't know about the dominoes though because the spots would be *very* small and there might be a lot of arguments, you know, and disputed points—'

'You idiot!' She clashed her knife against his.

'*En garde!*'

The sword fight carried them all round the hut, with Geoffrey whooping after them. Stella won it at last by seizing the flour bin and throwing the whole lot over him.

'Not fair!' Richard cried. 'Douglas Fairbanks never did that!'

'All's fair in love and war,' Stella gasped, holding her sides.

'Well, I never said anything about *war* . . .'

The moment's swimming pause that followed alerted them to something. They had been making a lot of noise in the hut, but now they were quiet the noise went on – up above them.

'What on earth . . .?' Richard said, shaking flour out of his hair.

She thought at first that the noises on the roof must mean Cecil and Ivy, who had the tearaway compulsion to climb up everything; and she ran outside preparing some suitable fishwife reprimands.

Instead she ran into a small and ribald crowd watching Auntie Bea who, with a glaring display of beige drawers, was mounting gawkily up on to the felt roof of the hut.

Bea had made her way up, as was helpfully pointed out to Stella by a grinning spectator, by means of some crates and a dustbin; likewise she had seized the frying pan she was clutching from somebody's stove, and used it as a weapon to beat off anyone who tried to stop her. Why she was doing this was a more complex question, to which Stella tried and failed to get an answer from Uncle Will, who was standing helplessly below with his braces disconsolately dangling. 'She's done it before,' was all he would say, his face a mask of slightly sozzled despair. 'Last time it was the Bright Street bakehouse. They had to get her down with a fire ingin. She's done it before, you see.'

'Don't talk to him!' came Auntie Bea's uniquely carrying voice. She was now perched on the apex of the roof, and brandishing the frying pan with one hand whilst modestly pulling her skirt over her knees with the other. 'Don't talk to him, gel! He's the one! He put me up 'ere! Making a show of me – he knows what he's done! You ask him!'

'But don't talk to him,' said a wag.

Richard had followed Stella, and was doing a creditable job of looking unsurprised at the fact that her aunt was on the roof with a frying pan. Still, Stella couldn't help feeling a little mortified. Part of her thought it was funny, but part of her thought it wasn't funny at all.

'Uncle Will, what's happened? What did you do?' She buttonholed him, but he only groaned and made beseeching noises at Auntie Bea, who resourcefully responded by plucking a lump of moss from the roof and batting it at him with the frying pan like a tennis player serving an ace.

'They had a bit of a falling-out.' The speaker was a vast fat hoarse man from Wapping who never did any fruit-picking, but acted as the camp bookie. 'Down the boozer, it was. I was there. Something to do with whatshername.' He made a descriptive gesture at chest height. 'That Bloss woman.'

'He was carrying on with her!' screamed Auntie Bea, to an interested chuckle from the crowd. 'Right in front of me eyes! Don't talk to him! He's broke me heart!'

'I bought her a port and lemon!' Uncle Will cried, spreading his arms wide and appealing to the crowd.

'You were whispering in her ear! I came back from powdering me nose and there he was whispering in her filthy trollopy ear!'

'Talking!' Uncle Will matched her for volume. 'I was talking, that's all! It was a right racket in there – I had to get up close!'

There was a whoop of delight from the crowd at that one. For a moment Uncle Will looked like a man who realizes he has walked out without his trousers; then he flushed plum-colour and shouted, 'Get down here, Bea! Get down off there, you bloody daft woman!'

'Swearing now!' Bea shrilled, drumming her heels on the roof. 'Y'crude bugger!'

So Moaning Bliss was at the bottom of it. Knowing – or disliking – the woman as she did, Stella doubted whether her part in it had been entirely innocent: certainly she was nowhere to be seen. But it wasn't important: the main thing was to get Auntie Bea down, because she was getting hysterical – admittedly not a great emotional leap where Auntie Bea was concerned – and if she wasn't careful she was going to take an almighty purler.

'Auntie Bea. Please, come down now. We can sort this out. Just come down from there.'

'Why?'

'Because – because you're upsetting the kids.'

Demonstrably not true, however: Geoffrey was treating the matter in much the same spirit as the slapstick sword fight, whilst Cecil and Ivy had become engrossed in doing something unspeakable to a beetle.

'And anyway . . .' Stella cast about her, and hit on something – Bea's rather paradoxical love of propriety. 'We've got company, Auntie Bea.' She tugged Richard forward. 'You've got to come down, because we've got company.'

Richard took his cue. 'Yes, please, Mrs Tranter, won't you come down? Won't you come down and join us for tea?'

There was a muffled snigger, which it was not difficult to trace to Frankly Hopeless, who was lounging at a little distance. A hateful snigger, and his expression matched it.

Auntie Bea looked momentarily regretful, but then shook her head. 'I shan't have tea no more. I shan't have anything any more. I haven't the heart.' She fanned herself with the frying pan, mournfully.

'Well, then,' Richard said, 'if you won't come down for tea, we'll come up.'

He said it with such jaunty decision that Stella thought at first he was joking.

He wasn't: or if he was, it was a serious joke. He went into the hut, emerged with the tea things on a tray, and began climbing up the precarious crate-and-dustbin stairway, holding the tray aloft with the debonair disdain of a circus acrobat. Near to the top he paused and, turning, winked at her gravely. 'Coming, Stella?'

She decided he was mad.

She decided it was the nicest thing anyone had ever done.

With a ladylike hitch of her skirts, she mounted up after him.

Presently they were perched on either side of Auntie Bea, who didn't know whether to look abashed, flattered, or dumbfounded. Richard balanced the tea tray delicately on the top of the roof and urbanely asked if Mrs Tranter would pour?

'I'm a bit wobbly,' Auntie Bea said faintly.

'I know what you mean. It's a fair way up, isn't it? You get a nice breeze though. Been terribly hot today. I think we need a good thunderstorm to clear the air.'

'You get a lovely cool after a thunderstorm,' Stella said. 'And that nice fresh smell.'

'Yes, that's a wonderful smell. And all the birds start singing as if they're glad to be alive. Sugar, Mrs Tranter?'

'Three please,' murmured Auntie Bea, gazing at him as if he were a slightly alarming species of angel.

'Yes . . .' Richard handed the slack-jawed Bea her tea. 'Yes, sometimes it takes a storm to get things back to normal. Oh – thank you!' One of the spectators, who were watching the rooftop tea party with high enjoyment, had tossed up a paper bag of biscuits. 'Have one, Mrs Tranter?'

'. . . Ta.'

'Yes, it's like everything,' Stella said. 'You need a good blow-up once in a while to clear the air. Now me, I've got a terrible temper. Go off like a bomb – *you* know, Auntie Bea. But I don't mean the things I say when I do. It's just a lot of noise. People who love you, they understand that.'

'Of course they do,' Richard said. 'Anyway, show me someone who's never lost their head and I'll show you a crashing bore.'

'That fella down Durbar Street, Auntie Bea, remember him? Little mousy bloke with specs. Real Creeping-Jesus he was. Looked like butter wouldn't melt in his mouth. Turned out he'd done his wife in with a fire shovel and when they caught him he said he'd do it again. Shows you what was bottling up inside him all those years. Better to let it out, I reckon.'

'I remember him,' Auntie Bea said. 'He used to go round collecting for the Tragic Orphans . . . Ooh, I feel a fool.'

Stella gave her hand a squeeze.

'By the way, Mrs Tranter,' Richard said after a moment, 'I brought four cups. I thought we might ask Mr Tranter to join us. What do you think?'

Again Bea looked down at the drooping figure of Uncle Will. She made a wry mouth and then burst out laughing.

'Go on then,' she said, whooping and shrieking, 'go on then – if he can get himself up here!'

There was a great cheer and a round of applause as Uncle Will, beckoned by a wave from Stella, gamely toiled up to the roof, where Bea seized him in such a perilously wild embrace that little Geoffrey and his siblings were in some danger of becoming Tragic Orphans themselves. And Stella and Richard exchanged a grin over the flailing couple. It was like the grin of two people who find themselves simultaneously saying the same thing.

# *FIVE*

## 1

It was an idea typical of Richard, Helen thought. It was charming, it was kind, it was fanciful; and he had probably put more effort into it than he had ever put into his work at Cambridge.

The idea was to mark Walter Lutton's return home from the hospital with a sort of triumphal parade. With the enthusiastic help of Aunt Hamblin he had procured bunting and little flags, and had drilled the fruit-pickers' children carefully: on the morning of Mr Lutton's return, they were to line the drove leading to the farmhouse and sing a chorus of 'For He's A Jolly Good Fellow'. He was going to fetch Mr Lutton himself in the Riley, and somehow he had obtained a chauffeur's cap for the occasion.

It was, Helen supposed as she waited with the children on the appointed morning, a kind of gift. The gift of treating trivial things seriously. Life as one great Fabergé egg. The other side of that particular coin, she also supposed, was treating serious things trivially.

*I shall have to go home soon.* This thought occurred to her with such mechanical frequency that it had almost lost all meaning. For she hadn't gone home: she was still here. It was as if she were under some drowsy spell; but instead of the island of the lotus-eaters, it was this sunstruck land of orchards that had bewitched her – this place where one could fancy there was no such thing as cities, countries, great movements and upheavals of peoples, no stirrings and strivings of the individual mind or soul. Just the fruit to be gathered in, the children to be tended, each succeeding day to be stepped gently in and out of like a warm, scented, soothing bath.

And only now and then did her mind make that perplexed protest and ask her what she was doing here. A touch of Puritan in her, perhaps: but she preferred to think of it as her real self, the self that meant to do things in the world, asserting itself against this temporary suspension of identity. Yes, she would have to go home soon; but though she prided herself on clear thinking, she couldn't say whether the impulse had as much of flight in it as resolution. Going home, or going away?

At any rate, she had a lunch appointment with Olive Kingswell next Saturday, and she clung to that like a mascot. Olive Kingswell, and the things she represented, would surely break these bonds: she would be plucked out of these soft toils of confusion and set back on the path she had chosen.

'Miss. Miss, my flag's broken.'

'Oh, dear, is it? Well, here you are, have mine.'

She had been coming here for something like six weeks, but the children still called her Miss. Apart from that, they were at ease with her now; and to her own surprise, she found them a good deal more tolerable than she would ever have expected. Likeable, even: amusing.

Kate, she knew, was up at the house with her family, awaiting her father's arrival with a cake and a 'Welcome Home' banner painted on a bedsheet. She would miss Kate, when she did go home: she would have to keep in touch. Kate, she felt, had dignity, a quality Helen prized – though the girl would be the last person to believe she had it. She was peeping out of her shell, though, little by little. Helen was curious to know what would happen if she came all the way out – how differently the world might look to her.

Idle curiosity, however; because, after all, she was going home soon.

'No sign of 'em yet?'

Helen turned to find Stella Tranter beside her.

'Ernie Delph let me skip off,' Stella said. 'I didn't want to miss it. Here, he's a right showman, your Richard, isn't he? I reckon he ought to go on the stage or something.'

'Oh, he's not my Richard,' Helen said.

'No, well, I know what you mean. Drive you mad in the end, a fella like that. He does make me laugh, though – oh, here they come!'

The Riley, top down, was making a stately progress down the drove. Mr Lutton, stiffly reclining in the back seat, was playing up to it splendidly despite the neck-brace and giving a regal wave. His eyes, Helen noticed, were a little teary. And Richard was playing his part with typical thoroughness, maintaining a dutiful eyes-front. The chauffeur's cap suited him, as formal wear always did: at the Newnham garden party for May Week he had made the other men look dowdy, in spite of what he confessed was a crushing hangover.

I really will, Helen thought, I really will have to go home soon.

'Welcome home! Hooray!' Stella in her excitement had taken Helen's arm. 'Here, what does he look like in that hat? Daft beggar!'

Helen wondered about the excitement. Richard had been spending a lot of time with Stella just lately. Part of his compulsive sociability, of course. But the girl might not understand that. Stella, she thought, was too open-hearted for her own good. She would hate to see her get hurt.

'"For he's a jolly good fel-low, for he's a jolly good fellow . . ."'

The children's voices, ragged, shrill, and pitched in any number of keys, were yet curiously affecting. As the Riley drew level with them Richard's eyes swivelled over in Helen and Stella's direction and he smiled, a smile of pure, careless happiness.

'It's all right, duck.'

Helen came out of a daze to find, incredibly, tears on her cheeks and Stella regarding her kindly.

'It's all right – you're like me. Nice things make me bawl my head off. I can watch a right old tearjerker at the pictures and not feel a thing, but something really happy sets me off straight away. It's funny, isn't it?' She patted Helen's arm. 'You're just like me.

I shall be the same next Sunday when Geoffrey gets up and does his bit.'

'. . . Next Sunday?'

'The village feast. You will be here, won't you? Oh, go on. It won't be the same if you're not.'

'Yes . . . yes, of course.'

I shall stay till the village feast, Helen thought, watching the car drive on up to the house. I shall stay till then. And then I really must get away.

## 2

Kate's father was allowed home, but only at the price of complete bed rest. An energetic man, it irked him to be unable to do more than watch the progress of the fruit harvest from his bedroom window; it irked him also, perhaps, to see that they could manage without him.

In George Maxey's fields a more conventional harvesting was in progress, and Kate often saw him from a distance leading the three brawny horses that pulled the binder, his figure an almost exact human counterpart of theirs, head down, legs high-striding, big and tireless. Once they came across him on the road when she was in the truck with Richard: he was leading the horse and cart that carried the corn shocks, and Richard slowed the truck so as not to alarm the horse. George's head came up, and he lifted a hand; but it was at Kate that he looked. The gaze he fixed on her was so intense she felt it almost plucked her out of the cab.

'Devil of a worker, that George Maxey,' Richard said when they had passed on. 'Seems to run his place single-handed.'

'I think he would if he could.' Kate gave a shudder.

'Someone walk over your grave?'

'Just seeing that harvest waggon reminded me of something. When the field's nearly cut and there's just a square of corn left in the middle all the mice come running out of it. When I was little the boys in the village used to love that time. They'd go along and kill the mice as they came running out. Mousing they called it, like it was a great game. You could always tell when a boy had been mousing because you could smell it on him.'

'Boys are a vicious lot, aren't they? I see the newsreels of Hitler and his gang and I immediately think of my prep school . . . So, Kate, what about you and George?'

She would once have gone into a wretched blushing fit at such a question: but Richard's whimsical directness had helped to break that. 'I don't know,' she said honestly.

'Does he?'

'Oh, George always knows what he wants. He probably thinks I'm in love with you, though.'

'Ah.'

'I'm not, by the way.'

'Good for you,' he said laughing. 'Not advisable. But are you in love with George?'

'Oh . . . Do I have to answer that?'

'I wouldn't expect you to. Take no notice of me. My brother's getting married soon, by the way.' Richard's hand strayed to his top button. 'With characteristic exactitude Maurice has named the day. The lady is called Phyllis Coombes. Her father is a solicitor and a Rotarian and she plays a good game of tennis. Maurice wants me to be best man.'

'That's nice.'

'It is, isn't it?' he said bleakly. 'Oh God, it gets worse. He's coming up to Cambridge this Saturday. He wants to see me.'

'That's . . . not nice?'

'It should be, shouldn't it? But Maurice . . . I get the impression, from his letter, that he's coming up to talk some sense into my head. Which he's been doing since he was thirteen years old and it still hasn't worked. Oh God. Never mind. The point is, I shan't be able to come up here on Saturday. I'm so sorry to let you down, but a visit from Maurice is . . . is not to be got out of.'

'No, don't worry. You shouldn't feel tied, Richard. Anyhow the plums are nearly over now. It's the apples next and they don't need to be transported straight away; we store them. Saturday – Helen's going to be away that day too, isn't she?'

'Oh, of course, this Kingswell woman. Sounds an old battle-axe to me, but I'd rather meet her than Maurice . . . Oh, well. There's the village feast on Sunday, I shall just think about that. You'll dance with me on Sunday, won't you, Kate? Even though you're not in love with me, I mean.'

'I'll dance with you, Richard.'

'And George Maxey?'

'Well, you could ask him. But I really don't think he's your type,' she said, and in their laughter she felt the question she had not answered lift and blow away, for now.

There was another question, though, that had stayed with her since Helen had driven her to the hospital, and that night she asked it.

Or rather, she asked a modified version of it. For the question she had been about to ask – *Dad, why did you never teach me to drive?* – died on her lips as she looked at him. He was a man on his sickbed, after all; and though Kate was changing, confrontation was simply not in her. Besides, the question only had to be posed in her mind to be answered. He had not thought to because she was a woman. And with that realization came others: that a man did not have to be a household bully to create helpless womenfolk; that weak vessels were made as well as born; that she had colluded in her own stunting, accepting the little-woman role, wrapping herself up in it.

And so she put it another way. She simply asked him, when she took up his supper on a tray, 'Dad, will you teach me to drive? When you're better, I mean.'

'Oh, you don't have to worry about that, gel. I shall be up and about soon, and we can manage in the meantime—'

'No, I don't mean that. I just mean – I'd like to learn to drive anyhow.'

Her father regarded her quizzically. 'I never knew you wanted to, duck.'

And there was an answer to that, too; and she did not speak the answer out loud either. She just smiled and said, 'Well, I would like to. When you get the time. I'll be back for the tray.'

## 3

Richard saw Helen off for London at Cambridge station on Saturday morning. He was gloomy.

'I wish you weren't going,' he said as they had tea in the station buffet.

'Why? So I could protect you from the dreaded Maurice?'

'Oh, nothing could protect me from that. No, it's just . . . I feel as if I'm losing you.'

After a moment's silence, which she felt as an eternity, Helen said, 'How so?'

'Well, this is your first step on the road, isn't it? I've no doubt that this Kingswell woman is entirely serious about helping you and quite rightly because it's what you deserve. You're talented and you're determined. It's going to happen. That's what I mean by losing you. Call it losing you to your destiny.'

'Oh, Richard, for God's sake, you can't play in the fields with children all your life.'

He seemed surprised at the level of her irritation, but he nodded and said, 'I know. Just what Maurice is going to tell me, no doubt. But I don't mind it from you. That's different. It's different from a friend.'

'Well, look, if we're friends, as you say, then friends don't necessarily lose touch just because they're embarking on different ways in life. You make it sound as if I were going to the front and you were staying at home in Blighty. It doesn't have to be like that. You could—'

'No, no, it will.' He drooped over his tea, making little waves with the teaspoon. 'You'll go forward in life, and forget about me. It's inevitable. Today is just the beginning of the process. No use even in talking about it.'

When he got in one of these moods, there was no getting him

out of it: he would stubbornly stay at the bottom of the pit despite all your tugging. It was infuriating; and really, she ought not let it bother her. Today was an important day.

'What time's your brother arriving?' she said crossly.

'Eleven-fifteen.' He consulted his watch, then adjusted his cuff meticulously. His dress was immaculate: only his face gave him away. Or perhaps, she thought, it was his immaculate dress that gave him away. 'I may as well stay around here. He'll be on time. Trains with Maurice on them never run late. They wouldn't dare.'

And then, typically, just when she was quite out of patience with him, he came up with one of those gestures which, as Aunt Hamblin said, made you feel you were the only person in the world. He handed her a package: a book.

'I remember you saying you wanted it,' he said. 'I thought it would do for the train journey. One way, at least. Knowing you, you'll have devoured it before you get to London.'

It was *Pavements of Anderby*, Winifred Holtby's last book. Helen had loved *South Riding* and had been looking forward to reading this, though she could hardly recall mentioning it.

'Thought it'd be inspirational too,' Richard said. 'She did it, didn't she? Born in your part of the world. Wrote for all the papers, serious stuff, not *belles-lettres.* Remarkable woman. I wonder if Olive Kingswell knew her?'

'Probably . . . You are terrible, Richard. I was just feeling ready to strangle you, and then you come up with something like this and I don't know what to say—'

'I know,' he said. 'Planned it that way. Come on, your train's in.'

On the platform a thought occurred to her. 'Where will you be having lunch? With your brother?'

'Hm? Oh, I thought I'd give him lunch at my digs. Cold collation. Well, warm collation I suppose—'

She was shaking her head. 'No, Richard,' she said, 'please. Take him out somewhere for lunch. Promise me you'll do that.'

'All right. I say, we are going up to Monks Bridge tomorrow, aren't we? There's the village feast and everything.' For the first time there was animation in his tone.

'Of course.' She had, after all, made that bargain with herself. 'Well, good luck with Maurice. I'm sure it'll be all right.'

'I know. Great fusspot, aren't I? It's taking advantage, really.'

'What is?'

Richard took her hand, and looking down at it said, 'Well, you're the only person I can talk to like this. When you have something . . . something special with someone, you take it for granted that they'll always understand you. And you do, too – that's the wonderful thing. It was an amazing piece of luck, meeting you. Not a thing I've ever told you, perhaps, but . . . Well.' He squeezed her hand and then released it, his eyes meeting hers at last. 'Take care of yourself.'

That was a phrase of his, but he always said it as if he really meant it.

The train bore Helen away. She shared the carriage with a frothy matron in an unseasonal fur tippet whose corsets squeaked like trapped mice whenever she moved and who looked as if she was ready for conversation; feeling unequal to it, Helen took out her book and tried to read.

She couldn't concentrate. Perhaps it was simply because this appointment was important to her, and she was keyed up; but it didn't feel like that. It was as if she had more thoughts in her mind than there was room for. It was like the feeling of having forgotten to do something important, and anxiously waiting for it to come back to you so you could know how important it was. It was like the unease that resolved into illness.

It was like these, and yet it was not these. Helen stared unseeingly at the pages of her book and for several alarming seconds was convinced she was going to weep.

Good, though, in a way: it gave her an opportunity to exercise control over herself, a skill she prized and which, like most skills, gave satisfaction in itself. Sternly, Helen made herself be composed. Interior lives, like family lives, are all different, and Helen's was marked by a strictness and discipline that many would have found intimidating.

After a few moments she risked lifting her head from her book: the furry matron seemed to be dozing. She didn't know where she was – somewhere, anywhere, in the nondescript landscape south of Cambridge. She thought of Richard back in Cambridge, and Miss Kingswell in London ahead of her, and of herself in this gentle trundling no-man's-land; and some weak backslider within her made a curious wish that she should stay like this, suspended between them, for ever.

## 4

Maurice Marwood did not so much step down from the train as ponderously descend from it, as if he were lowering himself into a swimming bath.

Though he was only twenty-eight, and still played rugby and cricket as devotedly and well as he had when he was himself at Cambridge, Maurice had this groping stiffish manner about him, like an elderly person. He held up queues, and took up a lot of room in seats, and was slow and heavy in his dealings with waiters and porters. It was a characteristic Richard had noticed in a lot of young men, and women, of Maurice's type. It was something to do with assurance, he supposed. Or pig-headedness.

Richard went forward to greet his brother, groaning inside.

From this feeling, from the way he spoke of him, and from the way he quite genuinely dreaded this encounter, anyone might have supposed that Richard hated his brother. In fact Richard wished to love him, but could not, and this was what made him so out of sorts. With Richard love and understanding were inseparable. When people repelled him, he could not even begin to understand what went on inside them; and because other friendships came easily to him, he often did not try. It was perhaps a sort of emotional snobbery, and in rare moments of self-examination he acknowledged it as such.

But he did try, with Maurice. In his heavy-handed way, Maurice had always tried with him: always he had been the big brother, conscious of his responsibility, watching over Richard with frequent perplexity but never indifference. The fact that they were temperamental opposites didn't deter Maurice: he just trampled over it in his serenely elephantine way. A notable quality of Maurice's was patience. A keen gardener, as he enjoyed most solid English amateur pursuits, he had planted several young trees at home, and liked to contemplate them, puffing on his pipe, and remarking on how they would look in fifty or even a hundred years' time. It was an image that filled Richard with a cosmic horror – he half-wanted to tear the little trees up. But Maurice could wait. And perhaps he felt the same in regard to Richard: felt that sooner or later, no matter how long it took, Richard would grow up in the Maurice way.

'Maurice. You're looking well. Did you have a good journey?'

'Good Lord, you're as brown as a Hottentot,' Maurice said, breathing hard and staring. He was a large blockish man with a sleek sculpted head and lustrous black hair: he looked, in fact, a little like Oscar Wilde, a comparison that would not have pleased him.

'Must be all the fresh air. Outdoor living,' Richard said. His smile felt like a puppet's grin: already the familiar, wretched defensiveness was on him. 'How's everyone at home?'

'Father has lumbago. The doctor tells him to lie on a board, an old door perhaps.' Massively stationary, Maurice took out a huge handkerchief and mopped his brow whilst the other passengers made detours round him. 'How far is it to your digs? Should we take a cab?'

'Oh, it's not far,' Richard said. 'But I thought, if you'd like, we'd go for a spot of lunch—'

'Yes, soon. I want to see where you live, though. Off Huntingdon Road, isn't it? Mm, it's funny, I can't remember any digs down there when I was up, but I dare say things have changed.'

'Yes, of course.' His heart sinking, his smile aching, Richard said, 'Congratulations, by the way, on the engagement, and thanks awfully for asking me to be best man. I shall be delighted.'

'Well, you're the natural choice, of course. What *is* that tie? Is it a club tie?'

'This, no, just a – just a tie. Army & Navy stores, I think.'

'Mm. Mother wants to know, by the way, how many books you'll be bringing home. She's been getting your room ready and there's just the one bookcase in there.'

A seething wildness filled Richard's brain. How many books? Did he want an exact figure, or a round number? Did he want an index? The wildness too was dismally familiar – it was part of him just as much as the careless flippancy that Helen saw; but it was ages since he had experienced it, and the sensation was like the nagging of an old injury.

'Not many,' he got out.

'No? Of course, one doesn't need them after university. I disposed of a lot of mine to a bookseller in Petty Cury. Got five pounds ten for them, I recall.'

They walked to Richard's lodgings, Maurice turning his great head about and remarking on the changes in the town since he was here. He made Cambridge sound an age ago, remote as infanthood: something to be comfortably placed in the past. The eccentricity of Richard's still lingering here he did not directly allude to, not yet. Meanwhile Richard fretted and fumed. If he could have hated Maurice it would have been better, but all his natural tendency was to affection: half of him felt a despairing fondness for the great well-meaning bear beside him, the other half wanted to shoo him out of the town, him and everything he brought with him.

'Where will you live? When you're married?'

'We've our eye on a little place at Abbotsleigh. Very good order and about half an acre surrounding. Possibly a little cramped for family living in time, but there's potential for an extension. One's only real quibble is that they're building some sort of military camp near Abbotsleigh. Essential, of course, but it does have an effect on the tone of a place.'

Richard began to ask about plumbing, but the whole thing was only a diversionary tactic, because they were approaching his digs. Maurice, however, wouldn't be diverted.

'Good Lord,' he said staring. 'Do you mean to say you live above a shop?'

'Above and behind,' Richard said. 'Come on.'

Bleakly he led his brother down the brick passage at the side of the locksmith's shop. It smelt of tomcats and damp, though he had stopped noticing it. At the back door he took the key from its niche above the lintel. He was always losing keys from his pockets, and nobody ever came down here, so this seemed to him the most sensible arrangement; but Maurice had to make a comment.

'That's rather inadvisable, you know. I'm aware a lot of people do it, but really it's most inadvisable.'

'Please, Maurice.' Richard laughed sorely. 'When I get a house in Abbotsleigh I promise I will take the key with me, but until then . . .'

He fell silent as they went in. He could see, he could plainly see, that this place was by Maurice's standards an appalling mess, with its greasy gas ring and stone scullery and heaps of clothes; the trouble was, he did not expect Maurice to see that it suited him perfectly. He had a rapid image of his life with his family as a long series of such impasses, frustrating and exhausting.

And if some people – he was aware of it – accused Richard of making a fetish of the spontaneous and unpredictable, then here was ample reason for it in Maurice's reaction. It was Maurice through and through. Richard could virtually predict each word as it came.

'My God, it's practically a slum. This is where you've been living? I'm amazed the university authorities ever approved it.'

'I'm not at the university any more, Maurice, so it's nothing to do with them. It's just private digs.'

'I cannot conceive why you should choose to live in one squalid room like this when you have absolutely no need to.' Maurice stared affrontedly at a magazine photograph of Greta Garbo. Richard had pinned it up to offset the doleful portrait of Queen Victoria which came with the fittings.

‘It’s not one room. There’s another upstairs.’ Randomly Richard wondered whether Maurice stared at the tennis-playing Phyllis like that. The all-out stare seemed to be his only way of looking. ‘Anyway, it’s only temporary. Do have a seat, Maurice, and don’t fuss.’

Fastidious and frowning, Maurice lowered himself into the easy chair.

‘Will you have some tea?’

‘No. Look here, Richard, just what do you mean by temporary? I may as well tell you that Mother and Father are pretty well mystified by this business and so am I.’

‘And so you’ve been sent to spy on me.’

‘Good heavens, I wouldn’t put it like that.’ The trace of hurt was genuine: one of the baffling things about Maurice was that he really believed his heavy hand was a gentle one. ‘Mother and Father are concerned, and so am I. So I came up to see you. You must admit it’s all rather strange.’

‘Lots of people stay up in the vac. Reading parties and what have you, it’s a tradition.’

‘In the vac, yes. In between terms. But as you say, you’ve left the university now. This is the time when you should begin to consider your future. Why you should choose instead to run a mission to a lot of itinerant fruit-pickers I can’t think. You’re the last person I’d have expected to get mixed up in all that Christian Socialist business. Have you had your head turned by some of these evangelical fellows one gets at Cambridge? I know what they’re like.’

‘I assure you, Maurice, I’m practically pagan.’

Maurice’s frown deepened. ‘Is it Communism? I remember when I was up there were some types who got involved in things like that. Went off and pooled their possessions and so on. I believe it was a front for free love.’

‘It sounds very nice,’ Richard said: he couldn’t help it.

Maurice harrumphed and began to fill his pipe, a process which brought out all his weightiest deliberation. Richard allowed himself to dream a moment. The thought that came into his head, like a gulp of clean air through the fug of Maurice, was Stella. A tea party on the roof. Her big healthy laugh. The glint in her green eyes. He had hardly realized the transcendent value of these things to him, until now when their end was being mooted.

'Now look here, Richard,' Maurice burst out again – and Richard saw that his whole great head was suffused with red. 'Is it a woman?'

Richard felt a jolt, then the wild anger again. 'Is what a woman?'

'You can tell me, you know. I know these things happen. Sometimes . . . ahem, sometimes a fellow fresh out of university will fall in with a woman, older perhaps, and it may be, I only say it may be, that he makes rash promises to her which in the nature of things can hardly—'

'Oh, God in heaven, Maurice, will no one accept that I am doing what I am doing because I enjoy it and not because I've been inveigled into it by Baptists or Communists or – or some sort of fenland Traviata! Is that too much to ask?'

'Well, frankly, it is.' Maurice didn't lose his temper – he never did: he just plunged doggedly on. 'You're living like some sort of gypsy here. I dare say there are people who are under the necessity of living in this manner, but you are certainly not one of them. Phyllis often asks about you – now what am I to tell her? Well, never mind that. The fact is, I've been making some inquiries for you in the City, and there've been some very favourable responses. But the point is, one must strike while the iron is hot. There are plenty of other Cambridge men besides you looking for a good position.'

'I don't recall saying I *was* looking.' This was what he hated: the way he ended up speaking in this frosty, priggish tone, unnatural to him.

'My dear fellow, you will have to sooner or later. You can't live off Father. I'm sure you wouldn't want to.'

'And Phyllis would be so much more comfortable if she were marrying into a family that didn't have a gypsy in it, is that right?'

'I'd rather you didn't bring Phyllis into this, if you don't mind.'

'I didn't. You did.' Richard blew out a long breath and ran his hands through his hair. 'Oh, God, Maurice. We're quarrelling.'

'Are we?' Maurice looked upset. 'Well, I'm sorry. I didn't mean to.'

Richard made an effort. 'Look. I promise I will come home soon, of course I will. And then I will . . . buckle down. But I can't say exactly when it will be. You know you can't tie me down to time like that.'

'Yes,' Maurice said, rueful. 'I know that all too well.'

For a moment there was a palpable affection between them, somewhere in the room; but it was rarefied, an atmosphere too thin to support life. The thought of Stella came back to Richard again, brief and sharp, like a glint of sun on water.

'Come on,' Richard said, jumping up. 'I'll take you to lunch. Get you out of here before the rats start biting you . . . No, no, Maurice, only joking . . .'

## 5

'My dear, you can have art or you can have life. You can't have both. Yes, I include journalism in art because it makes the same demands. We've become very snobby about journalism. It used to be called letters and it was what some of our greatest writers did – Defoe, Addison, Johnson.' Olive Kingswell waved a hand at the bookcases behind her. 'You can think of more. But don't suppose I'm just speaking from a feminine perspective. Obviously that adds an extra dimension. Babies or career – you know the arguments. No, I mean as a general human rule. Henry James recognized it. He made the choice: art instead of life. Observing, not participating. I met him once, by the way. I was a very green young reporter covering a literary luncheon and there he was, the grand old man. He was very infirm and I'm afraid I rather came away with the impression that he was gaga. I realize now that he carried his search for the exact word to such lengths that all he could do was make a sort of gasping noise. Anyhow, that is the *sine qua non* – don't use Latin tags when you write, by the way, it's pretentious. You *must* be heartfree. That's a beautiful word, isn't it? Not always a beautiful experience, though. Everyone has their longings, their moments of doubt. I once considered marrying a man I met in Washington. He had a ranch, a real ranch like in the films, out in Colorado. I was going to throw it all up and live there with him and, oh gosh I don't know, wear gingham skirts and make pies, I suppose.' Olive Kingswell gave her loud gravelly laugh. 'And then I came to my senses and, as they say, got the hell out of there. Shall we take our coffee in the garden? It's such a splendid day. And the doctor prescribes fresh air for these wretched tubes of mine.'

They moved from the sitting room – which was a perfect lair of books, leathery and tobaccoey – to a sunken wilderness of garden beyond the French windows. Miss Kingswell cast a frowning glance up at the windows of the floor above.

'Best make sure she's not peeping out . . . My upstairs neighbour is mad, I'm afraid. She delights in calling me a bitch whenever we run into one another. I hope that chair is clean – oh, well, it'll do. You're quiet, my dear: have I put you off with this stern talk?'

'No, no. I rather like stern talk.'

'Good! Because you've come to the wrong person if you want comforting flannel, my dear. It is not an easy profession to enter: it is wearing, dispiriting, and dreadfully insecure; and there certainly isn't any money in it – unless you want to write slop for the retarded like Godfrey Wynn. That isn't your aim, I take it?'

'No. Though I will take whatever work I can get.'

'Oh, my dear, you'll have to. For years, it seemed, I did nothing but cover the weddings of bankers' daughters. So patience is yet another virtue you've got to possess. I make it sound like taking the veil, don't I? Well, call it doing you the honour of taking you seriously. I read your *Granta* pieces – oh yes, I followed you up. Very good work. You write clearly – which is a matter of thinking clearly. I can never emphasize this enough when people ask me for advice on writing. It begins in your head: the words on the paper are just the end result. If there's muddle in your mind, then your writing will be muddled. You don't strike me as having any muddle in your mind, Helen – do you?'

'I hope not,' Helen said, a little uncomfortably. 'But I . . . I doubt myself sometimes. I feel that I'm not an extraordinary person and that I need to be to succeed.'

'My dear, do you think me an extraordinary person?'

'Well, yes. Yes, I do.' Helen felt able to be frank, even affectionately so, simply because there was no other way to be with Miss Kingswell. It was plain that she either liked you or she didn't: if she didn't you would get nothing out of her, if she did you were friends at once. The side-stepping hesitancies and evasions of new acquaintanceship were not for her, it seemed: probably because they wasted time, about which Miss Kingswell freely admitted she was a miser.

And she was an extraordinary person, to Helen: there was no disappointment in this meeting, except perhaps in herself; for that feeling of being unable to concentrate, of not bringing her whole self to bear, was still present. No, Olive Kingswell was all she had expected. Not a large woman, though handsome in a dark strong-boned way, and dressed in clothes that might have been thrown together from a jumble sale, and in imperfect health, she yet had a formidable presence. Seeing her here, in her cluttered Bayswater flat with its overflowing ashtrays and cat-haired upholstery, only added to the force of the impression. Here was the woman who had met Mussolini, whipping up a very palatable lunch in her own kitchen. Helen was stirred with emulation. The old feeling of rightness – *this is what I want to be* – was with her again. And yet somehow it was tainted. Miss Kingswell's reference to taking the veil was apposite. Helen felt rather as a novice nun must feel who knows she has not shaken off worldly thoughts. An imposter.

Miss Kingswell was saying something about not being at all extraordinary but Helen was not listening. For several long seconds she was wholly occupied by an intense self-revelation. It had burst upon her, like a delayed explosive, from that word Miss Kingswell had used: *heartfree*.

Helen was not heartfree. She knew it, suddenly. And such was her belief in knowledge as the highest good that even this, which must carry momentous consequences for her, gave her a sensation of intellectual satisfaction. Other feelings would follow, of course. She knew that too.

She snapped back to attention.

'. . . In a way a good journalist should be very ordinary. By that I don't mean common-minded. It's more to do with openness to experience. If you have an axe to grind, my dear, then keep it well hidden. Do your sharpening in private over a glass of whisky. If you think your scribblings are going to change the world, then forget it. It's hard, I know. Especially in these times. My friends call me a dreadful Cassandra and think it's my age, but I say to you what I say to them: we are in for trouble, not just us but the rest of the world. These gangsters in Germany are not going to settle down and turn into good statesmen if they get what they want in Czechoslovakia. They're Dark Age barbarians with tanks and aeroplanes. We are heading for interesting times, as the old Chinese curse has it: times we shall be very lucky to come out of, at least with our world intact. Well, there I go again. But that's what so refreshing about meeting you. Here at last is someone who doesn't want the world to go away while they flirt in the arbour. But come, tell me why you doubt yourself. What are your people? Are they pulling you back?'

'Not at all. My father is rector of a village in Lincolnshire: there's old money in the family. Very county, I suppose one might say.' Helen was able to go on talking normally, despite the new knowledge inside her: revolutionary as it was, her discipline was equal to it, for now. 'And yet they're not in the least hidebound. They've backed me to the hilt, in fact. I've always had the . . . the luxury of choice.'

'A wonderful thing, isn't it? And a responsibility too. Sometimes it frightens people. You can even take it away from people and they'll feel gratitude: something of that sort's happened in Germany.' Miss Kingswell regarded Helen narrowly, assessingly. 'Don't *you* be frightened of it, Helen. Always remember – seize the day. I'm fifty-three years old, but when I look back I don't see fifty-three years stretching hugely away. The whole thing seems to have gone by in about a fortnight. It's *that* quick. Believe me, my dear. Seize the day.'

Helen smiled. 'Yes. Yes, I will.'

# 6

That Saturday evening Kate did something she had never done before. She got roaring drunk.

She had been a little tipsy at Christmas parties, and had felt the effect of the wine that Helen sometimes brought to the orchards; but she had never been on what Stella, who called at the farmhouse to propose it, called a regular beano. Nor had she ever been to a pub.

'Get out of it,' Stella said as they walked down to the village. 'Not even for half a shandy?'

'Well, I've been *in* the village pub lots of times. To talk to people, visit the landlady when she's sick, you know. But I've never actually gone there to have a drink. It never really occurred to me before.'

'Gawd, I hope I'm not leading you astray!'

'No; I really would like to go, you know. I've been working all day. Why not?'

'That's the spirit. I'll tell you what, I've got a belter of a thirst, so if at some point in the evening you can't find me, just look under the table.'

Kate had a feeling she might be there herself. But somehow she didn't care. She felt free and exalted.

The pub they chose was the smaller and more unconventional of the two in the village. It was kept by two elderly sisters called Kitty and Alice who also did market gardening. They were lean grim-mouthed old bodies who spoke to each other in curt jerks –

'Kitty. There's more ale wanted' – much as if they were at daggers drawn, though everyone knew they were mutually devoted. The pub was known as the Corner, though there was no signboard, just as there was no bar or beer pumps; only a large bare room with sawdust on the floor where you waited, on hard smooth benches like church pews, for one or other of the sisters to bring the beer up from the cellar in tall jugs. But there was also a table outside – it was actually an old rosewood dining table, crazed and foxed with exposure to the weather – with a couple of rush-bottomed chairs, set on a lawn juicy with dandelion clocks, and it was here that Stella and Kate sat to enjoy the cool evening air.

And the cool beer, which the sisters kept wonderfully in their stone cellar. Kate followed Stella's prescription, which was half-and-half: half mild and half bitter. 'Slips down easier,' she explained. It certainly did: Kate had never tasted anything so thirst-quenching. Why she should still be thirsty after drinking a pint of it did not occur to her as a question worth examining.

'Well, tomorrow's Geoffrey's big day. I hope he doesn't make a show of himself. No, hang on, I don't. That's like Richard says, it's underwhatsname, underestimating him, that's why he gets pulled back. Wonder how he's getting on today? Richard, I mean. Didn't seem too thrilled about meeting this brother of his. I wonder if he looks like him?'

'I do like your hair, Stella,' Kate said, out of a sort of amiable trance.

'What? My old carroty nob?' Stella flicked at it disdainfully. 'Ruddy awful. Can't do anything with it.'

'No, it's striking. I wish my hair was that colour.'

'You're mad. I wish I had your colouring. Just like Jessie Matthews.'

'Richard said that, didn't he? That was a nice thing to say. Shall we have another?'

'Go on, you twisted me arm.'

Kate went inside, walking with a curious confidence, careless of the interested eyes of the drinkers inside. Alice served the beer without comment. Kate thanked her fulsomely and made her springy way back outside, where she found Frankie Hope, alias Frankly Hopeless. He was leaning over Stella with one hand on the back of her chair and giving her the smile, which plainly wasn't working.

'No, you can't buy me a drink,' she was saying with suppressed exasperation. 'I've got one coming, thank you very much.'

Frankie looked up at Kate's approach with a marked unfriendliness that then melted into cheery ingratiation.

'Well then,' he said, 'I can buy you both a drink, can't I? The more the merrier. Room for a little one here, ain't there?'

'No,' Stella said.

'I don't mind having somebody on me knee, if that'd help. What d'you say, girls?'

Plainly he could keep this going all night: Frankie was a living demonstration of the fact that talk is cheap.

'Sling your hook, Frankie,' Stella said, with a glare that made Kate feel she would not like to get on the wrong side of her.

'All right, if you insist,' Frankie said, holding up his hands. It was that look of humorous innocence, Kate decided, that got him his conquests. 'No harm in asking, is there? Just don't like to see two lovely ladies out here on their own. Like the Babes in the Wood or summat.'

'And don't tell me – you're the wolf,' Stella said. She wasn't bantering: the look she darted at him was venomous to the point of hatred.

Frankie, however, couldn't see it. 'Well,' he said, moving in again, 'you'd certainly get me howling at the moon, princess, any old day of the week.'

Stella turned on him. 'Listen, Fido, you move your arse out of here pronto else you'll get such a clout across your smarmy chops you'll be spitting teeth for a week. It ain't just that I'm not interested, sonny, I *really* can't stand you and I'd set fire to meself before I'd let your clammy hands anywhere near me. Now have you got that through your thick head?'

For a moment Kate was fearful for Stella: Frankie, though he did not move, went pale and a hooded, dangerous look came down over his eyes. But then he moved away with a sort of retreating swagger and seemed about to go into the pub without a word.

On the threshold, however, he paused and looked back. Like most men with ready smiles, he conjured up a sneer very easily too.

'Awfully sorry, old girl,' he said. 'Toodle-oo. See you at the hunt ball, what?'

He didn't do the posh voice very well, but the meaning was plain. Stella stared seethingly after him for a few moments, and when she transferred her gaze back to Kate her face was still livid.

Kate put up her hands. 'Don't shoot!'

It worked: Stella laughed, relaxed, and took a deep draught of beer. 'You still sure you want to be a redhead?' she said. 'Coh dear. Gave him the brush-off, didn't I?'

'You could say that,' Kate giggled. Now that he was gone it didn't seem important: it just seemed hilarious.

'Well, he gets on my tit. Carrying on like he's the dog's knackers.'

'Stella!' Kate shrieked.

'I'm sorry, I speak as I find, always have.' Stella looked devilish. 'Right, who's next? Who's next for the treatment? Come on, Moaning Bliss, wherever you are, I'm ready for you . . .'

Next, however, was not Mona Bloss: it was George Maxey. He came up the cinder path towards the pub with his jacket over his shoulder, whistling under his breath, his head down. In his short-sightedness he didn't recognize Kate until he was right beside her chair, and then he gave a tremendous start.

'Kate!'

'Hullo, George.' She felt a little, but not very, embarrassed: in fact she had to hold in a giggle. 'How are you?'

He disdained the question, peering at Kate and then at Stella in the evening gloom. Though the air was cool now, he seemed to carry something of the heat of the day about him still, like a south wall after sunset.

'Is everything all right?' he said.

'Oh, yes, thank you.'

'Your father?'

'He's feeling a lot better.'

'Hm. I thought I'd come and see him some time.'

'He'd like that.'

George's eyes dwelt on Kate and on the glass of beer in her hand as if they formed some puzzle that he would presently work out. 'Well! Looks like we'll have nice weather for the feast tomorrow.'

'Yes. Is your barley cut now?'

'Nearly. Well, I dare say I'll see you tomorrow.'

He walked into the pub with abruptness: this was usual, but Kate felt subtly annoyed.

'I'm sorry about that, Stella.'

'Wha' for?'

'He was rude. He never said a word to you.'

'That's 'cos he's only got eyes for you!' Stella laughed.

The sudden muddled solemnity of drink came over Kate. She drew patterns on the table top and said, 'I don't know what to do. I do like him but I wish he'd sort of flirt with me a bit.'

'What, like Frankly Hopeless?'

'Oh, no, not like him. Like . . . I don't know, with George it's as if he already sees us as married and with three children. All set out already, just got to get the formalities over with. Do you see what I mean?'

Stella nodded earnestly, then snorted. 'Catch me having kids.'

'Why? Why not, I mean?'

'Oh, I've got nothing against 'em as such. I dare say it's all right if you've got pots of money. But look at my lot. There's me and Dot and then there's Edie, she's married, and there's me brother Les who's at sea somewhere and Vic who's God knows where and the two little boys at home; and that ain't a very big family where we come from but can you imagine? All of us in that little house and Mum worn to a frazzle. And they call kids a blessin'. A bleedin' curse more like.' Stella's face grew tragic. 'Oh, I feel awful saying that. That's a terrible thing to say, ain't it? It sounds like I hate my brothers and sisters and – and wish they'd never been born.'

'No it doesn't. I know what you mean.'

'You're kind, you are.' Stella fetched a big sigh, then fetched more drinks. The beer tasted different, Kate decided: she hardly noticed the bitterness now.

'I wonder if Helen's back yet,' Kate heard somebody say, then realized she had said it herself.

'She's a smart one, ain't she?' Stella said. 'I thought she was a bit, you know, toffee-nosed at first, but she ain't. Knows what she's about, that's all. She'll go far, I bet you. In years to come we'll read about her in the papers.' A moth paid them a fluttering visit. Stella watched it with fascination and murmured, 'I wonder how Richard is.'

'Richard again.'

Stella nodded; then propped her chin on her hand and regarded Kate with a whimsical, stricken, helpless expression.

'Here!' Kate was transfixed. 'Here, you're not, are you?'

'Not what?'

'You've fallen for Richard.' Kate felt herself possessed of a marvellous acuteness, also a boundless, angelic sympathy. 'Oh, Stella, you have, haven't you?'

Stella shrugged, her elbow nearly sliding off the table as she did so. 'I don't know, Kate. He's got me thinking . . . oh, he's got me all ways, that one. I'm in a right old state. He's different, ain't he? Not like your regular run of blokes. Old Frankie there would reckon it's just 'cos he talks posh, but it ain't that. I don't know what it is. He gets under your skin somehow.'

'Oh . . .' Kate lifted her glass, found it empty. 'What are you going to do?'

'I'm not going to do nothing. Anything. Oh no, I'm out of that game. It ain't worth the grief. Anyway, he don't think nothing, anything, of me so it's daft even to think about it.'

'Oh, he do. I'm seen what he's like with you.' Kate was lapsing into the broad fen speech that a particularly exacting village schoolmistress had ironed out of her. She didn't notice it: she was only conscious of a tremendous burst of insight, in which a kaleidoscope of hints and signs suddenly formed an unmistakable shape. 'I'm seen it. You can tell.'

'No, no – that's just the way he is. Like the other day out in the field we started messing around, throwing rotten plums at each other and what have you, and then I landed one right on his nose and he chased me and got one down my neck, and when he caught me it was like he was going to . . . you know, for a second there . . . But that's just the way he is.'

Kate shook her head gravely. 'Plum down your neck, that's a sure sign.'

'Is it?'

'Definitely. Mind you, not as much as a pear in your hand.'

They were howling like monkeys when George Maxey came out of the pub.

He seemed about to carry on past them down the path, but then he paused and fixing Kate with a look said, 'Are you all right, Kate?'

'Never better,' Kate said, suppressing a mutinous giggle.

'Does your father know you're here?'

It was like a bucket of cold water. Anger followed it.

'Of course he does. Not that it's any of your business, as far as I can see.'

George's rigidity of expression gave little away, but he could not have been more surprised than she felt. Such an outburst was so entirely unlike her she could not have been more startled if she had found herself floating off the ground.

'Fair enough,' George said, walking away.

He was gone quickly – too quickly for the apology she tried to make, and which Stella could not comprehend.

'Why? Serves him right. After all, it *isn't* any of his business, is it?'

'No, but . . . he wouldn't think of it like that, you see . . .'

'Then he should. Listen, Kate Lutton, don't let people like him walk all over you. Doesn't matter if he reckons you and him are meant for each other, that's just his lookout and it doesn't give him any sort of right, do you see what I mean?'

'I've never spoken like that to him.' Kate felt despicable. 'Or anyone.'

'High time you did then. You can't be sweetness and light every minute of your life, duck – it ain't natural.'

'No . . . no, of course you're right. But – well, I must apologize to him tomorrow, when I see him at the Feast.'

Stella gave her a kindly look. 'You remind me of my mum, you do. She's the same – feels bad if she lets herself slip for a minute. D'you know – oh, I feel awful saying this, but I can say it to you – I've seen her whole face change, like she's two different people, when we've been out together just the two of us and then she thinks about going home to Dad and everything. I remember we went up the fair on the Downs once – you should have seen my mum. Like a kid she was. A real hoot. She gets these giggles, you see, and can't stop. She even had the barkers in fits. And she tried so hard to win this little china dog on the hoop-la that they gave it to her in the end. Funny little thing it was, a little dog with a top hat on. And then when we were walking home – that's when her face changed. She started to feel awful about Dad sitting at home and how hard he worked and all the rest of it. And she said she couldn't take that china dog home. "Your dad'll think it's silly," she says, "and I suppose it is," and she went and left it on somebody's doorstep. And by the time we got home all that fun was gone out of her.' Stella was quiet a moment and then gave a small smile. 'Love 'em both though. What can you do?'

On the way to fetch more drinks Kate thought of something tremendously wise and apposite in answer to that, but she forgot it on the way back; and presently she was joining Stella in a soaring duet of 'I Dreamt That I Dwelt in Marble Halls', full of pathos and harmonic daring. She was still crooning it some unguessable time later, when she fell into bed the wrong way round, solemnly notifying her clucking mother that the stars shone for everybody.

## 7

The Hamblins were having a musical evening when Helen arrived home – after leaving Miss Kingswell she had roamed the West End shops and had tea at an A.B.C. before catching the last Cambridge train – and when they pressed her to join them she pleaded a headache and went up to bed.

She undressed, and sitting up in bed opened *Pavements of Anderby*; but again she found her attention wandering, and soon she lay back and gazed at the window, where the top branches of a cherry tree rubbed and tapped at the glass. It had fruited, she noticed, but feebly compared to the cherry trees in Mr Lutton's orchards, which drooped and quavered like blowsy old women with the weight of their fruit.

Miss Kingswell's parting words came back to her.

'Well, my dear, I'm off to Malvern for a fortnight to try the air for this wretched chest of mine. But when I get back, I want you to come and see me again. Let's see – the fifth of September. Can you do that? I want to introduce you to a friend of mine at the *News Chronicle*. No, no, my dear, it's just an introduction and I don't make promises. But let's just say that my friend doesn't give away his time for nothing, any more than I do.'

So here it was. The fruit at the top of the tree was within her grasp, the fruit she had so long coveted. And it had happened just as another longing – more powerful, even? – had thrust its way into her consciousness, a besieger exultantly smashing through the gates at last and prepared to wreak who knew what havoc.

An irony. Helen liked tart flavours, and should have appreciated this one. But it was sweetness rather – an unearthly, cajoling sweetness with something of the drowsy orchard-spell about it – that she seemed to taste as she sank towards sleep, and there were dreams that night in which she acknowledged all and was granted all, and the fruits of both heaven and earth fell into her outstretched hands.

14

The Monks [illegible] a large feast, an ancient tradition, coupled with the more modern 'Hospital Sunday', when money was raised by a subscription for local hospitals. In the morning a marching band [illegible] accompanied by as [illegible] as the public could [illegible] from the [illegible] up to the church and back, leading a procession of decorated [illegible] floats, and each of the local Friendly Societies in their [illegible], and bearing their floral banners. In the afternoon there was an open-air tea for the [illegible], provided [illegible] by the Sunday school teachers, and again [illegible] in the [illegible], and a [illegible] in the schoolroom to round off the evening. [illegible]

[illegible]

[illegible] Little Ralph often [illegible] remarked, it was as if it were a very long wig stuck on either [illegible]

And this year was no exception; in fact all commented on the splendid turnout, not least the part played by the [illegible] in the procession. Somehow Richard had found time not only to finish the [illegible] but to [illegible] a set of wheels to mount it on, and [illegible] towed it from his car, with [illegible]

# SIX

## 1

The Monks Bridge village feast, an ancient tradition, coincided with the more modern Hospital Sunday, when money was raised for a subscription to local hospitals. In the morning, a marching band of such amateur scrapers and blowers as the district could boast made a progress from the clocktower to the church and back, leading a procession of decorated waggons, children's floats, and men of the local Friendly Societies in their Sunday best bearing their florid banners. In the afternoon there was an open-air tea for the children, presided over by the Sunday school teachers, and a garden fete in the church grounds, with a dance in the schoolroom to round off the evening. Most fen villages had their version of this, and all went at their jollifications with a will; but the Monks Bridge feast was usually lent a special flavour by the presence of the fruit-pickers, who joined in the proceedings with gusto, and made resourceful additions to the procession. The village still talked of a feast a few years ago when a beauteous young visitor from Rotherhithe had borrowed Ernie Delph's carthorse and caused a general sensation as Lady Godiva. And as Ernie Delph often reminiscently remarked, it wasn't as if it was a very long wig she had on either.

And this year was no exception: in fact all commented on the splendid turnout, not least the part played by the fruit-pickers' children in the procession. Somehow Richard had found time not only to finish the wooden pirate ship but to cadge a set of wheels to mount it on, and he towed it from his car, with the riotously costumed children swarming over it and running alongside.

Surprisingly, he hadn't donned any sort of costume himself, and wore sober shirt and flannels; nor, though he offered the odd smile as the procession made its way through the village, did he look overjoyed to be there. It was Helen, sitting beside him in the front of the car, who seemed to have entered most into the spirit of things, appearing in a swashbuckling hat and cloak and looking, Kate thought, almost radiantly happy.

For her part, Kate looked on dully, the excited squeals of the children going through her temples like skewers. She had done her bit towards the festivities this morning – rising early to help prepare the children's spread in the village hall, an experience that had sent her racing tight-lipped for the lavatory more than once – and now all she wanted to do was feel quietly dreadful on the sidelines. Stella had joined her to watch the procession, but she too was, fortunately, in subdued mood, merely remarking that it would get better eventually.

'Will it?' Kate said weakly.

'Be right as rain this evening,' Stella said, pale and rather hoarse. 'Be ready for a hair of the dog, you'll see.'

'Oh, don't.'

Stabs of memory kept penetrating Kate's numbness, and one of the sharpest was of her drunkenly snapping at George Maxey. When he marched past her carrying the banner of the Farmers' Union she tried to shrink behind Stella, but his eyes sought her out as ever. He looked very handsome in his Sunday suit. Kate had an obscure feeling of having been caught defacing something valuable.

It was not, as is so frequent with occasions greatly anticipated, a very easeful day. For Stella the hangover was not as it was for Kate a grimly novel experience, but she seemed quite as chastened – perhaps because of the way the beer had betrayed her into incautious confession. The air was still and humid – made you feel like a steamed trout, Stella said – and teeming with midges; and when a nervous Ernie Delph made a speech on behalf of the hospital fund at the clocktower, a task that usually fell to Kate's more nimble-tongued father, it seemed to go on and on like a long slow train at a level crossing.

They were not the only ones out of sorts that day, as became plain when they met Richard and Helen outside the church before the special service. Helen was unusually talkative: Richard by contrast was listless, and his heavy-lidded eyes seemed to have no life in them at all.

'Oh, a wonderful woman,' Helen said when Kate asked how she had got on with Miss Kingswell. 'She was very kind and encouraging. But realistic too. I mustn't set my sights too high and I must be prepared for a hard struggle and least of all must I expect much money from it—'

'Sounds like you're going down the mines,' Richard said. The flippancy was inserted a little too sharply.

'Is she going to help you, though?' Stella said.

'Well, yes.' Helen beamed: it made her look much younger. 'I have another appointment with her in a fortnight's time. She's going to introduce me to someone from the *News Chronicle*.'

'The office boy, probably,' Richard said.

'Coh, does that mean a job, then?' Stella said, ignoring him.

'I don't know. It's certainly an opening. And everyone has to start somewhere. Perhaps they'll tell me to go and report church bazaars or something, but—'

'Oh, come on, Helen, no false modesty,' Richard said. 'The great world beckons. Just don't imagine it's going to alter its prejudices on your account. Whatever happens they'll still have you doing the woman's angle. What hat Mrs Chamberlain had on and the cut of Signor Mussolini's breeches. You'll be condemned to scribbling feminine trivia.'

Strangely, Helen seemed to respond to these remarks only with a bright, dry interest; but Stella was irritated. 'You don't know that,' she said. 'This Miss Kingswell, she did it, didn't she?'

Richard clicked his heels together and made a little bow. 'I stand corrected.'

'How was your brother, Richard?' asked Kate, who was no less observant for the hangover.

'He was very well, thank you.' Richard was acidly formal. 'We had a long chat. Covered a lot of ground.'

Helen's eyes dwelt on him. 'Was it *very* ghastly?'

Richard wouldn't soften. 'What in life isn't?' he said, shrugging and walking into the church.

'He's a right little ray of sunshine today, ain't he?' Stella said as they followed.

'Don't take any notice,' said Helen. She seemed to have settled herself on a high plateau of calm. Everyone was perspiring, but she looked cool: in fact, Kate thought again, the only word for her was radiant.

Richard did bestir himself when it was time for the children to perform the little turns he had coached them in; but even that did not go smoothly. Their tea had been set out in a marquee in the church grounds, and the performance took place in front of it, before the official opening of the fete. The decision to have the performance first, followed by the tea, had seemed a wise one – Richard felt they might be sleepy after eating – but as it turned out, the thought of the spread behind them distracted the children's minds and made them impatient. One little girl who had elected to sing 'Twinkle Twinkle Little Star' cantered through it so fast she didn't even draw breath, and then shot into the marquee for her reward.

Nobody in the crowd who had gathered to watch minded this: they were in holiday mood and disposed to like anything; Auntie Bea could be heard wildly clapping and cooing 'Aaaah!' even when one or two of the infants got stage fright and fled without uttering a word. But Richard, hovering in the entrance to the marquee like an anxious impresario, looked more and more dissatisfied; and when two little boys abandoned their very amusing Laurel and Hardy routine to dash for the food, he caught hold of them and pushed them back, audibly hissing, 'Do it again. Come on. Do it again.'

The atmosphere was so generally unpromising that when Geoffrey Tranter stumped forward to do his bit Stella sucked in a sympathetic breath, and Helen murmured prayerfully, 'Come on

Geoffrey. Show them how it's done.' The sight of so many faces regarding him seemed to dumbfound Geoffrey, who merely stood for some moments absently scratching at a mosquito bite on his leg; but then without any prompting he hitched his chin and began to recite his poem, slowly and clearly.

> '"Come live with me and be my love,
> And we will all the pleasures prove,
> That valleys, groves, hills and fields,
> Woods, or steepy mountain yields . . ."'

Geoffrey won them. Even those who had no idea that this was a child dismissed as backward, incapable of achievement, sensed that they were witnessing a little triumph. When he hesitated over the fifth verse, there was a suspenseful murmur as if a tightrope-walker had wobbled, and a sigh when he negotiated the obstacle and forged on to the end.

> '"The shepherds' swains shall dance and sing,
> For thy delight each May morning,
> If these delights thy mind may move;
> Then live with me and be my love."'

Geoffrey didn't stay around for his applause, but it didn't matter. Auntie Bea, using her great elbows, made her way over to Stella. 'Did yer see him, gel? Did yer see him? I'm filling up.' She honked into a handkerchief. 'Will's piping his eye an' all. Our Geoffrey. Who'd have thought. He's not quite right, you see—' this to Helen. 'He got the cord wrapped round him when he was born but you love 'em the same, don't yer? You'll know, duck, when it comes to you.'

Geoffrey's success had partly lifted the cloud from Richard's brow, at least. But he was still like a coiled spring. After the fete was officially declared open by a flower-hatted lady who had been imported from the shires for the day and who seemed to have only the dimmest notion of where she was, Richard prowled the tents and stalls like a man who had lost something precious, at last coming up to Kate and demanding, 'Isn't there anywhere you can buy a drink at this damned affair?'

'Not alcohol.' The fens, boozy enough when workaday, betrayed an old Puritan streak when it came to ceremony.

'Dear God.' Richard glared gloomily about him. 'Well, I suppose I can wait till the dance.'

'Not then either, I'm afraid,' Kate said. 'There'll be refreshments – lemonade and ices and things.'

This was a moment at which, under normal circumstances, she would expect Richard to burst out laughing. Instead he grumped something and then, looking over her shoulder, muttered, 'Here comes your George, I'd better absent myself,' before wandering away.

Kate wished she could have been a little more prepared to face George Maxey, but he was upon her in a moment, presenting a chestful of clean-smelling blue serge to her view.

'Kate. Haven't had a chance to speak to you all day.'

She raised her eyes. The sun was right behind him, and his great head had the look of a bronze, carved and glowing.

'No. It's ever so hot today, isn't it? Muggy.'

George disposed of the weather with a brusque flick of his hand. 'Kate, is everything all right at home?'

'At home, yes, why shouldn't it be?'

'I just wondered with your father still laid up and all – whether it's a bit of a strain for you. I could do more for you, you know. I've got plenty of time – don't worry about that. If you need any help—'

'Thank you, George, it's very kind of you, but we're all right, really. I . . .' She fought down a sick wave of embarrassment. 'Last night, George, I – I'm afraid I was a bit short with you, you know, at the Corner – I was a bit tipsy to be honest—'

'Oh, I know that wasn't you,' he said briskly. 'I know you better than that. That's really why I was asking whether everything was all right.'

'Well, it was me,' she said, still trying to piece out an apology,

'I was the one who said it, and—'

'No.' He was emphatic, even by his standards. 'Look, I've nothing against these people you're mixing with, I dare say they're very nice, but obviously they're different, and that's bound to have an influence on you. You might say that that's none of my business either, but it is.'

'How?'

'Oh . . . because of the way I feel about you.'

His hesitation had been only momentary, and he seemed not to regret it at all once it was out. The conversation had taken such an unexpected turn that all Kate could do at first was grope along the old track.

'These people are my friends—'

'I know, but they won't be here for ever. I will, for you.'

Even when he was rocking her to her foundations with such a sudden and uncompromising demonstration as this, there was something massively reassuring about George. Because he took it all out of your hands: acquiescence was all his stark certainty required.

Curiosity moved her to speech, as a lesser emotion often will when the greater is paralysing. 'Have I changed, then? Am I different?'

'You'll never change for me. Pip, how are you, old son?'

He handled the arrival of her brother beside them much more adroitly than she, but she was grateful for the interruption. She used it, in fact, to steal away. It was a mean trick, perhaps, but this was all too much for her blurred and aching mind; and when she glimpsed George later about the fete, he did not appear to be searching for her, nor did he appear to have the slightest regret. His robust figure, standing hands on hips and head thrust forward as he cocked an ear to some vague chitchat from the flower-hatted lady, seemed to say to Kate more clearly than any words that he would wait. He had spoken, and that was that: farmer-like, he had sown the seeds and would await the harvest.

'You all right, gel?'

Stella came upon Kate skulking around the lemonade booth.

'Thirsty,' Kate said.

'Me an' all. That's what the booze does to you. Don't ask me how. It's wearing off, though. A drop more of this should set me up.' Stella bought another glass of lemonade, but it did not seem to refresh her. She stood dabbing at her face with a handkerchief and frowning out at the milling people. There was an acidic smell of bruised grass from the ceaseless trampling of Sunday boots. 'I don't know. I feel funny today. Not just liverish . . . Oh, maybe it's just that. Life's a bit too complicated sometimes, ain't it? Too many things in it, and they don't mix. D'you ever wish you were a kid again?'

'I feel like I am a lot of the time.'

Stella perplexed and subdued, Kate absent and almost careless with so much to think about, Helen seeming to carry around a strange, secret distillation of happiness, Richard edgy and dark in look and word: if the summer friendship between the four had been a process of mutual revelation, then here it had come to a bizarre turn, with each of them showing a side uncharacteristic to the point of deformity. They were as awkward as badly cast actors; and, with hindsight, what happened later at the dance was simply waiting to occur. The combustive elements were all in place, and it only needed one further ingredient to set them off. The ingredient appeared, in the shape of Frankie Hope.

The shilling-ticket dance which rounded off the village feast was held in the schoolhouse. A four-piece band, who in boaters and blazers had been playing arrangements of Strauss and Suppé in the church grounds throughout the fete, metamorphosed into a tailcoated dance band for the evening, and most of the village underwent a similar transformation, going home at seven to change into evening clothes and dancing shoes, if they had them. Early in the day Kate's mother had invited Helen and Richard up to the house to have a bite to eat and change there when the evening came, but in the end it was only Helen who did so.

'You go,' Richard said as the four of them walked away from the fete, where the tents were being dismantled. 'I'll see you at the dance.'

'But you'll want something to eat,' Helen said.

'Oh, I'm not hungry.'

'Where are you going to change?'

'Change? Oh, that. I didn't bring anything. I'll do as I am, won't I? Look, it's only a bob-a-throw village hop, it's not the ruddy Savoy.'

'Oh, Richard, don't be a snob,' Helen said, though indulgently. 'It's going to be a lovely evening, I know. Aren't you always telling me that life's too short?'

If she had not been so distracted, Kate might have been offended by Richard's sour dismissal of what was, after all, her own world; but it was Stella who frowned and said, 'Don't put yourself out on our account, Richard.'

'Look, I'll see you all at the dance,' Richard said. 'I just want a bit of – of breathing space.'

Nobody mentioned, jokingly or otherwise, that the pubs would be opening shortly – an index of the curious, listless tension in the air between them.

'Well, all right,' Helen said with a shrug. 'Just let me get my bag from the car then. I'm going to get changed, anyway.'

'Me too,' Stella said. 'I'll see you all at the hop.'

And that was how it went on. Up at the house, where they changed in Kate's bedroom, Helen was talkative, hardly seeming to notice Kate's abstraction; she even flirted gently with Pip, who at the sight of the willowy figure in a silk evening dress wafting into their homely kitchen turned untypically abashed. When they arrived at the schoolhouse they found it already well filled, for many of the fruit-pickers, regardless of whether they could muster suitable clothes, had jumped at the chance of a shindig. Mona Bloss was there, her neckline so plunging that some of the village boys could only stare at it, despairing and paralysed, wherever it went. Auntie Bea and Uncle Will were there, and were amongst the first to take the floor, Bea's great height and vast feet forcing Will to adopt a strenuous dancing posture, as if he were climbing up her. Stella was there too, sitting out on one of the diminutive school chairs that lined the olive-green walls; and when she saw

Kate and Helen, made for them as if they were her saviours.

Which they were – from Frankie Hope, who had been pestering her for a dance.

'Unbelievable, isn't it?' Stella said. She seemed almost ready to cry with vexation. 'After I gave him such a mouthful last night. I thought *that* had finished it good and proper. But no, he goes and gives it another go. And when I say no, just polite this time, he starts turning nasty.'

'Perhaps he was hoping you'd feel bad about what you said, and give in to him out of guilt,' Helen said. 'He sounds as if he knows all the tricks.'

'What did he say to you, then?' Kate said.

'Oh . . . stupid things.' Stella bit her lip. 'It doesn't matter.'

There he certainly was, at any rate, brilliantined and jaunty, sauntering about the room and giving that so-nearly convincing impression of a good sort with a deal of cheek but no harm in him. But it became clear as the evening went on that Frankie Hope had more than ingratiation in his repertoire. Trying it on with other girls, dancing with them, swapping jokes with his friends – he did all this whilst keeping his malice trained on Stella like a hidden pistol. It was partly a matter of staring at her whenever he wasn't looking at someone else: partly a matter of placing himself in her way whenever possible and then moving aside with an exaggerated bow, of bumping into her on the dance floor with such remarks as 'Whoops, sorry, Duchess, hope I didn't break your fan.' That he was able to keep up a steady stream of resentful nastiness whilst also being his normal self said much about him.

'Do you want to leave?' Kate asked Stella. 'I'll come with you, if you want to go.' She had her own reasons for wishing to quit this particular field – and they were not, this time, anything to do with the shyness that usually made dances a torture for her. That was scarcely a factor now: more pressing was what George Maxey had said to her, and the knowledge that, with someone of George's character, it could not simply be forgotten or disregarded. He was not here yet – he was probably fitting in a little work on the farm, having a brisk disregard for the Sabbath – but she had no doubt that he would be, later. And the old urge to hide herself away from disruption and difficulty was on her now with a vengeance.

But Stella, thanking her, firmly said no. 'I'm not going to let a little skunk like him stop me enjoying myself,' she said; though she was plainly not enjoying herself at all.

All this time there was no sign of Richard. He couldn't, Kate thought, have simply driven back to Cambridge, because that would leave Helen stranded; and she was just about to suggest going to look for him when he appeared in the doorway.

He stood there in an arrested posture, looking across the heads of the dancers, hair wild from the hot night breeze and his eyes very black against the pallor of his face. The moment of suspension gave something intense and dramatic to his appearance, as if the aimless dissatisfying evening were about to break into significance; but Kate, with the sensations of last night's toping still fresh within her, recognized at once that he had been drinking, and that that pause on the threshold was the drink swooping inside him and making him steady himself like a man about to cross the deck of a heeling ship.

And then he descended on them and he was all animation. His earlier bleak mood might never have been. There was something almost feverish in his high spirits.

'Hello hello hello, what have I missed? Helen, look at you – and Kate, you look . . . and Stella . . . Oh, to hell with the compliments, who's going to dance? As long as it's not a tango. Anything but a tango – I can never keep a straight face. Phew! I had the most beastly headache but it's gone, thank goodness. This band's pretty good, isn't it? Where are they from, do you know? Well, who's it to be? Helen – alphabetical order, how's that – will you?'

'Well, something's perked him up,' Stella said as they watched Richard and Helen take the floor.

'I think he's had a few.' Kate smiled as Richard swung Helen round in an extravagant arc. Normally she would have laughed at such a typical Richard gesture, but any laughter just now, she felt, would have been like the strawberry ice she was trying to eat – too cold, each mouthful setting her teeth on edge.

'More than a few,' Stella said.

Stella was not happy, and had given up attributing it to the remains of the hangover. It was something to do with last night, though, and the way she had betrayed herself. Also surprised herself: for it was only when she had found herself speaking aloud her feelings about Richard that she had seen them for what they were. Confession had made real what before was only shadowy.

Of course, the shadows were where it belonged. It was daft, and impossible. But even as a recognized daydream, an admitted absurdity, it imposed on her a burden of wretchedness. She could have borne it, perhaps, if it hadn't been for the presence tonight of Frankie Hope. The way he concentrated on her – no matter that it was now with malice instead of calculation – forced her to a dismal conclusion: that it was with the likes of Frankie Hope that she really belonged. The arrival of Richard only reinforced the lesson. The dance in the schoolroom might have been planned specifically to present her with the most eloquent contrast of what could never be with what grimly, drearily was.

And as if this wasn't perplexing enough, Richard himself had been, to say the least of it, very odd all day. She had even begun to entertain a superstitious notion that he had by some magical means – for Kate, she knew, would never break a confidence – found out what she had said last night and that his cussed mood represented his reaction to it. Yet now here he was, the life and soul of the party. Or striving to be. He was cranking it up, she could tell. Perhaps he was simply tired of them, tired of the orchard summer, tired of being away from people of his own sort.

Well, that might be for the best. After all, he wasn't going to stay here for ever. Neither was she, for that matter. A desolate sense of ending haunted her: she felt the treadmill of time beneath her feet. Stella was so accustomed to living for the moment – it was, in fact, her creed – that this new perspective shook her, to the extent that she doubted everything.

And then, in the midst of this – almost against her will – she found herself laughing. Richard had asked Auntie Bea to dance and, bridling like a girl, Bea was taking the floor with him. There was one crucial thing you had to be aware of when dancing with Auntie Bea: she led. Uncle Will had never got the hang of leading, so they had come to this arrangement which suited them both. But it was rather a shock for a new partner – as was clear from Richard's face as they began. For a moment he seemed to be wondering whether he was more drunk than he thought. And then all at once he recovered. With what must have been a good deal of concentration, he performed the lady's steps as if he had never danced any other way in his life. Meanwhile Auntie Bea, taller than him by an inch or so, adopted her usual dancing expression, which was a sort of dreamy skywards gaze imperfectly copied from Anna Neagle. The two bright red spots on her cheekbones were attributable to the youth and comeliness of her partner, which she suavely pointed out to Mona Bloss by cawing as she foxtrotted past her, 'See, I can get 'em an' all, you mucky ole trollop!'

For a second it looked as if Richard was going to curtsey to Auntie Bea when the dance ended, but instead he kissed her hand. Even now, Stella thought, he could still make her laugh.

And then with that almost hectic swiftness that characterized him tonight, he had swallowed down a glass of lemonade and was beside her asking her to dance the next with him.

'Don't you want a rest first?' she said, for he was sweating.

'Rest, no! I want to dance every dance. Come on.'

'There isn't any music,' she said, laughing with a curious pain inside her.

Richard clapped his hands and whistled at the band. 'More! Bravo, more!' Over in the corner Frankie Hope's groomed head turned.

'You're a funny one,' Stella said as they moved out on to the floor, which was slick with damp chalk in the humid atmosphere. 'Like a bear with a sore head all day and now this.'

'Eh? Oh, rubbish. Just had a bit of a headache. All right now . . . Sorry, was I? Bear et cetera?'

'Well, a bit . . . I didn't feel like I could talk to you today.' Stella didn't know why she said that or quite what she meant: her words were stepping stones, both tentative and treacherous, leading to a place she didn't know.

He looked at her, inquisitive. 'You've very serious tonight.'

'I am allowed to be, sometimes, you know.'

'No, you're not. You wouldn't be the person you are.'

'Oh, you don't know anything about me.'

'Doesn't matter. You like someone or you don't. You don't have to read a biography first.'

'You wouldn't like me if you really knew me.' She stopped, realizing she was talking in the sort of deadly self-communing spurts that Happy Harry infuriatingly used to indulge in; but she experienced a flicker of understanding for that almost-forgotten figure from a world that seemed very far away.

'I don't believe in all that. I think people who go in for soul baring are common.'

She glanced up: it was a word she had never heard him use and in her current mood it twanged a nerve. But he forged ahead, explaining.

'You meet them everywhere. At Cambridge there were whole sets of people who never did anything else. They clubbed up in dim rooms with coffee and just delved. What did Helen call it? Psychological nudism. Such rubbish. As if, by just digging hard enough, you could get to what you *really* think or what you *really* feel. As if such a thing exists! Do *you* know what you really think or feel?'

'No,' she said. It was true, though she also felt it to be untrue at some level that with his quickness he had passed over.

'There you are then.' He swung her round. His dancing, whether it was the drink or not, was more flamboyant than the sort of shuffling she was used to. She began to enjoy it. 'I kept thinking about you yesterday,' he said, surprising her. 'When I was with Maurice.'

'Did you? Do I look like him, then?'

'Oh, God,' he laughed. 'If only you knew. No, no, you look – ' his slightly foxed eyes dwelt on her – 'you look like . . .'

'Here, you, don't start.' She seriously did not want him to

start, but the tone of the remark at once established the old rapport between them, closing up great distances: not what she had intended, but too natural to be resisted. They began talking nonsense.

'Hard woman, Stella, that's what you are.'

'Better than being soft in the head.'

'Oh, not soft in the head, eh?'

'Not a bit of it, so don't think it.'

'Soft anywhere else?'

'You're starting again . . . I told you . . .'

They were still like this when the dance ended, and were the last to leave the floor. So it was obvious to Stella what happened when Richard tripped and very nearly fell on his face. It was Frankie Hope, who was seated to the side, and who stuck out his leg in pure schoolboy fashion as Richard walked past him.

Richard didn't realize. Being drunk, he put everything down to that: he simply laughed, colouring, and said, 'Sorry, old man.' If he heard Frankie repeating behind him, in his poor parody of a posh accent, 'Oh, sawry, old men,' he did not show it.

Stella knew this sort of business. In the pubs back home it went on all the time, and she hated it because you never knew where it would stop. No deep thinker, she saw instinctively what most people never grasped: that women were the first to come out of the cave, and that men still had a foot in there. And so she suggested that they should leave. But she suggested it feebly: she gave no reason, and her own heart tugged her the other way because in spite of her confusion she wanted to dance with him again. Richard, not unnaturally, dismissed the suggestion, and supposed it to do with his being pickled. 'I'm all right, really,' he said. 'Got chatting to somebody in the pub and had a few gins too many, you know how it is. I'll drink some more lemonade, that'll flush it out.' Soon he was dancing with Kate, and Frankie Hope got himself wrapped up with some girl from the village who gave a single screech of laughter, like the caw of a caged parrot, at everything he said; and Stella supposed that things would be all right.

Helen meanwhile had gone outside, and was walking up and down the schoolyard smoking a cigarette. She had bought a pack after visiting Miss Kingswell, and was trying to like them, though not getting on very well. It was for the luxury of thinking that she had really slipped out. She had had a moment, hearing the massed clumping of feet on chalked floorboards, when she had wondered what on earth she was doing here, but it had quickly passed. Because of her father's position as rector of an old-fashioned parish, she was quite used to village halls and all that polite paternalistic English awkwardness that had, she supposed, just kept off revolution: had she been more bourgeois, she would have felt more aversion.

As it was, she was almost wholly preoccupied with the thing she had discovered within herself yesterday. Far from cancelling out what Miss Kingswell had said to her of renunciation and independence, it seemed to harmonize with it: there had been two beginnings that day, and so they must surely come together. Normally so strict in her reasoning, Helen let the fuzziness of this pass, and searched the great fen sky for stars. Their gleams were few and reluctant: muggy cloud still infested the sky, refusing to break.

Curiously, for the present all she wanted was to contemplate the revelation inside her. The emotion was new, or newly understood, and as such required examination: its object had long been around, was here now, would exist in the future – that was all that mattered, for Helen was comfortable with the broad perspectives of time that appalled Stella. In fact, if anything she preferred to be a little away from him for the moment: they had danced, and talked as of old, but the proximity had seemed to Helen too much, like eating a whole banquet all at once. For now her self was enough, because it was an envelope containing beauty. She had long had a suspicion of 'beautiful feelings', believing them to be an indulgence of sentimental natures, but she saw now that she had simply never had any – indeed, had believed that beauty and herself had nothing to do with each other.

She ground out the cigarette, which had made her feel a little queasy. She supposed she ought to go back in – make sure that he was all right. He had had too much to drink, and would be suffering in the morning. This too did not seem to matter: she felt full of an expansive understanding.

She went in, and found Richard and Kate and Stella together, close to the dais. The band had just struck up a noisy schottische, and for a moment she did not grasp that there was trouble.

'You said yes. You did. You did, don't lie.' That was the young Lothario, Frankie Hope: he kept trying to say this, aggressively, into Stella's face; she, distressed, kept trying to turn her shoulder to him. Richard, not quite comprehending yet, was putting a tipsy cheerful oar in. 'A mistake,' he said, waving his arms vaguely about, 'just a mistake – never mind.'

'Who asked you?' Frankie turned at once to him, as if this was an opportunity he had been waiting for. 'Who asked you, smartarse?'

'No need for this,' Richard said, both smiling and frowning. 'All a mix-up, that's all.'

'I never said I'd dance with you,' Stella said, pale and vehement. 'I never did. Leave us alone.'

'Oh, it's us, is it? Oh, la-di-dah, pardon me, milady. I suppose I'm not good enough for you. Just because I'm not some stuck-up nancy boy—'

'That's enough, there's no need for that.' Richard wasn't smiling now. 'You heard the lady.'

'I don't see no lady. Just a cheap tart and a nancy boy.' Frankie put his face up close to Richard's. There was a sparkling exultation about his belligerence. 'You keep your nose out of it. Else you'll get what's coming to you.'

'Look, look, all right, I'll dance with you,' Stella cried, though the situation had gone past that.

'No, why should you?' Richard said: he had gone white. 'If this man won't see reason—'

'You come outside!' Frankie hissed it out: a little saliva touched Richard's face. 'Little pisspot – come outside . . .'

'Ignore him, Richard.' It was Kate, who looking dogmatic and rather fierce was trying to push herself between them. 'Don't take any notice . . .'

Plainly, Frankie fancied his chances. He had reason to, for Richard's looks and physique proclaimed him no fighter. But he had reckoned without the volatile chemistry of emotion that had been going on in Richard all day: Richard had been like a man on the edge of something and now, suddenly, he went over it. When there was no reply to his challenge Frankie took a step back, sneering, starting to say something, and Richard flew at him.

The shock of it so disarmed Frankie that he was on the floor and being pummelled in the face before he knew what had happened. Perhaps Richard's pallor should have warned him: it was the whiteness of pure rage. Now Richard was crimson, windmilling his fists like a goaded boy, and the peak had been passed. People began yelling: the band raggedly stopped playing. Having recovered himself Frankie began giving as good as he got, and the two scrabbled viciously in the dust. Helen and Stella struggled in vain for handholds on their flailing jackets, and in the end it was Kate, darting in with her violet eyes blazing, who pulled them apart.

By that time others had gathered around, and there was a lot of shoulder patting and soothing advice, while the two men, dusty and bedraggled as fighting cocks, glared and gasped; but they could not have gone on anyway. It was the sort of confused uncinematic fight in which real damage is done: both Frankie's eyes were puffed and he was winded, and blood was pouring from Richard's nose and mouth.

'You bloody fools!' Stella cried, in real anguish. 'Oh, you bloody fools!'

'Literally, in my case,' Richard said, looking down at his shirt: the blood-letting seemed to have brought him back to himself. He reeled, and Helen guided him into a chair, then felt helpless. This, after her starry thoughts outside, was beyond her: she was in a foreign land.

And then Kate stepped forward and, taking out her own

handkerchief, began to wipe the blood from Richard's face.

The band had struck up again, but not many were dancing. Auntie Bea was flapping and wailing around the figure of her former partner: Frankie too had his supporters, and Stella feared a free-for-all. But it was Kate who prevented the forming of two camps. She called for a jug of iced water from the refreshment tables and then crossed over to Frankie. She bathed his swollen eyes and made a cold compress from a napkin and Frankie, mutely, submitted. Gradually the fumes of violence evaporated and people began to drift away.

But the evening was in ruins and it had unpleasantness yet. Richard, all the wildness gone from his eyes, offered an apology to Frankie and tried to shake hands, but Frankie, scowling through his shiners, was having none of it; and Mona Bloss, never one to miss an opportunity, strutted by and pausing before Stella like an inspecting officer remarked, 'Beggared if I can see what there is to fight over meself.' It was Helen who suggested that they ought to leave, but agreement was unanimous.

Outside, the night reproached them. The sky was a deep plum colour: crickets were conversing chirpily in the grass, and cottage-garden scents hung in the warm air like sweet powder. Richard's car was parked over by the church, and as a group they made an aimless, speechless way over to it. They had reached that point where the resources of friendship are at an end, and silence and separation are needed to replenish them.

'I'll drive,' Helen said.

'No, no, it's all right,' Richard said, but she ignored him and got into the driver's seat.

'Lip's still bleeding,' Kate said.

'Oh, is it?' He put up a vague hand to his mouth.

'Here.' Stella gave him her handkerchief.

'Thank you . . .' He looked at it frowning and said with a jerk, 'I'm really – I'm really most awfully sorry about this, I can't – I can't begin to apologize, and . . . Oh, hell.'

'You go home and get some sleep,' Kate said.

'Yes,' Stella said, 'that'd be best.'

'I've left my things at your house, Kate,' Helen said. 'All right if I pick them up tomorrow?'

'Yes, of course.'

Richard started to say something, then got in.

A streamer from the procession still dangled from the rear door handle, and Stella reached out and held it as the car moved away, until it tightened and was plucked from her grasp.

# SEVEN

## 1

Helen was not in the habit of recounting her dreams, but the one from which she woke the next morning could hardly have been told even to someone as confessedly broadminded as Mrs Hamblin.

Its unsubtlety and directness surprised rather than disturbed her; then came a certain reassurance. She had sometimes wondered, viewing the world and the way people carried on in it, whether she were not rather cold – lacking, perhaps; the dream showed otherwise. She was interested, but that other revelation – which was connected with it, of course, but not identical with it – still took precedence in her mind.

And here was her first real opportunity to be alone with it, and think it through – for Richard, not wholly to her surprise, did not call that morning to take her to the orchards. She wondered how he was feeling today, though she wondered mildly, without the hard perplexity with which she used to try to fathom him. This was one curious consequence of her discovery: now that she knew her feeling for him, the impatient probe dropped from her hand and she found herself content to let things lie. Love, it seemed, opened wide gates of acceptance.

Even the fight and the blood and the animal stares did not trouble her, not as a memory, though she had been shocked at the time. It was merely one evening, one eddy in a stream that would soon broaden and flow on to finer places. It added, besides, to her knowledge of him, and to Helen all knowledge was good.

It was a day of serenity for Helen, solitary and strangely beautiful. Thunder made grumbling passes over thc roofs of Cambridge, and the sultry air was lifeless, waiting to be stirred: even sturdy Mrs Hamblin, perspiration beading her moustache, found it oppressive and was at last driven in from the garden by midges; but Helen found the external world powerless to touch her. She spent much of the day in her room, writing a grateful letter to Olive Kingswell and looking forward to their appointment in a fortnight's time, but even this did not seem urgent and she had not finished it when the bouquet of flowers arrived.

*These are part of the apology. Other part later, if behaviour not considered unforgivable that is. Can you keep six o'clock free? R.*

It occurred to her that if any apology was required, it was to all three of them; but it was a point that in her state of serenity did not trouble her.

Late in the afternoon the storm broke, fierce and thorough. Lightning made garish snapshots of the Hamblins' dusty lofty rooms, and when the rain came it pounded so hard it might have been the thunder liquefied. Mrs Hamblin's garden exhaled rank, grateful scents, and when the rain stopped it was as if the day had been wiped clean and replaced with a new one, fresh and pure. And the transformation in Richard, typically, was just as complete. He arrived at the house on the stroke of six, impeccably dressed, impeccably behaved, and so much his old self – despite the swollen lip – that the events of yesterday might have been the feverish dream of a humid night.

Helen had dressed with her usual care, and when he saw her he nodded approvingly. 'Just right,' he said.

'For what?'

'We're going to dinner. At the Bull. I've booked a table for four for eight o'clock. No alcohol-amnesia for me this time, unfortunately: I remember vividly and in great detail that I acted like a perfect pig yesterday to everybody, singly and *en masse*. Don't deny it.'

'I wasn't going to,' she said, smiling.

'Jolly good. Treating you all to dinner is, of course, a craven attempt to buy my way back into your good books, as were the flowers which I also despatched to Kate and Stella. And of course, it won't work.'

'Of course.'

They laughed.

'God, it's good to see you,' he said, taking her hand and smiling into her eyes.

'That won't work either. Come along. We're picking the others up, I take it?'

'If they'll come. They may not be as forgiving as you. There, how's that for flannel?'

'Keep it up. By the way, you didn't send flowers to Frankie Hope, I take it?' Momentarily she wondered whether this was out of place, but Richard made a wry amused face: she had not broken the mood. It seemed, in fact, unbreakable. Yesterday, with all its murky tensions, was an age ago, and all was freshness.

And so it remained. Yesterday had been a day long anticipated and planned – overcooked, in fact: it had come out sour. Today, conjured out of nothing, was all that yesterday should have been. Motoring up to the Marshland to fetch Kate and Stella, Helen remembered the first time she had made this journey: her mind drew a meaningful pattern between the two, and she did not mistrust it, as she once would have done, as woolly sentimental thinking. Yes, this was how it had started: here had commenced the process of awakening that was now complete. Now was the time to move on to another stage; and when in her calm, rarefied state she questioned herself as to whether she was ready for it, she found that she was. Yes, ready.

Once on the journey she took Richard's cigarettes from his breast pocket, lit one for him, and passed it over: to do so simply had a feeling of rightness. He smiled into her eyes. 'You're a mind-reader,' he said. Otherwise they did not talk a great deal on the way – there was rightness in that too: little was needed.

The orchard country, rain-washed, was paradisiacal, mingling scents of apples and late plums, roses, rich stirred earth. The fen sky, never dull, had come to a glorious ripening as the sun descended. The Turner comparisons that sprang to mind were inadequate, invidious even – the most delicate pigment was harsh and acid compared to the fascinating pink radiance that not only filled the sky but seemed to suffuse the foliage of the trees and even to transform the grass, as if it too might blossom and fruit in time. 'Beautiful,' Richard said, 'beautiful evening', and when they picked up Kate and Stella, who were both waiting at Kate's house, the beauty of the evening was like the restoration of a missing piece to their friendship. The awkwardness of last night was present for the first few moments, as Stella and Kate got into the car; but when Stella, sitting back, said, 'Isn't it lovely tonight?' it was as if a burden fell away.

'Well,' Richard said, 'shall I start grovelling now, or shall I leave it till we get there?'

'Where are we going?' Stella said.

'To wine and dine,' Richard said. 'Or just dine, in my case.'

'Oh, Gawd, is my frock all right?'

'You look ravishing. All three of you look wonderful. Shameless flattery, by the way, is part of my apologetic strategy for tonight. I warn you, I shall be laying it on with a trowel, so—'

'Oh, get away with you,' Stella said. 'Everybody's allowed to get in a barney once in a while.'

'No, you're being easy on me. That's no good. I want you to be hard. I really must insist that you be very hard on me all night—'

'I shall be hard on your bonce if you don't shut up,' Stella said.

He turned in appeal. 'Kate – you're my last hope. Say something nasty.'

'You great oaf,' Kate said.

'Not bad. More.'

'Oh . . . How's your poor nose?'

'I give in,' Richard said, amid the laughter. 'I give in.'

'Anyway,' Stella said shrewdly, 'if we're nice to you, that'll make you feel worst of all, won't it? There you are then.'

They were very merry together that night. Everything fell into place, nothing was unsatisfactory. The white flame of emotion burning within Helen cast its glow in other directions, and she felt she had never enjoyed the company of Kate and Stella so much. Recalling Kate mopping the blood last night, she saluted a small victory: the girl had steel in her. Stella she had found overly rumbustious in the past, but tonight she noted what good company she was: adult also, for though Helen suspected still that Stella was half-smitten with Richard, she did not seem to take his flirtatiousness any more seriously than it deserved. The Cambridge hotel was a good choice for dinner, Helen thought: not too formal to overawe the others, it had a feeling of plush old-fashioned comfort, and the waiter brought the champagne with a certain pleased flourish, as if it were a special occasion for him too.

From time to time throughout the evening she caught a secret glance from Richard – a glance that said *Everything going all right?* – which she answered with a glance that said *Perfectly.* Communication without words: one read of such things, and tended to scoff; she perceived now that with Richard she had long had it. She thought back over all the glances and hints and gestures that Richard had given her over the past weeks and which only now did she understand as confirmation of the love that had grown up between them. For now they were a foursome, and very nice it was, but presently the others would drop away, leaving the bond that she now saw as no less than magical. That it should have begun in friendship pleased her: it suited her view of the world.

Richard would have refused the champagne altogether if they had not pressed him; as it was, he limited himself to one glass. 'I'm giving my liver the day off. It's been complaining about being overworked. Even threatened to go on strike. Bolshie innards, what can you do with them? Besides, I want to drive you all home in one piece.'

'Oh, don't worry about that,' Stella said. 'Another drop of this and I shall just curl up under the table for the night.' She had the characteristic, Helen noticed, of reflecting her mood very faithfully in her appearance: her body expressed her. Yesterday she had been pale to the point of waxenness, the bones of her face staring through the skin: tonight she fairly glowed, and it was as if she had put on flesh with the revival of her spirits. She was revelling in the occasion – the faintly shabby chintzy furnishings of the hotel, the array of silver on the table, the ritual movements of the waiters: her restless green eyes were drinking it all in.

'Ever tell you about the time I did that?' Richard said. 'My second term, it was. I'd joined some sort of dining club, Lord knows why, where these fellows went out to dinner and jawed all night about the League of Nations or something. We went to this little place off Sidney Street and it was so deadly boring that I simply nodded off. Well, they left me there snoring, can't blame them, I suppose, and when I woke up the place was empty except for a waiter sweeping up – and worst of all it was past midnight.'

'Why, what would happen to you then?' Stella said. 'Would you turn into a pumpkin?'

'Worse than that – get caught by the bulldogs,' Richard said.

'Blimey, sounds nasty!' Stella said, choking.

'They don't set bulldogs on you, surely,' said Kate, who Helen could see had been hit by the champagne in just the right way – it had floated dreamily straight to her head.

'Well, they're fierce enough,' Richard said. 'They're college servants. They go out with the proctors trying to catch undergraduates up to – well, not up to much, really. They can fine you six bob for not wearing your gown. But staying out after midnight's the worst – even if you never meant to.'

'Here, you never got caught by the bulldogs, did you?' Stella asked Helen.

'Not me. They've got no jurisdiction over the women's colleges.'

'Don't need to,' Richard said. 'You should see the lady dons.'

'Caught by the bulldogs,' Kate said, a champagne giggle bubbling up inside her. 'Ooh . . .!'

'Sounds worse than a prison,' Stella said. 'However did you put up with it?'

'It wasn't so bad,' Richard said. 'It's like everything – friends make all the difference.'

'My best friend was called Eileen Pickles,' Kate said. 'We fell out when I hit her on the head with a glass marble.'

There was such a shout of laughter that other diners turned to look. 'Kate!' Helen said. 'You bully!'

'I know,' Kate said. 'I still feel awful about that. I don't mean I threw it at her, you know – I just sort of held it in my fingers and –' she became helpless for a moment – 'clouted her on the head with it.'

'Why, why?' Richard was rocking in his chair.

'She stuck a hatpin in my dolly's behind. Well, she did . . .!'

'Oh, no!' Richard wept into his napkin.

'It was mean, wasn't it? I think it was mean.' Kate tried to compose herself and eat some bread. 'Anyway, we fell out.'

'What happened to her?' Stella gasped.

'She married a chap from Wiggenhall St Germans, I think.' There was uproar. 'Well, there *is* a place called Wiggenhall St Germans! It's near – ooh! – it's near Wiggenhall St Peter . . . honestly . . .'

It was that sort of night. Every tale amused, every name was ridiculous: everything fizzed like the champagne. They were all young, and a sense of it ran through them: its ripples touched the other diners, who were not young, and who registered it with irritated and regretful looks. When another bottle of champagne appeared, Helen wondered at the cost, and whether she should covertly offer to help pay; but then she let it drop, because the champagne was having an effect on her too and she just wanted to enjoy it. It was long since she had indulged, and she could trust her head. She refused a pudding and sank into the cushion of wine: Stella, she noticed, was no great eater either. Only Kate worked her way through everything with a countrywoman's appetite, growing more pleasant and drowsy all the time. 'I shouldn't eat any more, you know,' she kept saying over her second helping of lemon torte. 'I'm a pig. I shouldn't, you know.'

After dinner they moved to the hotel lounge, a dark ferny place smelling of shrivelled compost, for coffee and brandy: Richard allowed himself a glass, after a hesitation. 'Go on,' Stella said, 'it won't hurt you.'

'Yes, do, Richard,' Helen said. 'Your sins are shriven now.'

'Are they really?' He was laughing but serious. 'Or shall I do some more grovelling? I feel I should really. Last night—'

'Oh, it was a funny old night all round,' Stella said. 'Best to forget it. I have.'

He looked closely at her. 'Have you?'

'Pouf. Gone. Shan't forget this one, though.'

'Me neither,' Kate said from the depths of the armchair. 'Thanks ever so much, Richard.'

'Here,' Stella said, 'you're still eating!'

'Just a mint,' Kate said, 'there was one left on the table, you see . . .'

'Kate Lutton, you'll pop!'

Richard offered cigarettes. Helen benefited from her recent practice, and Stella smoked like a veteran, but Kate just sat there with surprised brimming eyes, and that set them off again; even worse was the arrival in the lounge of an ancient turkey-necked lady, mottled with rouge, who sat a little way off and proceeded to look with infinite slowness all round the room, her head turning right round like a wobbly periscope. When she had taken in the full view, she started all over again. They went into silent red-faced hilarity: Stella crammed her handkerchief into her mouth.

'I feel like kissing everybody,' Richard whispered: brandy had brought back his devilment. 'And I shall too. Hold on.'

He waited until the old lady's head had turned away from them, like an escapee waiting for the searchlight to pass, and then darted a kiss at Kate: then he sat back and talked blandly while the periscope came round again. He repeated the performance with Stella, who flapped at him and nearly let out a yelp of laughter. Last he kissed Helen, his eyes glinting. With the kiss it was as if a shaft of thrilling sobriety went through her, cutting through the filigree that the champagne had spun in her brain: it re-formed shortly afterwards, but its shape had changed, and the kiss seemed to linger less on her lips than in her thoughts, where it was like the completion of an idea.

When they went out to the car at last, Kate was walking with the exaggeratedly precise steps of a ballet dancer, and Helen felt a little dizzy herself at the taste of the outside air. It was not late, but Cambridge was quiet, and the many stars gave a feeling of midnight.

'Oh, dear, you've got to drive us all the way home now,' Kate mourned. 'Perhaps we could get a bus.'

'If you could I wouldn't let you,' Richard laughed. 'Jump in. Helen, your aunt's? Or can you face the drive again?'

'No, drop me off at my aunt's,' Helen said. This, though the champagne obscured it, was the completed idea at work. 'I'm asleep on my feet.'

They were outside Aunt Hamblin's, where all the lights were burning, in a couple of minutes, and Helen said warm goodbyes. 'It's been a lovely evening – just lovely.'

'We'll see you tomorrow, won't we?' Stella said. 'You're still coming up to the orchards, aren't you?'

'Of course,' Helen said, exchanging a glance with Richard. 'I shan't be leaving just yet.'

'I hate the thought of it all ending,' Stella said – musing rather than maudlin. 'I wish it didn't have to.'

'Not everything does,' Helen said. 'Goodnight, everyone.'

She had a key, Mrs Hamblin insisting in her modern-minded way on her coming and going as she pleased; and it was in her hand as she went up the steps to the Hamblins' front door, turning to give a last wave to the departing car. But Helen did not insert the key in the lock. Instead she waited until the car was out of sight, and then returned down the steps and walked briskly down the street.

It was a good half hour's walk to Richard's lodgings off Huntingdon Road – ample time for second thoughts. None came, and there was no surprise in this, for the conclusion that Helen had arrived at, though reached by the road of passion, was clear and unequivocal, and it was only vagueness that she distrusted.

The air and the exercise blew away most of the mists of champagne, but there the idea still was, pure and diamond-like in the centre of her consciousness. It seemed, indeed, central to her whole life.

The narrow street off Huntingdon Road seemed deserted, and she jumped when a man in a trenchcoat and trilby suddenly loomed out of a doorway: he had a cigarette clenched in his mouth and he seemed to puff at her like an angry dragon. She came to the locksmith's shop. The brick passage to the rear looked very dark: as a child, fear of the dark had caused her considerable suffering, and for a moment she knew its potency again. But the passage was very short, and soon she was standing before the back door and feeling above the lintel for the key. She had visited him here several times, and knew where it was kept.

She turned the key in the lock, and the door opened to her with rather alarming promptitude: somehow one expected resistance from a door that was not one's own. Going in, the instant feeling of intimacy rocked her too. To be in a person's home, especially so idiosyncratic a one as Richard's, was almost more evocative than being alone with them.

There now occurred to Helen, as if from the voice of some sensible kindly parent, some excuses she could make if she did not wish to go through with it; and she gave them respectful attention for a few moments. She could, when he returned, pass off her presence by claiming she just wanted to be sure he had got home safely. Pretend, perhaps, that she had had some baleful premonition: she was of course the last person in the world to have such things, but Richard was not exacting. Or she might claim that the Hamblins were having some awful musical party or some such, and she had had to escape for some peace. This too was shaky, but the point was that the excuses would do, if she wanted them.

She did not want them, however. They were untruths not merely in the superficial sense. She had come here for a reason and the reason was everything, or nothing. Helen was excited, but at least part of the excitement was the sense of crisis about the enterprise. For nearly twenty-two years she had been one person: now metamorphosis approached.

The downstairs room, typically, was a mess, but her new eyes did not see it as such. It was a collection of essences. She moved slowly about it, touching things. Her body performed this as an instinctive prelude. Finding drinks in a cupboard, she poured herself a weak one, and then went up the steep staircase to his bedroom. The bed was unmade: she tidied it. From nowhere came a delusion that a ghastly creature was creeping up those stairs to her, and for several moments she could not turn round to look. It passed, and she realized that what had made it pass was the thought of telling Richard about it later, when he was here with her.

The consideration of whether to lie on the bed and wait for him occupied her for a while. Musing, she toyed with his hairbrushes on the dressing table, and at last decided to go downstairs. Her rigorous mind acquitted her of any two-faced modesty: it would simply be nicer to see him as soon as he came through the door.

Helen looked at herself in the dressing-table mirror. Though it was cracked and foxed, her reflection appeared supernaturally clear. It was as if another person were in the room with her.

There was a book by his bed, and without even looking at the title she took it down with her. She sat in the armchair with the book in her lap, but she did not open it. Listening to the silence without, listening to the pounding within, Helen waited.

## 2

Kate was three parts asleep when they pulled up at the end of the drive outside her house, and as soon as she got out of the car she leaned in again and gave both Richard and Stella a hot-faced kiss like a drowsy child. They watched her into the house, waved as the door closed.

'I feel awful sitting in the back on my own – like you're chauffeuring me,' Stella said as he started the engine again.

'Come in the front then.'

'All right.'

They drove slowly back down the drive. The orchards were still: a deep sumptuous darkness lay beyond the nearer trees. Across the fen sky the stars were dizzyingly numerous.

They had been together all night and most of yesterday: but to Stella it felt as if there had been a long absence. She had had a wonderful evening, but only now did she fully feel herself, and Richard, as reality: it was as if at last everything had come from fuzziness into focus.

'Shut me up if I'm banging on about it,' Richard said quietly, 'but I do feel I should offer you an apology most of all. I ruined things for you last night.'

'No. I've been thinking about that. Old Frankly Hopeless was spoiling for a fight, and everything was going to end up horrible whatever happened. His sort – they just can't let it alone. Make you end up thinking you did encourage 'em somehow.'

'Not him. He knew quite well what he was about. You could be in a nun's habit and he still wouldn't get the message . . . It's a funny business, though. Sometimes it is hard to read the signals.'

'Yes . . . Well, don't think about it any more. That's an order. I've had a lovely time tonight and that's what matters. Bad times are bound to come along in your life, so the best thing is to get 'em over with and then concentrate on the good times. They mean more.'

'Thank God,' he said.

'What?'

'Suffering's supposed to be good for you and educate you and all the rest of it, isn't it? So they tell you. I think it's rot, the worst rot that's ever been foisted on us, but nobody seems to agree.'

She studied him in the dimness. The dimness excused the long gaze – then she didn't care any more, for she just wanted to look and look. She realized that all night her eyes had been careful, resting on his shirt cuff, his collar, a space just beside his head. 'That visit from your brother,' she said, half-consciously.

'Yes?'

'It was that. You weren't the same after that.'

His fingers tapped nervously on the steering wheel: then he smiled a little, turning to look at her. 'You've got me.' He faced the road again and then said, tentatively, 'Am I the same now?'

'More like yourself,' she said. The impulse to reach up and stroke his hair, and the act itself, were simultaneous, so that they were both surprised. Their eyes locked. The business of driving suddenly seemed an intolerable distraction. 'Shall we stop?' he said, and she, 'Let's stop,' – simultaneous again.

They had just turned into Long Lane, and he parked the car on the verge close to the meadow where the children played. The shutting off of the engine was like the cessation of a nagging voice, and in the silence thought and feeling seemed to leap up in Stella, expansive and free.

'How about another cigarette?' Richard said.

'Yes, please.' She lit first, and in the light of the match his face, formerly just shadowy planes, seemed full of more expressions than she could count: the world suddenly teemed with richness. She passed him the box of matches, then wouldn't let it go: they tugged and wrangled, laughing in a breathless way, until all at once the horseplay fell away of its own accord like a flimsy disguise. They clutched at each other fiercely, so forceful that it was as if each were trying to push the other out of the car.

'Oh Gawd,' Stella said, coming up for air out of a sort of kissing whirlpool, 'oh blimey, I've lost me head. I've completely lost me head.'

'Have you? So have I. Doesn't matter.'

'No. I don't care any more. It's you, you . . . Oh, I don't know – you devil.' Grabbing him again, she nearly burnt his ear with her cigarette: they laughed uproariously with their mouths close together, then got lost again.

'Sorry,' he gasped, 'sorry, is this awful?'

'Does it feel it?'

'No.'

'Well then . . .' Nearly burning him again, she tossed the

cigarette out of the window. The clean breath of the orchards reached them: they quizzed each other with their eyes, then got out of the car. Feeling a little unsteady on her feet, she held his hand as they crossed the verge to the meadow. The hand was wonderfully warm and smooth: it seemed a miraculous thing. Light-headed, she said, 'Woo, is this what champagne does to you?'

He was lightly serious a moment. '*Is* it just the champagne?'

She considered a moment, but didn't need to. 'What do you think?'

'I think you're very beautiful. And I only had one glass.'

They smiled at each other. Crickets were chirping in the meadow grass.

'We never had a proper dance yesterday, did we?' he said. 'Oh, I know we danced, but it wasn't – it wasn't the way I'd thought of it.'

'No . . . I know . . .' The remembered disappointment seemed as remote as the stars now.

'Here then.' He stopped, held out his arms.

'No music.'

'We can dance without music. *We* can, Stella. Can't we?'

It was true. She fitted herself to him, and they danced through the grass. When they stopped – again with that spontaneous unison, as if they had only one will between them – her eyes had so adjusted to the dark that she could see his face clearly, could see indeed that the pupils of his eyes too had expanded, cat-like.

'Look at your eyes,' she breathed.

'Hm, that's the one place I *can't* look.'

'You've never serious, are you?'

'Never,' he said emphatically, holding her.

'Good . . .' She began kissing him, half laughter, half tumult. 'Good . . .'

Like cats, glowing-eyed and noiseless, they moved across the meadow together, towards the receiving darkness of the apple trees.

* * *

# 3

It was the book, dropping from her lap as she fidgeted in her uncomfortable sleep, that woke Helen; and for that, at least, she was eternally grateful. Five minutes more, and she would have had to face him.

As it was, it took her a full minute to comprehend where she was and why her neck ached so. The interior of Richard's room presented itself to her blinking eyes as what it was – a jumble: her thoughts got mixed up in it and would not form. She remembered touching these things, ties, books, cups; then she remembered everything and in the same moment knew why she was blinking. The clear light of morning was streaming through the window, penetrating the flimsy curtains. The old tin alarm clock on the mantelshelf confirmed it – six o'clock: the time was exact, and the way the hands formed a vertical slash was strangely ominous.

And then Helen knew everything. A sound escaped her – something between a gasp and a moan; she bit it down, and it was the last complaint she made. She stood up, staggering a little, as if the crashing blow that had fallen on her were physical. It was imperative that she get out – now; but imperative too that she leave no trace of her ever having been here. What had she done whilst here? There was the book – she ran panting up the stairs and flung it down by the bed, averting her eyes from the sight of it. But the bed too – she had made it. Fumbling, shuddering, she scrabbled the blankets and pillows into disorder, then fled down the stairs. It was the merest chance that she did not break her neck, taking those abominably steep stairs like that, but this was of no importance to her.

Glass: she had poured herself a glass of gin, though she hadn't drunk it. She tipped it down the stone sink in the scullery, rinsed the glass, checked it for lipstick, then put it back in the cupboard where she had found it. She looked round, checking for signs: she was also taking leave of the place of her humiliation, every detail of which would be etched on her memory for years.

She went out, locked the door, and put the key in its hiding place. Then she paused: a voice in her spoke.

*Perhaps he crashed his car – is lying hurt somewhere – that's why he didn't come home all night.*

When she realized that she actually preferred this thought to the idea that he had spent the night with Stella, Helen swiftly reviewed herself, and saw a very hateful and perhaps sick person. So: it was good that he had not come home, found her there ready to inflict her love on him; a sick person should not foist her sickness on others.

The moaning sound nearly escaped her again, but she kept it in: she was good at keeping things in.

Helen began to walk down the empty street. She did not really believe in such a thing as a sixth sense, but it must have been something of the kind that alerted her to the very faint throb of a car engine and made her duck into an alleyway. From there, pressing herself against damp gritty brick, she watched Richard's Riley come puttering down the street and draw up outside his lodgings.

Probably it was unwise to look at him; but her time of madness was nearly over and she might as well follow its self-lacerating course to the end. She watched him get out of the car and stretch, jacket over his shoulder. His clothes were crumpled, and she could see grass stains on his shirt. He yawned vastly and went down the passage to his lodgings, ambling, and whistling a tune.

Helen stayed there, pressed against the wall, for a few moments longer. Well: that revelation in Miss Kingswell's garden, which had seemed to burst through to the very heart of truth, had not after all played her false, though it had led her on to such disaster. The mask had certainly been lifted from her own feelings, but she had remained blind in other directions – wilfully blind, perhaps, for now it was drearily plain to her that something had long been brewing between Richard and Stella Tranter. Plain now, why not before? She attacked the question as if it mattered – nothing did now – and soon came up with a familiar conclusion. The preoccupied ego had seen what it wanted to see. Snobbery might have been mixed up in it too: she had seen Stella as simply outside Richard's class, therefore . . . Therefore nothing, actually: here was another blindness, for she should have known Richard didn't give a damn about such things.

There was some knowledge that did not come from books or experience or reflection: it just was. And so she *knew* that Richard had spent the night with Stella. Ghastly and graphic speculations forced themselves on Helen before she could stop them; but when the gross images had passed, the knowledge remained. It was the first time Helen had ever hated knowledge and wanted to drive it from her. An impossible task, of course: she must concentrate on others, or die.

She would have to face the Hamblins. Aunt Hamblin, a fanatically early riser, would be up by now, and would find that her sensible niece had been out all night. This, of course, would also have been the case if her plan had come to fruition instead of catastrophe – but that wouldn't have mattered. There would have been triumph, joy: she could have hugged them to herself while the scolding went on. Instead there was her humiliation, which was like a knife: but Helen hugged it to herself all the same. It must never appear – never. The vigil in Richard's lodgings must be her eternal, lonely secret. In a paradox that her cool mind would normally have appreciated, her pride, which had been practically annihilated, was also all that remained to her.

And she felt this to be literally true. When her mind turned instinctively to Olive Kingswell, to the bright world she was poised to enter, Helen found no consolation. She found ruin there too. Was that not merely another girlish dream, with a disastrous wakening at the end of it? Belief in herself was what had sustained her through the struggle for a career; but now her belief in herself was so comprehensively shattered that she could not see it ever being rebuilt.

She began to walk home through the quiet streets. Such people as were about moved with the unhurried expansiveness of early morning, but Helen walked quickly. She wanted plenty of time to bathe, change, make herself ready, because they were supposed to be going up to the orchards as normal today, and Richard would no doubt call for her as normal about nine – and normal she was going to be, even if it broke her inside. Not for a single instant did she consider crying off today. It seemed, in fact, desperately important that she should go.

She found Mrs Hamblin up, as she had thought, and at once presented the startled old lady with an implausible tale of having stayed by the river, thinking, and at last deciding to stay and see the dawn come up . . . It was designed to be the sort of thing Mrs Hamblin must sympathize with, or else reveal herself to be an old-fashioned fuddy-duddy, and perhaps didn't deserve to succeed as it did. Her aunt clucked her tongue and said she wouldn't scold, looking curiously wistful: Helen felt the lie to be dirty, and ran upstairs to bathe.

Always fastidious, she washed herself till she smarted. Dressing, she remembered that she still had some clothes at Kate's house: the memory brought back images of last night – laughter, champagne – and for a moment she wanted to slam the shutters and hide in everlasting darkness, howling. She resisted this as she would have resisted the devil, and was soon sitting at her dressing table, applying her lipstick: such victories would have to be her soul's food from now on. By the time she heard Richard's car, a little later than usual, she was as smart, poised and correct as she had ever been, and there was nothing to show as she walked downstairs to greet him that she had been secretly preparing to give herself to him just a matter of hours ago.

He looked frankly tired. This suited him: fatigue, which aged some men, made him look both boyish and sensual. He said something about what a good night it had been, and she replied quite levelly, thanking him again: she even asked if he and the others had got home all right, not from bitter irony, but because it was what she would have said under normal circumstances. He was brief rather than evasive in reply, and she made herself see the flush on his cheeks as a mere objective phenomenon like a cloud in the sky.

'Ready for the off, then?'

'Ready. Glorious day, isn't it? Thank goodness that humid weather's broken.'

A kind observer might have told her that there was no need for this sad strength: that life, unforgiving enough, does not call for it. But kindness was the one thing that would have been insupportable to Helen just then. If anyone could have known of her situation, and offered sympathy, she would have fled from them.

They drove up to Monks Bridge. The orchards, green and fresh under the bright sun, seemed to mock her with their beauty – but she denied herself even this correspondence between outer world and inner: it was a fallacy, the orchards were as they had always been. She felt a sort of hate for them, because they had altered her life – yet that was another fallacy, for they had merely been the scene of the alteration.

As for the man beside her, she supposed she should have felt hate, but she didn't, and to summon it seemed a futility. He had created no illusions about himself – that had been her doing: he was her friend, and had pretended to be no more. Was this leniency prompted by her love for him? – the love that burned her with lonely intensity while she sat a matter of inches from him in the front of the car. Was she acquitting him too easily? Surely she would never have done what she did last night without some strong encouragement – she who was normally so little given to impulse, so careful to base her conclusions on firm evidence . . . And yet that was just it: she couldn't trust herself any more, if her judgement had failed her so badly in this, how could she count on it in the future? How could she become a journalist when she was so blind . . . so pathetically stupid . . . ?

This didn't alter the fact that being with him now was hell – hell such as she had never known; and if in her self-loathing she felt that hell was what she deserved, she doubted her capacity to withstand it. Precisely where he stood with Stella Tranter now, what would happen to the two of them, whether it was an irresponsible fling or a furtive affair or something full-blown and romantic – these were questions from which her mind turned away, not only because they were unbearable to address but because they seemed curiously irrelevant. The thing had happened; and the sympathetic interest of a friend, which would surely have been engaged, perhaps with misgiving, by such a mismatch, was no longer possible to her. Whatever was going on, let it go on without her: the idea that she might be made privy to it at some point, perhaps even entrusted with confidences, was horrendous. Thus Helen came by another route to a decision her heart had already taken. She must leave. Coming to the orchards today was an essential gesture of pride – inconsequentially she thought of aristos dressing and powdering their hair before going to the guillotine – but the gesture once made, she must flee. The only condition was that he must not suspect for a moment the real reason for her flight. She would rather die than have him know it.

Meanwhile there was today to be got through – this journey, first of all, which after a period of quietness he was enlivening with his usual genial flow of talk. Just for a second Helen suffered a violent wish to rip the whole thing apart – destroy this quite remarkable self-possession with a few acid words to the effect that she knew about last night. The wish died swiftly away – Helen could not contemplate the uncivilized even now – and she continued making conversation as if it were pleasant to her instead of agony.

They came to Monks Bridge, and he parked the car by the Long Lane meadow as usual. Some children were there, and Knatchbull and Neeve, who had softened a good deal of late, were playing rounders with them. Unusually, there was no sign of Geoffrey, who usually galloped to greet them, nor the other Tranter children. More unusually, as they got out of the car they found themselves being hailed by Uncle Will, who came hurrying from the camp at the end of the lane.

'I don't like to ask,' he said, panting, and trying to get his mutinous teeth in order. 'I wouldn't ask normal-like. Only you've got the car, you see. And if you could – if you wouldn't mind – seeing as you've got the car . . .'

To her astonishment, Helen saw that Uncle Will was weeping.

'My God,' Richard said, 'what's happened?'

'Our Stella,' Uncle Will gulped, and Helen saw Richard turn white, and the feeling that went through her made her hate herself even more.

'What? For God's sake, what about Stella?'

'Her mum.' Uncle Will whispered it. 'Her mum passed away.'

Over on the far side of the meadow there was a cheer as one of the children playing rounders hit the ball with a firm whack. The sounds were summery and cheerful. Helen wondered if she would wake in a moment: evil dreams were like this.

'No,' Richard said – flatly, as if declining something. 'No, no.'

'Telegram from her dad came this morning.' An absurd little man in braces whispering about the dead, Uncle Will had somehow a vast dignity. He did not wipe or hide his tears. 'Poor ole Connie. No age. Not fifty. Heart attack she had, just like that. She was at home. She was at home when it happened.' Sobbing, Uncle Will seemed to grasp at some comfort in this. 'The gel's in a state. Poor gel. She's fit to fly. Bea's doing her best with her—'

'When?' Richard almost barked it. 'When did it happen?'

'Yesterday,' Uncle Will said obediently. 'Last night. They took her to hospital, but no. Her poor ole dad must be in a state an' all. So I thought . . . what I wanted to ask . . .'

He hesitated, because Richard had covered his face with his hands. Helen made a supreme effort: she touched Richard's arm, patted gently. 'Richard,' she said.

'Sorry,' Richard snatched his hands away, came up with a face that was almost normal but for the ashen pallor. 'God, what a dreadful thing. I'm – I'm just so sorry. Please, what were you going to ask? What can we do?'

'I wondered if you could just drive us into Wisbech, so we can get the train home. She's got to go home, of course, poor gel. I'll go with her, make sure she's all right. And her dad – he's me brother, see. Poor ole Jack. I can come back after the funeral. Bea'd want to go too but she's terrible at funerals – break her up, they do – and, well, we can't afford to lose the earnings, and we'd have to take the nippers and there'd be buying train tickets for 'em all, so it's best if she stops here and . . .'

'I'll drive you down to Peterborough,' Richard said, cutting him off. 'You can get a train direct from there, it'll be quicker. Any time, whenever you're ready.'

He had mastered himself: fleetingly, too late, Helen saw a new aspect of Richard, a self-discipline not unlike her own.

'It wouldn't half be a help,' Uncle Will said. 'You've got the car, you see. That's what made me think – you having the car – I thought about the car straight off.' Uncle Will kept insisting on the car: it was as if the car could almost overcome death. 'Shall you – shall you come and see if she's ready? Bea's packing her things.'

They followed Uncle Will down the lane to the camp. Richard was silent and stiff. Helen said, 'Poor Stella . . . what a dreadful thing,' and while she meant it, her sense of herself as a hateful person was no less, and she felt her words were dross. She was almost relieved when they came to the Tranters' hut, and the tortuous writhings inside her could give way to a simple common emotion – the helpless ache that all feel in the presence of the bereaved. Stella, white-lipped, her eyes raw and naked, was finishing her own packing, moving like an automaton about the hut while Auntie Bea wailed and the children sat solemn, trying to fight down their wish to escape.

'Stella . . . I'm so dreadfully sorry . . . it's . . .' Richard said, and then gave it up. Hating herself to new depths, Helen watched his face as he looked at her. Yes, yes.

'He's got the car,' Uncle Will explained. 'So that's all right. He's going to drive us down to Peterborough. That's summat.'

'My dear, anything we can do—' Helen began, then stopped. Poor, even for a contemptible person as herself. Do? Such as what – bring her mother back to life?

And yet Stella, typically and heartbreakingly, responded. 'Thank you,' she said, 'thanks ever so much – if you could just give us a lift to the station . . .' And she looked at them both – included both Richard and Helen in a sad, defenceless glance, full of unconscious trust. I want to hate her, Helen thought, and she has just learnt that her mother has died. And Richard, she thought and knew, wanted to love her, wanted to offer himself to make things better and could not. Seeing him, paralysed and wordless, she saw the feelings that her madness had craved, and they were not for her. She made an excuse of being in the way, and went outside.

Around the quadrangle a few people were standing outside the open doors of huts, holding their faces and quietly talking – not many: work went on. One of the few was Frankie Hope, who was lounging against the wall a couple of doors down. His eyes were still blackened: Helen was strangely glad of this. Turning her face from him, she took out her cigarettes and lit one: they still made her sick, but she understood they were supposed to help in such moments as this.

Frankie Hope was suddenly, ingratiatingly, beside her.

'I say – do you think I could have one of those? Only I'm right out.'

She passed him one, at a distance. After a watchful moment he produced his own matches, and lit it.

'She's had a bit of bad news, apparently,' he said, standing near to her, and cocking his head at the Tranters' hut.

Helen nodded, not looking at him.

'Funny how it happened, really. Last night, so they say.' He inhaled smoke delicately. 'Just about the time she was over in that field fucking his lordship.'

The obscenity was meant no doubt to be like a slap in the face, and Helen felt it so. All she could say for herself was that she did not – she was sure – flinch, or grimace, or betray any emotion whatsoever.

'I mean to say,' Frankie said, studying her, 'they should be a bit more careful, if that's their game. Anybody could've seen 'em. *I* saw 'em, and I ain't a nosey sort of bloke by nature. Still, there you are. It's funny how things turn out, ain't it? It's cramped her style a bit, I'll bet. What a time for her poor old ma to snuff it. Just when things were getting interesting.'

It was confirmation, and her pain was extreme; but Helen was not beyond answering him, fiercely. Only she couldn't tell whether that would be best, or silence; and she never knew, for just then Stella came out of the hut.

Uncle Will was with her, and Auntie Bea in floods of tears, and Richard following, suitcases in his hands, with a sort of tall, braced remoteness; but Stella, whether it was simply the sanctity of loss or some more personal emanation, seemed to walk out quite alone, like a figure in a desert; and Frankie just melted away.

'You stay here,' Richard said, setting the cases down, 'and I'll fetch the car round.'

Life did not offer neat schoolbook lessons, Helen thought. Her own grief ought to have appeared small beside this, but it didn't work like that: experience was not like some bracing efficacious medicine. All she could conclude was that people were not even united in their sufferings. All the same, the sight of the grieving Stella made her look more closely at herself – made her look, indeed, almost with the eyes of another person. What would Olive Kingswell, for example, think of the creature that Helen had become last night? Contemptible, surely. She was certainly not the woman Miss Kingswell had thought her. In fact, standing outside the huts in the sunshine, Helen saw herself as nothing more or less than a fraud. And with that revelation the glorious future she had envisaged began to take on a different shape too. It was tawdry, fake, not to be trusted. And now she was murmuring again to Stella that she was dreadfully sorry, so very sorry . . .

'S'pose we'd better say goodbye really,' Stella said, with her hand absently in Helen's. The car was coming. 'I don't think I . . . you know . . .'

'Of course.' Hellish, hellish. 'Look after yourself.'

'Could you say goodbye to Kate for me? And – explain and everything . . .'

'I will. Perhaps—' She didn't know why she said this, for it seemed as unlikely as undesirable. 'Perhaps we'll see each other again some time.'

Richard put the cases in the car. He was still stiff and correct, as if the situation had robbed him of his identity, and all he could do was be a chauffeur. Once more Helen found herself wondering, as the car drove away, what he was thinking – a meaningless reflex, curable only by time, like walking in the direction of a lost home.

## 4

The train that had brought Stella to the orchards had been full and boisterous with holiday voices: the train that took her home was almost empty, and the carriage was haunted by two drowsy wasps which Uncle Will kept slapping at with a rolled-up newspaper, over and over again. 'I shall get them jaspers,' he kept saying, bobbing up and down and uselessly flailing, 'I shall get them jaspers, don't you worry.'

It was irritating, but it kept him occupied. Though he had been kindness itself, there was only so much kindness could do, and once or twice she had had to stop herself screaming at him not to fuss over her: it had been worst at Peterborough station, where he had steered her around as if she were blind. That sounded ungrateful, and she wasn't: she was just bruised and aching inside almost beyond bearing. And Uncle Will's overwhelming presence had, at least, effectively smothered any communication between herself and Richard, who at the station had simply taken her hand and said goodbye before walking away. It was best – indeed, she couldn't have borne anything else.

It wasn't that she wanted nothing to do with him. The fact that last night she had been lying careless in his arms beneath the trees whilst far away her mother had been dying – well, that was a fact like any other, a fact that would have to be thought of, lived with, its consequences felt and understood, but not yet. Now it merely rebounded from her stunned mind like everything else. What made Richard an irrelevance just now – and by 'Richard' she meant everything about him, the place where she had met him and the things they had done and the feelings he had aroused in her –

was the change which this morning's news had wrought. And that change was complete. There was a person called Stella Tranter who had existed before the opening of that telegram, and there was a person called Stella Tranter who would, she supposed, have to go on existing after it: but they were wholly disconnected.

Indeed in her shock and grief she could only see the change as an ending: vast blackness yawned before her. What would she do? It was the refrain that had stuttered through her first wild burst of tears, but now as she sat red-eyed and exhausted, feeling as if she had been squeezed dry by a giant fist, the question presented itself to her with a profounder resonance. The loss of her mother was unthinkable: that pretty tired twinkling-eyed woman from whom she had parted a couple of months ago, suddenly gone . . . Oh, it couldn't be! Stella's spirit beat baffled fists against the monstrous knowledge.

'Buck up, gel,' Uncle Will said, pausing in his wasp-hunt to bestow his hopeless kindness on her once more. 'See yer dad soon, eh?'

Yes, Dad: he would be devastated, his prop knocked away; and then there was Dot and the younger boys – however would they manage? What would life be like for them all now?

With a new convulsion of pain, Stella caught herself up. Dear God, she was doing it – doing what they had all done, unwittingly and well-meaningly perhaps, while her mother was alive: thinking of Connie Tranter not as a person in her own right, but as someone who was there for others. And now she was no longer there, up went a wail as of betrayal. But what of her poor mother's thoughts, as her heart gave up and the world dimmed on her sight?

Probably, Stella thought, in fact without a doubt, they would have been for those she left behind. Dear God!

'You let 'em out, gel,' Uncle Will said – for she found, to her surprise, that the tears she had thought exhausted were running afresh down her cheeks. 'You let 'em out. It doesn't matter.'

'I wish she'd kept that china dog,' she murmured. Uncle Will wouldn't understand, but that too didn't matter. 'I just wish she'd kept it.'

# 5

'Poor Stella,' Kate said. 'I wish I'd been able to say goodbye to her.'

'Well, I think she wanted to go home as quickly as possible,' Richard said.

'Of course. I'll write to her – though I don't know where . . .'

'Her Aunt Bea'll have the address, no doubt,' Helen said.

They were in the garden at Kate's house. She had asked them in for some lunch, though none of them had eaten anything, and now they were wandering dully amongst the flowers, which ought to have been beautiful but which struck Kate as deathly and oppressive. As they walked each maintained a little distance from the other, as if to admit a fourth person.

'I've been thinking,' Helen said, 'that I ought to be going home too.'

'Yes,' Richard said, his hands in his pockets, his eyes cast down. 'Yes . . . it's not the same any more, is it? One can't . . .' Whatever he had been going to say seemed to absorb him: he was silent with it.

The sun blazed, Walter Lutton's garden flourished, out in the orchards fruit remained on the bough – yet their summer was ending; Kate could feel it dissolving around her, swiftly decaying with a sickly smell of honeysuckle.

'When will you go?' she said; she was so determined not to let her voice tremble that it came out almost breezy.

'I think I shall go first thing tomorrow morning,' Helen said.

Fast, it was all finishing so fast: a strange selfish voice within Kate protested at their leaving her as if they had solemnly promised to stay for ever.

'What about you, Richard?' she said.

'Mm? Oh, soon, soon. Yes, I'd – better go home soon. It's probably best.'

'You'll keep in touch, though,' Kate said after a moment, 'won't you?' and this time there was no disguising the tremor in her voice.

'Of course,' Helen said.

'Yes, of course.' As Richard said it he gave Kate a friendly look, his old look – yet it seemed to come from a long way off. Something had happened, Kate thought, something beside the tragic news that had taken Stella away, but she could not pick it out from the general feeling, winding itself insidiously about them, of loss and ending.

'Richard, would you mind – could we go back to Cambridge now?' Helen said. 'I really ought to see about my packing, and telephone my parents.'

'Yes, whatever you like.'

As they turned to go in, Helen turned her ankle slightly on the hummocky grass, and Richard put out a hand to support her. It seemed to Kate, following, that she shrunk from him. Strange, but another thing she could not grasp, and let go. All she knew was that last night had been perfect, and today was ruin; and even the parting from Helen, which if she were to leave for Lincolnshire in the morning would be final, seemed somehow perfunctory and unreal, as if its significance had got lost in the dismal shock of it all. They kissed, and murmured some more useless things about poor Stella, and promised to write, whilst the car engine throbbed, ready to sever them; and only at the last moment did Kate find herself saying with sudden urgency, 'And good luck.'

Helen looked quite nonplussed. 'What with?'

'Oh – Miss Kingswell, you know, your meeting – the newspapers, and everything.'

Helen gave a remote smile, and said thank you; and then the car drew away down the drove, and when Kate came to herself she seemed to have been standing on the porch steps watching the empty distance for long, empty hours.

It was the last of Helen: she went home the next morning just as she had said. It was not the last of Richard, though. He came to the orchards next day, after seeing Helen off at Cambridge station, and invited Kate to a drink at the Corner.

'Saying goodbye to everybody,' he said.

'You're going home, then?' She knew, but it was still wretched to see him nod.

'I suppose I've only been putting off the inevitable. And something like this . . . well, it breaks things up.'

They were sitting outside the Corner, as she and Stella had sat the night before the village feast. Kate remembered Stella's confession, and wondered what might have been.

'It was sad saying goodbye to Geoffrey. Poor kid must feel as if he's losing everybody at once.'

'I can't believe it, Richard – two nights ago it was all so happy, and now . . .'

'It was, wasn't it?' He looked away – far away – and then said with sudden violence, 'That's the way it is with this damned life. You have to – oh, you have to grab things so damned quick or else whoever's up there's going to snatch it away from your hands as sure as eggs is eggs – supposing you even get the chance.'

The darkness was about him, rather as it had been on the night of the dance; remembering this, and moved by her instinct to smooth things over, she said, 'By the way, did you remember to say goodbye to Frankie Hope?'

He turned the black look on her for a moment; then he burst into laughter. 'I shall probably even miss Frankie Hope. Frankly Hopeless, as Stella called him. Did she have a secret nickname for me, I wonder?'

'She never told me it if she did.'

She was glad that they had had a little laughter, at least, on their last day: it seemed to her important, and not at all inappropriate. It was one in the eye for whoever was up there, as Richard phrased it. He left in the early afternoon. 'It's been – well, you know . . . I shan't forget it,' were his last words. She leaned into the car and kissed him.

'And then there was one,' she said, which made him smile: she was glad about that too.

And then there was one. And when they sank in, her own words appalled her.

* * *

## 6

About a week later, Olive Kingswell received a letter from Helen Silverman, which said she would not be able to keep that appointment Miss Kingswell had so kindly made. There were regrets and apologies, but no explanation; and after the first surprise, Olive Kingswell did not trouble to look for one. She had liked Helen Silverman, been impressed by her, and seriously meant to do something for her; but Miss Kingswell was a busy woman, and not sentimental. Presumably the girl had her reasons for changing her mind, and that was that. The Czechoslovakia crisis was coming to a head, the fate of the world, as she saw it, hung in the balance: it was no time to be bothered with trivialities. She never thought about Helen Silverman again.

# Part Two

## *November 1938*

# ONE

## 1

'Uncle James, my dear? I'm not sure whether he's well enough to travel. But we can send him an invitation, by all means, he'll be delighted,' Mrs Silverman said.

'Effie Jarvis, there's another,' Helen said, writing. 'Effie Brooks, I should say.'

'Who was it she married? Not that awful Clive Brooks, surely?'

'No, no. Another Brooks – from Derbyshire, I think. Army man. Though now I come to think of it I'm sure I heard she's expecting a baby soon, so perhaps that's out.'

'Oh, well, dear, there's plenty of time. After all by the time of the wedding she—'

'Actually, Mother,' Helen said, laying down her pen, 'I've been meaning to say – we were discussing it last night, and we've decided we want it to be soon. Next month. Before Christmas.'

'Goodness!' Her mother was not a woman given to extreme reactions, but Helen could tell how surprised she was. Frowning a little, Mrs Silverman put aside her needlework basket. 'My dear, that's very soon. There's so much to arrange, and these things take time. Wouldn't you rather wait at least until the new year?'

'We'd rather not. We discussed it fully and – well, we both agree we want to be married next month.' Recalling last night's conversation, Helen allowed her words to be true. They *had* agreed: no matter that it was she who had raised the question and suggested the date. 'We thought the fifteenth. That should be far enough away from Christmas so there'll be no problem of people being away and so on, and we should be able to book the White Hart for then. As for the marriage service, I thought one of Father's friends would surely . . . Canon Cunningham, perhaps?'

'Oh, I'm sure he'd be glad. Unless your father took the service himself – I *think* it's allowed.'

'No,' Helen said quickly, 'no, I – I'd like Father to give me away.' The thought of her father performing her marriage service was strangely abhorrent to her: something about having to face him at the altar.

'Of course. Well, my dear, if you think it can be done . . . I must say I don't quite see the need for such hurry. I know there were quite a few hasty marriages a while ago, with all that Czechoslovakia business, but that's all died down now surely. And if there is a war—'

'There will be a war, eventually, but we're not getting married because of that.'

Many people, unknowingly, are at their sharpest with their parents, but this brusque tone in Helen was new, or recent. Mrs Silverman put it down to leaving Cambridge, which she felt must have been an anticlimax, especially as the grand ideas of a career seemed to have been dropped. Helen's mother was a woman of some beauty and taste who devoted herself to crafts and good works, and whose only sin was imagining the world to be a nicer place than it really was. She believed in backing people to the hilt, and let this belief conquer other feelings. So while she felt Helen was rather rushing into marriage, she did not pursue the matter, saying instead, 'Well, it is rather romantic. And I don't think we need to have these long engagements nowadays. I'm sure it can be managed if we all put our heads together. Let's see, there's your grandmother's wedding dress, she was very keen that you should have it, though she was quite a small lady and I think it would need altering—'

'Too much altering, really,' Helen said. 'I was thinking I could go into Louth tomorrow and see about a dress. Just something simple and modern. Also have invitations printed. Which is why I wanted to get this list finished. Will you have a look? See if you can think of anyone else?'

Her mother got up and came to the bureau where Helen was writing. The last thin sun of the autumn afternoon filled the Rectory sitting room with weak gold, and the smell of burning leaves penetrated the warped old windows. Mrs Silverman felt it was rather beautiful: this moment, the planning of her only daughter's wedding ought to have been rather beautiful too, and she did her best to persuade herself that it was.

'Groom's side, too, remember,' she said, looking over Helen's shoulder.

'Yes, we're going to do his list tonight. The Hamilton-Pooles, do you think?'

'If they'll come. You know their airs. A bit thick if you ask me, when she drinks like a fish and is always in and out of sanatoriums for it.'

'Sanatoria, Mother.'

'Those too. Good heavens, Grace Gale, wasn't she that rather plump girl you were at school with?'

'Thin as a rail now.' Helen stroked her mother's hand where it rested on her shoulder. 'Teaches gym at a very Spartan girls' school on the south coast.'

'How strangely life turns out,' said Mrs Silverman, feeling happier. 'Now what about that friend of yours at Cambridge? Richard, wasn't it? There's one you've missed.'

'Richard Marwood,' Helen said.

'I thought he was very nice when we met him at your graduation. What's he doing now?'

'I really don't know. We haven't properly kept in touch. The odd letter, you know how these things go . . .'

'Well, here's your chance to catch up, anyhow.'

'Oh, I don't know, Mother. I think I'd rather have a quiet sort of wedding. Otherwise you end up inviting everyone you ever met and it just gets ridiculous. I always think it's rather artificial when people keep up these university friendships out of context.'

'As you like, darling.' Though Mrs Silverman saw more than

Helen gave her credit for, she saw less than she might have: an almost exaggerated respect for the privacy of other people's minds obscured her view. There was a tap on the window, which made Helen jump: the poor girl was nervy. 'That'll be Mr Digweed. He must have finished early today.'

Mrs Silverman opened the window to speak to the gnarled old man waiting there. It delighted Helen's parents, who were humorous people, to have a gardener whose name really was Digweed: it was perhaps their chief reason for hiring him, for he was not a very good gardener, and pruned everything to extinction. The 'Mr' was characteristic of them too: they detested snobbery, and in their quiet way were just as forward-looking as Aunt Hamblin; Helen's father, the Rector, took a mild pleasure in scarifying country society by defending the Labour Party.

For all that, a highly genteel peace reigned over the Rectory, a gabled building as thick-walled and solid as a tithe barn, secluded from the rugged wold village by tall horse chestnuts. It was a place where voices were never raised, and life flowed on easy currents. In Helen's mind it was always intimately associated with the seasons: autumn, as now, suiting it perhaps best of all, with the wind off the wolds sighing down the chimneys and tossing gold leaves at the windows; in winter, opulent wood fires and a thoroughly traditional Christmas; in spring, the high windows catching a dazzling morning light that seemed to have about it something of the harsh freshness of the North Sea, away to the east. And in summer, a combination of ripe beauty and domestic pleasantness, with her father optimistically venturing on to the dumpy tennis court whilst hollyhocks, impervious even to Mr Digweed's depredations, rose to the sky like brilliant beanstalks.

Different this summer, of course: Helen hadn't been here and she rather regretted that now. It might have been nice to spend the summer at home instead of frittering it away as she had done; because, after all, she was to be married now and that would have been her last chance. But of course there was no telling how things would turn out: even lives as smooth and well-regulated as those of the Silvermans turned up surprises. Her becoming engaged to be married in the three months since she had come home was one such surprise, and Helen suspected that it had caused more of a stir in that quiet household than either of her undemonstrative parents would admit.

Well, she could understand that in a way; it had been something of a whirlwind romance, though she disliked that glib phrase and its associations, which did a disservice to her fiancé and their feelings for each other. Also, no doubt, there was a certain puzzlement over her seemingly abrupt change of mind in regard to her future. She supposed she could understand that too, though she had been unable to disguise a certain irritation whenever her parents had referred to it, which they had now, fortunately, ceased to do. Yes, she had had fanciful ideas of a career in journalism, independence, all the rest of it. But they were just that – fanciful ideas, a conflation of the extravagance of youth with the blinkered idealism of Cambridge. One changed: one saw more clearly. And besides, back when she had that unrealistic bee in her bonnet she had yet to meet Owen.

This was not strictly true. Society in their part of the world was not large, and in one's own class there were few complete strangers. She had a dim memory of talking to Owen once at a cricket match, shortly before she had first gone up to Cambridge, and her father knew him quite well, as he had dealings with Owen's firm of solicitors in Louth. But as far as she was concerned her real acquaintanceship with Owen had begun at an evening party in Horncastle, shortly after her return from that nonsensical summer in the fens.

The party was given by a family who had made a fortune out of the Grimsby fish trade and had built a pretentious cupola-crowned villa on the strength of it: here they feasted their guests on anchovy toast and champagne and gin cocktails, in noisy overheated evenings that often ended with carpet-dances to the sound of the great mahogany-clad wireless and riotous party games led by the hostess, a jovial rouged woman who would shake with laughter until the pompadour front of her hair waggled like a fat sausage. There were many people who wouldn't be seen dead there and Owen, as he ruefully confessed to Helen that first evening, used to be one of them; but he had been pleasantly surprised and found them delightful people, though he did look subtly out of place, with his quiet austerity, when the gin had done its work and the shenanigans started.

In this Helen was quite in accord with him. She had no taste for unbridled hedonism. The accord, in fact, was deep and complete: if she had not concluded this by the end of that first evening, in which they talked together almost to the exclusion of everyone else, she was sure of it by the time of their second meeting, in the very different atmosphere of a county ball. Each had thrown out hints to the other that they would be there; and from then on, tentativeness was abandoned. Owen was a cautious lawyer and a cautious man, and might well have proceeded more cautiously than he did if Helen had not been so open, certain, and decisive on her own side. They were right for each other, and so there was no point in wasting time. He need not fear any hesitancy over such a commitment on her part: she was quite ready for it; she told him so.

Her memories of his proposal were both highly distinct and strangely vague. He had come to the house for Sunday tea: afterwards they had gone on a walk together across the wolds, and had stayed leaning against a stile at the top of a slope that gave a wonderful view across to Somersby, where Tennyson had been born. An enormous crow had startled them by passing low overhead and seeming to rasp its grim cry right in their ears: she remembered that. They had talked of Mozart, whom they both preferred to the beetle-browed strenuousness of Beethoven: she remembered that; and she remembered too that a country bus had been crawling slowly across the skyline at the moment of their first kiss. What she was unsure about was how the subject of marriage had come up. She had a feeling of having met him at least halfway, which was as it should be in what she viewed as a partnership of compatible minds; yet sometimes the feeling shaded into a suspicion that she had come as close as possible to proposing herself, without actually doing so.

Did this matter? It should not: though she had abandoned the pipe dreams of Cambridge, she retained strong ideas about the relationship of the sexes, and the cramping effect of conventional roles. Owen was, besides, no dashing blade – his reserve was one of the things she liked him for – and probably appreciated being helped towards the point. If she had any unease, it must be at the thought of people saying she had rushed into marriage, thrown herself at him, snapped him up – all the usual catty stuff. But who, after all, would say this? No one whose opinion mattered. The carping was entirely notional. All their mutual friends and acquaintances thought it an excellent match.

No, there was nothing equivocal in her engagement to Owen: indeed it marked a return to truth, reality, the clear light of day, after a curious period of groping about in hazy and unwholesome dreamscapes. Thank goodness, in fact, that Owen had rescued her! She had been drifting: he was solid ground. While her mother talked to Mr Digweed in her fluty soothing voice, Helen let her attention wander from the wedding list and concentrate on Owen, the man with whom she was going to spend the rest of her life.

His name was Owen Harding. He was thirty-seven years old, and a partner in a firm of solicitors in the market town of Louth, where he had a pleasant bay-windowed house which he had bought from an aunt who had retired to the coast, and which he shared with a large collection of gramophone records and two affectionate springer spaniels. He was tall – over six feet: Helen's height disappeared when she was with him, which pleased her; and he was handsome in an austere way. His grey eyes had a tired, knowledgeable look, which also pleased her. Marriage meant looking at the same face day after day, and she thought it would be restful to look at one that was not bright with unlikely hopes. He was cultured, which was a prime consideration for her; he was quite well off, and they would be comfortable, which was not a prime consideration but one which she felt it would be foolish to disregard. He dressed well but soberly, and he drove a nearly new

Vauxhall Twelve: he liked privacy and he disliked sports.

Also, he was no digger and delver. They shared their thoughts and opinions, but there was no search for essences, no requirement that the heart be continually laid out to inspection: things that she had done or felt in the past he gave a loverlike attention if she chose to mention them, and she did likewise, but in the main their lives before they met played no part in their relationship beyond the anecdotal. This was the way she liked it. Her past self she regarded as both mysterious and tiresome. She wished to begin life, not continue it.

And as she looked down again at her list of wedding guests, Helen felt a flick of impatience as she recognized that this could not be, not quite. It was silly to think of inviting the people she had spent the summer with: it had been a mere interlude, a holiday diversion. Richard had been simply a university friend and she doubted that Kate and Stella would be able to make the journey . . . no, it wasn't even worth thinking about . . . And yet Kate had written – and Richard too, a faintly amusing undergraduatish letter, she hadn't given it much attention – and she should, really, nonsensical as it was, write to them all and let them know she was getting married. It was a point of etiquette and she would have to find time for it.

She was drooping over her list, scribbling jagged doodles down the margin, when her mother at last closed the window and came over to the bureau.

'Well, darling, thought of any more? One often finds with these things that one's missed out someone terribly important right at the last minute.'

'I don't know . . . I'm tired of it – so tired of it,' Helen burst out, throwing down the pen. 'I wish to God we could just get married tomorrow.'

Mrs Silverman was surprised, for her daughter had never been fractious even as a child. But she was not very surprised, for she put it down to love, which, she knew, did not necessarily make people nice.

* * *

# 2

'I've just got Peggy in the bath, Bea – will yer come and have a look at her?'

These cryptic words were spoken by an elderly neighbour of Auntie Bea's, who poked his bald head round the ever-open front door to deliver them just as Stella had nerved herself to ask her shameful, desperate question. She had been round at Aunt Bea's for half an hour now, absently chatting while she tried to pluck up the courage; and now she would have to wait a little longer, because Bea hollered, 'Yes, I'll come, Arthur – I'll come and see if she's got 'em. Shan't be a minute, gel,' she added to Stella. 'There's more tea in the pot. I said I'd have a look at Peggy and see if she's got 'em.'

The children were at school and Uncle Will was at work – when the family had finally returned home from the fruit-picking in October, Uncle Will had had some luck at last and landed a reasonably secure job in a shoe factory – and Stella was left alone while her aunt went on her enigmatic errand of mercy. There was nothing to do but sit tight, a wise course in any event in Bea's house, which was literally crammed to the ceilings: even the wireless was high up in a corner of the living room, as if pushed there by the rising tide of debris. Will and Bea not only never threw anything away: they collected the things that other people threw away, and they put them all in this house, which was about the size of two potting sheds. Once you had cleared yourself a seat it was best to stay there and not move, in case you started an avalanche.

Stella sighed and sipped cautiously at her tea – Bea's brew was strong enough to pull your cheeks in even when it was fresh, and when it had been standing it was like liquid iron – and idly scanned the photographs crowded on the mantelpiece. Bygone relatives of Bea's mostly, easily recognizable as such by their height: even the bonneted old ladies towered like guardsmen. When her eye fell on a photograph of her own mother, Stella thought – just for a second – how odd it was to see her there amongst all those dead people. The horrible knowledge came flooding back immediately afterwards, but it was not the first time this had happened. She would see something in a shop window and think: 'Mum would like that – I shall have to show her'; she would hear thunder and hope the storm would pass over because her mother was afraid of them. The bludgeoning grief that had reduced Stella to a hollow-eyed waif in the first weeks after her mother's death seemed almost straightforward compared to these excruciating little refinements of pain. And yet in a way she dreaded the day when they didn't happen any more: the day when she no longer automatically called out her mother's name on entering the house because her mother was dead and every fibre of her knew it. There would be a second death in that.

Her mother looked happy in the photograph, at any rate: that was something. Was she aware of it, at the time when the picture was taken? Stella had begun to wonder whether happiness was something you simply couldn't be conscious of: whether it only took shape when you looked back at it from a distance.

'She's got 'em.' Auntie Bea was back. 'I told her, you've got 'em, duck, no two ways about it. Poor old stick.'

'What's she got?'

'Shingles, gel,' Auntie Bea shouted benevolently, peering into the teapot. 'I knew 'em straight off. I should do, my grandma had 'em. I reckon it was them what finished her off in the end. I nursed her, see. Well, I had to. There weren't nobody else. Me poor ole mum had already passed away. There was me Aunt Jeannie but she was no good. Trollopy piece she was. Do it for a bottle of Mackesons. And poor ole Uncle Dick got taken before his time an' all, he fell off the gasworks. Mind you, there was summat the matter with him – you know, down there. He had a motorbike and a sidecar.'

Used to Auntie Bea's somewhat disjointed thought processes, Stella did not take this to mean that Uncle Dick was genitally endowed with a Harley Davidson. 'Auntie Bea,' she began, then stopped. It was so embarrassing having to ask this, but she could see no other way.

'What, duck? Oh – oh, my Gawd!' Bea slapped a hand to her

face. 'I've gone and set you off again! Here's me talking about people dying and your poor mum hardly cold in her grave – I should be shot, I should—'

'It's all right, Auntie, honest—'

'Hit me. Go on, you hit me.' Auntie Bea thrust her wrist in Stella's face. 'Go on. Slap it. Give it a good slap, gel, I deserve it . . .'

'Oh, Auntie Bea,' Stella said, weakly patting Bea's leathery hand, 'I can't very well hit you when I was just going to ask if you could lend us some money, now can I?'

'Money, gel? Whass matter?' Bea said, sitting down close to her and peering beakily into Stella's face. 'What sort of money are you talking about?'

'The usual sort,' Stella said unhappily. 'It's just till Dad gets his pay at the end of the week. Only – he doesn't know, you see. About me asking. It's just that I've run out again, I can't seem to make it stretch . . .'

Forced again to confront her own inadequacy as a housekeeper, Stella felt a familiar mixture of shame and irritation. Of course it was terrible that she couldn't make the money go round like her mother used to, and it pained her to see the kids' look of disappointment at the meals she dished up; and yet, another part of her protested, why should the whole burden fall on her? She hadn't reckoned with looking after a whole family when she was only twenty. It wasn't fair.

Yet she felt this failure more keenly because of another. She had no work. An unspoken reproach hung in the air at home: if she couldn't bring in a wage to make things easier, couldn't she at least keep the house properly? The worst thing was that she had come very close, just the other day, to landing a job that she greatly fancied.

Violet Drew kept a hairdresser's in the Hackney Road. The salon was upstairs above a pork butcher's but this did not affect its reputation as a pretty high-toned establishment: practically every bride in the district had had her wedding-day coiffure created by Violet Drew, who was admired for the stiffness of her pin curls

– the general opinion being that the more your hairdo resembled a crash helmet the more you had got for your money. Violet Drew employed two assistants, one an apprentice who was leaving to get married. The vacancy didn't need to be advertised: like everything here, the news simply got around, and when it reached Stella she had paused only to put on her best frock and dab on a little make-up before running down to the Hackney Road. Well-turned-out but not tarty, pleasant but not familiar, that was how Violet Drew liked her assistants: rumours circulated, in fact, that she could be a bit of a dragon, but what did that matter? It was a better job than Stella had ever had; and her age was on her side, because Violet Drew was known to dislike young flibbertigibbets straight out of school who would only giggle and moon over film magazines. Here surely was Stella's chance to land a decent job, bring in a wage, and be free of her frustrating imprisonment with the mangle and the rolling pin. The housework would still have to be done; but she would rather make a hasty fist at it when she got home from work than spend the whole day with it and still end up with crinkled shirts and a pie that tasted like a shoebox full of greasy string.

She didn't get the job. She would have – Violet Drew said as much, in her regretful ladylike way, patting at her shelflike bosom with fingers puckered from setting lotion. She took to Stella, but she had already promised the job to a girl who had applied that morning. Stella's heart, already low, sank further when she heard the girl's name. Muriel Peasgood – an unbearable Little Miss Perfect who at school had always been held up as an example to be followed, who made her own frocks, who was walking out with the universally fancied, godlike son of Fred Clark the butcher, who could no doubt make delicious pies with one hand whilst putting knife-edge creases in her father's shirts with the other . . .

It was a blow, and she would have felt it even more if the loss of her mother had not dulled the impact of such things. As it was, the setback was another obstacle on a dark road, and Stella could be forgiven the self-pity that wondered if light would ever break through again.

Auntie Bea, of course, had heard about it; and being Bea, she couldn't forbear mentioning it now. 'Ah, short again, are you, gel? Course, it's harder with you not working, ain't it? Shame you never got that job at Violet Drew's. Would have suited you down to the ground, that would, I was just saying to Will the other day. That Muriel Peasgood got it, didn't she? Well, she would, you see. Sort who always does well for herself . . .'

Well, she could have done without being reminded of it, but it was fair enough: she was the one cadging money, after all. Stella's opinion of herself, usually robust, was low, and if Bea had told her she was hopeless she would probably have agreed. Bea, however, was not the type to judge, at least not when it came to her own family. She rhapsodized a little more over the virtues of Muriel Peasgood – who was also, it seemed, a champion ballroom dancer and could do miraculous things with pressed flowers – but at the same time she was hunting through a sort of leaning tower of biscuit tins atop the sideboard, and when the rattling and crashing was over she emerged with five shillings.

'I promise I'll pay you back, Aunt Bea, I promise.' The promise was heartfelt, even if the prospect was a hazy one.

But what prospect wasn't, Stella thought as she made her way home after listening to some more anecdotes of Muriel Peasgood's achievements (nursing not one but two neighbours through life-threatening illnesses – a bedpan in each hand presumably). She hadn't known, until it was taken from her, just how much the presence of her mother had brightened life here, sweetened what was essentially a monotonous diet of experience with scant nourishment for the soul. Perhaps it was simply the dullness and apathy consequent on grief, but Stella seemed to cast a new and discontented eye on Corbett Street and its hugger-mugger community. 'You're never on your own round here,' was the approving formula spoken by oldsters who had refused the opportunity to move elsewhere; but Stella, regarding the open front doors, the heads that turned to follow you, the pinafored threesomes of gossiping women, none of whom dared to leave in case the other two talked about her, began to feel that the price you paid in respect of privacy was pretty steep. If she had scarcely begun to articulate her sense of dissatisfaction, it was because the words for it didn't really exist here, not without laying yourself open to that gravest of charges: being a snob. 'Think they're too good for us' – woe betide anyone of whom that was said in Corbett Street. She had joined in the same unthinking condemnation herself in the past, but now she chafed at the too-easy prescription. Thinking there must be more to life – did that make you a snob?

Perhaps it did. It was her home and it was where she belonged and that was that: she knew what the reply would be. But so much of what had made it a home, she saw now, was gone. Remembering her mother's funeral, it occurred to her that a stranger mingling with the mourners might have been hard put to it to guess which were the deceased's family. They loved each other, but there was no centre now. Her father was an exemplary parent as far as beatings went – he had never lifted a hand to any of them; but Dot and Archie and Lennie still looked on him with awe, and there was no question of their turning to him for some of the warmth that their mother had supplied. Jack Tranter had made such a point of carrying the wrongs of the world on his shoulders that his children scarcely dared to press their claims on him. He was more legend than father – a sort of Father Christmas without the presents.

They were a sorry lot, in fact, and Stella was burningly conscious of her failure to make them any less sorry, for all her efforts over the past three months. The house in Corbett Street was a sort of joyless chaos, and even the absence of Happy Harry Fisk and his family, who had moved from next door to Bethnal Green, didn't amount to a blessing worth counting. The money difficulties gave a new poignancy to her memories of her mother, who had never given away any hint of the worry these must have cost her. She must have racked her brains as Stella did now, not just for three months but for years and years; and it had only showed in the two faint little vertical lines between her brows, which Stella had always thought rather added to the prettiness of her face.

*And* she could make a tasty pie – which Stella, Aunt Bea's five bob jingling in her purse, decided she wasn't even going to attempt tonight. Instead she bought scrag-end at Fred Clark's, where the butcher's son, godlike intended of bloody Muriel Peasgood, gave her a beautiful remote smile over the bacon slicer, dreaming no doubt of his ballroom-dancing, flower-pressing future of wedded bliss. 'That'll stew up lovely,' Fred Clark assured her. Stella was sure that it could, but whether it would for *her* was a different matter. Arriving home, she set to work on it; when the kids came in from school shortly afterwards, she shoved lumps of bread in their hands and shooed them out to play, because she got flustered enough in the kitchen as it was.

Well, she didn't see what could go wrong: it was in the pot, with potatoes and an onion and some dripping that she had saved for a stock; surely time should do the rest. Stella sat down at the table and counted out what was left of Aunt Bea's loan, then made notes on the back of an old envelope. It hadn't turned really cold yet so they could do without coal, but they were nearly out of tea and sugar, say one and six for those . . . Archie needed new shoes but there was no chance of those this week, maybe next week they could go down to the Woolworth's in Whitechapel High Street and see . . .

Almost without volition, Stella found herself slipping the letter from her purse and unfolding it. She had read it any number of times, but that didn't matter: it was what the letter stood for that was important, rather than what was in it.

It was from Richard Marwood and had come last week. He had written before, a sympathy letter at the time of her mother's funeral – they all had, though she had been too upset to take much notice of them; but this was a proper letter, probably the first proper letter she had ever received.

It was an ordinary enough letter, she supposed. He condoled with her again, and enquired after her welfare, and mentioned the orchard summer and how wonderful it had been; and he told her that he was having to knuckle down and seek employment, or a position as he called it, 'else my father will cut me off with a shilling – whatever that means – always sounds rather excruciating.' It was like that – vague, warm, humorous: ordinary, in fact; and not seeming urgently to need a reply, though she had several times begun and abandoned one.

And yet it was special too, special enough to keep in her purse like a talisman. Stella was glad that he made no explicit reference to what had happened that last night in the orchards – neither apology nor avowal – because that seemed to her to reflect an essential truthfulness that was beyond the power of direct words. After she had come home it had been a long time until she had been able to think of that night, and when she finally did it was with a sort of shrinking dread: in crude terms, she half expected a voice to boom out that by lying down with him in that starlit meadow she had killed her mother. As it happened, no such curse rang out: if anything, there was only a sad murmur to the effect that life was full of bitter ironies, and the bitterest irony of all was that none of them was so very meaningful. It was chance: it was what happened. Which was not to say that she could ever feel again as she had felt when she had walked into the long meadow grass with Richard. Between her self then and her self now a chasm had opened up: in fact she found it difficult to picture the Stella Tranter who had existed that night, and to fathom her heart. She was sure that something true and real had led her to that spot in the meadow – for otherwise she would have died since of self-loathing; but much had been true and real under that strange spell of the orchards. A pirate ship had been real, and a tea party on the roof; and a bond, too, between four people whose paths would never normally have crossed.

Love? It might have been; but everything had been broken apart by the news of her poor mother's death, and was still broken, and she had yet to put the pieces together and see if love was amongst them, or merely passion – the dizzy abandon of a summer's night far from home. No knowing, either, whether she would ever put the pieces together. But it was in this regard that she understood and was grateful for the letter and what it did and did not say. It did not erase what had happened, but it did not thrust it upon her: it acknowledged that it belonged elsewhere. The memory was a curious one, because it was like a memory of something that had happened to someone else; but it was a beautiful one too, and it was to be treasured, stored up against the grimness. And, like the letter, taken out just occasionally, when she was alone.

Which she so very seldom was. How long did they give me there, Stella thought irritably as there was a knock at the door jamb, all of ten minutes? She just had time to scramble the letter back into her purse, and then Lilian Catmore was upon her.

'Ah, I thought you'd be in. I saw the little ones out in the street and I said to Archie was his sister in, he said yes she's there but they were playing a game you know, all wrapped up in it, so I wasn't sure whether he was really listening. You know what children are like, they'll say yes or no and they don't really know what you've asked them, they're so lost in their own little world. Lennie's growing, isn't he, it doesn't seem two minutes since he was only just walking, they change so fast at that age, I remember with mine it seemed like their clothes only fitted them for a few weeks and then they'd outgrown them. Of course when there's more than one you can hand them down, that's the blessing of it really, say if you've got a five-year-old and a seven-year-old the younger one can wear the older one's things that he's grown out of and it's not as if they'll be worn out at all, you know, because they only fitted him for such a short time that nine times out of ten they're still in good condition. Maybe not like new, you know, but still good enough to be worn and I don't think children tend to notice that sort of thing, although sometimes you do get a bit of complaining that they're having to wear something their brother or sister used to wear and they think it's a bit unfair, mainly girls really, I think that is true that little girls are more fussy about these things than boys, though I don't remember either of my two girls being like that, they were always pretty sensible. So how are you keeping, dear, you look well, a lot better than last time I saw you.'

That, for Lilian Catmore, was relatively concise. For Lilian

Catmore, that was practically silence. Stella managed, 'I'm very well, ta, are you?' before the next onslaught.

'I hope you don't mind, only I brought you a little something, I was doing some baking and I had some left over so I thought I'd use it up and then bring it over because I hate to see things go to waste, you know how it happens that you end up with more than you think because you haven't judged the right amount, I find that with pastry especially. My Dulcie was there, she'd just come over from Stepney Green, she was just seeing a friend of hers over there who's expecting her first and a bit down in the dumps apparently, her husband's working nights and she feels like she doesn't see much of him, you know, it's a shame really and so Dulcie dropped in and she was just about to start helping me clear away, she's always been like that, you know, not one of these people who has to ask but I don't mean she's pushy, you know, because that would be different, and I said no, wait a minute, because I wanted to make a little something with that and take it round to the Tranters', I know what a man's appetite's like when he comes home from work and they haven't had it easy that family . . .'

The most monstrously hypnotic thing about Lilian Catmore's speech was not how dull it was, how achingly empty of all form and content, how maddeningly repetitive and insistent in its chasing down of some entirely uninteresting details – it was how *slow* it was. She wasn't a chatterer: she didn't flutter or gabble it out. Her nasal monotone had no pace at all. To call it a drone would be misleading, because a drone might conceivably be soothing. Listening to Lilian Catmore talk gave you the feeling you had in nightmares when you tried to run and your legs moved like dead weights and you wrestled with a scream that would never come.

She was Welsh, but that couldn't account for it – Stella had met several Welsh people and they didn't talk like that. She was just Lilian, a unique and immovable fixture of Corbett Street, a large dimpled dewy-faced woman with a neat shingle of grizzled hair and an endless capacity for making herself useful, or for busybodying, whichever way you wanted to look at it. Her life had been eventful, to the tune of uncountable children and two marriages – in her own frequent phrase, she had 'lost two husbands'. She always reported this with a sort of complacent resignation, as if it were a piece of accidental damage that had been covered by the insurance. There wasn't much that Lilian Catmore didn't know about having children, rearing children, making gravy, gathering curtains, destroying cockroaches, saving marriages, and every other branch of domestic expertise, and even less that she wouldn't tell you, freely and at great length.

'Oh, it smells like you've got something cooking anyway,' Lilian went on, advancing towards the stove. Stella darted in front of her and did some brisk stirring. The smell, she now noticed, was less than appetizing; and the whole concoction, colourful enough when it was merely ingredients, had turned elephant-grey. It had also shrunk.

'Well,' Lilian said, her face appearing with bovine inquisitiveness over Stella's shoulder, 'like I say, you never can tell with quantities. When there's a hungry man in the house you can never have too much, that's what I always found. They need their strength, don't they, because of the work they have to do. It's not the same with women somehow. I haven't got a very big appetite myself. Sometimes I'll just make do with a piece of bread and butter. I'll leave this anyway. It'll eat just as well cold if your father's still hungry later on.'

It was, of course, a pie: a shapely, golden-crusted, aromatic pie, a pie of the sort that Minnie Mouse put out on the windowsill to cool. It even made Stella's mouth water, traitorously. 'It's very kind of you,' she managed.

'Oh, it's no more than anyone would do really, you know, to help out when a family's struggling a bit, I don't see it as anything more than common neighbourliness, really I think it's just natural, I couldn't understand anybody who didn't feel that way,' Lilian said, attacking Stella's conversational commonplace with all her deadliest thoroughness. 'How's your father bearing up under it? I suppose he's trying to carry on and be strong, men do, don't they, I suppose they have to in a way because they still have to be the breadwinner and you can't just give in, even though you might feel like it sometimes, I know I felt like that when I lost my second husband but you've still got to think of the future because life goes on, doesn't it, and you never know what the future will bring. Well, I'd best be leaving you.' Throughout this Lilian had been making a slow circuitous glide in the direction of the door, eyeing everything like a motherly vulture. 'You'll be wanting to do your tidying before your father gets home, you're like me I expect, like to do it all in one big go, it's the best way to clean I think rather than doing it in dribs and drabs because that way it never really gets done . . .' She was still talking when she reached the street outside, and didn't stop there: seeing someone she knew, she just switched targets and went on firing without drawing a breath.

Meanwhile Stella 'did her tidying', which turned out to be a rather furious affair: the beating of the rug was especially vigorous, perhaps because Stella was imagining Lilian Catmore's face in the middle of the pattern. Awful woman! Formerly Stella would have laughed it off, but just now she hadn't the heart, and by the time her father came home – the two boys having undone the results of her tidying in about two minutes – she was in a black mood.

Dot, who came in at about the same time, didn't help. Stella's younger sister had work of a kind, skivvying a few days a week in the kitchen of a pie shop down near the docks; and she certainly made a meal of it, groaning about her hard day and expecting Stella to wait on her as – well, as her mother had waited on all of them. She was full of it tonight, wanting to know if Stella had washed and ironed her other apron, and sitting expectantly down at the table alongside her father. The way Stella was feeling, this was not wise.

But Stella kept her temper. Even when the stew had been served up and half eaten with, on her father's part, various pained and puzzled expressions, she kept her temper: she kept her temper too when Archie spotted the pie – after briefly considering passing it off as her own, Stella had put it out of the way on a high shelf –

and it was brought down and eaten with smacks of approval. Keeping her temper, in fact, became vitally important to her. If everything else she did was a failure, she might at least accomplish that.

And then, in spite of all her efforts, the quarrel came: not with Dot, but with her father. Since his wife's death Jack Tranter had become if anything more serious, deliberate and undemonstrative: knowing him as Stella did, she understood that this was the way grief worked on him, and there was no doubt that the loss of his wife had hit him badly. But a consequence of this was that he became even more bleakly and doggedly preoccupied with putting the world to rights. Perhaps Stella should have sympathized with this too – it was only the revolution that was keeping him going – but her reserves of patience were not unlimited, and when after tea he stationed himself in his chair with his newspaper and began to hold forth about the industrial proletariat, she snapped.

'Oh, Dad, for Pete's sake, what would you know about the industrial proletariat? You work for Mr Milstein in a two-room furniture workshop and you've never been north of Enfield in your life.'

Her father was stunned for a moment – and so was she. For anyone to tackle him on this ground was unheard of, let alone his own daughter. But he soon gathered himself.

'The struggle's everybody's struggle, Stella. Everyone who's been oppressed by international capitalism, every worker who's been forced to give his sweat and blood to feed the parasitic growth of the imperialist exploiters. But the struggle has to be led somewhere and it's historically inevitable that it should be here, right in the centre of the so-called Empire. Look at when we fought the Fascists in Cable Street – I remember standing shoulder to shoulder with Alfie Goldman . . .'

It was unfortunate that he should mention this. Two years ago there had been a pitched battle in Whitechapel when the British Union of Fascists had tried to stage a march through the Jewish areas. Many of her father's friends had been there, but to his eternal sorrow Jack Tranter had been laid up in bed that day with a hernia. As time went on, however, he had overcome his disappointment at this by means of a sort of creeping fib. First he had watched it from a distance, having been carried there by two comrades: then he had been there shortly afterwards and helped tend the wounded . . . But he had never yet claimed to have actually taken part, and this was what goaded Stella beyond endurance.

'Blimey,' she said, 'there must be more to this revolution lark than I thought, if you can do it while you're lying in bed.'

This was cruel and hurtful: if her father had been angry she would have been apologetic. But even now, though he coloured, he didn't get angry.

'Ah,' he said, lifting his big square forefinger in that infuriating schoolmasterly way, 'now I see what this is. You've been got at by somebody. Somebody's put a lot of reactionary stuff in your head, Stella – now I don't blame you, because it's easily done. Look at Trotsky, even he went wrong. Perhaps it's those people you got mixed up with this summer. Yes, I should think that was it. You've had some wrong ideas put into your head and that's what's made you—'

'Oh, yes, that's right, nobody can think for themselves, they only think something because somebody's told them to. That's what it boils down to, don't it? Well, I don't see you as any different from Hitler's lot.'

'You take that back, my girl!' Now he *was* angry. 'Don't you think just because you're taking your mother's place you can talk to me like that in me own house! Your mother never would have – never in a million years!'

'That's because she was too bloody frightened! Frightened to do anything in case you didn't like it and made her feel guilty about it with your miserable pious ways! And I don't want to take Mum's place, I don't, I'm no good at it and I just want her back . . .'

They stared at each other.

'Well,' her father said, dropping his eyes, 'so do I . So do I, duck.'

'Oh – shush, Lennie,' Stella said, as the youngest boy, whose face had gone from startled to tragic throughout this, gave a loud sniff. 'I mean – oh, come here. Come and help me make a cuppa . . . Would you like one, Dad?'

'I would, please, duck,' her father said stiffly, looking at his paper. 'You know, I don't expect . . . I mean, it was nice, you know, that stew. Quite nice really.'

'Just gets in your mouth, that's the trouble,' Stella said.

They managed a shaky laugh; but it was a relief when there was a coo-ee at the door, and distraction appeared in the shape of Auntie Bea.

A more than usually excited Auntie Bea, in fact, who hurtled in and to Stella's everlasting astonishment avoided falling over Archie, who was squatting on the rug, by vaulting right over him like a headscarfed hurdler.

'You'll never guess!' Auntie Bea squawked. 'You'll never guess what I've heard! I bet you'll never guess!'

'Well, tell us then,' grumped Stella's father.

'You'll like this one, gel,' Auntie Bea said beaming. 'This'll put a smile on your face, this will. You know that Muriel Peasgood?'

Stella groaned. 'What now, invited to the King's garden party?'

Bea gave a shriek of laugher, piercing even for her. 'I doubt it! She won't be going anywhere much before long!' Bea adopted her whisper, which was about the volume of normal conversation. 'Up the spout! Muriel Peasgood's up the spout!'

'Whassat?' Lennie said.

'Got a bun in the oven,' Archie informed him.

'And no prizes for guessing who put it there,' Bea went on. 'Fred Clark's going spare. Muriel Peasgood's lot are going spare. Doesn't surprise me, mind you. I always thought she was all red hat and no drawers meself. So what d'yer think of that?'

'Gawd,' Stella said. She couldn't think anything for the moment: she was too busy gloating, and then reproaching herself for gloating.

'Well, there goes her job at Violet Drew's, that's for sure,'

Auntie Bea said, with a great wink at Stella. 'Violet Drew won't even have a gel in her salon with earrings on, let alone . . .' Bea performed a vivid mime. 'What d'yer reckon, gel? Eh? What d'yer reckon?'

'I reckon, Auntie Bea,' Stella said, 'I shall be able to pay you back quicker than I thought,' and she found herself smiling for what seemed the first time since she had walked beneath a strawberry-coloured sky.

## 3

November was rather late for a harvest-home supper, and the tradition of the harvest-home or 'horkey' had pretty much died out in the fens in recent years anyway; and the last person anyone would expect to celebrate it would be George Maxey, who never entertained and had even been known to work through Christmas Day. And it was typical of George that he should not only disregard all these considerations when he decided to hold a harvest-home but invite everyone in the district, lay on a vast quantity of food and drink, and generally carry the thing off as if he had been doing it all his life.

'And then – round about half-eight, say, when everybody's moved on to the punch – I thought I'd make the announcement,' George said.

'What – right in front of everybody?' said Kate.

'Oh yes, of course. I want everybody to know. That's the point of the whole show really,' he said, with one of his rare smiles, which gave a look of tightness to his big face.

That was it, of course: he wanted to show off their engagement – shout it to the world, in fact. And although the prospect of being exposed to view like that still made Kate tremble a little, and would once have had her screaming, she defied anyone not to feel overpoweringly flattered. Loved too: that went without saying.

Looking deeper, she saw that the harvest supper was not entirely a pretext. It became clear to her as they made plans for the evening that this marked something of a return to the world for George. Since the death of his parents he had been an essentially solitary creature, working his farm with monklike devotion, not in the least shy but not social either, his relations with other people entirely workaday and pragmatic. Once married, she saw, he intended things to be different. People had been wide of the mark when they had referred to George as a confirmed bachelor. He had been as thorough about bachelorhood as he was about everything, but it was plain that he saw it as a strictly limited state of being, and that the real business of life began with marriage.

To Kate, only: here was another overpoweringly flattering consideration. George had had chances aplenty to marry before now, but he had waited for Kate. Whether he would have waited for ever was perhaps a question she should not have asked herself. Academic, anyhow: he had meant to have her, he had asked her, and she had consented.

He had moved with characteristic swiftness and directness since first speaking out on the day of the village feast. He had found it easier, no doubt, because what he always referred to as 'those other people' were out of the way now. In a curious way, in fact, it was 'those other people' who gave Kate the nudge over the edge of acceptance and – she couldn't help thinking of it in these terms – sent her falling into an engagement to marry George Maxey.

The occasion had been a dark October day of ceaseless rain. Her father, just mending, had tried to do some work, set himself back, and retired again in a foul mood made worse by the fact that his truck would not start. George had come over in the late afternoon to see what he could do with it, and Kate had kept him company in the garage while he worked. She had been in a frame of mind as dull and grey as the day. Though the picking of the autumn apples went on, and a small number of the fruit-pickers were still at the camp, there was a distinct feeling of finality about the orchards: soon there would only be the pruning and washing of the bare fruit trees, with everywhere that acrid creosote smell of the washing solution that was like a dismal essence of winter. The departure of her friends, the suddenness of their loss and the sense, saddest of all, that their meeting at all had been ultimately meaningless, had left Kate low and dispirited, and today seemed the lowest point of all. The garage had once been a stable, and after that a mushroom shed, and there were still signs of its former uses to be seen by the light of the oil lamp – odds and ends of horse-tackle, crates and chip-baskets, rotting and covered in cobwebs. Everything seemed to belong to the past, to have faded and had its day.

And then George, his head under the bonnet of the truck, started muttering something about the transmission and about 'that Cambridge chap' who had driven the truck when her father was laid up. 'That's where the trouble started, I shouldn't wonder,' George said, wiping his hands on a rag. 'When that chap drove it. You have to be careful with an old model like this.'

Kate didn't know much about trucks or cars, but she didn't think it likely that Richard could have ruined the engine, as George seemed to be suggesting. She thought it was just spite, and made uninhibited by gloom, she said so.

'Eh?' George stuck his head up, and his expression was one of sheer surprise. She knew he was no dissembler, but she couldn't stop now: it came pouring out of her.

'You're always being nasty about Richard – and Helen and Stella – you know they were my friends but you still do it. Well, I liked it when they were here and I miss them and I don't see anything wrong with that. They never did anything to you and it just – it just sounds petty and childish when you keep making remarks about them. They're gone anyway, they've all gone and so I don't see why you can't just leave it.'

He stared at her, and there was a bleak silence which he then broke with two words that startled her.

'I'm jealous.'

'There's . . .' All of a sudden she couldn't look at him. 'There's nothing to be jealous of, they're not here—'

'I know. But you know what I mean. I'm jealous because I'm in love with you and they took you away from me.'

He threw down the rag and spanner and came away from the truck, swift decision in every line of him. Kate saw then – and her admiration was the greater because it was a quality she believed she crucially lacked – that George was a person who would never, ever wriggle out of anything: he had a harsh, bright courage; if he committed a murder he would own up to it – perhaps even feel that lying about it would be the worse crime.

'I know I'm unreasonable about – those people. That Richard one especially. I just can't help it. You know why – you remember what I said that day at the feast. I've been wanting to say something more and that's why I've kept coming round and – well, I knew you were sad when they left and that made me jealous too. Anyway it doesn't matter. You're all that matters, Kate – you're all that matters to me in the world.'

It didn't come out trite or melodramatic when George said it: he made it a peculiarly uncompromising statement of fact, like a confession of bankruptcy.

'I'm sorry,' she said – grasping at the first words that came. 'I shouldn't have spoke like that, it was—'

'It was true, but now you know why. Oh, I don't give a damn about those people one way or the other. If they stood between me and you I'd – I'd drive them out of the way, and if I had you then I'd think they were the greatest people in the world – or whatever you wanted me to think. That's how I feel. That's what you mean to me.'

In confusion she turned away from him and looked out of the open garage door. Even the house looked grey and comfortless today, the smoke from the chimney seeming scarcely to rise in the rainy air; and the surrounding fen had so little form or colour it might have been returning to its primeval state, dissolving and liquefying, sloughing off its unnatural burden of crops and trees and houses. A world of shapeless vacancy confronted her, and was terrifying because so ordinary; whilst behind her an ardent and loving man focused the beam of his whole self upon her, and was all that the lifeless scene was not. He seemed, in fact, little less than a world in himself: certainly she knew that that was what he would try to be, if she wished it of him.

'If you don't want this, say so.' Deep feeling, rather than roughening his voice, made it more even, and almost metallic. 'I'm going to ask you, I've got to, it's all I've been thinking of . . . I can't absolutely promise that I won't ask again if you say no, but I will respect what you say – I'm a serious person and so are you and I don't think either of us believe in messing people around . . . Kate, will you look at me?'

She did look at him, turning: she found him closer to her than she had thought, and his presence was like a dark lamp in its intensity. And just then it seemed to her that the blankness of the weeks since the feast and the loss of her friends, the drifting and the dissatisfaction, had not many causes but a single cause only: she had been mentally evading this question that George Maxey was about to ask her. If she had had a feeling of groping about in dimness, it was because she had been living in its huge shadow.

And all she had to do now was step out of it. It was this simplicity, after so much complexity, that was immensely appealing to her.

She saw George check himself in a sudden movement, and then stuff his hands with touching awkwardness in his pockets. 'You see,' he said, 'you must – you must know what it is. I want to ask you to marry me.' Having said it, he took his hands out of his pockets and stood braced as if for a firing squad.

He wasn't quite close enough for her to feel the warmth of his body – but it was warmth she seemed to feel nonetheless, an enfolding and reassuring warmth that she found she did not want to leave. If she was vastly flattered at his offering himself to her as a lover, what struck even deeper was the way he offered himself, at that moment, as a saviour. In an amorphous, colourless world this rocklike figure stood forth and beckoned to her; and gratefully, with a sense of inevitability that was also reassuring, she came to him.

Comforting too was the way the news of their engagement fitted in, as it were, at home. Kate had a curious superstition that to surprise her parents would be to hurt them. That she was to marry George Maxey did not surprise them, pleased them greatly, and caused them to congratulate themselves on their clairvoyance; thus Kate felt she had given those she loved a share in her happiness. Which was real: her feelings for George were far from crystal clear to her, but that in itself suggested truth, which is never facile, and there was no doubting his magnetic effect on her. Being with him, planning their future together, gave a positive pleasure that also had something of relief in it, as if something alarming and threatening had been about to occur which he had put a stop to.

Planning, especially, took up much of their time. George did not dally over the past and reminisce over her in pigtails: he had always loved her and that was that. It was on the future that his eyes were fixed, when Kate would be his wife and mistress of his farm. Unusually for the fens, where place names were many and resonant, the farm had no name despite being the largest and oldest homestead on the map of Monks Bridge. It was just known as George Maxey's place. When Kate mentioned this, George took notice, first with amusement, then seriously. 'Yes, the old place ought to have a name now,' he said. 'Why don't you choose a name for it? You're good at that sort of thing. We could have a little sign made.' And she saw then that it was she who was to confer identity on the place: saw that up till now he had only been existing there, waiting for it to be made whole. It showed, for all his self-confidence, an affecting modesty in George that made her feel she loved him very much.

The farm was very different from the cosy home at the end of the apple-tree drove that she had always known. The prospect from its front windows was all barley fields, bare now, with the main fen drain running at their rim like a straight steely rail. Too large for one, the house contained several rooms that had been shut up and unused since George's parents had died: going through it with her, George flung open doors and yanked back drapes, letting light pour in. 'This stuff's donkey's years old,' he said, with dismissive prods and kicks at the fumed-oak furniture: his tastes were modern. 'We'll get new. Everything up to date. I want you to choose everything the way you like it.'

This, she soon discovered, was far more than loverlike obligingness. The house was a place that had served him, as a workshop might, but there were no associations or attachments in it for him. It was to be made over in Kate's image. The domestic arrangements were to be, very literally, her province. She felt that if she had said she would like hammocks instead of beds and a ship's galley instead of a kitchen he would have gone along with it quite happily.

And this was attractive, very attractive to Kate – so much so that she mistrusted the attraction like a drinker eyeing an unopened bottle. She could imagine herself very easily making a little domain of this house – transforming it into a smoothly functioning little world, neat and self-contained and safe. It would be so pleasant and so easy. She would not have to worry about anything: George was insistent about that and she believed him. Times had been so poor for Anglian farmers that there were plans for taking the unprecedented step of a mass protest rally in London, but George, through fanatical hard work and diversifying his crops, had added to the natural advantages of Marshland soil, and was as secure as it was possible for a farmer to be. They would lack for nothing. A bower was being prepared for Kate and all she had to do was take her devoted swain's hand and walk into it. She was very willing: no one, after all, is averse to having all their problems solved at a stroke. The trouble was, Kate had a good deal of self-knowledge, and knew that she was more susceptible to such a temptation than most people. To close the shutters and stir the fire and feel oneself snugly protected from the outer world – that was her version of the drunkard's binge. And here was a man offering, as it were, to stand drinks for ever more.

She wondered if she were looking into it too closely. Everyone else seemed delighted with the match. At the harvest supper, there was a general awareness of what was to come even before George made the announcement, as if it were an event that everyone had been long expecting. The supper was held, traditionally enough, in the barn, with trestle tables set out along its earth floor; and though George had not stinted with the food and drink, and had even engaged the stiff-backed sisters, Kitty and Alice, from the Corner to lay out the spread, the occasion did betray his inexperience at entertaining. Oil lamps did well enough for lighting when the dusk deepened, but a single brazier could not keep off the chill of the evening. George did not notice it, but one or two of the older residents of the village ate with chattering teeth, and Kate saw her father surreptitiously press a baked potato to the tip of his nose to warm it.

The sight made her smile – also ache a little, because presently she would be leaving him; but only a little. Marrying George, she realized, would be as near as one could come to leaving home without leaving home at all. Well, that was nice too: nothing wrong with it. She drank a glass of ale with her meal, and it was perhaps the ale that made her think with sudden lucidity that there was nothing wrong with any of it, as long as she and George were all right. That came first: she must remember that.

She felt an urgent need to say something of this to George. But though she was seated next to him at the top table, it was out of the question in front of these rows of munching people. It was a public occasion and they were on show.

Then George was getting to his feet, clearing his throat, tapping on his glass with a knife to get their attention.

'Now then,' he began, and it came out so gruff and auctioneer-like that there was a general laugh, in which he joined.

Kate looked up at him. He looked large, flushed and handsome; and in the solidity of his lines, not quite real, like an illustration of a hero in a book fending off sharks with an oar.

'What I wanted to say,' he went on, his voice echoing round the high roof of the barn, 'is thank you all for coming – and how nice it is to see you all here, and I hope everything's to your satisfaction. I'm a bit of a newcomer to this sort of thing, as you know – ' another laugh – 'but I'm hoping this'll only be the first of many harvest suppers we'll have here, once we're . . . Well, you've probably guessed that there's more to this than meets the eye, so I'll come straight out with it. I've asked Kate Lutton to marry me, and I'm proud to say she said yes.'

The noise of approval startled Kate. It was as if it were a piece of wonderful news that everyone had been waiting for. Smiling, she tried to meet a few of the interested eyes that were fixed on her down the long white perspective of tables, but she was dreadfully uncomfortable.

'And so – I just wanted to say that I'm the happiest man alive – and we hope you'll all come to the wedding!' George concluded hastily, beaming.

'Well, that's saved the price of the invitations, George!' someone called out, to more laughter.

George sat down, reaching out for Kate's hand; then, egged on by calls of 'Goo on, she woon't bite!' he kissed her. Not for the first time she registered surprise at the softness of his face: though so generally rugged, George had almost no beard. Strange. It was all strange: the light of the oil lamps on the familiar village faces, the stiff collars and strawy smell, the momentousness of the occasion and its paradoxical, drowsy, undemanding quality. Her father got up to make a little speech, and that was strange too, yet easy also: he was in his element here, making the guests roar with laughter, Walter Lutton in fine and typical form. Everything was out of her hands. She did not have to do anything.

But that was all right too: there was no reason why getting married should be strenuous. Still, as she drank another glass of beer and absentmindedly received the congratulations of the people around her, she again experienced that spasm of urgency. Something needed saying to George: something in their contract needed to be underlined.

She supposed the time would be later, when the guests had gone and they would be allowed a little time alone together before he took her home. But what happened at the end of the evening was unexpected – quite out of the blue, in fact. They sat talking companionably for a while by his kitchen fire – he had closed the barn door firmly and said the clearing-away could wait till tomorrow – and warmth and fatigue quite dispelled Kate's feeling of urgency. Soon it was time for her to go home: they both stood and stretched, idly debated the merits of walking or of riding in his truck, and then inclined together for a kiss which suddenly became eager and passionate. On George's part, at first, and to her astonishment; his attitude to her thus far had been almost chivalrous in its respect, but now he clutched fiercely at her, huge, boyish, almost feverish, and she found herself responding. No one knew, no one could see: folded to George's great body, she felt herself to be effectively hidden from the world, beyond its power, and yet also as if she were being received into the earth. The probing of his tongue, which momentarily seemed an obscenity, then had the inspiring rightness of ritual: in the surge of it she forgot who she was, though George remained George to her.

They were both people capable of a good deal of self-control, so it would have been surprising if neither of them had broken off. In the end she was not sure which it was, but presently they were drawing away from each other, tousled and red-faced, though not awkward. He drove her home, and kissed her good night in an everyday fashion, and neither referred to what had happened.

She thought much about it, however, when she went to bed; and wondered whether it made what she had been going to say unnecessary, or more necessary than ever.

# *TWO*

## 1

*Dear Kate*

*I believe it's bad form to begin a letter with an apology, but nevertheless do accept my apologies for not having written since I left your part of the world. Believe me I often think of you, and of that lovely orchard country – bare now, I dare say? – and of the most enjoyable time I spent there.*

*You may excuse my dereliction a little when you hear my news, and understand how busy I have been in consequence – I am to be married: in ten days' time no less! The name of my intended is Owen Harding. He is a partner in a law firm in Louth, which is not far from here. We shall live in Louth. I am not very good at pen pictures, so you must take my word for it that he is a wonderful man and I mean to be very happy with him.*

*I dare say this may come as something of a surprise – but then one never knows, does one? We met and found each other eminently suitable – and there it is. I know I said much to you, very grandly forsooth, of what I was going to do in life, and it didn't include this. But then we can never tell what's going to happen in our lives. Sometimes it seems quite pointless to plan at all, things are really so out of our hands. The main thing is I am very sure of Owen and that this is what I want. The journalism idea was only one among the many that a person naturally has when young, and which are bound to include foolish and mistaken ones. Owen by the way does not wish me to work when we are married and of course I shall respect that.*

*And my goodness what a lot of work is involved in planning a wedding, even a very quiet family one such as ours is to be! I think I shall be quite exhausted by the time the day comes. We shall honeymoon in the south of France, over Christmas I think. It will be strange spending Christmas abroad.*

*Kate, I do hope all is well with you; also that your father is recovering well. Please give him and all your family my best regards. I remember my summer with you, Stella &c with great affection. Please forgive the shortness of this letter – and do write whenever you have time.*

*With all good wishes*

*Helen Silverman*

Kate could not remember anything which had ever surprised her as much as this letter, which came in late November.

'You didn't know her all that well, after all,' her brother Pip said with a shrug, when she told him about the letter. Kate felt this was not true, but she lacked anyone to back her up. The fellowship of the summer was disbanded: even Knatchbull and Neeve had folded up their tents and gone. She was curiously shy of writing to Richard, and temporarily shy of writing what could seem merely gossip to the recently bereaved Stella. All of that rare intimacy was so utterly vanished, in fact, that she began to doubt whether it had ever existed. Perhaps Pip was right: perhaps she hadn't known Helen as she had thought.

Then not long after she received the letter she saw something that set her thinking harder about it, and revived the initial astonishment. Her father's winter pruning tools were brought out of the sheds wrapped in newspaper, and unwrapping them she spotted an article bearing the byline 'Olive Kingswell'. She remembered the name at once, and read it through attentively. It was about the Civil War in Spain, and the sort of thing she would normally have found hard going. But it impressed her with its salty style and clear-headed view of things. It strongly reminded her, in fact, of the way Helen used to talk. In her letter, by contrast, she could hardly see anything of Helen at all.

She told George about it, showing him the newspaper article. 'This Olive Kingswell – she was the one who was going to help her get started,' Kate told him. 'That was Helen's ambition – to be like her.'

'One of these career-type women, eh?' George made a face. 'Well, that wouldn't have been much of a life for her. All on her own – having to fend for herself. They tend to be old dragons anyway, don't they? I didn't really know her, but she didn't seem that sort.'

'I still don't understand it,' Kate mused.

'People change their minds,' he said hugging her. 'So what about tomorrow? Still game? Speaking of old dragons, I mean. No, that's unfair. Aunt May's a dear old stick, I'm sure you'll like her. I know she'll like you.'

George's only family was an elderly great-aunt who lived in genteel seclusion in Ely. He wanted to introduce his fiancée to the old lady: he was punctilious about such things. It would be a bit of a day out for them too, he said; and in honour of the occasion he shed his customary work clothes for a suit and got out the old Humber saloon that rested, barely used, in an outhouse at the farm. It was a lordly old car with plush upholstery and burnished woodwork, more like a coach than an automobile. Kate wondered aloud why George didn't use it more.

'Oh, I shall in future,' he said. 'This can be our runaround – if you like it, that is. Just the truck was all right for me, when I was on my own.'

It was almost as if his bachelorhood had been an exercise in deliberate self-deprivation. Kate felt she should not be thinking this, but she could not rid herself of an image of George eating solitary Spartan meals at his kitchen table, going to bed amongst a heap of ugly furniture, going out in a rattling oil-smelling truck . . . and not really minding any of it because it was all going to change when he married. Why this made her uneasy she could not say, except in very bald terms: in essence, it seemed to her wrong, profoundly wrong, that one person should affect another's life in that way. And when that person was herself . . .

Occupied with such thoughts, she was quiet on the drive down to Ely. George didn't mind, taking it for nervousness at the thought of meeting his great-aunt. 'We needn't stay long,' he said. 'She's a bit cheesy in the ears these days, so you have to shout rather. Don't worry, I can do the talking.' Kate's shyness rather pleased him than otherwise: it gave him the opportunity to take more on his shoulders.

She kept thinking too about Helen's letter, and especially the words *things are really so out of our hands.* For some reason they caused something like a cold flush of fear to go through her. Was it true? Did you merely move along through life like a target at a shooting gallery, waiting for whatever the world cared to inflict on you?

'George – shall we go for a drink somewhere?' Kate said as they came to Ely.

'Dutch courage, eh? Tell you what – we'll pop in and see the old girl first, and then we'll have the day to ourselves. All right?'

It was Saturday, and tiny Ely was busy, the marketplace and quayside teeming noisily beneath the vast vertical silence that was the cathedral. George's great-aunt lived in part of a narrow Georgian house that with its many decayed window frames and spiked railings looked like a slice of a jail. 'She lets most of it,' George told her as he knocked, 'and lives down at the bottom . . . Hullo, Auntie May! How are you?'

Kate had expected someone small and frail, but George's great-aunt, though very old, turned out to be big-boned and tall like him: she would have towered over Kate if her back had not been humped by age. With her cottage-loaf hair and ropes of jet beads and strong voice she was formidable in a schoolmistressy way. Her eyes were sharp too, and Kate was thoroughly studied.

Approval seemed, if not actually withheld, to be conditional.

'Have you had the measles?' the old lady shouted at her, as they sat in her dim and flyblown sitting room.

'Yes, when I was little,' Kate shouted back.

'Chicken-pox, mumps, tonsilitis?'

Having satisfied herself that she had been through all the childhood ailments, the old lady softened a little towards Kate. She sent George into the kitchen to make tea and made Kate sit down on the threadbare ottoman beside her.

'I haven't been out to the farm for years,' she boomed. 'I dare say it needs a woman's touch. You know George's parents died young. I think we need some healthy stock. He's talked about you before, of course. He visits me every week without fail. Do you like my view?'

Kate's eyes had strayed to the window. The old lady's rooms were on the basement floor, down a set of area steps, and the window gave an oddly truncated view of the street outside. People were continually passing by, but all that could be seen of them was their legs.

'I can look out, you see,' the old lady said, 'and watch everybody go by. But I don't have to see their faces. That's the beauty of it. You can watch them without seeing their faces.'

Why this should be a matter of satisfaction to her Kate could not understand. While they had their tea, and even while the old lady was showing her a photograph album full of square-jawed Maxey faces, Kate's eyes kept straying involuntarily to that square of dirty window with its parade of legs, trousered, skirted, booted, high-heeled, old slow legs and quicksilver children's legs, busy, purposeful, and inscrutable. And what she felt was a sort of suspense of frustration, like holding your breath against the hiccoughs. Not seeing the faces of the passers-by was unbearable: she wanted to run out and confront them.

'You must come to the wedding, Aunt May,' George was shouting. 'I'll hire a car to take you there and back – you don't have to stay any longer than you want.'

'Yes, do, please,' Kate said. It wasn't just that she was George's only family: she wanted the old lady to be taken out of this room, up to the outside world where the people had faces.

'I'll see,' was all she would say, 'I'll see,' and turned back to her photographs, giving forth stern snippets of family history. She seemed to like the past best, but before they left she spoke again of the need for healthy stock, and said to Kate, 'I like your colouring. It will be good if your children have your colouring.' And Kate saw she was not much interested in the wedding. Her eyes were fixed on long perspectives of time, backward and forward, generations rising and falling.

'Terribly stuffy in there – she ought to air the place out,' George said when they left the house, noticing Kate's expression; and she lacked the words to explain that her feeling of suffocation was more than physical. It didn't matter, though, with George: creeps, moods, sulks meant nothing to him. Though he was hugely possessive, he also had a remarkable respect for the privacy of your thoughts. 'As long as I am his,' Kate thought, 'I can do and think and say whatever I like.' All her thoughts seemed to be formed in precise words today, clear and yet cryptic. And that line from Helen's letter was most prominent and baffling of all: *things are really so out of our hands.*

They had beer and sandwiches at a little place down by the quayside. The day was cool and misty, and the few boats on the river had a ghostly look, as if they might steer away by themselves. An artist with an easel kept scrubbing at his sketch of the scene, stepping back, beginning again. Above it all the cathedral soared, austere and serene, like a profound question satisfactorily answered.

'Never been in the cathedral?' George said. 'It's a wonderful place. I'm not churchy myself, but it's a thing to see inside. They do say from the top of the tower you can see all the way to Cambridge – and the sea on a good day.'

'Oh, shall we?' The idea seized her at once, she didn't know why: perhaps because it would be the very opposite of the old lady's sunken room with its views of nothing. 'Let's do it – go up the tower.'

'Heck of a climb – two hundred feet, I reckon.'

'I don't mind. You can give me a piggyback if I get tired.' He laughed affectionately at that, but she knew there was nothing he would like better.

They were the only visitors to the cathedral except for an elderly professorial man who was plying the verger with antiquarian questions. The loftiness and solemnity left Kate impressed but unmoved: what struck her most were the figures in the Lady Chapel. They were all headless. 'Cromwell's lot knocked the heads off, I reckon,' George murmured. 'I'll just ask this chap if we can go up top.'

The climb up the stone staircase of the west tower scarcely troubled her, so eager was she to see the view from the top. When they finally emerged on the tower roof, she thought for a moment, with an odd disappointment, that they were not alone: she could hear a grumbling voice. But it was just the flagpole, moving in the strong breeze that could be felt up here, though the day down below was quite still.

'Well! Better on a clear day, but still—' George said, leaning on the parapet. 'How's your head for heights?'

Not good: looking straight down over the parapet at the cloister turned her dizzy. Stepping back a little and looking straight ahead she was all right, at first. And then something about the view began to horrify her. The furthest horizons were lost in grey-blue mist, but still it was plain that what her eyes were taking in was literally scores of miles. She was seeing with one glance what would have been a fair-sized area on a map of England, yet it all looked random and meaningless. The straight fen roads and dykes made a pattern without order: distant villages were eruptions of brick, indistinguishable from one another. There were few trees in the fens, but the inclusiveness of the view erased even that fact: the trees were there to be seen, no more or less significant than anything else.

She turned away, and put her hands out to the flagpole as if for support; it moved in her hands. She felt ill. With that appalling sight it was as if a last cracked bell tone had been added to the jangling in her head set up by Helen's letter and that old aunt with her window on an incomplete world.

'Here, are you all right?' George was at her elbow. 'Feeling a bit queasy?'

'I am a bit.'

Having longed to get up to the top of the tower and see the view, all she wanted to do now was get down again. She was, she thought, behaving very badly. But George didn't and wouldn't think so. 'Come on,' he said cheerfully, 'let's go down. You go first. I'll be right behind you. Shout out if you want to stop a minute.'

So they descended. It seemed much longer this time: the stone steps began to hurt her feet through her shoes and her calves ached. But George, as he had said, was right behind her and every now and then would put a large gentle hand on her shoulder reassuringly. And through the intolerable jangling in her head Kate saw that it would always be thus. George would cherish her frailties. He was preparing, with robust gladness, to be her eternal shelter. He was going to nurture that part of herself that she had tried to conquer, the shyness and the shrinking and the urge to hide away from all unpleasantness: kindly, he was going to water its sickly foliage until it smothered her.

The clanging in her head deafened her. Emerging into the main body of the cathedral, she sat down in the first pew she came to and hid her face in her hands.

'Poor old girl.' George crouched down beside her. 'You look done in by it all. You sit there and get your breath back.'

'George, I can't marry you.'

She kept her face hidden as she said it. This was cowardly, and she made herself take her hands away and say it again, looking into his face.

'How do you mean?' He looked as if she had posed him some highly abstruse and complex question. 'Do you mean not yet?'

'I mean not ever,' she said, feeling as if a brutal club had been placed in her hands. 'Oh God, I'm so sorry, George. I made a mistake. I should never have agreed to – I don't expect you to forgive me for this. If there was any way that I could – but I can't . . .'

'Here, here, you're just tired and upset, that's all it is. Wait a minute, was it something Aunt May said? While I was making the tea? She can be a bit sharp—'

'Please, George, it isn't your aunt and it isn't you – that's what you've got to understand. It isn't you, it's me . . .' A frequent plea, which always sounds ignoble, perhaps because it is never entirely true: feeling its cheapness, she changed tack. 'I just don't want to get married, George, and it would be wrong if I did, wrong on both of us . . .'

'But we're engaged,' George said with sturdy logic, frowning. He was still crouching beside her, holding a position that most people would have found excruciating by now. 'Do you want to postpone it? Cool off for a while? I don't mind—'

'No. More than that. More than that, George. Oh, I am so sorry, there's no excuse for this . . . but I had to tell you . . .'

George's face had changed. Though deliberate, he was not a slow man: a swift shadow across his eyes showed that he had grasped, understood all, and seen his whole plan of life overturned. A lesser person might well have staggered and howled. Instead he became grim and pedantic.

'When exactly did you decide this?'

'I don't know . . . it doesn't matter. George, I know it's awful but a person has to be sure, absolutely sure, and if not—'

'You had that letter from that Cambridge woman. I wonder if that was something to do with it. Hmm?'

She struggled, trying to translate the clanging in her head into words that would make sense to him. *Things are really so out of our hands* . . . The old lady watching the world go by, the meaningless landscape, the panic and futility . . .

'Reminded you of those people, perhaps,' he said bitterly. 'And I can't measure up. I see.'

He was entitled to this, but at least here was something she could answer. 'I swear to you it's nothing like that. I don't want anything that you can't offer, and any girl would – would probably think I was mad—'

'What *do* you want, then?' Though so hurt, he still cared to know: that was the worst part.

'I don't know. I honestly don't know.'

His mouth grew tight: he liked things clear, and this probably seemed shabby evasion. 'You're afraid, that's what it is,' he said, his voice breaking a little. She was no longer his, and he felt free to attack. 'You're afraid of committing yourself to anything – afraid of giving yourself.'

Kate habitually believed other people's judgements to be superior to her own, and so she accepted this one without demur: indeed it stayed with her, lodged deep. And yet it did not alter her feeling, because she had a crucial core of stubbornness that did the duty of self-belief.

Further down the nave the professorial man, still exploring, gave them a curious look before returning his attention to traceries. The intense pair were at a painful crisis in their lives, but in his were only a peripheral distraction: recognizing this, they hated him for it and glared at him a moment before their wretched situation dragged them back.

'I don't understand you,' George muttered. 'I thought . . . Obviously not. God, I've gone and announced it. What will people think?'

'It doesn't matter what they think.'

'It's all off then. Oh, Kate – damn you, I . . .' He tried to take her hand, she half-tried to evade him, and their touch was hostile without either of them intending it. There was a sharp silence, full of ruin and collapse. 'God,' he said, shielding his eyes, 'what an ending . . . I can't believe it.'

'I'm so sorry . . .' She was suffering too, acutely, but such advantage as there is at these times lies with the other, and she accepted it: moreover, the clanging in her head had stopped at last, and there was a bleak relief in that.

He stood up, not looking at her. 'We'd better go home,' he said.

He could, of course, have just left her there to make her own way back to Monks Bridge: she thought she might have done something like that if she were in his shoes. But George remained chivalrous to the end. Tough also: he did not flinch at having to drive fifteen miles home side by side with the woman who had just rejected him; he even managed to talk, doggedly pursuing a narrow trail of neutral subjects.

But she was not fooled: gritted teeth did not constitute a smile, and she denied herself the luxury of believing that because he was brave he would not suffer. When he dropped her at the drove leading to her home she had scarcely stepped out of the car before he was grinding the gears and speeding away, and she knew that today was for him a beginning as well as an end. He had empty deserts to cross, and knowing George as she did she could not pretend to herself that the journey would be short.

She might perhaps still have rescued him, but did not contemplate it for a moment, and it was this absence of regret that triggered her first real quarrel with her father that night, when she broke the news that the engagement was off. Her father could not understand it, and grew heated. Kate suspected that he was disappointed less for George's sake than for his own, because the arrangement had suited him so admirably. When in frustration at her inability to explain she shouted, 'You can't marry somebody just out of gratitude!' he took this as feminine whimsicality, and was acidly sarcastic with her as he sometimes was with her mother.

It was, in a way, the scene that she had not had with George, and it ended in tears all the noisier for having been postponed so long. She was glad, though, that she had not shed them earlier: George would have felt he had caused them, which was not so. Her father, feeling the same, was instantly contrite. 'It'll get sorted,' he kept saying, anxiously soothing, when she went red-eyed to bed, 'never mind – it'll all get sorted.'

She had no doubt that it needed to be: but not in the way he thought, and not easily, and not here.

* * *

# 2

'I hear you're leaving us, then,' Mr Gathergood said, daintily digging the little brass shovel into the sack of brazil nuts.

'Yes. Right after Christmas.'

'Right after Christmas, eh? That soon?'

'Well – new year,' Kate said. 'I start training in the new year . . . And half a dozen oranges, please.'

'Training, eh? Sounds like you're going in for it good and proper. My sister Nellie was a volunteer nurse in the war, but she had trouble with her feet and they sent her home. Think there's going to be a war, do you?'

'I don't know. It's not that really. It's just something I want to do.'

'*Is* it now?' Mr Gathergood sniffed at an orange, goggling at her over the top of it. 'Well, there's a thing. And how much, if you don't mind me asking, do they pay you for being a nurse?'

'Not very much. Very little when you're a probationer. But you get your meals and a bed, and after three months you get a uniform.' Kate recalled the stern stare of the Sister who had interviewed her at Addenbrooke's. It had been plain that she thought Kate a slip of a thing who would faint away when she learned what was involved. 'The typical working week of a probationer, Miss Lutton, amounts to fifty-two hours,' she had said, watching her reaction. 'This is to say nothing of your studies.' When Kate had not only not fainted but seemed to welcome the prospect, there was a look in the Sister's eyes that might have been respect or might have been a gloating anticipation.

'Uniform, eh? By crikey. I should think you're nervous, en't you? Going away from home and all. Mind you, perhaps it's just as well. You know. After all that's happened. Getting away. Must be a bit awkward. You know.'

Kate gazed at Mr Gathergood levelly.

'I just thought – you know – not that I'm saying . . .' Mr Gathergood gulped like an embarrassed tortoise. 'Any figs?'

Well, she thought as she left the shop with her purchases, he was only expressing in his insinuating way what the whole village thought of her. The heartless jilt who had made a fool of a wonderful man whose only crime was to think the world of her: no one had said it to her face, but she got the idea. None of this, she knew, came from George: whatever bitterness he was feeling, he kept to himself.

She supposed they were entitled to their low opinion of her, but she was rather tired of standing in the dock, especially when there was no chance of her putting a case for the defence. And now that she was going away, they had an opinion on that too. Her decision to go and train as a nurse was being viewed as a penance – one step away, as it were, from taking the veil.

Well, she didn't much care if they thought that either; because she had already examined herself very carefully on precisely that point. Was her decision some curious form of self-punishment? She knew it was not when she compared it with the prospect of staying here in Monks Bridge, where she would be continually running into George, where every sight and sound was heavy with association and memory would prey on her daily. That would be punishment indeed.

And she was, besides, simply excited at the thought of the new life ahead of her. Apprehensive too, and not without strong doubts about her capacity to make a success of it: not so long ago the very idea of her doing nursing would have been horrifyingly unthinkable, and her mother and father could still hardly believe it. Strangely enough it was her brother Pip who in his light-hearted way came closest to understanding. 'I suppose it's a bit like putting your head in a lion's mouth,' he said. 'Once you've done it, you'll never be scared any more.'

Christmas was only two days away now: her old life at home would soon be over. 'Now if you don't like it, you come home,' her father said, more and more often as the time for parting approached. 'You don't get on with it, you come straight home, now do you promise?' She promised, but she did not think it would come to that. This was not something she had to do, or was expected to do. It was something she chose to do, and that in itself was a new and fulfilling experience for her.

She had written to both Stella and Helen about it, and had had a reply from Stella full of an earthy encouragement that showed she was getting back to her old self. *I can see you with a bedpan in your hand now,* she concluded, *which reminds me I'd better start dishing up my stew. Good for you, Kate, and God bless.* From Helen, of course, there was no reply yet – she would be on her honeymoon. But Kate was impatient to hear from her. Helen above all would understand what she was about. Or would she? If that last letter was anything to go by, she had changed, and disappointingly.

The village felt she was slinking away because of what had happened with George. But what they didn't see – what was only dimly apparent to her – was that she would not have been going away to start life alone if she had not met Helen, and Stella, and Richard. They supposed she had changed her mind, and did not suspect that her mind had changed. The wide street of Monks Bridge was empty as she walked home, but if there had been anyone there to see they might have noticed a new purpose in her step. For too long she had drifted with the current: now she was about to take the oars into her hands.

# Part Three

## *August 1939*

Gazing out of the bay window at the barrage balloons floating above the rain-soaked roofs, Stella couldn't decide which was worse – Violent Spew, Lily of the Valley or Hitler.

No, she corrected herself, that was unfair on her employer. Violet Drew could be irritating with her airs, and if you got on the wrong side of her she was capable of being a pure unadulterated bitch, but most of the time they rubbed along pretty well together. Besides, she was going through what Doris, her fellow assistant, called in an ominous whisper, 'The Change' and you had to make allowances. Stella hoped she never had hot flushes like Violet Drew's; the only thing the poor woman could do when they came on was sit panting in the back room with two slices of cucumber pressed to her cheeks.

In fact, as long as you could put up with her talking through her nose and putting on a [illegible] [illegible] [illegible] when Stella reached the point of mentally calling her Violent Spew were relatively few.

Unfortunately, today was such a day.

'Stella, don't stand there dreaming, thank you very much. There's plenty of sweeping to be done if you wouldn't mind picking up a broom.'

It would have been better, Stella thought, if she'd just talked in her natural accent, which was pure Docklands. The combination

# ONE

## 1

Gazing out of the salon window at the barrage balloons floating above the rainy roofs, Stella couldn't decide which was worst – Violent Spew, Lily of the Valleys or Hitler.

No, she corrected herself, that was unfair on her employer. Violet Drew could be irritating with her airs, and if you got on the wrong side of her she was capable of being a pure unadulterated bitch, but mostly they rubbed along pretty well together. Besides, she was going through what Doris, her fellow assistant, called in an ominous whisper the Change, and you had to make allowances. Stella hoped she never had hot flushes like Violet Drew's. The only thing the poor woman could do when they came on was sit panting in the back room with two slices of cucumber pressed to her cheeks.

In fact, as long as you could put up with her talking through her nose and putting on a sort of garden-party smirk for her posher customers and munching greedily on a chocolate while she peered over your shoulder, Violet Drew was all right. The days when Stella needed the relief of mentally calling her Violent Spew were relatively few.

Unfortunately, today was such a day.

'Stella, don't stand there dreaming, thank you very much. There's plenty of sweeping to be done if you wouldn't mind picking up a broom.'

It would have been better, Stella thought, if she had just talked in her natural accent, which was pure Docklands. The combination of fishwife and Greer Garson was deadly. Glad of an occupation, she swept the floor. Violent Spew was doing a manicure and Doris was occupied with an ancient crone who came in every week to have her wisps done in an outstandingly unflattering crinkle. She always fell into a deep sleep under the dryer: once Stella had prodded her in a sudden apprehension that she had pegged out under there. It was Saturday, and Monday was a Bank Holiday, but they had hardly any bookings. Something was putting people off having their hair done, whether it was the wretchedly unseasonal weather or the knowledge that war might come at any moment.

Strangely, there didn't seem to be the feverish dread that there had been a year ago, when Mr Chamberlain had flown to Munich to suck up to his nibs. Everyone seemed to agree that this time it was really going to happen: you picked up your gas-mask case as unthinkingly as you picked up your handbag, and when planes flew over, as they often did, you instinctively looked up to see if Goering had jumped the gun. Even the people of Corbett Street seemed to have been deemed worthy of saving from imminent bombs; most of their backyards had Anderson shelters, and everyone had received a leaflet carefully informing them What to Do if War Breaks Out, which more than one wag had amended to the single instruction Put your Head between your Legs and Kiss your Arse Goodbye.

Yet there was more resignation, it seemed, than fear. It had been coming for a long time: Stella sensed that there would even be a sort of relief when the day did come. It would have been untrue to say that she had no fear for herself – she sometimes woke in the night with cold sweats, imagining a horde of bombers droning overhead – but what chiefly troubled her was the thought of her little brothers, Archie and Lennie, being in danger. There had been some evacuation exercises and it was rumoured that schools were not to re-open next month, but it was still not certain, if the children of London were sent out to the country, that Archie and Lennie would be amongst them. Her father held out against the idea: he thought it was some sort of government plot.

Stella wanted them as far away from the capital as possible if there was a war, and she thought that her mother, though she would have ached at parting with them, would have felt the same. But that, of course, was an argument she could not use: it would have been unfair under any circumstances, and with the changed situation at home it was unthinkable.

Home: if you could call it that now. Stella sighed deep inside. It wasn't Violent Spew that was making her feel like a dog left out in the rain. It was the thought that when she took off her overall and dragged her tired legs back to Corbett Street it was to a house made dreadful by the presence of Lily of the Valleys. Who had been Lilian Catmore, and was now Lilian Tranter.

Of course it was traditional to dislike your stepmother, and Stella knew that she would not have taken kindly to anyone who had proposed to take her mother's place as if they were filling a job vacancy. Indeed the very idea of her father marrying again, and less than a year after her mother's death, had set off a blaze of resentment that had still not died, two months after the wedding. But she had managed at least to dampen the flames by forcing herself calmly to consider, again, what her mother would have thought of it. And she had to conclude that yes – God bless her, and God help her – Connie Tranter would have wanted her husband to be happy no matter what. That was the way she was.

And in the same considered spirit Stella had to admit that her father had not rushed into a second marriage in a spirit of amorous abandon. He had deeply loved Stella's mother in his dour fashion and it was plain that he did not feel about Lilian in anything like the same way. But he had, as he haltingly informed Stella, needs: not least the need for someone to look after him. And Stella would have been the first to admit that she was no homemaker.

So taking everything into account Stella sincerely believed that she could have reconciled herself to the fact of having a stepmother. If only it had been *anybody* but Lilian Catmore.

She had tried to be fair to the woman. More precisely, she had tried to disentangle from her dislike of her the elements that were rooted in simple envy – envy of the way she effortlessly turned the chaotic house in Corbett Street into a model of smoothly functioning domesticity in which the luscious glaze on the treacle puddings was rivalled only by the shine on the children's shoes. She even tried to leave aside the memories of how her poor mother could never keep on top of the chores the way Lilian so serenely did: and even to disregard the suspicion that her father was quietly making comparisons in Lilian's favour – a proper wife at last. It was no good. Even when all that was left aside, she was left with a huge and unconquerable loathing of the buxom, slow-blinking, ever-talking creature who haunted the house Stella used to call home. She didn't hate Lily of the Valleys for what she represented. She hated her for herself.

'Yes, cerise is rather outdated now,' Violent Spew was saying to her client. 'This year's shade is definitely maroon, with taupe for the accessories . . .'

This year's shade, Stella thought gloomily, is black.

The trouble was you didn't just get Lilian, though that was bad enough. You got the whole brood into the bargain. Lilian's children by her previous two marriages were all grown and flown, but none of them had flown further than the Mile End Road and they all possessed what seemed to Stella an excessive amount of family feeling. A day seldom went by without a visit from at least one of the ten, or was it eleven? Stella preferred not to make an accurate reckoning. The important thing to note was that they were all as awful as Lilian thought they were wonderful, with marks for exceptional repulsiveness shared between Olwen, a spirit of pure malice attached to a pair of ponderous breasts whose idea of endearing herself to her stepsister was to call her Sheila to her face and Whatshername to everyone else, and Norman, a young man with an old face who not only stared fixedly at Stella's legs but repeatedly dropped his dandruffy comb on the floor so that he could hunker down and try for a glimpse up her skirt. And all ten (or eleven) had already bred precociously, so that they came armed with numerous small ill-behaved children on whom Lilian could practise her motherly skills. Lilian's motherly skills were sickening in their proficiency. You might have thought that she was up for a cup in being indulgent, patient and self-sacrificing, not to mention doting. 'It's nice to see them with so much energy,' she would drone, whilst some demonic brat trampled across her lap swinging the bread knife over its head and screaming for a tenth helping of jam tarts.

'. . . Yes, we shall be closed on Monday, of course,' Violent Spew was saying. 'I remember my father telling me there was no such thing as Bank Holidays in his day. People weren't afraid of hard work then. They have things too easy nowadays in my opinion . . .'

Stella didn't much like children and never had. She was perfectly capable of loving children as individuals – Archie and Lennie, and Auntie Bea's little Geoffrey, for example – but as a species she found them and their ways highly resistible. There had never been any difficulty about this before. But once Lily of the Valleys was under your roof you had to convert to child-worship or else be persecuted as an unbeliever.

Amazingly, even her dour father had fallen for it. 'Ah, we've had a little monkey round ours today,' she had heard him say to one of his friends, in reference to the jammy fingermarks on his pullover – and he said it fondly, sentimentally even. She supposed she should have been pleased at this softening in him. But she couldn't help remembering her own childhood, when she had had to tiptoe past the door of the front room where he and his comrades were setting the world to rights. Back then you hesitated to go to him with a cut knee in case such a triviality impeded the revolution. Now he romped around with his brand-new grandchildren on his shoulders singing nonsense rhymes. It was a rum world, and she couldn't pretend she wasn't a little bitter; but she could have borne her father's belated transformation into the Jolly Miller if they had only left her out of it. But something about Stella's indifference to children – and also perhaps the fact that at twenty-one years of age she hadn't had any of her own – got the collective goat of Lilian and her tribe. They wouldn't let it alone, and just the other night it had driven Stella almost to snapping point.

The monstrous Olwen was visiting – she was the most fertile

of the lot, and there were children hanging from the curtain rails – and she and her mother were pitying the fate of a mutual acquaintance who had omitted to reproduce and now, old and ill, relied on kindly neighbours to get her shopping.

'She's very down in the dumps all the time, poor soul, but she would be, wouldn't she?' Lilian said. 'Look at her – she never had any children. She's got nothing. No grandchildren, no one to look after her now she's old, of course that's not a reason for having children, you have them because you love them and because it's natural, but that's a sort of extra, you know, that they'll always be there when you get old, and then there's the grandchildren who perk you up when they come to see you. I mean I think that's partly her trouble, a lot of the reason why she's poorly is because there's something missing in her life.' Lilian paused to blow the nose of a passing infant, examining the results in the handkerchief with a connoisseur's appreciation. 'I mean, she did get married, her husband's dead now but I think they were married for something like twenty-five years and yet she's nothing to show for it, the only thing I can think is perhaps they couldn't have children which must be a terrible thing, don't you think, Stella?'

'Well, at least they won't be gathering round her deathbed hoping to come in for her spoons,' said Stella. It was harsh; but the warm sweet porridge that was Lilian's conversation always brought out the vinegar in her. 'Hoy – don't touch that, you'll break it,' she added, as the snotty child bore down on a little vase on the mantelshelf that had been a favourite of her mother's – about the only nice thing she had been able to keep.

'Oh, Sheila, he's only playing,' whined Olwen, giving Stella her most thorough, head-to-foot look. 'He won't hurt anything, will you, duck?'

The brat gave an evil sidelong glance and then lunged at the vase. Just in time, Stella snatched it away from the outstretched paw.

'I'm going to put this out of the way,' Stella said, and did. The child had screaming tantrums all over the room, whilst Lilian and Olwen fawned over him like courtiers, apologizing for the fact that the world was not exclusively tailored to suit his every whim. His grandmother pacified him at last with home-made toffee. It was no wonder the whole clan was so well-fleshed. The child was no more than four and already had a behind like a sandbag.

'You just have to be patient with them,' Lilian said, caressing the gnawing head. 'You have to remember they're only children.'

'Small chance of forgetting,' Stella said, discovering that her handbag had been ransacked. 'Someone's been in my ruddy bag now.'

'They're just curious,' Lilian crooned. 'Shows their little minds are developing. Into everything they are. You're little scamps, aren't you? What'll you be like when you get to school, I wonder? Do you want to go to school?'

'No, I'm not going,' the child said, stickily.

'He's not going, he says. Listen to him.' Lilian and Olwen began their monotonous, mirthless, bosom-quaking laughter. It went on and on. Tears streamed. You'd think the kid was Max Miller. 'Stella, did you hear him? I said did he want to go to school and he said he's not going. Oh – oh they do make me laugh . . .' On they chortled. The child looked smug: no doubt he was thinking up another entirely commonplace and unamusing thing to say. This time they would probably give him a standing ovation. They'd throw ruddy bouquets.

'Oh dear,' Lilian said, wiping her eyes. 'That's what I mean. I can't imagine life without children.'

'It's easy if you try,' Stella muttered, refilling her handbag. There was definitely sixpence missing.

'Ah, you'll find out,' Lilian said. Stella knew what was coming: they were always saying it to her; but she wasn't sure she could stand it today. Don't say it, she silently begged. Lilian said it.

'It'll be your turn next.'

It was the way they said it as much as the words: the mixture of dolefulness, archness and grim satisfaction. And then Olwen topped it by lifting her chins and informing her, 'I used to be like you, Sheila. Didn't think I wanted them at all. But it's different when they're your own. You'll find out.'

Stella did not at all enjoy being told that she was like Olwen in any respect; but it was the mindless, cooing certitude of it all that made her wild.

'I've got nothing against children,' she snapped, 'but I don't see why I should start popping them out like some bloody sausage machine just because it's what everybody else does. If I thought life was as – as predictable as you make it out to be I'd chuck myself in the river, I swear I would.'

Lilian and Olwen did nothing but look at her like two faintly affronted sheep; but Stella suffered for her outburst nonetheless. That night her father tackled her alone.

'I hear you lost your rag with your stepmother today,' he said. 'What was that all about?'

'Oh, nothing. Just don't like being told what to do with my life by people who've never done anything but rinse nappies.' Stella's anger was usually as swift to die as to rouse, but not today.

'I don't like it, Stella. I thought we'd talked about this. I know it might have been hard at first, getting used to Lilian as your stepmother. But she's been good for me and good for this family.' For some time after his wife's death Jack Tranter had been diffident, almost feeble; but now he was very sure of himself. He had a new wife who thought he was the bee's knees – Lilian liked men manly, which meant strong, silent and out of the kitchen – and who waited on him hand and foot. Possessing no opinions of her own, Lilian was devoutly respectful of his political activities, which she admired as men's business: the front-room committee meetings were now regaled with home-made refreshments. It was no wonder that he was feeling pretty pleased with life, and sufficiently confident to tick off the daughter whose temper he had always been a little wary of.

'It's when they talk about kids like that,' Stella said. 'Like I'm just the same as them. It gets on my wick.'

Had he not seen the world in terms of absolutes, and had he been a little more receptive to the idea that emotions can be mixed, her father might have recognized that this was the moment to temporize: to express some sympathy, whilst asking her to bear with Lilian, and so on – she would readily have met him halfway. But he wouldn't: unaware that he was steadily losing his daughter, he took up a fixed position, from which she could only grow more distant.

'That's no excuse, Stella. You wouldn't have talked to your mother like that.'

'Mum would never have said anything so damn stupid.'

He frowned. 'I don't like that tone, Stella. I don't know – something's changed you. Sometimes it's as if you think you're too good for us.'

It was, she knew, as strong a condemnation as was possible to her father, with his intense class loyalties. It also struck her, irritated as she was, as every bit as dull and narrow-minded as Lilian's droning about babies.

'Well, roll on the revolution, Dad, that's all I can say,' Stella answered. 'If that's what it'll take to knock that chip off your shoulder then it gets my vote.'

It was a hateful thing to say: hurtful also – her father was silenced. She felt guilty, and the guilt ground at her again now, as she finished sweeping the salon and began collecting the towels for the laundry. But the guilt was unproductive: such a thing couldn't be unsaid. In reparation she had tried to be nicer to Lilian, but it was all fake: to truly get along with her you would have to become like her.

Never, thought Stella, never will I have children.

The ancient woman's hairdo was finished, and having tied a headscarf around the brittle curls she tottered off. Doris, a sighing wrung-out young woman in spectacles, sidled up to Stella. Violent Spew frowning on chitchat amongst her staff, they had evolved an almost soundless manner of talking, like convicts.

'Going anywhere nice tonight?' Doris never did anything, and took a sort of plaintive pleasure in other people's experiences.

'Don't think so. Just go to bed early, I reckon.'

'Eh? What about that fella you were seeing?'

'Oh, that's nothing.' Stella had been desultorily walking out with a pleasant pale young man who worked in a tripe-boiling factory and had to bathe for an hour every night in consequence. There were whispers about him because he had been seen to wear suede shoes, an apparently infallible sign of being a nancy boy; but Stella doubted this. He was just a bit eccentric, and generally not interested. They enjoyed each other's company, and parted without pain. Of course, that was another thing they wouldn't understand – that a woman and a man could simply be friends.

'Miserable weather for going out, anyway,' Doris said. 'It doesn't seem like summer at all, does it?'

'No,' Stella said, and a sigh deeper than any of Doris's went through her as she thought of orchards, and of a handful of well-worn letters, the most recent several months old and with a look about it of being the last of its kind. 'No, it's not like summer at all.'

## 2

Richard stood on the steps of the National Gallery, looking out at Trafalgar Square and wondering how this scene would look in a year's time.

But for the unseasonal rain, it might have been any August Saturday. Visitors thronged the square, pointing box Brownies, feeding the pigeons, posing with Landseer's lions. The only sign of anything untoward was in the sky, where the fat fishlike shapes of barrage balloons diminished into the distance, and it was remarkable how quickly the eye got accustomed to those.

To Richard, though, everything today seemed to have a heightened and artificial look. The familiar landmarks were like larger-than-life models of themselves: Big Ben, seen from a window of the gallery foyer, might have been itself a painting, framed and glazed. This was doubtless a consequence of his feeling, which was strong though undefined, that a crisis was imminent and that its consequences would be greater than anyone guessed. This was partly why he had come into town today, to see the National and the British Museum: he felt this might be the last chance to see them, perhaps for a long time, possibly for ever.

Richard expressed himself flippantly, but he was capable of feeling profoundly, and he possessed an intuition that served him quite as well, for example, as the reasoned deductions of Helen, who followed events with a historian's attention. This time last year he had shrugged off the talk of war because he did not feel it would happen, but now he knew it was coming and had no illusions about it. His generation had been chosen for the fire. It did not strike him as worthwhile being bitter about this. He supposed that mistakes had been made, perhaps catastrophic ones, and that the stupidity and greed now at large might ultimately crush them all. But he didn't think himself immune. He couldn't even have said with certainty that he wouldn't have been a Hitler, if placed in that wretch's position.

This was the sort of contention that would have set off a tremendous discussion with Helen, back at Cambridge; and would probably have ended with her accusing him of lack of principles. He did have these, but he regarded them as a fortunate gift rather than something to be smug about. Life was wholly random – that was his creed in a nutshell, intolerable to Helen's orderly mind.

Helen. He often thought of her, though he had not seen her since the orchard summer and she had scarcely returned a letter since writing to inform him of her marriage. Helen's abrupt transformation into provincial *hausfrau* had greatly surprised him: that he was not even more surprised was due to his belief that people were not required to be consistent. As it was, he still admired her ability to make clean-cut decisions. Journalism, ambition, independence, these were no doubt part of Cambridge; and once she was out in the real world and committed to another course she had neatly disposed of them. And him too, he presumed, as he had not been invited to the wedding.

He had been disappointed about that, for he had wanted to wish her well, but in view of that decisiveness he accepted it. He had always seen Helen as a person superior to him in all respects, her friendship with him engaging only a very small part of her. That, at least, had been the Helen he knew: what she was like as the wife of a solicitor in a country town he could only guess, with a certain perplexity. One thing he was certain of: she would do it well.

Besides, she must have fallen in love with the man – head over heels, judging by the swiftness of it; and Richard was romantic enough, or realistic enough, to believe that this altered everything.

Well, he had seen the British Museum and the National . . . What now? There was the Abbey – but he decided on lunch first. His reasons for this trip were real enough, but he had other reasons for drawing it out. He hesitated to put it so crudely even to himself, but the fact was he wanted to postpone for as long as possible the moment when he would have to go home to his parents' house.

Since the beginning of the year Richard had been employed as a junior master at a prep school on the south coast. Such a post was the traditional refuge of middle-class young men who had not distinguished themselves at university. Richard's predecessor had been found dead in the bath after breaking his shaving mirror and cutting his wrists, as his fellow masters had eagerly informed him. Richard did not fear being driven to a similar fate. The school was no worse than most such establishments – a little dingy, rather draughty, very gossipy, and not at all as grand as it pretended to be. He didn't mind it and was faintly amused at the comic-novel appropriateness of it all.

His parents, and his brother Maurice, were not. All they could say of it was that it was respectable – which wasn't saying much, as they routinely averted their eyes from anything that wasn't. It certainly wasn't anything to boast about – a consideration that weighed heavily with his mother in particular: the salary was a pittance and, most importantly, the post had that air of lurking failure about it. 'Well then, I'm perfectly suited to it,' he said to them, in that angrily frivolous tone which they always called forth in him, and which he hated himself for. They shook their heads, deploring the taste of such remarks, and understanding was as far away as the moon.

'You don't need to place yourself in this position, that's what baffles me,' Maurice told him. He was married now, with a little Maurice safely deposited within the healthy womb of the tennis-playing Phyllis, and there was a new severity about his pronouncements. 'You had the chance of an excellent position in the City. I went to a good deal of trouble to keep that offer open for you, but never mind that now. The fact is you could still get quite a promising post there – I could arrange it for you with a word in the right ear. This schoolmastering business may be all very well for chaps who really haven't the family or the connections, but for someone like you it just looks like – well, I'll be plain with you, Richard, it looks like you're deliberately throwing it in our faces.'

He was stung by this; but here his habit of flippancy backfired on him, because he could not explain to them that he genuinely liked teaching – they would think he was mocking them. Besides, it was a skill that he had stumbled on by mere chance, when he had looked after the fruit-pickers' children last summer, and lucky accidents were not in his family's scheme of things. One planned the future. And presumably, therefore, knew everything about oneself: knew at eighteen what would satisfy at fifty.

Well, one disadvantage of being a prep schoolmaster he was prepared to concede: in the summer holiday he had to go home. Foreseeing this, he had thought of spending the summer in seaside digs near the school, such being all he could afford, but had unwisely mentioned it. The idea had caused such an outburst of consternation at home that he had given in. They wanted him there so they could work on him.

He was being unfair, of course. He always was: sometimes it seemed his life was one long unavailing struggle to be fair to his family.

Richard went into an A.B.C. off Charing Cross Road and ordered one of their shilling lunches: Cornish pasty with mash and cabinet pudding. The place was full of typists and counter clerks and headscarved shoppers. Richard pictured his mother's shudder of loathing, and wondered whether that was partly why he liked coming in here so much. Was he such a misfit? Were even his everyday habits merely feeble gestures of rebellion?

Richard had long ago concluded that his family was mad, and tried to adjust his ideas accordingly. However, perceiving that your family was mad did not make it any less your family.

He and Maurice were late children. Their parents had prudently postponed reproduction, and as a result were now elderly. Though this cannot have been the intention, it increased the burden of expectation. When they had waited so long to have you, you ought to turn out well; and not to turn out well was to break their old hearts. Maurice's father was mostly retired now. He was well off, and suffered from dyspepsia. He was still nominally a director of his old broking firm in the City, and occasionally went there to offer the benefits of his experience and, as he said, keep his hand in. What these activities consisted of, Richard had only the dimmest idea. His father's profession had always been to him a mystery without allurement.

As for his father's days of leisure, they were mostly spent in a curious and rather touching assault on the classics of English literature. When younger, Mr Marwood had never cultivated any hobbies or pursuits, which in his retirement he would have had the opportunity to broaden and expand. He had to start from scratch. So he set himself to read his way steadily through all the books that an Englishman ought to have read, but for which he had never had time. Classic novels attracted him particularly, perhaps because they were weighty: reading them really felt like doing something. He went head-on at Scott and Thackeray and Dickens and George Eliot. He said, quite baldly, that he wanted to fit it all in before he died. He had moved on to Trollope now – the complete works. Richard had diffidently suggested that he sample just a few books from each author, but Mr Marwood would not entertain that idea. He seemed to think he might miss something – as if writers were confidence tricksters. By his reading chair he kept slips of paper on which he noted down the names of the numerous characters in the books so as to keep track of them. Sometimes Richard had the notion of secretly adding invented names to the lists to see what would happen.

But he was fond of his father, and would have been even fonder if encouraged. Unfortunately Mr Marwood was almost fanatically undemonstrative. When younger he had treated fatherhood as an exercise in setting an example – an example of upright, stiff-collared, unsmiling, practical masculinity. He worked hard, made much money, earned the respect of his peers, had an adoring wife, and had his unassailable place in the world. Richard was as impressed by this household god as his father wanted him to be, and it was only later that it occurred to him that there was an element of evasion in it. Simply by being so conspicuously successful, you got out of having to give advice or guidance. What should you do? Be like me. I have never put a foot wrong: just look and learn.

It worked very well as long as you wanted the same things as he did – like Maurice. When Maurice and his father stood side by side in front of the fire with their pipes, chins jutting, unspeaking, they were communicating at a level beyond words. Unfortunately Richard, not wishing to be a facsimile of his father, had only words to attempt communication, and they were not the right ones.

Paradoxically he often found himself rather at ease with his father, simply because there was such a gulf between them. Though Mr Marwood disapproved of everything Richard did and in his costive way seemed actually to dislike him, they did not quarrel, because a quarrel requires at least some common ground to be fought over. Sometimes Richard took a fantastical delight in their conversations: his father's conservatism had so hardened with age that he came out with quite delirious suggestions. He advocated the reconquest of Ireland. He wanted to do away with trial by jury, saying the verdict should be delivered by judges, whose moral authority would make them incorruptible.

It was pure Lewis Carroll – but at least he could bear it on that level. With his mother it was more difficult. Being affectionate, Richard had hidden from himself what his mother was really like: the only alternative was to see that she was a monstrous, irredeemable snob. This he could not do without partly destroying himself, and so he took refuge in bafflement – even struggled to find her amusing.

This was just possible with regard to her mania for cleanliness, which might have been a family joke if they were the sort of family who had them. But even interior laughter had a bitter edge when the cause of it was a woman in her fifties crawling about the floor on her hands and knees inspecting the sitting-room skirting boards for specks of dirt. Not that she did the cleaning herself, of course: even in these times the Marwoods still kept a maid, though the current slave was a Jewish refugee from Austria and, naturally, unsatisfactory. To hear Mrs Marwood talk about the servant problem was to be wafted into a world that should only have existed in back issues of *Punch*. She talked about declining standards, but the fact was her standards were insanely exacting. The obsession with the skirting boards was the crown of it all. Insofar as Richard was aware that there were such things, he supposed they were meant to trap dirt. For his mother they were an emblem of character. Dust on them meant, presumably, moral decrepitude. Hence the crawlings and peerings. The expression on her face as she did this was far from lovable. What made it worse was that she was a woman of rigid decorum, who would cut a person dead for wearing the wrong shoes and would have jumped out of a second-floor window rather than be seen without her permanent wave, face powder and matching accessories intact.

Richard had dipped into Freud at Cambridge, where the good doctor had an enthusiastic band of disciples, and had not found it difficult to apply what he found to his mother's Lady Macbeth scrubbings; that he had never known his parents so much as peck each other on the cheek probably fitted in somewhere too, but he did not care to follow up his conclusions. He already felt disloyal on account of a leap of perception that he had made as a public schoolboy at the age of fifteen, when the mannerisms of the headmaster's wife had reminded him of his mother. The headmaster's wife was a grocer's daughter who had married above her. From then on he knew what his mother's exaggerated gentility meant and, to his shame, noticed its crudities. Previously, with a child's ingenuousness, he had supposed his mother to be what she made herself out to be – pretty much on a footing with the King and Queen. In truth she was as vulgar as only an idle and wealthy woman without cultivation or taste can be. He knew this in his secret heart, and would have knocked down anyone who had dared to say it to him.

As to what she felt about him, it was hard to tell through the screen of pretentious propriety; but her feelings seemed to depend on what he did rather than what he was. She was waiting with a pained patience for him to do the right thing: in the meantime she talked of her friends' sons who were already doing it. She was rather fond of young men, and even fancied, when they condescended to her, that they were smitten. With a slight change of emphasis, this might have been charming and amusing. A step across the line into eccentricity would have made her a more rounded human being, but Mrs Marwood loathed eccentrics. Convention with her was not a set of received ideas, unthinkingly taken on board, but a dogma. She was strenuous about it.

'Richard, you *cannot* wear that jacket to the Watsons'.'

'Why not? I have a tie.'

'But it is a sports jacket.' She had a thumping way of talking. 'It's not the correct wear for the afternoon.'

'Oh, nonsense, I wore it for the open day at Felling Court. That was in the afternoon.'

She raised her eyes, long sufferingly, at the mention of the school where he worked. 'Schoolmasters wear any shabby old thing. No one expects any different. For an afternoon party, if there is to be tennis, you should wear a blazer.'

'Oh, I'm not going to play. Just loll about. Anyway the Watsons aren't like that. They know better than to insist on that sort of formality.' Perhaps unconsciously, he was trying to needle her.

'You should wear a blazer with flannels. Or else whites. Whites are acceptable even if you're not going to play.' She was all serenely pained determination.

'Well, don't take me wrong, I'd like to play. Just the difficulty of getting a partner. I do lose so. Usually they send me to look for the lost balls in the weeds. I think they hope that, like Captain Oates, I won't come back. It's quite nice out there though. You can botanize and chase butterflies. Find the source of rivers and so on.'

She took no notice. This sort of talk was part of her son's general unsatisfactoriness to Mrs Marwood, who believed that men should be boastful and keen, also straightforward. She made him change the jacket.

If only, he thought as he put aside his pudding and lit a cigarette, if only . . . The thought stopped there. If only what?

He liked teaching, but he knew that he favoured certain pupils: self-confident little beasts he left to their own devices, which was not the right way to go about it. Prep school was in the main a fairly tepid bath before the freezing plunge of public school, but still tradition and convention ruled, and he had tried to make innovations that were reproved: he did not think his tenure at Felling Court would be long. If he chafed at his family's designation of him as a black sheep, he was no less dissatisfied with himself for his inability to find his own garden and cultivate it. If only . . .

Well, his thoughts did tend in a certain direction at those words, but it was backward rather than forward. The experience that had meant most to him was the summer he had spent in the orchard country of the fens.

Richard paid his bill and tipped the waitress and went out into the damp rackety streets. The memory of that summer went with him, and he indulged it.

It had, of course, come often to him in the past year: but at Felling Court it had seemed like a dream, and at his parents' home it was scarcely to be admitted even as a silent thought. There were pursed lips at the very mention of that summer. Recalling, in the chintzy rooms at Abbotsleigh, that he had met and loved a fruit-picker from the East End seemed like an invitation to an earthquake or a thunderbolt.

Loved: yes. It had been a while before he had allowed himself to admit this, because of his self-hatred. The night he and Stella had spent together in the meadow had been directly followed by the news of her mother's death: she had given herself to him whilst her mother lay dying. He had added ghastliness to tragedy, and poisoned the purity of grief, and whatever there had been of good between them had been turned foully inside out. She had, of course, said nothing of this to him: she did not need to; his self-disgust was complete.

While this lasted, he could not see his feelings for her in any clear light. He was sure at the time that he had lain down with her in a spirit of sheer love . . . but then love was all too easily used by men as an excuse for behaving badly. That she had acted of her own free will carried no weight with him either. The fact remained that she had gone home in anguish and that for at least part of the anguish he was responsible, and there was no dignifying such a mess with fine words about love.

He supposed moreover that she must hate him, and felt it reasonable that she should. He had made tentative attempts at writing, to which at first she could reply only incoherently: her grief was all. When a letter that made sense did come, it was friendly and neutral and superficial, as if she had decided that forgetting the whole thing was the only option. He took his cue from this and warned himself not to pester her with letters; but he wrote all the same, and that was when he began to mistrust himself less, and to trust the feelings of the orchard summer more.

And the memories of that time had been insistent this summer. The mere fact of it being summer was responsible perhaps, for the weather this year had been no idyll, hot enough to buckle railway lines in June and now a stormy downpour. Certainly spending a month at home was enough to drive him into the arms of memory. Disastrously as it had ended, the summer of the orchards and strawberries, of Kate and Helen and Stella, of a tea party on the roof and a pirate ship in the fields, was a time when he had felt intensely alive. At Abbotsleigh he felt three parts dead, and the remainder was itching frustration. There was only the same old circle, and newcomers were carefully vetted. A widow with a young marriageable daughter had recently moved to the district and after a due period of inspection been accepted: Phyllis, Maurice's wife, had begun good-naturedly matchmaking for Richard when he came to tea one day. Phyllis was rather a kind and jolly person who adored Maurice and wore the expression of a smacked dog when, as often happened, he was short with her. 'Now I wonder how we can throw you together,' she had said, cheerfully plotting. 'Perhaps dinner – with no other guests . . .'

'Poor woman,' Richard said, 'what has she done to deserve that?'

'Oh, I think she likes you, Richard. Women can tell. And I'm sure you'll like her when you get to know her. You're awfully well suited—'

'Don't talk nonsense, Phyllis,' Maurice said with finality. 'Richard can't afford to marry on his salary.' He shook his newspaper and breathed hard, glaring. That was the end of that. Richard felt sorry for Phyllis. She was still a big, hearty girl, but in twenty years' time there was going to be nothing left of her.

Richard was a dreamer, but not as much of a dreamer as his family chose to believe. Retreating into memories of the orchard summer did not mean he thought there was any way back there: he knew perfectly well that it could not be more than an interlude, which was why he had plunged into it so deeply. But if he was not about to go and live in a tent beneath the apple boughs, he certainly felt himself impelled towards an emotional decision. There was no practical choice to be made between the orchards and Abbotsleigh, but it was a different matter inside him.

He was wandering about theatreland and thinking of these things when all at once he saw Stella.

He had paused outside Drury Lane, where *Dancing Years* was playing, and was wondering whether he could get a matinee ticket. The rain was coming down hard now, and there were many umbrellas out, and it was under one of these that he glimpsed the face of Stella, across the street.

Darting out, he nearly went under the wheels of a cab. By the time he had got to the other side of the street, amid shouts and squealing brakes, he saw that she was already crossing the next street. She had on a black coat, and seemed to be in a hurry, walking fast with head down.

She had fifty yards on him, the streets were busy and noisy, there was no chance of shouting to her. But he managed to keep her in sight and at the entrance to Covent Garden he caught up with her.

'Stella!' His heart lifted as he said it and then sank horribly as she walked on. He reached out to touch her arm and she looked round at him from under the umbrella.

'Oh – I'm terribly sorry – I thought . . .'

He stood stammering in the rain while the woman who looked very like but was not Stella frowned at him and hurried on her way.

Same shade of hair, he thought, same shape of face, but different eyes: wholly different. Dull, narrow eyes, with no spark.

People were staring at him: he was drenched. He didn't care. He found that his heart had recovered that buoyant feeling. The woman had not been Stella, but it made no difference: the impact on him was explosive just the same.

He began to saunter through the market, thinking, or rather letting thoughts wash over him like the rain. Without actually believing in fate, he felt there was such a thing as meaningful coincidence; and the way that the memory of Stella had thrust itself upon him, in the midst of his gloom and dissatisfaction, was surely one such. His feeling was rather like that of at last remembering a name or a tune that has been eluding you for days – yet vastly more intense. And it was that very intensity, he realized, that had been missing from his life since the parting in the fens: indeed, once locked in the dreary prison of his family one could forget that it ever existed. One got used to the dimness and dust – almost took them as natural. But now a window had been thrown open, and he saw again what he had lost.

It didn't have to be like this: not at all. He came to a stall bearing punnets of strawberries, and it was as if he had seen a vision.

'Where were they grown, do you know?' he asked the stallholder.

'Kent,' the stallholder said. 'Or somewhere.'

Richard laughed. Well, there were limits to coincidence. He bought three punnets of strawberries and then, sheltering under the portico, fumbled in his wallet for the letter he kept there.

# TWO

## 1

It was the most dismal Bank Holiday anyone could remember, with leaden skies and almost incessant rain. For Stella, however, the day seemed to be bathed in the same magnificent sunshine that had marked her days in the orchards.

It had really begun on the Saturday before, when she had made her foot-dragging way home from Violet Drew's to find a gift awaiting her. It had come in a delivery van, which was such a rarity in Corbett Street that everyone had turned out to look at it. The only van they ever saw there was a steely grey affair that periodically came to take away Mrs Noakes at number sixteen when she had one of her turns, which usually involved taking off all her clothes and trying to throw Mr Noakes out of the window.

The bouquet was beautiful but it was the accompanying strawberries that appealed most eloquently to Stella. The scent and colour of them brought back many feelings – she was surprised how many. Richard's note was short.

> *I thought I saw you in London today – mistake. If I should come into town again on Monday, do you suppose I could see the real you? I'll be outside Liverpool Street Station at eleven. Don't worry if you can't. Richard.*

That was her first thought: she couldn't. The flowers and strawberries and the rush of pleasure they gave her were all very well but she couldn't meet Richard because . . . well, because it wouldn't do. Whatever they had had together belonged to another time and place, if to any time and place at all. Life was real and life was earnest and life did not include Richard. And that was to say nothing of the dreadful way it had all ended. They couldn't meet again after that – could they?

She shared the strawberries with her family. Only her stepmother declined to eat any: strawberries brought her out in a rash. This fact gave Stella a curious satisfaction. Lilian was very keen, however, to know where they had come from. 'An old friend' would not do for her, understandably enough. Old friends did not send such gifts, at least not where they came from. But Stella had kept the note to herself, and wouldn't be drawn. Lilian's influence was already overpowering. She wasn't going to be party to Stella's memories as well.

She learned something that night: your mind carried on working when you were asleep. She went to bed glowing, touched, reminiscent – but wholly convinced that meeting Richard was not a good idea. She woke in the morning to the sound of Dot's snores, and to a firm conviction that she would meet him no matter what.

If she had dreamt about him and the orchard summer, she did not remember the dreams. But something had been settled within her. Most importantly, she found she could think about that last night in a light no longer made garish by her mother's death. It was significant on its own terms. So significant, indeed, that she didn't know how she would feel when she met him – whether, for example, she would be crushed by shyness and embarrassment. They were lovers who had separated without properly parting – or ever acknowledging themselves to be lovers. It was all very strange. But Stella was not a person who needed to have things cut and dried. And even though she could not begin to imagine what the meeting would be like – she was prepared for the possibility of its being a complete disaster – she was determined on going through with it.

Sunday bolstered the determination. On Sunday mornings Lilian attended some peculiar tin-roofed chapel that offered the religion of her homeland, but she was always back in time to begin the ritual of Sunday dinner. In the Tranter household there had nearly always been some sort of meat on a Sunday, even if it was bread and margarine the rest of the week, a fact for which Stella was appropriately grateful. But the way Lilian made, as it were, a meal of it was enough to put you off Yorkshire pudding for life. Whatever the cut of meat, Lilian would discuss its advantages and shortcomings at length. She would discourse on potatoes. 'I like a nice floury potato myself. I don't mean the sort that all just crumble away to nothing, you know, they're not very nice and the funny thing is you can't even make a good mash out of those, which you'd think you would but the thing is they go soggy and really it's a good firm potato you want for mash, but for roasting I like them a little bit floury inside but nice and brown on the outside . . .' There was no respite when she took the joint down to the baker's on the corner to be cooked. A lot of women would sit outside the Feathers shelling peas while they waited for their joints, but Lilian came home and polished up the cutlery. She favoured vinegar for this, but there were many other methods and she discussed them all. Stella understood now that 'bored to tears' was not just a phrase. Sometimes when Lilian showed no signs of ceasing to talk, ever, she felt an actual sob rise up in her chest.

But the thought of meeting Richard tomorrow, she found, helped a great deal. Also it was a sort of flag of no surrender. Lilian peppered her domestic monologues with references to Stella's future. 'You'll have your own way of doing that when you're married.' 'You'll find that out when you have children of your own.' In Lilian's mind Stella's destiny was mapped out. She was going to get married, live round the corner like all Lilian's progeny, and be part of one big baby-rearing cutlery-polishing family who all knew each other's business from morning to night. In this scheme of things, Richard and everything connected with him had no place. That alone would have been enough to have drawn her to him.

It wasn't that alone, though. The scent of strawberries and a few words on a sheet of notepaper acted on Stella like a revelation: she had never supposed her memories of that summer to be anything but vivid, but now they surged in on her as if a mental dam had burst. It seemed to her that they were all good: it seemed to her that she had hardly been living at all since that summer.

She couldn't have that time back, of course. But she would snatch eagerly at even a fragment of it. The times fostered the mood. At any moment war might fall upon them. A single day, a single hour, could have the significance of a lifetime – this was something Stella had always believed.

If Richard was an exotic in the pinafored scenarios of her stepmother, he was no less so to her father. Jack Tranter could be hugely obtuse, but he cottoned on to the meaning of the strawberries, and when on Sunday night she mentioned that she was going out tomorrow he only hesitated a moment before pronouncing, 'It's that posh fella you met last summer, ain't it? When you went to the country with Will and his lot.'

Uncle Will, the country, posh people – everything he disliked was in that speech except Trotskyites.

'Yes, he – wants to say hello, you know, for old times' sake.'

'I don't like it, Stella. I don't like it at all. What's he after?'

'How do you mean?' Stella said, though she knew what he meant. Whilst he rhapsodized about electrification and steel production, her father had a curiously old-fashioned morality. The paper he read carried cartoons of toffs in top hats and monocles, and he had an idea of the upper classes as continually bent on having their twirly-moustached way with young working girls. She was momentarily amused then, remembering the night in the meadow, grew uncomfortable. Her father's solemn, pale eyes dwelt on her.

'He's just an old friend. It's not anything,' she said. Faced with her father's unsmiling grimness, she grew defiant. 'We used to have a laugh together, that time in the fens, so we thought we'd meet. God knows there aren't that many laughs around these days.'

'All very well to laugh when the Fascists are on the move,' her father said. 'All very well to laugh when the working people of this country are going to be thrown to the wolves once more to save the face of their capitalist masters . . .' He was away, and she was free. He would forget all about her while he ranted.

She wanted to look her best for the day, but her resources were limited. Round here people couldn't make much of themselves. Women wore the same print frock until the armpits rotted away, and the men's best suits were permanently creased crosswise from being folded up in the pawnshop. Stella had one decent tailor-made skirt that she wore to Violet Drew's, and a secondhand jacket that looked halfway smart when she tied it with a belt that had belonged to one of her brothers. What would really complete the outfit would be a soft beret, which she didn't possess. Dot did, but she was notoriously mean about lending her things. Stella spent much of Sunday night plotting bribes and blackmail, but in the end Dot surprised her by saying simply, 'Here, take it.' Adding afterwards, however, with an evil look, 'It ain't your bonce they're interested in looking at, you know.'

As it turned out she was not the only one gallivanting that day. Most of the local pubs had Bank Holiday beanos: the regulars clubbed together to hire a coach, loaded it with beer and went off to Southend or Margate for the day. Stella's father had never participated in such events, but this time he was persuaded at the last minute by Lilian's dreadful leg-watching son Norman, who was a regular at a specially unsavoury place called the Exhibition. It was strange how Lilian's lot could persuade her father into these things. Stella's poor mother would get moralized at if she so much as suggested a pot of cockles as a treat. Stella felt both sad and angry when she thought of it; but she also felt relieved that her father was going to be off on a junket today too. Lilian, of course, was staying at home to do wifely things whilst being climbed on by grandchildren.

And the Bank Holiday morning came, rainy, strange, war-threatened: and, for Stella, wonderful. She never forgot that day and even as it was happening she had a sense of its events as clear and separate and shapely, like memories in the making.

Richard was waiting for her outside Liverpool Street, under an umbrella. A man with an umbrella often looks hangdog and even foolish, but what struck her was that he appeared exactly as he had done in the fens, under the summer sun. Then they met under the umbrella and after an awkward moment made a grab at each other's hand, laughing.

'It is good to see you – you look awfully well.'

'So do you . . . I should have brought a brolly, shouldn't I?'

'What a day!'

The rain coursed and streamed. It was what Auntie Bea called 'that wet rain', noisy and penetrating. But instead of depressing, it made them laugh.

'There's a Territorial camp near us at home – the poor chaps are flooded out. I say, shall we go somewhere? You don't look wet at all. I'm so glad – I didn't know whether you'd come . . . Was it difficult to get away?'

'Not really . . . I'll tell you all about it.' She took his arm. All at once it seemed to her that the lack of someone to tell all about it – about home, about her father and Lily of the Valleys and Violent Spew – had been the worst deprivation of the past few months; and that without this meeting she would have gone mad.

But she didn't tell, not at first. The very fact of being with Richard diminished it all. Even her initial shyness was pleasurable and seemed to belong to a better world.

'Where shall we go?'

'I don't mind,' she said, and didn't. 'You choose.'

He studied her, faintly smiling. 'D'you know, it's so strange meeting you here. It feels like there ought to be – you know, sun, and fields . . .'

'I know. And instead it's dirty old London in the rain.'

They sighed over this and recalled open cloudless skies, but happily; and dirty old London in the rain was an arena for them just as the orchards had been. The empty day was theirs to move around in.

They went to the zoo. The animals looked patient in the rain. A serious little boy held his father's hand and said, 'Daddy, what will happen to the animals if there is a war?' They didn't hear the father's reply, but it raised a subject neither of them had yet mentioned.

'I dare say they'll wonder what on earth we're playing at,' Stella said. 'First we stick 'em in cages, and then we drop bombs on 'em.'

'Funny old crew, aren't we? Most dangerous animals of all. It'll be hairy in London if it comes. Will your family stay put?'

'I want the kids to go. Dad ain't sure . . . I've got a stepmother now, Richard.'

'Hell,' he said; and with that one word there was perfect accord between them. Whilst there had been no discomfort thus far, there had been a sort of bashfulness, as if they were not grown-up people. Now distances closed – perhaps ranks too. 'How long?'

'Not long after I last wrote to you. It didn't seem . . . I didn't want to . . .'

He squeezed her arm. 'Can you describe it?'

'Well . . . she's not a wicked stepmother and I ain't Cinders. It's . . . it's hard to say . . .'

'I should think,' he said after a few moments' silence, 'you still miss your mother a lot.'

'God,' she said, her voice roughening. 'I miss her something terrible.'

They were looking into a cage of monkeys, but it was the spectacle of that last night in the fens that was really before them, and much depended on how the sight affected them. But Stella found that it faded away before her eyes. That last night did not determine everything: life could not be reduced to a series of frozen symbolic moments. Life was continual renewal. The monkeys gazed, elvish and wise. Stella said, 'Thanks for being so nice that time, Richard.'

'I wasn't sure there was anything I could do that would be nice.'

'You left me alone, but you didn't leave me alone.'

'I thought about you. After you went home. Even thought of coming to London – descending on you. Wouldn't have been right, I think.'

'No. This is, though.'

The umbrella, a hindrance in their shyness, became an ally. Huddled close together under it, they made the circuit of the zoo, seeing little, locked in talk. They griped contentedly: the resemblance to schoolchildren remained insofar as they were both playing truant from lives they did not like.

'Schoolmastering's all right,' he said. 'I'm hopeless at the discipline, though. I can't see myself being a Mr Chips in fifty years' time. If I did it would only be to – no, I shouldn't say that.'

'Go on.'

'To spite my family. There, it's out,' he said laughing a little uneasily.

'Why, whatever's wrong with being a schoolteacher?' A neighbour of Auntie Bea's had been a scholarship girl and gone on to be a teacher: she was considered round their way as having gone thoroughly, even dizzily, up in the world.

'Lord knows,' he said looking glum; then brightened. 'It was your Geoffrey who gave me the idea, you know. The way he responded. How is he?'

Geoffrey had slipped back. He was regarded once more as a dunce and his teachers merely awaited the day when they could get him off their hands, but Stella did not want to tell Richard this. 'He's doing ever so well. Often talks about that summer . . . and he still remembers that poem, you know.' This at least was true. 'Here, you ever hear anything from Helen? She sent me this sort of card announcing she was getting married, and I wrote to say congratulations, but I never heard any more from her.'

'Nor me. Well, Helen always did know where she was going. No nonsense. And what about Kate, eh? Who'd have thought she'd go in for nursing?'

'She's stuck at it as well. She wrote me the other week. Apparently they're getting a lot of these volunteer nurses now and she's allowed to boss 'em around.'

'Good old Kate. I should think the military hospitals will snap her up now, if it happens – they'll want trained nurses . . .' He sighed. 'Separate ways!' But this was nonsense, because their ways had always been separate. They glanced at each other, recognizing this, and laughed. Melancholy began to seem ridiculous to them, which was an index of their happiness. They left the zoo and walked in Regent's Park, getting soaked despite the umbrella, whilst Stella told him about her work for Violet Drew. He moaned in sympathy, countered with terrible tales of Abbotsleigh. They exaggerated everything, but the stark shapes of dissatisfaction showed plainly through, and under a tree he took her hands and said, 'I wish things were different for you.'

'Well, they are today.'

'They are, aren't they?' The awareness of being about to kiss stopped them kissing. They laughed instead. 'Come on.'

'Where to?'

'Don't know. Boating.'

This too seemed hilarious, with the world liquefying around them. There were searchlights and trenches in Hyde Park, where they took a boat on the Serpentine. Richard rowed whilst Stella tried to hold the umbrella over both of them.

'Do you ever feel you want to scream, really scream at the top of your lungs?' he said, grinning and dripping. 'You could do it here. Think about your stepmother.'

She did: threw her head back and screamed. It felt wonderful. Then he screamed, though he did not tell her what he was thinking about.

Richard was so wet when they disembarked that the old boat keeper took pity on him and invited him to dry off in the boathouse, where there was a brazier. 'A fire in August,' he kept saying, shaking his head, and reminisced about the scorching August Bank Holiday of 1914. 'The park was full of people with flags. Jam-packed. They wanted the war. Next day they got it. Thought it was going to be a ruddy picnic.'

This sobered them a little: so did the recruiting posters on display when they walked up to Marble Arch. Richard paused in front of one. 'SALUTE – to adventure. JOIN THE R.A.F. Write to Air Ministry Information Bureau, Kingsway, W.C.2.'

'Think they'd have me?' he said.

'I . . . don't see why not.' It seemed a question beyond answering.

'One of the other masters at Felling Court applied. They wouldn't have him because of his eyesight. He'd set his heart on it . . . I think I ought to set my heart on something.'

They ate in a Fuller's teashop, and Stella gorged on walnut cake. They recalled the meal they had had with Helen and Kate in Cambridge – again the memory of that night and of their lovemaking under the stars was present. But it was as if it were simply a third party at their table, neutral – with a question to ask of them, certainly, but prepared to wait before it posed it.

'Where now?' he said. 'Or – sorry, have you got to get home yet?'

'Not yet. How about the pictures?'

'All right.'

Either of them could suggest anything that day: they were always in agreement. When she complained in the cinema queue that he shouldn't keep paying for everything, he shrugged it off: it genuinely didn't matter. The day was a gift to both of them. They had been chattering all the time, and the enforced hush of the cinema was strange at first: then it took on its own rightness. They sat with their hands and their knees lightly touching, and this too had a sweet sufficiency: she was learning that there were many kinds of intimacy.

The darkness too gave her the opportunity to think about him – which she could not do when she was looking at him. She thought about how she didn't really know him and yet knew him again at once. He was not in the least changed, and she felt she could say anything to him, yet he was also a mystery to her. They came from separate worlds, but were still wonderfully at ease with each other. In fact she felt more at ease today – more on her own ground, as it were – than she ever felt at home; she recognized, from the half-flippant, half-awkward references to his own home life, that he felt the same.

Did he? Her thoughts were leading her to conclusions that seemed too rapid and urgent for the spacious day. She let them fall gently into quietness, and he was quiet too when they left the cinema. The rain had stopped and a little late sunshine was filtering through, an apologetic fragment of the day that should have been. They went up to St James's Park and walked amidst dripping trees and lustrous grass, tired, but wanting to do nothing else.

'When do you have to go back to the school?'

'First week in September. Depending on whether the schools open at all, of course.'

'You know what you said – about joining up? Would you do that?'

'Yes, I would. I remember Helen asking me about that once. I think she was surprised, didn't suppose I could feel strongly enough about anything to fight for it. Maybe I don't, really. But I know what I'd fight against . . . I wish I could take you dancing.'

'I've got to be up early in the morning,' she said mournfully.

'I know.'

'We danced in the grass last time.'

'. . . I know.'

They exchanged a glance, of the sort unreadable to onlookers.

'I'd still like to take you dancing though. When you haven't got to get up in the morning. But it depends.'

'Eh?'

'Well – I've popped up in your life again, Stella. And I like it and I want to stay popped. But you might want me to pop down again. D'you see?'

She was laughing. 'Pop goes the weasel,' she said. 'No, I don't want you to pop down again.'

'Good,' he said, smiling on her. 'Good, good. Lot of things I haven't said.'

He did not say them now, however: neither of them felt impelled to say anything weighty. This was part of the perfection of the day. It ended with more rain, but that too was fitting: the rain was as memorable as the sun of the orchards. When they parted at Liverpool Street they kissed, their faces cold: his eyes looked shadowed, he hung around and nearly missed his train, and Stella felt wretched when he was gone. To a degree, at least. It would have been intolerable if this had been the end.

## 2

At the time she put the row down entirely to Norman, Lilian's least lovable offspring, who carried his lecherous activities a little too far that day late in August. Only later did she begin to see that Stalin might have had something to do with it too.

It was a shattering row, and Stella did not have tender nerves when it came to such things. She had lived all her life in crowded houses with walls made of paper and spit where there were too many children and not enough comforts: in Corbett Street, 'respectable' working-class as it was, backyard screaming matches were common and outside the Feathers men with inflamed faces and hearts full of frustration regularly went at each other with bottles. Stella supposed herself toughened against everyday abrasiveness, but this row left her shaking.

Partly that was because the rage of it would not die. The rage was not only at Norman, though it began with him. The young whelp with the narrow face of a foxy old man had turned up early in the evening – plainly, to touch his mother for a few bob and to get away from the squalls of the new baby he had at home; but Lilian had done a lot of dimpling and droning about how good her boys were to her, and Stella was glad of the excuse to escape to the washhouse and rinse out her work overall for tomorrow. She was pegging it out to dry in the yard – the bad weather had broken at last and produced a late summer of almost unreal beauty – when she became aware that she was not alone.

'C'n I help you wivvat?' said Norman in his invidious way; then, hardly bothering to disguise what he was about, he made a grab at the overall and got hold of Stella's breasts instead.

He was easily got rid of – the elbow in the chest had him stooping and grovelling – but the filthy cheek of it . . . Stella was wild. She was being mauled about in her own home and suddenly it seemed to her that she had been mad to put up with even the least of this. She stormed inside and interrupted Lilian in mid-maunder.

'I don't suppose he'll listen to me,' she shouted, 'because I'm not part of your bloody clan – so *you* tell that son of yours to keep his eyes *and* his hands to himself in future.'

'Oy, oy, what's this?' her father said. 'Who do you think you're talking to, my girl?'

'I'm talking to *her*.' Stella found herself breathless, and quite beside herself. Lilian was sitting there like some fat martyred madonna – looking at Stella as if *she* were the intruder. Her temper went up in a white blaze. 'While I can get a ruddy word in edgeways, I'm telling her what her precious son's like. And if he doesn't keep his grubby paws off me I swear I'll give him something to remember me by and you needn't expect any more snotty grandchildren out of him after I do—'

'Now you watch your mouth, lady,' her father said, 'I won't have you—'

'No, Jack,' Lilian said, 'it's all right. Let her say it. It doesn't matter, she's never liked me anyway. I don't really mind, I've tried my best but you can only do so much.' She turned her swimming eyes on Stella. 'I don't see why you have to tell lies about Norman. Take it out on me if you like, not on Norman. He's never done you any harm.'

Norman slunk in then. He looked like what he was, a guilty skunk, but that was neither here nor there.

'What's all this about?' Jack Tranter demanded.

'Eh?' Being gormless, Norman hardly needed to act. 'Wha'?'

'Stella reckons you've been misbehaving,' Lilian mourned.

'Dunno whatcha mean. Came up behind her and went Boo and made her jump, if that's whatcha mean.'

'Was that how it was, Stella?' her father said; and even in the midst of her fury, she felt a sadness of loss. He had to ask. If he had to ask, there was no point in telling him.

'It depends who you want to believe,' she said distinctly, looking at him.

Perhaps in those words and that look there was more reproach than she meant: perhaps he felt that she was taxing him, as she had never done yet, with betrayal of her mother. Certainly his own temper, normally so sluggish, flared at something, and he began shouting. 'I don't like the way you're carrying on, my girl! I don't know what you think you're trying to do to this family – but I've got my eye on you—'

'Oh, that'll only encourage her, Jack,' Lilian said, laughing regretfully.

'And just what do you mean by that?' Stella cried.

'I just mean it's funny you of all people cooking up a story like that about my Norman. I'm not one to gossip, but it's common knowledge that you're a bit of a one for the men, and I think it's a bit of a cheek dragging Norman into it when he's a happily married man and not some fly-by-night—'

'I'm not the one who goes through husbands like other people change their drawers!'

'You take that back, gel,' her father roared, jumping to his feet.

'No, no, Jack – don't quarrel,' Lilian moaned, putting up a saintly work-roughened hand, 'don't quarrel on my account – I won't see that happen – I'd rather go myself, that'd be best—'

'You're not going anywhere, Lil. I won't have her speak to you that way. She'll say sorry for that.'

'I will not say sorry.' Stella was on a high horse now, and would see it buck and throw her down before she would move. 'She can go to hell for all I care.'

'I'll go. It's me. I'll go,' Lilian crooned, making some feeble efforts to rise out of her chair.

'You stay where you are, Lil. It ain't you. It's this girl of mine. God knows how it's happened, but she's turned out all high and mighty and reckoning she's too good for us.' For the first time in Stella's remembrance, her father looked mean and spiteful. 'She never learnt it from me. All I can think is it's this toffee-nosed chap she's been seeing, putting ideas in her head.'

'You don't know anything about him,' Stella snapped.

'Ah! Dead right I don't!' her father cried with a sort of acid triumph. 'None of us know anything about him because she's never brought him to see us! *Oh* no! Ashamed of us, she is – ashamed of us because we're honest working people! Ashamed of the home she grew up in—'

'I wouldn't have been ashamed when Mum was here. But I'm ashamed of that fat cow.'

Vindictive and unforgivable – perhaps. It didn't matter what remorse reflection might bring, because she had meant it at the time, wholeheartedly. She meant it still when she ran stormily up to bed, after the row had abruptly fallen apart with her father threatening to belt her one and then withdrawing into shocked silence at himself. She hated Lilian and perhaps her father too: she certainly hated her life here. If Hitler's bombers came over right now, she thought as she flung herself down on the bed, she wouldn't turn a hair. She'd cheer.

It was then that it faintly dawned on her why her father had so uncharacteristically lost his temper. She knew he had had a shock that morning, when the news broke that Nazi Germany and Soviet Russia had signed a non-aggression pact. Everyone had had a shock: suddenly war was very close, and old Hitler even had the Russians on his side, it seemed. But what she had neglected to bear in mind was what a blow this must be to her father. He sincerely venerated Soviet Russia and looked on it as the beacon that would lead the world to a better future. And now Stalin had gone and jumped into bed with the Nazis. Stella could not imagine being personally grieved by the machinations of a gang of foreign politicians, but she had sympathy enough to know that her father was. Deeply enough, in fact, to lash out in a way quite unlike him.

It was insight of a sort, but it didn't lead her anywhere: her own anger, and anguish, stood in her path, and she could not see past them. The misery of the night, which came slowly on with distant palpitations of thunder and then the snores of Dot beside her, could and should have been alleviated by one factor. Unfortunately that had been part of the row. The beauty of the last fortnight, in which she had met Richard at every opportunity, had been besmirched.

It wasn't that she feared truth in what her father had said – that she was ashamed. Her time with Richard was simply something separate, and valuably so. Now a new and desolating light had been cast upon it. It was finite. It always had to end, and when it did the loathsome tentacles of home clawed her back.

They had had wonderful times. There had been a visit to the theatre -- her first, and not to the Hackney Empire: Ivor Novello at Drury Lane, and supper and dancing afterwards. She had floated. But she was certain that it was not a mere matter of her head being turned. Just as wonderful had been the evening they had spent simply walking by the river, with egg sandwiches and a mug of tea from a cabman's stall at the end of it.

It was the way he made her laugh. It was the way he made her spirits bubble, no matter how murky they had been all day. It was the way they both found the world funny and sad and beyond them, and not a wheel to break your soul upon. This was what they could not know at home and it was this which now seemed fastened to her only by a thread whilst Lilian and her father and Violet Drew and Corbett Street held her like a vice. *We are real. He's not,* they said. *You'll see. It'll come home to you. It'll be your turn next . . .*

She writhed and tossed, sweating, and recalled the day last week when they had watched as a huge formation of bombers had moved overhead: an RAF war exercise. 'We're very small, aren't we?' Richard had said.

'Like little candles,' she had said: she didn't know where the picture came from.

'Just like that . . . The only thing to do, I suppose, is burn at both ends.'

She slept, and woke late to find Dot up, dressed, and sour, holding out a bunch of flowers.

'These come for yer,' she said, throwing them down as if hoping to break them, and stomped downstairs. There was a call of 'Coo-ee!' at the front door; Olwen, with children in tow.

Another day was beginning, and Stella had half an hour to get to work.

She sat up in bed just looking at the flowers, their colour and shape, for some minutes. Then she noticed the note and opened it.

A ring fell out.

She picked it up and looked at it as she had looked at the flowers. Then she read the note. All it said was:

'*Come live with me and be my love.*'

And Stella Tranter thought: yes, yes, I will.

# *THREE*

## 1

Helen was sitting at the bureau staring at a blank sheet of letter paper when the telephone rang. She picked it up without expectation, and for the first time in a year heard Richard's voice.

'Hullo, Helen? Hullo! This is a wonderful instrument, isn't it? Only I never use it. How are you?'

'Good heavens. Richard.'

'I rang your mother first. She gave me your number. I say, have you heard our news?'

'Your letter came this morning. I was just about to write back to you. Congratulations.'

'I suppose it must have been one heck of a surprise.'

'Oh . . . yes.'

'It was to us too, really. But I know you'll understand how these things just happen. One minute you're – I say, still there?'

'Yes – I'm here, Richard. Sorry. Bad line.'

'It's our landlady's telephone. Lets us use it with great reluctance. As I said in the letter, we're just in digs at the moment. The cockroaches don't bother you if you don't bother them . . . Just a moment. Here's Stella.'

Helen closed her eyes.

'Hullo, Helen? It's me.' The voice was almost shy.

'Hello, Stella. Many congratulations.'

'Thank you – coh, you sound ever so close, just like in the next room. This is funny, talking to you again. I'm not used to talking on the telephone . . . I dunno, you must have thought we'd gone mad when you heard. It's a shame you couldn't have been at the wedding – only it was all so quick – Richard got a licence and before you knew it there we were. I still can't believe it – we got this old lady who was sitting in the park to be a witness, and she piped her eye even though she didn't know us.'

'It sounds very romantic.'

'It was that all right. Here, we shall have to meet again, I don't know how, depending on Adolf, I s'pose – and Kate too, all of us like we were before – we shall have to get her married next!'

'Yes.' Helen attempted a laugh. 'Yes, I suppose we will.'

'How's life treating you, then? What's it like up there? It's all a bit grim in London, a lot of long faces. I feel like I shouldn't really be happy what with everything.'

'Well, it's quiet here. Much the same sort of feeling, though, I think. Rather glum. I've been busy sewing this wretched blackout material. We bought yards and yards, it still isn't finished . . . My dear, of course you should be happy. Now more than ever. Don't lose a moment of it.'

'No, you're right . . . I won't . . .' Stella's voice sounded shy again, and touched. 'Richard's waving at me, I think he wants you again. I'll say ta-ta. Look after yourself.'

Just in the way Richard always said it – as if she earnestly meant it. 'You too, dear.'

'Hullo, blushing bridegroom again. Well, how did she sound? Been married to me for three days now, she should have gone round the twist.'

'I was just saying to Stella, it all sounds very romantic.'

'Romantic and hectic. Actually we weren't the only ones going through a rush job. Lots of service weddings just now, as you can imagine. Looks as if it's all going to blow up, Helen – you were right a long time ago.'

'I wish I'd been wrong . . . Well, yours was practically a service wedding, it seems.'

'Oh, well, they haven't accepted me yet, as I said in the letter. But I was talking to a pal who was in the Air Squadron back at Cambridge and he thinks I've a fair chance. There's a medical and some bumf to be got through yet. Things grind exceedingly slow even with the situation as it is. It's what I want to do though: one hundred per cent. It's odd being married, isn't it? You become a sort of instant grown-up. How's Owen? I'd very much like to meet him. We really must try and meet up if this show lets us.'

'He's very well. At work just now. And your family?'

'Oh, don't mention them. All right, I suppose. There's an almighty huff in that general direction on account of my running off and getting married without consulting them.'

'They haven't met Stella yet?'

'Not yet.' The lightness in his voice did not fool her. Involuntarily and for the first time she pictured him on the other end of the line, with Stella beside him.

'Oh well . . . these are times when you have to – act quickly and take your chances. It puts everything in proportion, in a way.'

As soon as she had said it, it seemed to her the height of incoherence, but he answered, 'That's right – that's absolutely it, I knew you'd understand,' and there was not only warmth but gratitude in his voice. She still had the skill – which appeared natural and was actually hard won – of saying the correct thing.

'Well, I wish you all the happiness in the world, Richard. And Stella too,' she said, continuing with the correct thing, twining the telephone cord round her fingers. She noticed that the flowers in the vase nearby were dead, and reminded herself to throw them out.

'Thanks, Helen. I'm glad you don't think we've gone completely mad. I said to Stella, let's ring Helen, *she* will understand.'

'Oh, yes, I know you like to act on impulse, Richard. Though it – was a surprise, I . . .'

'Sorry, can't hear—'

'I was just wondering, what are you living on?'

'Hope and air just now,' he laughed. 'No, I've a few bob left. And Father sent what I suppose is a sort of wedding present of a small cheque. Which – I don't know, I want to pay him back really, if that doesn't sound strange. If the RAF take me I'll have my pay, and then . . . but I don't know, it's a tricky point.'

'Yes, I suppose so.' She suddenly felt very tired, and incapable of advice.

'Anyhow, look, I'd better go,' he said dropping his voice, 'the landlady's hovering about rather. It's been awfully good to talk to you – we'll let you know as soon as we're settled somewhere more permanent.'

'All right, Richard. It's been lovely. And thank you for your letter. Say goodbye to Stella for me.'

After she had put the receiver down Helen hummed a tune and set about disposing of the flowers. Then she returned to the bureau and scribbled on the blank sheet 'Wedding pres. for R & S?' She supposed that they had not received any, and it must be rather wretched living in digs. Something that was a little luxurious yet practical too . . . she would have to think.

She spent the morning with Lucy, the daily help, hemming the last of the blackout material. The endless black made her head ache, and she was glad of the fresh air when the time came to take the dogs out for a walk. Another brilliant cloudless day: this late summer had a wonderfully serene quality, and around the market town of Louth the sandbags, the taped windows, the white-painted kerbstones, the gas-mask cases carried like shopping bags, seemed preparations not for cataclysm but for some minor event – a little local flooding perhaps. All was provincial ease – coach-built perambulators, family butchers, elderly cars parked anyhow in the marketplace, well-dressed children buying ice cream from a Wall's tricycle, the fine spire of the church rising above massy horse chestnuts, and here and there glimpses between roofs of the green wolds beyond. Helen saw many people she knew, as she did every day. She also passed close by the premises of Seymour and Harding and thought about Owen working away inside, though she did not know which was his own office: she had never visited it.

When she came back Lucy had made her lunch, and had tidied the house with her usual efficiency. Of actual cleaning there was very little to be done: though the house itself was old, Owen had installed all the newest conveniences, with furnishings in a modern style; and they were both very orderly people. Even the dogs hardly seemed to shed hairs. There was a Sadia water heater and a Jackson cooker that ran on electricity and under the stairs a Hoover vacuum cleaner. In the dining room there was a brand new dining suite of limed oak: the sitting room was similarly up to date, with a tiled fireplace and a low three-piece suite and standard lamps in opposite corners. Pride of place was given to the radiogram, which Lucy had polished to coffin-like brightness. Owen always turned it on as soon as he came home from work. On either side of it he had built shelves to hold his collection of gramophone records, which he kept in alphabetical order, beginning with Auber and ending with Weber. The place made her father's Rectory, with its draughts and bad drains and vault-like kitchen, seem impossibly inconvenient.

Lucy came to Helen with a question. Her brother was at a Territorial Army camp and was being kept there in case of emergency. Did that mean he might be sent overseas? And would she see him before he went? Helen didn't think so and tried to reassure her; but really she was pretty much at a loss herself. The great events taking place in the world seemed quite beyond her now.

Helen had a question too. 'Lucy, what do you think would make a good wedding present for a couple starting out with very little?'

'Haven't they got a list, mum?'

'No, nothing like that. It was a very quick wedding. They haven't even a proper home.'

'Well, I don't know. Sounds as if they're just happy with each other for now . . . What did you say, mum?'

'I said never mind. I'll have a look round when I next go into Lincoln.'

She had to go out again this afternoon, and sitting over her coffee she felt a little tired and cross about it. The local Women's Institute was rehearsing a pageant of inspiring scenes from British history. It was due to be staged in the Drill Hall on Saturday, though Helen suspected the Drill Hall might be needed for more urgent uses by then. The pageant was the usual pleasant nonsense with stalwart ladies holding a pose as Florence Nightingale with her lamp or Queen Elizabeth at Tilbury and trying not to wobble: Helen had agreed to take part – as she had agreed to join the W.I. in the first place – because it didn't do in a small town like this to be seen as offish, but she found it rather a bind. Mrs Seymour, the wife of Owen's partner, was portraying Britannia and bossed the proceedings. The woman talked in a unique way that one could often find amusing and even quotable – 'Tom and I took the Wolseley up to Cleethorpes this weekend – found the sea air a sovereign remedy for the cobwebs and dear old Winky was absolutely tail-on-end after weeks in the doggy doldrums' – but one could easily have enough of her. She had cast Helen as the Duke of Wellington – 'because you've *such* height, dear, you can carry it off.' Rehearsals chiefly consisted of getting into the costumes and then just standing there, but Mrs Seymour treated it like a West End premiere. It was all rather tiresome and Helen, nestling in her chair with a spaniel snoring near her feet, was half-inclined not to go. It was so easy to surrender to this odd listless fatigue that seemed to creep up on her so much lately. But in the end she resisted, put on her hat, and walked down to the Drill Hall.

The place was already full of milling ladies, tramping on the floorboards and shouting, and there was a mingled odour of face powder and perspiration and mothballs. Helen felt the beginnings of a headache and hoped it would not be a migraine. Soon Mrs Seymour bore down on her, Britannia-clad, and began booming something about a sash. Helen did not understand for a moment.

'The sash, my dear. You must remember. You promised to run up a sash for your Wellington costume. *Don't* tell me you've forgotten.'

'Oh – heavens, I did. It went clean out of my mind, I'm sorry. Oh, well, as long as we have the red coat—'

'The red coat will do for *now*, but one would really hope for the finished effect by Saturday. Detail is *so* important in things of this nature and one simply can't do everything oneself.'

Helen got out of the way while they ran through the first tableau. It was Boadicea defying the Romans. The bank manager's wife was playing Boadicea. She was nervous of her chariot, which creaked ominously, and became flustered when Mrs Seymour reproved her for forgetting to take off her clip-on earrings. Helen longed for a cigarette. She seldom had the opportunity to smoke as Owen disapproved, and to light one here, in a semi-public place, was doubtless unseemly. A couple of boys had sneaked into the hall and were sniggering at the back. 'Mrs Harding,' came Mrs Seymour's voice, '*would* you be so good as to eject the interlopers? One wishes to bash on and "noises off" are *not* called for.' Being called Mrs Harding still struck Helen oddly even after nine months of marriage. She shooed the boys away and looked back at the stage where King Alfred, the vicar's sister, was burning the cakes. At the front one of the ladies was enthusiastically knitting whilst wearing her Oliver Cromwell costume. All at once Helen found herself unable to find any of it amusing or touching or quaint or even tolerable. Horror filled her. The racket of gossiping voices scraped her nerves and the echoing clomp of heeled shoes on bare boards was like a thunder of futility. She sat down on one of the folding chairs at the back and put her head in her hands. It must be a migraine – that was all. Closing her eyes and breathing deeply sometimes helped to fend off the attack.

'. . . Mrs Harding! Are you with us, my dear?'

'I'm sorry – what?'

'My goodness, one is quite the Dreamy Daniel today. We're ready for Waterloo, my dear, and we have a Bonaparte but no Duke so one would appreciate skates being put on if at all possible.'

'Sorry.' Helen hurried to the dressing room behind the stage to put on her costume. The doctor's wife was in there struggling out of her Queen Elizabeth gown and there was hardly any room. 'You've a pimple, dear,' she informed Helen, 'just below your shoulder. You want ointment else it'll turn nasty.' Helen thanked her and then wondered what on earth she was thanking her for –

being an interfering old crone? – and then was shocked at herself. What was wrong with her today?

'Well now,' boomed the voice of Mrs Seymour, 'one presumes the Duke will take the field eventually . . .'

Helen staggered out on to the stage. The boots were Mr Seymour's fishing boots and hurt like the devil.

'Hmm,' said Mrs Seymour. 'Do we not have a hat?'

'Oh – I couldn't find it,' Helen said, and then with ungovernable irritation, 'For goodness' sake, it's only a rehearsal.'

Ladies gave her stately stares, and she told herself to calm down; but it was all so ridiculous. Mrs Seymour came up with a new idea: Napoleon should be shown handing something to Wellington. 'An instrument of surrender – we might have a rolled-up document of some kind.'

'Napoleon didn't surrender to Wellington,' Helen found herself saying. 'They never even got near each other on the battlefield.'

'Oh, I don't know about that, my dear,' Mrs Seymour said jovially. 'One is sure there must have been some form of surrender. But of course one would wish for accuracy. Mrs Ibbotson, your husband's quite the history man, isn't he? Perhaps you could ask him to consult the relevant volume and give us the gen.'

'I know my history, Mrs Seymour. I have a first-class degree from Cambridge in the subject,' Helen said: suddenly she was speaking without volition. Wild, seething, she didn't care what they thought of her – didn't care for anything. 'The whole thing's a farce – a boring farce and I hate it – for God's sake let me out of it,' she cried, ripping off the red coat and throwing it down. Horsey English faces goggled at her. She ran off the stage biting back tears. In the dressing room the doctor's wife started on the pimple again. Helen told her to go to hell, flung on her clothes, and fled from the hall.

'I can't go home – I simply can't go home.' This was nonsense, and alarming. Some other identity than that of sensible Mrs Harding, the solicitor's wife, had taken command of her. But there was no resisting it. She wandered vacantly about the town, dried tears on her cheeks. At the sight of a display of cut glass in a shop window, sensible Mrs Harding came back for a moment, and murmured something about a wedding present. Then she fell away again, and Helen found herself wanting to throw a brick through the window and smash everything.

She wandered again, and when she looked at her watch it was six o'clock. Owen was usually home at half-past six. The doors of the George Hotel stood open.

The fact that you were married made no difference: drinking alone in a public bar if you were a woman was still tantamount to declaring yourself a prostitute, even the lounge bar of a stuffy hotel like this one. For a moment she was appalled at herself. This was not the behaviour either of sensible Mrs Harding or of Helen – whoever that was. Then a white-coated waiter greeted her and she lost volition again. Surrendering, she ordered a large whisky and soda and drank it down swiftly, seated in a corner. The place was empty still, quiet as a library: there were hunting prints on flock wallpaper and a smell, curiously comforting, of old beeswax and tobacco. She felt she understood why men liked these places – some men at least. Owen drank at home but would never have dreamt of entering a pub. He could only relax within his own four walls.

Helen had another whisky. She felt she could go on doing this for ever: sit on in this dingy tapestry armchair that was wholly neutral and did not belong to anybody, gaze around this room that was nobody's home and required nothing of her, drink, and think – or avoid thought, depending on the effect of the whisky. At first it merely cushioned her mind, and that was wonderful; then after her third she fell into a sort of painless consideration of how unhappy she was. Fragments of the debacle at the Drill Hall came back to her, and she saw that she had stored up trouble for herself: in a place like this the ripples from even so minor a gaffe would go on and on. But she was resigned to this. The whisky, rather than confusing her, lent her a rather ruthless sense of priorities. It was not the gossip of ladies that was making her lurk in here but the fact that she was married to Owen and did not like it.

Having pretended to herself for a good while that this was not so, she did not inquire even now into what it was that had awakened her. The fact sufficed. Facing it gave her a sort of bitter exhilaration, like swallowing the whisky. She was able to look back upon her marriage and see it for what it was, an unhappy one: though she still stopped short of examining why it had happened in the first place.

Two men in loud check suits had entered the bar and were being jovial with each other over gin chasers, rattling the change in their pockets and stamping in amusement. Occasionally one would slide a curious eye over in Helen's direction. They were strangers to the town and did not know her – what would they think, she wondered, if they learned she was the wife of a prominent citizen, partner in a law firm, and until recently considered its most eligible bachelor? Looking at their fat necks and wet laughing mouths, she felt she could guess what they would think. Discontented wife of a man who had been a bachelor too long and probably should have stayed one – the stuff of comic postcards.

There was some truth in this, perhaps, but not enough to give any clear picture of what her married life was like. It was not that simple, and she doubted whether she could have found any coherent terms to describe it. The ruthlessness given her by the whisky forced her to admit that she found her husband intensely limited; but there were many limited personalities who were also capable of inspiring great love. Her own mother was limited in her refusal to believe ill of anybody: she was also a delightful person adored by her husband. But with Owen all Helen ever seemed to see now were the limits. Having gladly entered the neat enclosure of his personality, now she kept coming up against the fences, pressing herself against them – and perhaps soon would begin flinging herself against them.

Gazing at the cold fireplace, she had a recollection from when they were first married. On winter evenings at home Owen would often stand with his back to the fire, and after a while she would mischievously pull the knees of his trousers forward so that the hot cloth at the back scorched him. He would yelp and laugh, and she would laugh – and it would seem to her that they were doing something right. She felt instinctively that married life was a work of imagination, to be spontaneously invented by the collaborators as they went along, and that such details were important – like pet phrases and private jokes. But these they did not have. Owen's mind worked along its own paths. He knew what he thought about everything: he had settled it all long ago. Where they agreed there was harmony, as in preferring Mozart to Beethoven, but he wanted no voyages of mutual discovery. To talk about something, genuinely to talk all round it, batting the subject about like a tennis ball, was beyond him. 'You know what I think about that,' he would say, with a frown like the closing of a door.

She gathered that he had been unhappy as a child. His father seemed to have been a domineering man of some brilliance, who had spoiled a career in government science through drink. Helen guessed that, despite the general perception of Owen as a successful man, deep down he believed himself to be otherwise. He had a peculiar animus against what he called 'cleverness'. When he brought home a tale of someone who had slipped up in spite of their 'cleverness', he was as waspish as an old woman: his mouth would draw tight when he heard of achievement. 'It won't get them very far without money,' he would say, or 'All very well if they can keep it up,' and Helen would feel the cold touch of the fences, high and unyielding.

At first she had despised herself for minding about these things; for surely this meant that she had fallen into the awful trap of supposing that her future husband was perfect and then being disappointed when he turned out to be human. Lately she had modified her ideas about this: it was not true that she had ever supposed Owen to be perfect. She had merely supposed him to be perfect for her.

Perhaps he was, she thought: perhaps the coldness, the black withdrawn moods, the prim habits were what she deserved – for her self-esteem was a light that had dwindled and almost gone out. And it was not as if he had led her to the altar only to spring a series of nasty surprises on her. Their life together was just as she could have predicted it to be. Indeed it was really Owen's life as before, with her added to it. When they went to bridge parties, he partnered Helen rather than any other single person as he used to: when they attended Rotary Club affairs, they talked dull small talk with golf bores together instead of separately. The conclusion to be drawn from this, and from his sexual lukewarmness, was that he had married her for companionship. 'Which would be fair enough,' she thought, 'if he actually enjoyed my company.'

She gave a start: she was afraid that, drunkenly, she had spoken those words out loud. But the noisy men at the bar were taking no notice of her, so it could not have been . . . Knowing it was unwise, knowing it was wrong, she had another drink, and yielded to self-pity. She was no pessimist and her normal response to a problem was to seek a swift solution, but today had seen something like a collapse of personality within her: all she could do was bewail her lot. Her life was so dreary and stifling! She concentrated on this, though a suppressed part of her knew that the real torment lay in the fact that her life was loveless. That part of herself knew also what it was that had triggered all this off – but even with drink it remained ruthlessly suppressed.

'What a failure,' she thought, resolving that this would be the last whisky, 'what an utter failure!' She really believed this of herself, and did not see that her recent life, though miserable indeed, had actually been heroic. For she had been living without food for the soul and without food for the mind, and yet had kept going: starved of all that made life valuable, she had not ceased to value it; and until today, she had never turned and lashed out in her disappointment. It was scarcely to be wondered at that her courage had finally failed her, but she saw only the failure and not the courage.

It was past seven o'clock. Owen would be home now, and wondering where she was: she knew how he hated any divergence from routine. Reluctantly, Helen left the hotel and began walking home, unsteadily: the fresh air made her realize that she was plain drunk. She dreaded the return, though even in this unheard-of condition she did not fear Owen's anger. When he was displeased with her there was only sour weariness, as if he could not be bothered with her: when all was well he found her acceptable, otherwise he seemed to wish she would disappear. It was something of this sort that she expected as she opened the front door, but for once Owen surprised her.

She found him seated in his usual chair with Richard's letter in his lap. She looked at it, then at Owen's face; and the memory of a voice down the telephone, which she had been warding off all day, hit her a blow of terrible bluntness. With a grunt she sat down heavily, turning her eyes from him. Even someone without Owen's fastidious perceptions could have told at once that she was stinking drunk.

'Well,' he said in his quiet way, 'I suppose one is entitled to ask where you have been.'

'I went into the George for a drink,' she said.

He regarded her with distaste, then looked again at the letter in his hand. Something about the way he held it infuriated her. That was the way he held a book when reading – between finger and thumb, up before his face, with a sort of lawyerlike mockery. She made a lunge and snatched it from him, muttering, 'So now you read my letters.'

'It doesn't normally trouble you,' he said. This was so, and his face registered a moment of tart triumph at having truth on his side. Then his jawbone stood out and his look was deathly as he said, 'This appears to be a special case, however.'

'I don't know what you mean.'

'Credit me with some intelligence.' He folded his hands and crossed his legs. 'The news of this man – this Richard getting married seems to have made quite an impact on you.'

'No, I—'

'Yes, I think, because I can't imagine why else my wife would suddenly go out and get stinking drunk. Can *you* give me another reason?'

She blinked at him, feeling naked. No words would come.

'. . . I see,' he said at last, and his face went stony.

She could only guess at what he was feeling – hardly knew what she felt herself; but something like an impulse of pity went out towards him. Then for a moment she wanted him to be outraged, to tear at the letter, to demand her love or vow to fight for it . . . But no. It died: she saw she didn't really want that, not now, and when he stalked out it didn't matter. She had gone beyond that into a place of unique emptiness – caught between two loves, neither of which had ever had any real existence.

## 2

'Helen sounded different, didn't she?' Stella said, playing with Richard's hair.

They had not spoken of her for a good while after their phone call, for the simple reason that passion had carried them upstairs to bed immediately afterwards, and love had kept them there for a couple of hours. Now at last, drowsing over cigarettes and blinking at the weak shafts of sunlight that poked between the dingy curtains of their digs, they picked up the theme.

'She did rather,' Richard said. 'Not like her old self. But then you can never tell with the telephone.'

'Gawd knows what I sounded like on there,' Stella said, running her fingertip along his nose. 'Like some old squawking hen, I reckon.'

'Young squawking hen,' Richard said judiciously. 'Don't be hard on yourself, love.'

He was flat on his back, holding a cigarette. She reached out and tapped the end so that a fragment of burning ash landed on his bare chest.

'Ow! Look at that – my fair flesh, marked for life!'

'I shall mark you somewhere else if you ain't careful.'

'Oh, you will, eh?' He made a plunge beneath the bedclothes and began tickling. Stella was very ticklish, as he had already discovered. She squeaked and squirmed, and then an especially ticklish bit made her squeal aloud.

'Ssh,' he said, shaking with laughter, 'the landlady'll think I'm a wife-beater.'

'Well, you are. Oh, you devil.' The bedsprings quavered with their laughter. At last she sighed and putting a hand up to his face said, 'Guess what I want.'

Richard rolled his eyes. 'Now let me think . . .'

'Oy.' She pinched his nose. 'Not that. Not yet anyway. I want . . . something to eat.'

'The woman's insatiable. What's it to be? Fish and chips? Do you want to eat them wrapped up in newspaper, or would you rather just wear your nightie?'

'That's a terrible joke!' she said, going off into squeals again; then, snuggling close to him, 'Fish and chips is nice . . . but you'd be gone ages getting 'em. I don't want to let you go . . .'

They were both silent a moment as there was a noise downstairs. It was the front door closing, followed by the unmistakable stumping footsteps of their landlady going down the street outside.

Stella turned her eyes to Richard's. 'She's gone out,' she said.

'Amazing deduction, Holmes. Ow!'

'She's got some grub in her kitchen, I'll bet.'

'I dare say . . .' He gave her a look of injured innocence. 'Mrs Marwood . . . I hope you're not suggesting . . .'

She grinned at him.

'You *are* suggesting.'

'Well, she charges us enough for the rooms.'

'True. And she gives me cold shaving water. Probably because she's shaved in it first . . . All right.' He got out of bed and pulled on his trousers. 'I'd better be quick, though. She might only have popped out for a second.'

'Speaking of popping out,' Stella said watching him, 'I should do your flies up.'

He blew her a kiss, and she heard his bare feet padding down the stairs. She stretched her legs out in the bed – it was almost decadently comfortable as old beds often are – and looked around at the frowsy room. There was hardly an item in it that was not worn, chipped, foxed, broken, or just plain horrible; and yet the whole place sang with ecstatic association. This was happiness: she knew its flavour now, and knew she had never tasted anything like it.

She came out of a sensuous dream, and realized that Richard had been gone a long time. What was he doing down there – cooking a three-course meal? And then she heard the key rattle in the front door. Almost in the same moment there was the sound of Richard's footsteps on the stairs, moving at scarcely possible speed. He burst in and dived headlong into the bed like a swimmer.

'That was a near thing!' he said, surfacing cautiously. 'God – imagine if she'd caught me!'

'Whatever took you so long?'

'Well . . .' He grinned, shame-faced. 'It was that great big tom-cat of hers – you know what it's like, it was in the kitchen and . . . well, it didn't like the look of me, and in fact it got me pinned up against the wall . . .'

'Richard!' She had to cram the sheet in her mouth. 'I've heard of people getting pinned against the wall by dogs, but a – a cat – oh, my good Gawd . . .'

'Well, it's a ruddy big cat,' he said, laughing too; and then with a crestfallen look, 'Oh, damn – I forgot . . .'

From under the bedclothes he brought up something that he had been holding in his hand when he burst in. It was a single Scotch egg, rather crushed, and now very hairy.

'My darling,' he said, gravely presenting it to her, 'for you,' and as Stella laughed she tasted that happiness again and thought: Can anyone else ever have tasted this sweetness? Surely not, surely not.

## 3

Kate could count herself very lucky to get leave to visit home this weekend, as the Sister informed her, and she must expect a wire calling her back to the hospital at a moment's notice. She still looked as if she wanted to deny it to her, but Matron had given special permission and the fact remained that Kate had had no leave for weeks. Not even the fact that war might be declared at any moment could alter a decision made by Matron.

Kate's father came down to Cambridge in his truck to fetch her: catching a train would be a chancy business today, for evacuation from London had begun and East Anglia's railways would be packed with trainloads of children. It was Saturday the second of September, hot and still, with thunder in the air. Far away – though perhaps not so far – German guns were firing on Poland, and the papers on the Cambridge newsstands bore the stark headline WHY ARE WE WAITING?

'Terrible bad harvest this year,' Kate's father told her, as they drove out of Cambridge to the fens. 'Poor old crop and late. George Maxey went round the towns looking for people to come and help get it in. Our fruit's been spectac'lar, but we haven't had the labour – there's a few pickers still up from London, but mostly they went home when all this palaver started. And the prices are so low we'll barely break even. Hey-ho. Well, who knows what we'll be doing this time next year. George has had these letters from the Min of Ag saying to be prepared for changes. He reckons they'll make us plough up the grasslands for the war – maybe the fruit fields an' all . . . Well, here's one thing that don't change, any road,' he said, patting Kate's hand. 'Always a treat to see your face, my duck. How are they treating you at that place, now?'

She had been nursing for nine months now, but her father had continued to insist that she should come home if she didn't like it right to the end of her three months' probation, and even now remained anxious about her, as if she were at some Dickensian school full of bullies. 'We've been very busy,' she said. 'They're going to evacuate a lot of patients and staff from the London hospitals so we've got to make room. But . . . I don't know how long I'll be there anyway.' She thought it best to give him this news as soon as possible. 'Once I've passed my First Year Prelim I want to work in a military hospital.'

'What? Where?'

'Depends where they send you. Not necessarily far. They're bound to set up more when the war starts. And the military are desperate for nurses who've had proper training – they'll be swamped with volunteers who don't know anything, like last time.'

'Well . . . if it's what you want, duck . . . If you're sure it's what you want . . .' Walter Lutton kept his eyes on the road, thinking. Though he had spoken of her as the one thing that did not change, it was plain from this that there had been a deep though subtle shifting of the ground between them. He was troubled but respectful; and the change was not simply in his attitude but in the new sturdy confidence of Kate, which could not help but impress itself upon him. Still, she guessed what he was thinking: would she be up to nursing war casualties? For it was certain now, despite the government's last-minute havering, that the attack on Poland meant war. It was part of her new sturdiness that she did not resent this apparent doubt in her abilities. She had asked the same question herself: she had deliberately called up the spectre of Uncle Ralph, that mangled product of the last war, to pose the question again; but her answer had been prompt. Whilst much of her early training had consisted of skivvying in the sluice room, she had by now seen at close quarters most of what could happen to a human body, and she did not suppose that military casualties could be worse. The most ghastly thing she had seen was a syphilis case, which had demonstrated that the God of Love could outdo any barbarity of the God of War.

'It won't be just yet, anyway, Dad,' Kate said. 'We don't know how things will turn out.'

'Things'll turn out dreadful, I reckon. Worse than the last lot. I don't want to think it, but you can just see the way things are going . . . Bloody fools!' he said with sudden vehemence. 'They told us it was all finished last time, you know. Don't worry, chaps, you won't have to fight again. And now it's the kids in the firing line. Well, that's our news, by the way, duck – we decided for definite. We shall take some of the kids they're evacuating. They told us Monks Bridge was going to be a reception area and your mum was all for it straight away. We've got plenty of room and after all – ' he grinned at her – 'we're used to having a lot of Cockneys running about the place.'

'That's good, Dad. They'll love it here.'

'We thought three – but we could stretch to four, depending. If there's four from the same family, say, we wouldn't see 'em split up.'

Kate remembered Stella's Auntie Bea and her brood. Little Geoffrey, who had blossomed out here. She wondered if they were part of the evacuation. She would have to ask Stella when she wrote: she still hadn't had time to send her congratulations on her marriage, having heard the amazing news just this week in a chaotic joint letter from Stella and Richard. It would have been wonderful if Auntie Bea's children could have come to Monks Bridge, but she knew that the evacuation didn't work like that: you went where you were sent.

'We're expecting 'em to arrive tonight,' her father went on. 'They've got the schoolhouse all ready – though we're not to be surprised if it's this afternoon, tomorrow or never. They don't pretend it's going to go like clockwork. Ernie Delph's agreed to tek a couple as well. And Kitty and Alice at the Corner.'

'How about George?' Kate said.

'I don't reckon so. With him being on his own and all, I suppose he en't in a position to look after 'em . . .' Her father swallowed hastily. 'Tiddly-pom . . . Phoo, I wish this storm would hurry up and break, clear the air a bit . . .'

Cambridge, where Kate had been doing her training and living in nurses' quarters since the beginning of the year, had the signs of coming war all over it: precious college windows had been boarded up, blackout precautions were everywhere, and just that morning she had been helping to fill more sandbags to place around the hospital. But her old home, which she had visited only a handful of times this year, was just as it had always been. The orchard country shimmered in the Indian-summer heat as if no time at all had passed since she had walked here with Stella and Richard and Helen.

Her mother greeted Kate with warmth, shyness, and a certain abstractedness. The warmth was the way she was: the shyness was something to do with the nurse's uniform, which Kate had kept on in case of a sudden recall to duty: the abstractedness, the consequence of frantic preparations for the arrival of evacuees. Glad there was no fuss for her, Kate still reflected in a rueful way on its absence. In the past year she had remade herself, often painfully, sometimes exhilaratingly, as an adult woman instead of the shy girl who outside the warm bosom of the family shivered with cold: now she found herself accepted on those terms. And it was a little strange.

'Caster sugar – I knew I should have got more.' Mrs Lutton fluttered. She was doing a vast bake, for the children. 'And vanilla essence – there's a bit, but you don't know how long these things are going to be around now . . .'

'Now, now, Maud, you know what they said – no panic buying,' said Kate's father. He was keeping an ear cocked to the wireless, but there was no news – at least, not the news they were waiting for. German troops were moving into Poland: the Prime Minister had called an emergency Cabinet meeting. In the farmhouse kitchen the cats lolled in the heavy heat, and thunder whispered from a distant horizon.

'Just some more caster sugar,' Kate's mother said. 'If you give 'em a good feed when they get here it'll take off the shock.'

Kate volunteered to walk down to Gathergood's shop in the village: she wanted to be doing something. She was afraid, as she supposed everybody was; but she had been involved in a running battle with fear this year and it had a familiar face to her. It had not been easy. Moving away from home to a world of cold hostel rooms and canteen meals and sharp Sisters and loneliness had not been easy: learning to nurse had not been easy and for a long time had teetered on the edge of impossibility. If Kate had gone into it with some idea of confronting and conquering her old squeamish terrors, she had soon been disabused of any accompanying notion that one good sight of blood would effect an immediate cure. All she could say for herself was that the Sisters and Charge Nurses had never entirely lost patience with her, and that she had not fainted or been sick – on the wards, that is. She had mastered an art of postponing both until she was out of the way. As for the urge to run away and scream, that had finally stopped about a month ago. All the same, she was convinced that she would have been found unsuitable if she had not compensated for her latent squeamishness with a fanatical appetite for work. It occurred to her early on that laziness was the one thing that doomed a probationer nurse, and she drove herself accordingly. The senior nurses were understandably happy to delegate the dogsbody work to the juniors, who hurried like mice in a revolving wheel, fetching and carrying. The sluice figured prominently in all the leg-aching journeys. Kate had transported by hand, and washed away by hand, everything that could possibly come off or out of a human body.

As is the way, she was ceasing to notice it just as it was about to end. The threat of war had placed a premium on experience, and the bedpans would soon be washed by others. Kate was seeking to be employed in a military hospital because it seemed the next logical step: also, perhaps, because she was anxious that there should *be* a next step.

The welcoming committee was at the village schoolhouse, but there was no sign of the evacuees, and in Mr Gathergood's shop it was just another Saturday afternoon, with ancient Mrs Loos sitting on one of the bentwood chairs while she debated her purchases. Mr Gathergood, more solemnly bug-eyed than ever with the weight of events, ceremoniously wrapped the caster sugar whilst favouring Kate with some doubtful gossip about the Poles. 'The officers wear hairnets in bed,' he told her. 'And they've got some crack troops who wear skirts and shoes with pom-poms on. And they all get blind drunk before they go into battle. That's the Poles for you.'

'Did you say Poles, or moles?' croaked Mrs Loos.

'Poles, Mrs L. I'll be with you in a minute.'

'North Poles?'

'I dare say,' Mr Gathergood said easily. 'And so your mother's tekking in these London children, eh? Well, we all know about *them*. I'd advise her not to put sheets on the beds, if she's really set on it. They en't used to it. Sheets of old newspaper's more their line, I think you'll find.' The shop suddenly went dark, or darker than usual, and there was a salvo of thunder like a rip across the sky. 'You'd best stay here – wait till it passes,' Mr Gathergood said with relish, but Kate had had enough, and elected to hurry home before the rain came.

The storm was loud and fierce, but did not seem so very terrible compared with the gas and bombs they were all daily expecting. Soon it was rumbling away to the south, and Kate spun out the journey home, taking field paths. Far off she saw figures working in George Maxey's fields, and by his gait she recognized the one leading the laden waggon as George himself. She stopped and watched for a time, whilst the sky alternated between angry purple and sunlight and fat scattered drops of rain hit the stubble. Being only human, she wondered about what might have been. The news of Stella and Richard's sudden marriage had set her thinking a little wistfully about decisions, paths taken and not taken . . . Her thoughts became vague, and she wandered home through the orchards in a dream. She found Pip there, but not her parents: word had come that a busload of evacuees was on its way from Wisbech station and they had gone to the schoolhouse to meet them. 'Place'll be crawling with kids,' Pip grumped: he had begun courting, taken to brilliantining his hair, and wanted nothing to do with childhood.

'Yes, I suppose,' Kate said, wistful still. It occurred to her, as she sat down and took a storm-shaken cat on to her knee, that she was no longer the centre of anyone's picture. Certainly not here, as was right: she was grown and flown. To George Maxey she was receding into the past. At the hospital she was a nurse amongst many nurses, and a friend in a circle of friends. Helen was married and gone, and now Stella and Richard had married . . . She had an old and weary feeling, and a feeling also of having somehow missed out. She had burnt her bridges effectively enough, but where did the road lead now? Had she taken the wrong one entirely?

She was jolted out of these self-pitying reflections by the sight of four sombre little faces, shiny with rain, and perhaps tears, which had noiselessly appeared at the back door. They gazed at her with stoic expectancy, as if equally prepared for her to embrace them or eat them.

'Well, here we are,' her father said, appearing behind the children, and gently urging them to go in. 'Looks like that storm's gone, any road. In you go, folks. Mek yourselves at home. I'll tek your bags.'

'Four in the end,' said Kate's mother, making an expressive face at her over the tops of their heads. 'Now then, who's hungry?'

The two boys and two girls were not, as it turned out, from the same family. The eldest three were: the youngest boy was an only child and had been separated even from his schoolfriends in the evacuation. The other three had kept him with them all the time and staunchly refused to be separated from him even when it came to the billeting. 'How could we not take him?' Kate's mother whispered to her as she dispensed wedges of cake. 'Anyway, one thing's for certain – they must be nice kids to have taken care of him like that.' They certainly appeared so, though paralysingly shy, and seeming a hair's breadth from tears even while they were laughing at her father's jokes. What chiefly made them uneasy now they were here, Kate soon discovered, was her – or rather, her uniform. Of course: the place looked like a home, but it had a nurse in it, so perhaps grim medical treatment impended . . . She hastened to reassure them. 'I'm just visiting. I'm going back to the hospital where I work tomorrow.' They unbent, and began to talk shakily of their homes and pets, whilst Kate stifled a regret that she would not be here to get to know them: reproached herself too for her gloom, whilst feeling sadder than ever.

She slept that night on a camp bed in the boxroom – the two girls had her old room – and woke late from a strange dream in which it was actually Helen who had married Richard, and Kate had made a dreadful *faux pas* in her letter of congratulation.

Which she really must write, she thought groggily as she went downstairs. From the kitchen window she saw Pip, unbrilliantined, showing the children the hens and ducks. The morning was warm and sunny without sultriness. 'Well, how did they sleep?' she said. 'They look well—'

'Hush.' Her father was crouched at the wireless, his face wincing. The battery was nearly dead and he was having a job to get a signal. Then the unmistakable pinched tones of the Prime Minister came through, with startling clarity.

'. . . from the Cabinet Room at 10 Downing Street. This morning the British Ambassador in Berlin handed the German Government a final note . . .'

Kate's mother had a potato peeler in her hand, and she sat quietly down still holding it, with a little ribbon of peel that dangled but did not fall.

'. . . I have to tell you now that no such undertaking has been received, and that consequently this country is at war with Germany . . .'

'I think perhaps,' Kate said at last, stirring in the silence, 'I'd better go back to the hospital.'

# FOUR

## 1

Perhaps, Stella thought afterwards, it might not have been so bad if it hadn't been for those damned raspberries. And then she thought that was like saying going down in the *Titanic* wouldn't have been so bad if it hadn't been raining at the time.

But these reflections, in which she managed at least a little wry humour, came a good while after the fact: in the immediate aftermath she could not laugh, and her mortification was deep.

'You'll like it when we get there,' Richard said more than once on the train up to Abbotsleigh; but for the first time she could not quite read him, could not tell whether he was being elaborately ironic or just blithely hopeful. Neither helped her, because Stella was truly anxious about this visit and was desperate for it to go well: all the more so because the response of her own family to their marriage had been so discouraging.

Not all of them. Her sister Dot had surprisingly entered into the spirit of the thing and had got hold of some confetti to throw at them when they visited Corbett Street, the day after the little ceremony at the Islington Registry Office. Stella had been prepared for some awkwardness. She had accepted Richard's proposal when she was on very bad terms with her father and stepmother, she had run off to get married without telling them, she had deprived them of the thorough beano that was supposed to accompany a wedding: they had a right to be huffy. But a lot of people were going through quick marriages with things as they were – Richard might be summoned by the RAF at any moment, after all; and Stella had also assumed that the fact that she was enormously happy would count for a lot even with a father as solemn as hers.

She had assumed wrongly. It was because of Richard, of course. She had married out of her class. Already she had had her own simplistic view of things modified, and knew that as far as 'posh' went, Richard was not exactly in the top hat and monocle league. But to her father it was all one: she had colluded with the enemy. That was his personal view, which at least had a certain austere consistency about it – but now of course there was another influence at work. Lilian had plainly thrown in her own poisonous fourpenn'orth, which was the usual mush about thinking herself too good for them. The result was a welcome so chill that not even Richard could make any headway against it: thus he tried too hard and defeated his own object, as he recognized to his own disgust. 'Christmas Day in the orphanage,' he told her later, 'I was awful.' She tried to reassure him, but could not explain that easy manners were not the sort to work with her father; gruff and manly would have been better. But probably nothing would have worked. Wretchedly they perched in the little sitting room, whilst Lilian pressed saintly murmurings on Richard. Where was he from? Hertfordshire? Oh, she had never been there. She'd never had much opportunity to see the country. What with working to bring up children and all . . . Meanwhile her father sat blockishly with gritted teeth, as if imagining himself a political prisoner under interrogation. Having adopted this fixed position of disapproval, he moved from it only to get on his high horse or his soapbox. Richard, still trying, tackled the subject of how they would live – the rented digs must have heightened the Svengali aspect of the whole situation in her father's eyes – and mentioned his application to the RAF, adding that he would try for the other forces if he didn't get in. Jack Tranter had done some tortuous thinking around the subject of the Nazi-Soviet Pact, and found himself a new stance. The Soviets wanted peace: everyone else was warmongering. He informed Richard that a bayonet was a weapon with a worker at both ends, and sulked when Richard agreed with him. Only Archie and Lennie lightened the mood, readily taking to Richard as most children did. They had aeroplane fever and showed Richard cigarette cards of Wellingtons and Blenheims, whilst her father glowered and Lilian made maternal croonings about the state of their shoes.

'Well, that's my lot for you,' she said afterwards, not knowing what she felt.

'It's bound to be awkward,' he said hugging her. The hug made things seem better: in fact, everything seemed better once they were away from it all and back in their dingy, neutral digs near King's Cross. That was the way of it: together they were fine, indeed blissful. The set of rooms that belonged to neither of them formed the perfect space to laugh and make love and waste time; there the anonymity of London was their ally again as it had been during their brief intense courtship and their briefer wedding, where they had signed their names in a smell of floor polish and ink and emerged laughing into an indifferent street full of heedless strangers. And all Stella wanted to do for now was stay in there with him, making occasional sorties to buy fish and chips and sneak them up past the stony eye of their landlady, who was severe about smells. But the day after their nuptial visit to Corbett Street she decided she had better go there again, alone this time, and try for some sort of reconciliation with her father. It was little better. 'You've come for the rest of your clothes, I suppose,' he said: Lilian, of course, had ironed them perfectly and presented them to Stella with a look of suffering reproach, as if they were the bleeding hearts of her children. 'Just wish us well, Dad,' Stella pleaded, but her father was like a wall.

'I don't see as it matters to you whether we do or not,' he said in his most stubbornly argumentative way. 'You went and got married without consulting us. Didn't want anything to do with us, in fact. You're ashamed, that's why. Ashamed to show this chap where you come from.'

'Oh, Dad, I wouldn't have brought him round if I was.' It was no good. As far as her father was concerned, she had rejected them. Perhaps he felt the wrench more than he let on, for whilst his disapproval was usually expressed in the loftiest terms, now he stooped to unworthy sneering. 'You'd best go back,' he said, 'you wouldn't want to get your hands dirty hanging around here.'

It was distressing. Within Stella a flame of respect for her father guttered and nearly went out; and that the flame did not go out entirely was due to her distrust of Lilian, whom she suspected was behind much of it. She left the house almost in tears, and some instinct for consolation led her footsteps to the next street, where she called on Auntie Bea and was riotously received. Bea and Will regarded the match as of their own making – which was in a way true – and having no grasp of social realities, saw no difficulties with it. They at once invited the couple to a knees-up at their place, and so that evening there was something like an impromptu wedding reception in Auntie Bea's house, with crates of beer, Geoffrey shyly clinging on to Richard's arm the whole time, and Bea doing the can-can to their lodger's accordion, whilst the whole neighbourhood pressed itself into the tiny house until it seemed the walls bulged.

Jack Tranter, of course, did not appear. But estrangement from her father was no novelty, at least since his remarriage; and even when he drove her to despair, Stella was on home ground. When she finally agreed that they ought to go and visit Richard's parents, she knew she was venturing into territory that was unknown and also – judging by the sniffy communications Richard had received since their marriage – very probably hostile.

They made the trip in the first week of September – a few days after the declaration of war. They did not hear Mr Chamberlain's Sunday morning broadcast: they were still in bed when their landlady shouted up the stairs that it had finally happened. 'It's been on the wireless,' she shrieked. 'We're at war!' A few moments later sirens were baying across London and Stella was fiercely gripping Richard amongst a tangle of bedsheets to stop him going to the window. 'Bloody hell,' she moaned, 'that was quick off the mark!' It was a false alarm, of course, and the all clear sounded a quarter of an hour later, but for that quarter of an hour Stella was sure they were going to be bombed to bits and in a sort of wild fatalism would not even run down to the public shelter. 'We'll go like this!' she cried, squeezing Richard till he could hardly breathe.

Afterwards they laughed about it, but Stella felt the biting truth of war for the first time. It was real and it included them, and the truth bit more sharply the next day with a letter on Air Ministry notepaper calling Richard for another interview. The world was closing in and their odd honeymoon was coming to an end. And in spite of all her natural optimism, in spite of all Richard's assurances that they would get along just fine, when they set off a few days later to visit his family Stella could not rid herself of a suspicion that this was what would definitely end it.

The train journey up to Abbotsleigh was short, but it was long enough for Stella to notice a change stealing over Richard. They held hands, he was affectionate as ever, but he was restive: he flicked imaginary specks of dirt from his clothes and spoke in flippant bursts, glancing out of the window. Stella wondered whether this was her own nerves infecting him: she knew he did not get on well with his family, but he was at least on familiar ground, whereas she did not know what to expect. She could not, in fact, ever remember feeling more apprehensive. It might not have been so bad if they could have gone home again later, but they were to stay the night. There had been a hasty buying of clothes the day after the wedding as a sort of trousseau and she had on a new frock, but still she was worried about the matter of dress. Were they supposed to change in the evening for dinner or something? 'God,' Richard said, 'don't give them ideas.' He probably meant this dismissiveness to be comforting, but it did not work that way. When he said, 'Just be yourself,' she felt herself more adrift than ever, and would have preferred it if he had given a strict checklist of how to behave.

Abbotsleigh surprised her. There was very little of it: even dear old Monks Bridge seemed clustered and busy in comparison. They got down at a station that looked as if it belonged to a toy railway set and walked up an empty road between tall pine trees. Here and there a grey-tiled cupola showed, and there was a very clean-looking church tower. When they turned into a drive between brick gateposts, Stella gave a murmur of surprise: there was a sign on one of the posts. 'Holdfield – is that the name?' She was impressed. 'I never knew your house had a name!'

'Oh yes, that! Silly really, the postal address is just 5, The Avenue. At least they didn't go the whole hog and call it The Pines.'

The large redbrick villa came in sight. Stella would have admired it if it were not for the fact that she had actually had to go in there. She had an urge to run – but Richard, after all, had braved her father and Lily of the Valleys.

And then it was not so bad – at least, once she had got over her inner embarrassment at nearly saying hello to the maid who answered the door and whom she took at first for Richard's mother. Indeed it was less excruciating at first than the visit to Corbett Street. Whatever they might think of her, Richard's mother and father had the formal manners of their class, which meant that they welcomed her in and said they were glad to meet her and asked her if she would like to freshen up – which meant, as she had hoped, the toilet, because she was bursting to go. It might all be frosty and fake, but it got her through the first minutes, she thought, admiring the fittings of the bathroom. There was a mirror of startling clarity and she applied some powder: those damn freckles were showing. 'My in-laws,' she thought, and wondered how she had ever got here.

Coming down again, she couldn't see her overnight bag, and had a moment of panic – what had she done with it? 'Your luggage has been taken up to your room, my dear,' Richard's mother said. 'Do come and sit down.'

She did, but Richard wouldn't: he roamed like a caged cat, jingling the change in his pockets. Used to Richard being the one who was always at ease, Stella felt a little innocent triumph. Mrs Marwood gave her tea, and then wrong-footed her by talking to her while she was thirstily drinking it.

'Well, this is a very unusual way to meet a daughter-in-law,' she said. 'But I'm glad Richard's seen fit to bring you at last anyway. I'm afraid I don't know the first thing about you, my dear. You'll have to fill in the gaps for me.'

She was a tallish, plumpish, prettyish woman with dark eyes that seemed to stare even when they were lowered. Stella's Violet Drew-trained eyes could tell that her hair was permed very regularly and that she wore a lot of expensive make-up which would have looked garish if it had been cheap. She was at an age when she could have chosen to be an old lady but had decided instead to be neatly, carefully middle-aged. All her movements as she poured the tea were precise and slow, as if she were being filmed in close-up: she radiated an air of feminine expertise, and the room reflected her. Curtains and rugs were meticulously arranged. Wood shone. There were two equally spaced pictures hanging above the mantelpiece, invisible behind highly polished glass.

'Richard, sit down, won't you,' Mrs Marwood said. 'You can't have tea wandering about like that.'

'Yes, sit down, Richard. What on earth's the matter with you?' said his father. He was a big tweedy florid man with a silvery moustache. He had a rich suety voice that Stella found rather pleasant, but glared as if he found everything puzzling.

'Have you had the air-raid sirens here?' Richard said with an effort, sitting down. A silk cushion stuck up behind him and he tugged irritably at it. His mother watched him do so.

'If they dare to bomb us,' his father said, 'we shall repay them in kind.' He spoke hotly, as if someone had challenged him.

'You must find it rather inconvenient where you're living,' Mrs Marwood said, sweeping Stella with her eyes. 'Near King's Cross, I understand?'

'Well, it's just temporary, Mother,' Richard said. 'Just somewhere to stay until the RAF decide what they want to do with me.'

'There's another one of his little surprises,' Mrs Marwood said to Stella. 'Suddenly we discover our son is married. Suddenly we discover our son has applied to join the forces.' She laughed, smoothing her throat.

'Mother, you know I discussed it with you a couple of weeks ago, and told you I was thinking of joining up.' Richard set his tea aside and began running his hands through his hair.

'Well, that at least was mentioned,' Mrs Marwood said, chuckling. The chuckling did not fool Stella, nor did the way Mrs Marwood kept addressing her. It enabled the woman to have a good look at her, which she was doing very thoroughly. 'I must say I don't see why there had to be quite such haste. And as for these lodgings, I would have thought you would have known you were quite welcome to live here with us, until something more suitable could be arranged.'

'Oh, well – that's nice of you – but we didn't want to put you out,' Stella said. 'That wouldn't have been fair.'

'And as for something more suitable – who knows?' Mrs Marwood said, seeming not even to hear this. 'Presumably, Richard, you'll just have to go where the RAF send you. You've thought of that, I suppose?'

'Of course,' Richard said. 'That's how it is in the services. You just get lodgings wherever. It doesn't matter.'

'I don't mind,' Stella said, as Mrs Marwood looked at her again. 'You expect that, what with the war and everything.'

'That's it.' Richard spread out his hands and attempted to be breezy. 'What it comes down to is, we fell in love, and with things as they are it seemed the best thing to marry straight off and worry about the practicalities later, and – it's wonderful.'

There was silence. Listening, Stella noticed that it was complete. There was no traffic noise, no children's voices – nothing. Even the neat-bordered garden beyond the French windows seemed to be devoid of birds. And in that silence she saw something that she should perhaps have seen before. Mrs Marwood had said 'Welcome' because it was proper to do so, but she did not welcome Stella at all. She hated it when either of them said 'we': she hated the whole idea of their marriage. And if Stella couldn't say for sure that Mrs Marwood already hated her personally, it was because she had a strong feeling that her new mother-in-law was the sort who didn't like women much anyway.

Probably this should not have come as such a shock to her. Richard had gone and married a common girl, and she had gathered enough about his family to know that they would deplore it. But being in love with Richard had obscured this. She loved him with an overwhelming energy and directness and had supposed that everything connected with him would at least feel the force of this. Now she saw it was not so. Her love was irrelevant here.

'What part of London are you from?' said Mr Marwood suddenly.

'I told you, Father, Hackney,' Richard sighed.

'I don't know Hackney. What are your people?'

It was like talking to a dotty old judge, Stella thought. 'My mum's dead. My dad works for a furniture maker down the Hackney Road.'

'And does he approve of your marrying like this?'

'Well . . . it was a surprise to him, I s'pose. But he's a bit of an awkward old s . . . so-and-so at the best of times.'

Mr Marwood stared.

'Would you like more tea, my dear?' Mrs Marwood said. Stella was still thirsty, as the cup hardly held anything, but she thought it was politer to refuse, so she said, 'No, ta.' Then instantly regretted it, as everybody else had some.

'Well, I'm sure you understand it's been a surprise to us too,' Mrs Marwood said, delicately stirring. Her hands, small and manicured, always seemed to be on show. Stella noticed a couple of liver spots. 'Naturally one would like to meet one's son's choice of wife before the event, but the matter was really taken out of our hands.'

'The world's changing, Mother,' Richard said. He had his hands behind his head: the exaggerated ease was full of tension.

'The world,' Mrs Marwood said, 'has obviously gone mad. One looks in vain for standards any more. In my day one played the game of life by the rules. Very old fashioned, no doubt, but it seemed to work. And now look where new ideas have brought us.'

'Oh, Mother,' Richard said, 'surely you're not going to say that there's a link between the war and people getting married without a lot of hoo-ha first.'

'I am not saying that at all,' Mrs Marwood said in her heavy imperturbable way. 'But this hoo-ha, as you call it, was good enough for previous generations. It was good enough for Maurice.'

Stella saw a dangerous look in Richard's eyes at that, and piped up, 'Well, you know me and Richard did meet a good while ago – last year it was. Up in the fens. So – you know – we go back a fair way.' But she saw at once that the orchard summer was not a subject to please Mrs Marwood; whilst Richard's father looked more crustily puzzled than ever and said, 'I thought you were from London?'

'I am. I just . . .' At this moment Stella began to lie – not with outright untruths, but by trying to say things in a way that would go down better with the Marwoods. 'I just spent the summer there.'

'What an odd place to spend a holiday,' Mr Marwood said. 'I understand there's a lot of inbreeding in that part of the world.' Having said this, he then gave an abrupt glare all round him, as if someone else had spoken. It was a habit that Stella had already noticed and which she might have found funny under different circumstances.

But Mrs Marwood was no fool. 'Well, Richard has kept you very secret, at any rate, my dear,' she said, 'which is why it's such a great event meeting you at last. As I say, we really don't like to think of you and Richard living in lodgings, and one rather wishes he could have discussed it beforehand; and the matter of the wedding too, because then one could have planned in regard to presents and so on. But I dare say under certain circumstances a quiet wedding is best. As to joining up, I suppose that was your choice too, Richard.' She looked hard at Stella.

'It's only jumping the gun a bit,' Richard said. 'Men of my age will be called up soon anyway.'

'Well, I dare say you wouldn't have fancied living as a preparatory schoolmaster's wife, my dear, at any rate,' Mrs Marwood said, with a smile of acid sweetness.

'I wouldn't mind whatever,' Stella said promptly. She had felt that shaft hit home, and she knew it had been fired with malice.

Her instant impulse was to come out with the Eliza Doolittle stuff – 'Coo, imagine me in a school, when I can't even write me own nyme!' – because it would be the surest way of turning the tables on the woman; but she quashed it. All she had to do, she reminded herself, was keep up the sweetness and light till tomorrow, and then they could leave and forget about it all. It was she and Richard that mattered: she must hold on to that.

'You haven't been telling lies to this girl, have you, Richard?' Mr Marwood said, giving him the look he seemed to reserve for his son – a look of tetchy incomprehension, as if he were a strange dog or cat that had crept in and made itself at home.

'Good God, what a question,' Richard said laughing.

'In regard to money, I mean. The fact is you're hardly in a position to marry at all. I was over thirty before I felt myself able to support a wife and family in the proper manner. I just hope you haven't been giving a false idea of yourself.'

'Here's a turn-up, darling,' Richard said with a wink at Stella. 'They think you married me for my money. I don't know which of us should feel more insulted.'

'Rubbish, rubbish,' Mr Marwood said, his face glowing. 'You know quite well what I mean. You'll only have yourself to rely on—'

'I haven't got any money,' Richard said, 'and I won't have any except the King's shilling or whatever it is the government pays you nowadays for fighting their wars for them while they sit in their snug bunkers.' He couldn't help putting that in, Stella noticed: it was as if he had to needle them. 'Stella understands that and so does anybody who knows me.'

'I'm sure we'll be all right,' Stella said. 'And what with the war and everything – I mean we don't know how long it's going to last, so there doesn't seem much point in making too many plans.'

Am I talking Chinese? she thought. Everything she said was met with the same blank response.

'Well, the world seems to have gone mad,' Mrs Marwood said with a wave of her hand. 'It's such a dreadful thing that we should be at war again, though of course we have right on our side.'

'We had God on our side last time,' Richard said, 'but then so did the Germans.'

'There's no denying this Hitler has gone too far,' Mr Marwood said, 'but it is a pity it's come to this. Nazi Germany, for all its faults, has prevented the spread of Communism into Europe. It's acted as a bulwark against the Bolsheviks.'

'And Italy too,' Richard said. 'A pair of bulwarks, in fact.'

'Absolutely. Pity, pity it's come to this,' Mr Marwood muttered, then gave his glare of surprise.

It should have been one of those moments when meeting Richard's eyes without going into screaming fits was an impossibility – a moment for the delightful, almost telepathic complicity of lovers. But not here, not in this silent, bright, dustless house: here their glances were perplexed gestures across a vast space, and Richard himself looked subtly different, as a loved person will when seen in a mirror.

Mrs Marwood suddenly brought tea to a close by suggesting they go out in the garden. Stella wondered if this had been the first part of the test, and whether she had passed or failed it; then saw bleakly that there could hardly be any question of a test. She wasn't even a candidate, simply because of who she was. Yet a part of her still refused to be downhearted. There were worse things in the world than snobs, after all; and when Richard resolutely took her arm she felt a little of the distance there had been between them close up. 'Well,' she thought, 'they can be as snotty as they like – it doesn't matter. The worst they can do is pull a knife on me or something, in which case I shall give as good as I get.' The idea of her wrestling with Mrs Marwood in the shrubberies like something from a Bulldog Drummond story tickled her: she would have to tell Richard later.

'One tries to keep the place up to scratch,' Mrs Marwood was saying, 'but it's so difficult getting good help these days. We had a wonderful little man who did sterling service for years, but he's quite crippled with rheumatism now and though he wanted to keep coming, I wouldn't hear of it . . .'

The garden seemed vast and ornate to Stella, but dull too. The borders seemed to have been edged with a ruler: the stone path that led down to the apple trees at the foot had been scrubbed clean of any trace of moss and nothing grew in the cracks. It was as if nature itself was a sort of weed, to be kept down.

Mrs Marwood began to talk of cousins and aunts. The pretext was to say how disappointed they all were at not attending the wedding and how they sent their best wishes. Actually it was a game that quickly became obvious even to Stella, whilst Richard's whole body – she could sense it – went rigid with resentment. All the achievements, the unimpeachable character, the sheer rightness of the cousins was trotted out. Somebody called Cousin Herbert seemed to be especially approved. He was a full partner in the firm now – at twenty-six! – and engaged to a wonderful girl who had a brother at Sandhurst . . .

'Dear old cousin Herbert,' Richard said. 'I once saw him kick a hedgehog a good hundred yards down the road and then stamp on it. He must have been about thirteen then. Already full of promise.'

'Youthful high spirits,' huffed Mr Marwood. Richard's mother went on with the game, though with pursed lips and a look of inhaling some unpleasant scent. Richard continued to add barbed comments. It was deadly: Stella wished he would leave it and squeezed his arm significantly. But she sensed that there was something compulsive at work here. It was not all about her: she was a new element in an old conflict.

Beneath the apple trees she experienced a moment of exquisite memory, and when she caught Richard's eye she saw an answering twinkle. If only, if only . . . ! But the apple trees were not an orchard, and no careless summer stretched before them. They had to go back into the frigid house and make more small talk with these people from whom she found it almost impossible to believe that Richard could have sprung. The curfew had sounded and the gates of the real world had swung to with a clang and shut them in, as they must always do.

A few moments alone might have helped them. But life in the

high-ceilinged rooms of Holdfield was no more conducive to privacy, Stella saw, than the cramped conditions of Corbett Street. You had to be on view all the time. Even the slightest remark passed between the two of them was snapped up by Mrs Marwood, who would tilt her serene doll-eyed face and inquire, 'What was that, my dear? What did you say?' Somehow the time crawled by: dinner approached, and with it a new challenge to be faced – Richard's brother Maurice and his wife were invited.

They arrived early – to have a good look at her, Stella supposed. This was not as bad as she had feared. Mrs Marwood had temporarily disappeared – not of course to the kitchen, which was the province of the little scared-looking woman who crept about behind the stairs – Stella suspected she had gone to apply a fresh coat of make-up. Sherry had been produced, and she had swallowed down a couple of glasses, not caring if it was unwise, and she had received her first genuine smile of greeting. This was from Maurice's wife, Phyllis. She was a blooming big-boned lady, healthily pregnant; she looked as if she could have carried quintuplets with no trouble. 'I'm the family elephant,' she laughed, giving Stella a hearty handshake. 'And *you're* Richard's little secret. Not that I'm *very* surprised because I've been trying like anything to matchmake for him and got simply nowhere so I thought there must be something behind it. And so you absolutely toddled off together and got married! I think that's the nicest thing I ever heard, and so I'll forgive you for not letting me be there and see it and have a jolly good cry and so on.'

'I've never understood this business of crying at weddings. Surely they should be happy occasions.' That was Maurice.

'You must have heard of "crying with happiness", Maurice,' his wife said.

'I've heard of it, certainly. But it's not something I've ever experienced. One can only judge by one's personal experience, after all.' Burly, serious, pompous, Maurice stood before the fireplace cradling his unlit pipe and studying Stella whenever he thought she wasn't looking. He was as unlike Richard as it was possible to be, and plainly disapproved of her, but Stella thought there might be quite a nice person in there somewhere – unless the stuffed shirt had completely displaced him.

'Well, I can only say I would have been *more* surprised if Richard had got married in a normal manner like everyone else,' Maurice said. 'He seems to take a positive delight in foisting unpleasant surprises on us.'

'I don't call this an unpleasant surprise, Maurice,' Phyllis said, with a nervous smile at Stella.

'I wasn't referring to that, of course,' Maurice said, colouring. 'I mean the unpleasantness of being kept in the dark about things in general. Now, Richard – what is this about the RAF? Does it offer the best prospects just now, do you think?'

'I don't know about that,' Richard said. 'Best prospects of getting your behind shot off, I suppose.'

He was joking, but Stella winced inside. His decision to try for the RAF had seemed out of her hands, and she knew that the war would gather most young men into its perilous arms; still in spite of her natural optimism she suffered a shudder of dread whenever the reality of what he would have to do was mentioned, and she secretly hoped the medical board would turn up some unfitness in him.

'One could have seen about getting you a commission a good while ago, if it was the forces you had in mind,' Maurice said. 'As it is you'll just be caught up in the herd of recruits, but there we are. I dare say these aren't the times to be picky. I shall be happy to do whatever my country asks of me, if it comes to that.'

'I think the women should too,' Stella found herself saying: the sherry had buoyed her up. 'You know, like in the last lot, where they made shells and guns and what have you. We're all in it together, ain't we? Nothing worse than sitting at home twiddling your thumbs while the men are off soldiering. And it don't make sense – I mean, if Hitler means business, we shall need every pair of hands else we'll go under.'

'What are we saying about women?' Mrs Marwood said, floating in with her smile in place and a puff of eau de Cologne.

'Stella was just saying that women will have their part to play in the war,' Phyllis said, 'and quite right too.'

'Good heavens, one hopes it won't come to that,' Mrs Marwood said. 'Of course one is fully prepared to keep the home fires burning, because that's always been our contribution in time of war and very valuable it is. But one can't approve of women becoming directly involved. That would be just giving up the civilization we're supposed to be fighting for.'

'The trouble started with the last war. It was after that women got the vote, which should never have happened,' Mr Marwood said biliously. 'Led to all sorts. All sorts,' he told himself, and gave his puzzled glare.

'Well, women may have to step in as they did last time, if a lot of manpower is called up,' Maurice pronounced, 'but of course one wouldn't wish to see them doing men's work.'

'But they have been doing it for years,' Stella said. 'Ain't they? It's just they don't get paid the same for it. There's thousands of women been working all their lives in factories and sweatshops and what have you.'

'Not a good thing, though, my dear,' Mrs Marwood said, stroking her throat, 'surely?'

'Maybe it ain't, but most of 'em don't have a lot of choice. They have to work to make ends meet.'

'Well, of course, it's a great pity if their husbands don't provide for them properly,' Mrs Marwood said. 'But I think that says something about their choice of husbands, I'm afraid. No, I'm sorry, my dear, you can't convince me that it's a good thing for women to go out into the workplace. The experience coarsens them. And it spoils them for marriage.'

'Not every girl wants to get married, Mother,' Richard said.

'Oh, yes, I know, dear,' his mother said laughing. 'I've heard that very often – and always from the lips of extremely ugly girls.'

'Now, do I see someone who'd like another sherry?' Mr Marwood said, lumbering forward with the decanter.

'Oh, yes, lovely, I'll have a drop,' Stella said; and only realized too late that he had been addressing Phyllis, whose glass was empty. Phyllis passed it off for her as best she could, saying, 'No, not me – Stella's turn – I'd better not have any more – the coming event, you know,' but Stella caught a malicious glance from Mrs Marwood, and felt that she had showed herself up. With more sherry inside her this did not seem to matter as much as it might have, and she felt it was better to talk and make a few blunders than sit there like a mouse.

'Anyone mind if I light my pipe?' Maurice said, still looming at the fireplace. Obviously this was not a question he normally asked, but did so for Stella's sake. She thought this was nice of him, and was about to say something about liking the smell of a pipe when she was talked down by Mrs Marwood, who gushed, 'I am glad you took to a pipe, Maurice. A pipe suits a man. He can sit and think with a pipe. I wish you would try it, Richard.'

'Tried it at college,' Richard said. 'But I found it such a darn fiddle getting it lit, and hadn't the patience.'

'You get used to it with practice,' Maurice said.

'Yes, all it takes is a little practice,' their mother echoed. The whole family, except for Richard, had this way of hammering on at things – the very opposite of his own manner. 'I should think it's like second nature once you're used to it. I do think a pipe suits a man better than cigarettes. I always think there's something a little effeminate about cigarettes.'

'You don't like to see women smoking, and yet you think cigarettes are effeminate,' Richard said. 'You're like Humpty Dumpty, Mother. You make words mean what you want them to mean.'

'Men should be men and women should be women,' Mrs Marwood said with her smoothest complacency. 'That's what I mean, my dear, and I shall stick by it.'

A man's woman, Stella thought: poor old Phyllis doesn't get a look-in. She found that she disliked her mother-in-law very much, but she was still slightly in awe of her and of them all: they were so different, so assured, so difficult to measure up to. Without that touch of awe she might not have tried so hard, and the result might have been easier; but inexperienced as she was, she took them at their own valuation. There was no one to tell her, as

Helen might have done, that these people were nothing to be afraid of – that they were only a pretentious set of middle-class suburbanites, and that a woman such as Olive Kingswell would have found them as awful as she did. Richard could have told her, but he was so tangled up with them it would have meant tearing himself apart. All she could do was drink the sherry and try desperately to fit in, feeling more intimidated all the time. Whether it was the sherry that was her downfall it was hard to say. She didn't have a weak head and felt quite normal when they sat down to dinner. But something made her reckless enough to reach out for those raspberries.

They were in a large cut-glass bowl in the centre of the table, bright red and swimming in juice; she guessed they were for dessert. They looked enormously tempting, and all through the first course, which was some rather salty bony sort of fish, she was wondering how they would taste. She was separated from Richard: beside her was Mr Marwood, who seemed interested only in noisily going at his food, and nobody seemed to be taking any notice of her. Her intention was to put out her hand and pinch a raspberry and pop it into her mouth without anyone seeing. But somehow her fingers got hold of a whole clump of raspberries. Her hand jerked, and the next moment they were spattered across the snow-white lace of the tablecloth. The juice was scarlet as blood, and Mr Marwood lifting his head from his plate began shouting out in surprise.

'Good God, what's that? Is it blood? Good God – look here – on the tablecloth . . .'

There could hardly have been a greater fuss if she had hurled the raspberries round the room. Everyone craned to look. Maurice boomed, 'How on earth did that happen?' She sat red-faced and apologizing, whilst Mrs Marwood put on a calm hostessy performance that did not fool her for a moment. 'Never mind – not to worry,' she droned, examining the scarlet stains. 'I've had this tablecloth for years – something of an heirloom. It's remarkable the punishment it can take.' She got the cringing domestic to rub at the stains with a wet cloth. This only made them worse, as

Stella could have told her; but for Mrs Marwood, dirt must be attacked at once. And even when the fuss had died down and the main course had been brought in and Richard was valiantly telling a succession of wild stories, Mrs Marwood could not forget it. She did not mention it or try to clean it any more: but she did not take her eyes off the stains for more than a couple of seconds at a time for the rest of the dinner, and all her talk was absent-minded. The stains, glowing and undeniable on that expanse of white, possessed her.

She did not look at Stella: not once. After the first awful embarrassment was over it did not occur to Stella that Mrs Marwood might hate her for doing such a thing. In fact Mrs Marwood hated everything about her, and the stained tablecloth merely released what was hidden; but Stella did not find this out until after dinner was over, and by then, again perhaps unfortunately, she had had some more to drink. Maurice – or more likely Phyllis – had insisted on bringing a bottle of champagne for the occasion, and they drank some at dinner, Mr Marwood proposing a stiff toast to the happy couple. The whole thing was as awkward and insincere as could be, but Stella floated on the champagne and felt that the worst was over. Even when they moved to the drawing room and Mrs Marwood began being coldly and precisely hateful to her, she could not quite believe what was happening.

The woman had her in a corner, which made it easier for her. Mr Marwood was hunched at the wireless listening for the news, Phyllis was chattering to Richard, Maurice was going gravely round checking the blackout for chinks: the opportunity presented itself for a talk alone over the coffee pot, and Mrs Marwood commenced it by saying, 'Richard looks ill.'

'Does he?' Stella glanced over at the back of his dark head. 'I thought he looked all right.'

'I know my son,' Mrs Marwood said; and then, 'Of course this hasn't wholly surprised us, what's happened. He was always irresponsible.'

'Look, Mrs Marwood, we'll be all right, really – I wanted to marry him and I'm ready for whatever comes—'

'You will not be all right.' Up close the shape of Mrs Marwood's small mouth was visible beneath the large Cupid's bow of lipstick. She sprayed a little as she went on in a loud hiss, 'I mean that he has always been irresponsible and because of that he is always likely to be taken advantage of.'

Stella fell off the champagne cloud with a bump. 'I haven't taken advantage of him,' she said, more in bewilderment than anger.

'You know very well what you're doing.'

'Well, so does he. He's a grown man, in case you hadn't noticed.'

'Of course he doesn't know what he's doing. Look at him. Having to live like a petty clerk in some frightful set of rooms—'

'He doesn't have to do—'

'And this business about joining the RAF. That was never in his mind before you got hold of him. He doesn't know what he's doing – he's just thrown himself into it with no thought for the consequences and now God knows what will happen. You must think I'm a fool not to see it.'

Harsher things were in her mind, but all Stella said was, 'We're happy, so I really don't care what you think.'

Mrs Marwood gave her a glance up and down, which from a man would have been explicitly insulting. 'That's obvious,' she said.

'I think we should go home.'

'Oh, that's it – cause a sordid little scene and drag Richard into it—'

'Stella could drag me anywhere,' Richard said, appearing beside them and placing a hand on Stella's shoulder. 'But where am I being dragged in this particular instance?' His voice was light, his eyes hard.

'Richard, do you think we could go home? I'm not feeling very well,' Stella said. All she wanted was to escape.

'Being catty, Mother?' Richard said. 'You're a bit old for it, aren't you? But do tell – where am I being dragged?'

'It isn't worth talking about,' Mrs Marwood said, averting her eyes. 'You obviously can't see, so we may as well forget about it.'

'Richard, I'd like to go home.'

'Home, but I thought you were staying here?' boomed Maurice, butting in.

Mrs Marwood threw up her hands. 'They were invited to do so,' she said with a harsh little laugh, 'but who knows?'

'You don't invite somebody to your house and then spend the whole time insulting 'em,' cried Stella. She had lost her temper, and knew what her face must look like. 'At least you don't where I come from.'

'I wouldn't know about that, my dear. Never mind, I do begin to understand the secret wedding, anyhow. If this sort of behaviour is anything to go by—'

'Listen, my old duck, it wouldn't be my lot that would show themselves up – it'd be you, staring away like a lot of constipated pigs!'

'Oh, yes,' Mrs Marwood sighed, turning away, 'oh yes, here we go . . .'

It would take more than that to wound the old bag, Stella thought, but at once Mr Marwood began fussing over her. She was his little rose, to be protected: how stupid he was. Maurice was blustering something about an apology, but Stella was already moving.

'Richard! Where are you going?' Mrs Marwood said.

Richard had slipped his hand into Stella's. He was white, and she saw that he was as wild as she; but he was pulling at bonds that could not touch her. 'Home, with my wife,' he said. They collected their bags and ran to the station. The outside world allowed them a little kindness, and they caught the last train back to London with half a minute to spare.

## 2

They had not been together long, but already Richard and Stella had reached that level of unspoken communication which saves both energy and time. On the train home they did not talk much because they did not need to: a few glances and words reinstated the tenderness that the frigid atmosphere of Abbotsleigh had denied them. And once inside their digs Richard poured them each a stiff glass of gin and then sat down close to her, looking nakedly into her eyes.

'I'm sorry that I ever put you through an experience like that, my darling,' he said, 'but I did, and I can't change it. I'd give anything to be able to change it, but I can't. That's the awful thing. I'd move heaven and earth for you, but my family . . .'

'Are your family,' she said. 'And you can't change that either. And I suppose it's wrong to want to.'

'You understand,' he said, caressing her fingertips. 'You see, part of me – especially after tonight – wants to blow the whole lot of them up with a ruddy great bomb and—'

'I know, sweetheart,' she said. 'Gawd knows I feel like that myself tonight. But that part of yourself – well, it hurts you, doesn't it? I should know. Look at my lot. Look at the way my dad's carried on.'

'Preferable to my unholy crew anyway,' he said, his face darkening.

'No – it's no good thinking like that, duck. We can't turn it into a war and take sides and everything. It doesn't get us anywhere.'

He sighed. 'You're right, of course. Well, I can't be glad that you've seen what they're like. But I'm glad they've seen what you're like—'

'Blimey, you're joking.'

'No, no. I'm not, Stella. They're not quite as stupid as they appear, so I'm hoping it will sink in to them, somehow, just what it is that they lack that you've got. I'm hoping that they'll see why it is that I'm out of their clutches: because I've found happiness with you, real happiness. And it's that happiness that takes me away from them. It's that happiness that they can't understand.'

'I'm not very happy tonight,' she said truthfully, 'but I'm

happy with you, Richard. That's a different thing, ain't it?'

He kissed her.

'I don't want to speak to any of them or see any of them ever again,' he said.

'I know,' she said. 'I could see it in your face. And you'd do that an' all, wouldn't you? For me. I don't want it, though, Richard. It wouldn't be right and it wouldn't be – I don't know, it wouldn't be real, somehow.'

They went to bed and lay quiet, limbs touching, hands fitting together; discovering each other again, in fact, for at Abbotsleigh they had been as effectively separated as if they had been miles apart.

'Imagine if they had all been at the wedding,' she said after a while. 'Both lots, I mean. Blimey . . . I suppose she was right in a way. It *was* like a secret wedding. It must have seemed a bit odd to them.'

'God, don't go defending her. She doesn't deserve it.'

'I'm not. I was just thinking . . . both families must have thought that.'

'I don't give a hang what my family think. Especially my mother and especially about the wedding.'

'Well, you must do, else you wouldn't be all strung up now.' Though their limbs were still touching, there was a stiffness about the contact, and a strained dogmatic tone had entered their voices. To conclude a day of such tension without friction would have been superhuman, but they had been so loving and they did not see this. 'Anyway, that's all very well for you to say – as if she doesn't matter. You weren't the one getting picked to pieces by the old crab.'

'I wish I had been. Then I could have told her to go to hell.'

'No, Richard, you couldn't. Because I'd have felt like that was my fault. You'd be falling out with your family and it'd be all my fault and – oh, for crying out loud, I don't want that.'

'I don't want that either,' he said, sitting up and fumbling for a cigarette. 'But what would be much worse is if they made *us* fall out. And that's what they're doing right now and I won't have it.

I'm damned if I'll let them do that.' The lit match showed her his profile abruptly in the blacked-out darkness. He looked thin and drawn. 'Yes, I want the best of both worlds. Doesn't everybody? But if it comes to a choice, then there's no competition. If I can't make you believe that, then I'm stuck.'

'I do believe it,' she said after a moment. 'I do. But it won't come to a choice anyway. Will it? Not unless you decide to run away with Phyllis.'

It was a weak and shaky attempt at humour, and their laughter was weak and shaky too; but it was a signal, and Richard responded to it. They embraced, with the awkwardness of deep feeling.

'That's nice,' Stella said. 'Now give us a puff of that.'

They lay quiet, smoking. She felt heartsore; but also greatly loved. 'Just us two,' she said, when the cigarette was put out and they lay comfortably curled against each other. 'We'll just have to be everything to each other, won't we? That's all right.' Stella was brave, and did not flinch from even such an impossible task as this.

# Part Four

## *August 1940*

# *ONE*

## 1

Corporal Benham only dawned slowly on Kate's consciousness as an individual presence. At first he was an anonymous part of that suffering mass that had been brought back from Dunkirk and was referred to, in the Emergency Medical Services Hospital where she worked, as 'the men'. She was not dealing with 'patients' any more. While the hospital was not a full military establishment, it was run on military lines, even though many of the nurses had come like herself from the Civil Nursing Reserve. It had been hastily built from prefabricated blocks in the grounds of a derelict country house ten miles out of Peterborough, and everything down to the nurses' quarters had an air of the barrack. Since June its three wards had been filled with wounded soldiers who had been spirited back from the French beaches to a country ill-prepared to receive them. Many had undergone appalling experiences: some, shattered beyond the resources of the hospital, had been transferred, being moved covertly at night so as not to offend civilian sensibilities. Others had let go of their hard-won lives, but the empty beds they left were soon filled. Nursing – good nursing – required impersonality, even in a civilian context. At the EMS Hospital it was absolutely essential. In the urgent chaos of the men's arrival – some who had been burned and strafed on the crossing had arrived virtually naked – there had been no time for sentiment, and Kate had tried to maintain that detachment since. Military discipline helped, but so did the simple instinct for self-preservation.

And so, though she knew Corporal Benham as the man in the second bed from the end on the right of Ward B, as a patient who was now walking though still being treated for wounds to the back and right arm that gave him great pain and that would leave him perhaps sixty per cent fit if he was lucky, even as Jim because one or two of the other men called him that, Kate hardly knew him as a person at all and felt it right that it should be so. And when she did begin to be aware of him it was as a voice.

The voice was not noticeably different in timbre and inflexion from that of the other men. It was a plain voice with a touch of West Country in it: it did not stand out as did the voice of a fierce and touchy young man named Frobisher who, though a private, spoke like an officer and was gently mocked for it. Yet when the men were talking amongst themselves, it was Corporal Benham's voice that her ear singled out. Perhaps it was because he did not speak overmuch; and when he did it was with a sort of coolness that was somehow refreshing.

'Oh, thank *you* very much,' one man grumbled when the air was rent, once again, by the roar of a fighter overhead: he was recovering from an operation and needed sleep. 'See plenty of you now, don't we? Where were you when we needed you? Bastard Brylcreem boys.'

'Where were they, my old fruit? They were slipping it to your wife, that's where they were while you were getting your arse shot off on a frigging frog beach, and you know what—?'

'They couldn't be everywhere at once, Powell, as you well know.' That was Frobisher. 'And just suppose they'd lost any more planes in France, where would we be now?'

'Why, where are we now? Right in it, that's where we are. Don't talk to me. Can't be everywhere at once – balls to 'em. Nancies, they are. Bunch of ruddy nancies.'

'Well, if they're nancies,' Frobisher said with exasperation, 'then they're not going to be interested in anybody's wife, are they?'

'Perhaps Jerry'll beat them. Then we can all start liking them.'

That was Corporal Benham. There was something almost lazy

about the way he inserted this remark, which caused a moment's silence.

'We'll have no talk of getting beaten, thank you, Benham,' Frobisher said. 'That's the sort of talk that brought France down.'

'Well, we got beaten,' Corporal Benham said. 'Didn't we?'

'Bloody Frogs let us down,' someone muttered.

'Yes, Benham, we got beaten,' Frobisher said. 'But I don't see why you should gloat over it.'

'I'm not,' Corporal Benham said equably. 'But it doesn't bother me. You fight and you lose. Hard luck.'

'It's going to be more than hard luck,' Frobisher said, irascibly, 'if the ruddy Nazis get here. You've got rather a strange attitude, Benham, if I may say so. One wonders why you joined up at all.'

'I don't know why I did, really. Why did you?'

'To serve my country,' Frobisher said, very stiff.

'Well, I suppose that's a reason.'

'You're a damned odd fish, Benham. I wonder about you, I really do.'

They did not know what to make of him. Grousing was a way of life with them, and understandable after what they had been through; but Corporal Benham did not join in. Neither did Frobisher, because of his patriotic principles, but Benham seemed merely neutral. This was baffling to the men; to Kate, against her will, it began to be fascinating.

The others sometimes spoke of him as a loner. She noticed that he received very little post, and on visiting days, when wives and relatives were brought to the hospital in a special bus, there was never anyone for him. She wondered about this, but not with pity; her job required her to keep pity on a short rein in any event, and there was something about Corporal Benham that discouraged it, a kind of self-possession that did not, however, repel – he was just different.

It did not yet occur to her why he should strike her as different: she did not see this as a symptom of something in herself. Even her curiosity about him she suppressed, which was not difficult in the circumstances. Life was busy and arduous: the nurses were overstretched, the most junior having to do work that would normally have been the province of orderlies and even domestics; sitting up in bed in her hut, she could hardly keep her eyes open long enough to scribble a letter to her parents, and in the summer skies planes enacted a deathly ballet that had fateful meaning for them all. Tense and tired, with nerves tightened by raids and the daily apprehension of what was to come, Kate scarcely had room in her mind for speculation about the mysteries of another human being.

But life, she found, had ways of making room. Corporal Benham was not a patient who needed a great deal doing for him now, but still she was in daily contact with him, giving A.P.C. and changing dressings. While she was very correct in her dealings with all the men, the Ward Sister holding strong views on fraternization, there was inevitably a trickle of personal exchange. She asked him about the book he was reading: he asked her where the raid had fallen last night. It was all small stuff; but she found herself going over it in her mind when she went off duty.

'I think I'll have to take these apples away – they're rotting. The hot weather, I'm afraid.'

'Oh, that's all right. None too keen on apples, to tell the truth. I always think they're a bit of a let-down, don't you? They look nicer than they taste.'

'I shouldn't try telling my father that. He grows apples for a living.'

'Does he now? You don't sound like a West Countrywoman.'

'That's because I'm not. I'm from a little village in the fens – not too far from here – about twenty miles away. They all grow fruit there. I'm sure my father would convert you to apples. Oh dear, those pillows haven't been changed. I'll have a word with laundry.'

'Here, I'm sorry.'

'What for?'

'That sounded rude. When I said you didn't sound like a West Countrywoman. Like I've been listening to the way you talk or something.'

'Silly. Is that where you're from?'

'Zummerzet,' he said, in a quiet droll way that made her laugh.

'It sounds nice. Family there?'

He shook his head. 'I've got an aunt in Puddletown in Dorset. I wish I'd come from there. It'd be nice to be able to say you come from Puddletown, wouldn't it? Like something out of Beatrix Potter. Anyway, she sent me the apples . . . She's not much of an aunt, really.'

He gave a smile. To call it wintry would be unfair, for it was warm; but it was the fleeting, glinting warmth of sun on snow. Perhaps this was the effect of the wounds, but he looked as if he had always been a pale man. His eyes, heavy-lidded, were a strikingly light blue, his hair a cinnamon colour: he was slight though tall, with a pronounced bone structure, and had long beautifully shaped hands. This was the more noticeable because of the state of his right arm. The first boat he had boarded at Dunkirk had been blown up on the beach, and his arm had been pinned under the wreckage. It had been crushed from shoulder to wrist, and Kate knew from his records that he had very nearly lost it. Instead the surgeons had performed some wonder that had left him intact but fearfully scarred: the arm looked like sewn leather and would always be wasted, and he had only the feeblest grip in his right hand. Yet the hand itself was unmarked. On the end of that ragged arm it looked like a piece of marble sculpture emerging from crude stone.

Not much of an aunt: it was an odd phrase and she kept pondering over it. Then she reproached herself. Her duty was to minister to the men's medical needs and that was all. The effort of will that had carried Kate through her nurse's training had turned her into a rather stern self-disciplinarian: the advent of rationing had made little impression on her, for the habit of denying herself was fixed. So she set herself a strict ration when it came to thoughts of Corporal Benham; and felt it would be best if she could do without them altogether.

Then one day the army surgeon made the rounds of the wards. She was not on duty that day, and glad of it: she disliked the pompous military fuss that was made, and the way the men had to sit to attention in their beds seemed to her sheer nonsense. When she went on duty that night, however, she learned that the surgeon had scheduled another operation for Corporal Benham the next day.

'Not his arm again,' she said to the Night Sister. 'What more can they do? There's nothing on the X-rays.'

'Major Ridgeley detects certain sequestra in Benham's lower back and wishes to open for that reason,' said the Night Sister. 'The operation is scheduled for the morning, so it'll only concern the day staff, Nurse, not you.' She was a sour middle-aged woman who resented the way the war had thrust these inexperienced young nurses above their station.

Taking her place at the lamplit table at the end of the ward, Kate looked down the twin rows of narrow iron beds. At the near end a very young private named Evans was having another bad night. The brightest and liveliest of all when the men had first been brought in, he had suffered increasingly from a spinal injury: she wondered that the Major hadn't had him transferred. The rest of the men were quiet, including Corporal Benham. She could just see a faint line of light along his cheekbone.

Kate savoured the quiet. The hospital had escaped raids so far, but there were aerodromes not far off: all day the sky had throbbed and whined and the sirens had sounded three times. The orderlies had a wireless in their quarters and one had told her the day's tally of planes before she came on duty. The balance was still in our favour, they said; but the losses sounded terrible to her, and she doubted they were being told everything. In the darkness, with no sound but the troubled breathing of the rows of wounded men, it was impossible not to think sombrely of what might lie ahead.

At length she began to write a letter. It was to Stella and Richard. They had been married nearly a year now, and to their great delight had been living since the spring in the fens, not far from the orchard country. Richard had been posted to RAF Marham in West Norfolk, and they were living in a rented house near Downham Market. *Isn't it wonderful that we should end up here, near where we first met?* Stella had written. *About time something good happened to us!* They had had some hard times: marriage had estranged them from both their families, they had flitted from place to place during Richard's preliminary training with the RAF, and then he had been injured whilst with his Operational Training Unit and had had to kick his heels through a dreary convalescence. Now, however, they seemed to be as settled as any service couple could be; and though your mind could not be at ease about anyone in uniform just now, he was at least in bombers rather than fighters. He was a Pilot Officer with a squadron of Wellingtons. He had been flying ops since May and had found it, apparently, a piece of cake; but Stella's latest letter told a grimmer story. Things were really hotting up, she said, and she could tell that Richard was exhausted simply because he pretended so hard not to be. As for Stella's own state of mind, she gave no clue to the strain she must be suffering – except perhaps in one sentence. *I was in the garden the other day and Jerry went over and all of a sudden I screamed every swearword I knew at him till my throat hurt and then I felt better.*

Also, Stella was pregnant. She must have been six or seven months forward by now; yet though her letters were frequent, this was something she had hardly mentioned at all since first sending Kate the news. Kate restrained herself from reading between the lines, and felt it would be best to see Stella face to face before speculating. It would be wonderful to see them both again; she had promised them a visit as soon as she had heard they were living nearby, but the events of the summer had put paid to that, and it was rash to make any plans with the situation as it was now. *I hope to see you both soon,* she wrote. Hope was a commodity that everyone dealt in nowadays.

The letter was nearly finished by two o'clock, when the ward orderly brought her some hot milk. Young Evans was still restless, and she asked the orderly to give him A.P.C. At the same time she noticed movement further down, two beds from the end.

'What's wrong? Having trouble sleeping?'

You were entitled to call the men, who were still soldiers and not discharged, by their surnames, and some of the nurses did so with sharp relish; but Kate always avoided it.

'Afraid so.' Corporal Benham shifted himself up in the bed. 'I suppose you know they're having me on the slab again tomorrow?'

'Yes, and all the more reason you should get some sleep if you can. I'll get the orderly to bring A.P.C. if the arm's troubling you.'

'Thanks, it's all right.'

Kate felt rather than saw his eyes searching her face.

'You haven't anything to worry about,' she said. 'I was asking Sister about it—'

'Oh, I don't mind the knife. What I hate is . . .' He hesitated: she had never heard him speak with such feeling before, and he seemed aware of this for a moment before plunging on. 'It's the going under. You lose control so. You . . . you have to give yourself up.'

'You don't strike me as the sort of person who'd be bothered by that.'

'Don't I?'

She had spoken without thought: now she felt herself blushing. 'Sorry. Now I'm the one who's being rude.'

She saw him move his head in a gentle negative. His eyes were still fixed on her.

'After all you've been through, I mean,' she said. She began to tidy the top of his locker, needlessly.

'It's different,' he said. Some would find his manner oddly abrupt, but Kate recognized the bumpiness of thought. 'You see – even in France, when you realized you were in the middle of an almighty cockup, and you had Jerry swooping over trying to finish you off and it looked like you hadn't a chance in hell . . . even then, you were still sort of free. Your mind was your own, so it didn't matter.' He gave a low chuckle. 'That sounds as if I'm trying to pretend I wasn't scared, which is rubbish. Sorry – hard to explain. I have the most awful dreams when I go under, and the feeling of slipping away – of course, once you're out it's fine. I suppose that's like dying in a way. It's the dying you're scared of, not actually being dead.'

He had spoken not morbidly but with a sort of ruminating interest; but it affected Kate and she said at once, taking refuge in the nurse's manner, 'Oh, come along, let's have none of this talk of dying. You're progressing very well; I can tell you that because I've seen your notes, and now I think you should get some sleep.'

'All right. Sorry.'

She smiled, and a glint in the dimness showed her he was smiling too. 'We always seem to be saying sorry,' she said.

'Who were you writing to?'

'You haven't been sleeping at all, have you? A friend.'

'Boyfriend?'

She fell back on the nurse's manner again. 'I've far too much to do to have time for that.'

He looked at her, smiling still: he was a person who had no fear of silences. 'Very wise,' he said at last. 'I'll go to sleep now.'

He was sleeping when she went off duty at six. She did not eat but went straight to her hut, feeling acutely unhappy for no reason at all, and climbed into bed. To her surprise she woke six hours later after a long and satisfying sleep, and was even more surprised to be told by one of the other nurses that there had been a raid on. 'Going for the aerodromes again,' the nurse said, and Kate thought of Richard and Stella and how she must find a way to visit them soon.

She had a surprise when she went on duty that night. Two patients were still in the post-operative side ward. One of them was Corporal Benham. The morning operations had had to be postponed till the afternoon as the visiting surgeon had been held up by the raid. 'Neither of them have come round yet, so we'll leave them in the side ward till the morning,' the Charge Nurse told her.

Kate looked in on them soon after her shift began. The other post-op patient was a man of forty-odd who, pitifully exposed by the effects of the anaesthetic, looked as old as her father. Corporal

Benham seemed to have settled well: he looked peaceful, and also enigmatic, as if he were somehow not part of this war business at all. The Night Sister had given her to understand that all had gone well and it ought to be Benham's last operation.

Jim, Kate thought. Jim Benham. She reckoned his age to be twenty-five or -six, and wondered what he had done in civilian life. But really, she thought, it was none of her business.

Young Evans had another bad night, and in the end she had to ask the Night Sister whether she should give him a sedative. When he was finally settled she found the orderly at her side.

'Benham's come round, Nurse. Wants a drink – shall I give him some water?'

'Only a little. Wait, I'll come.'

Corporal Benham did not look a very robust man, but he must have had a strong constitution: he had come swiftly and without delirium out of the anaesthetic. He merely appeared a little tipsy, and gave her a lazy smile when he saw her.

'Hullo, how are you feeling?'

'Never felt better. I don't mind this bit. Not like the going under. I made a bit of a fuss about that, didn't I? Here, why's the blackout up?'

'It's past midnight.' She gave him a drink.

'It's amazing, isn't it? I only seem to have been out for a few minutes. Jerry up to much today?'

'About the same.' She ran her torch over the man in the other bed: he was still under. 'Let me just turn you this way. I want to check your dressings.'

'I was lucky with that, wasn't I? Another couple of inches and it'd have been the spine. Seen chaps like that. Can't move a muscle.'

'Yes, it was lucky.'

'Here, you're not going, are you?'

'No, I'll stay for a while. Try to lie still.'

'That's easy. Good at that. You're the ones who are always on your feet. We take it for granted, you see. Just like you're machines. But you must have a life too.'

'My work's my life,' Kate said; and the words seemed to thrust a dismal truth at her.

'No, no. You shouldn't let them do that to you. Sorry, if this doesn't make sense, it's the dope. But they shouldn't. You should – keep a bit of yourself separate from it all.'

'Is that what you do?'

He smiled at her. 'It's the only way.'

'Well, you know, it looks harder than it is. We get days off and so on.'

'Do you? What do you do?'

'I . . . visit my parents, if I can.'

'Fruit farmers – I remember you telling me. That must have been nice – growing up there.'

'Yes, it was. But I suppose anywhere's nice if you're loved.'

'Were you? Loved, I mean?'

'Yes.' How frigid and prim my ways are, she thought. I want to ask him about himself, how it is that he has no one, but . . . 'My parents have evacuees staying with them just now.'

'Do they . . .? That must be a bit strange for you.'

It was perceptive; but still she could not be forthcoming. 'Well, it's very nice to see them there, they're lovely children, and – to know they're safe and so on.'

'You say nice things,' he said, and then, 'I can't say the same about my parents, I'm afraid. Rather a bad lot. Dad ran off, and with poor old Mum it was the sauce. Finished her in the end. I think she was quite happy though. She just liked being pickled.'

'I am sorry.'

'No, no. Just the way they were.'

'What about you? What did you do before the war?'

'Carpenter.'

She at least managed not to let her glance fall on his mangled arm: but she should have said something, could think of nothing, and her silence teemed.

'It doesn't matter,' he said kindly. 'I wasn't a very good carpenter. Look – when I've had my stitches out, I should be due for a pass. If you were off duty, would you think of meeting me for a cup of tea and a wad or something? They have a bus into Peterborough. Only, you know, ignore this if you like and put it down to the dope, but I do like talking to you.'

'That would be nice,' she said, 'but we'll have to see. Try and get some sleep now.'

It was because he had no one, she thought: that was all. Of course that was no reason to turn down a perfectly normal pleasant suggestion. But it was a reason to be very careful with herself.

## 2

They met on a pass a fortnight later.

The time was perhaps not propitious. It was now the end of August, and the air onslaught had reached such a pitch that even at the EMS hospital, where there was a military strictness about loose talk, it was openly said that the German invasion would surely come soon. One had to be prepared for all leave to be cancelled at any moment. Jim Benham's pass was only granted at the last minute. And even then something occurred to cast a shadow over it. Young Evans suffered haemorrhaging of the brain, and died in the ward with the other men looking on. The general feeling, in which Kate shared, was that he should have been transferred long ago. It was a tense, simmering and unhappy place that they left early that evening to catch a bus to Peterborough.

And yet there was a sense of escape, of refreshment, that made them smile at each other like children let out of school. They had met up a good deal to talk in the past week. The talks were squeezed into the ordinary hospital routine – now that he was a walking patient again the shortage of staff meant he was detailed to some small fatigues in the kitchens and washrooms – but none the less rewarding for that. Indeed, it was how one had learned to live nowadays: each moment was distilled to the last drop. Rules on fraternization between nurses and patients would have made travelling on the bus together unwise under normal circumstances, but the situation made nonsense of it.

He looked well. She had seen it often: patients emerging from the grinding jaws of long pain would make a sudden spurt into health. He managed the arm very well: in the kitchens she had seen him, when he thought he was not being observed, try picking up forks and spoons with its baby-weak hand. He still had to wear it in a sling a good deal of the time, however, as it weakened so quickly and gave him extreme pain once overtired; he had the sling now, and on the bus an old lady kept looking at him sentimentally – he was still in khaki – and trying to catch his eye. When she got off at her stop, she made a point of patting his shoulder.

'Perhaps I should tell her I got my wound punching my sergeant-major or something,' he said to Kate.

He was embarrassed, of course. Still, there was a certain perversity in his reaction that was characteristic of him. Kate had begun to see why the other men, though they liked him well enough, did not get close to him. He would not go along with their ways. Their talk, with its grumbling and bravado, its undercurrent of sorely wounded pride mixed with bewilderment, tended naturally to extremes; but these he would not accept, and he would stick, not arrogantly, but stubbornly, to points of truth. If you did not mean a thing, you should not say it. Kate understood this as the other men did not, having her own stubbornness, and a fenland Cromwellian streak; though she also felt that there was such a thing as an emotional truth that bypassed words.

'She's just proud of you,' she said.

'But I didn't do anything,' he said. 'Except cop a shell blast, and that I didn't want. If I'd had my way, I wouldn't have been wounded at all. So she's proud of me for something I was trying to avoid.'

'She's proud of you for putting yourself in a position where you might be wounded,' Kate said. Stimulated by his company, she found herself thinking very clearly. They wrangled good-humouredly, continuing when they arrived in Peterborough and had tea at the Dujon Cafe. Kate remembered trips here with her father before the war. Plump ladies in their best hats and fur tippets would meet over fancy cakes, comparing purchases from shops with highly polished floorboards, where the sales assistants waited on them with Edwardian deference. There were no fancy cakes now, only a few buns: blast tape obscured the shop windows, and the ration book, that great leveller, had begun to rule. The past seemed not so much to have faded away as to have been rudely chopped off and disposed of.

'It feels as if there'll never be times like that again,' she said.

'Perhaps one day we'll say that about *these* times – if we get through them.'

'What do you think? Will we? Are you an optimist or a pessimist?'

'Now you're asking.' She had to cut up his food for him, a thing which in the hospital would have come naturally but which here made them both curiously shy. 'I don't think I'm either. The one thing I'm sure of is that things will always turn out differently from what we expect. That's the only thing you can bet on.'

'Oh, not always, surely.'

'Always. See – look back five or ten years, and ask yourself whether you'd have been surprised if a crystal ball had shown you what you're doing now. You would have been surprised, wouldn't you?'

'Well, yes—'

'Aha!'

'Some things must – sort of come true, though, the way you pictured they would.'

'What, like dreams and hopes?'

'. . . Yes.'

He was quiet.

'You must have had some,' she said.

'Well, I had this dream that one day I was going to have this farm near where we lived. It was going to be all mine and I would live there with a lot of farm animals, like the ones you get in a toy set, I think – I certainly don't think I ever imagined myself digging ditches. Anyway, then I found out that life doesn't work that way, and that was that.'

'I nearly married a farmer once,' she found herself saying.

He was attentive; but then, she reminded herself, he always was.

'Anyway, it didn't happen. It was just one of those things that wasn't right.'

'When did you discover it wasn't right?'

'I don't know . . . I probably knew it all along, which makes it worse really . . . You don't think you'll ever have that farm, then?'

He considered. 'Only if I stop wanting it,' he said; and then, as if to take the edge off these words, he smiled, with that effect like coolness and warmth at the same time.

By now even Kate's tight self-discipline had given way, and she had stopped pretending that she could feel towards Jim Benham only a neutral friendliness and interest. The interest was there, indeed, but it was part of something much greater. She was in over her head; her sometimes harsh honesty had won out, and she could now confess this to herself. But outwardly she was unchanged. There were two reasons for this, both connected to her view of herself. Her feelings for Jim Benham would remain inwardly tortuous and unrelieved because the spontaneous expression that came easily to others seemed beyond her. She had a weakness for hiding and cloaking herself, and there was no doubt that the nurse's uniform had furnished an opportunity of this sort. She had exchanged shyness for stiffness. Dried-up and spinstery, she thought, that's what I am. Presented with the heart's demands, she did not know where to begin. She could only long and suppress, but the suppression seemed to her both good and necessary – and here lay the second reason. Jim Benham was a man she had nursed, who had no family and was solitary, who needed sympathetic company – that was all. He was a singularly independent soul, but even if he had not been, there was no reason to think that he could feel anything for her. She had been loved once, and that had been exposed to the unfortunate man as an awful mistake that had spoiled his life. Such things were not for her.

And yet here she was, sharing a pass with Jim Benham and

loving every moment of it. Her reasonings were all very well, but they got tangled up in life, which just now was not reasonable, but chaotic. Perhaps this was what he meant when he said that nothing ever turned out the way you thought it would. She wasn't, couldn't be consistent, even though she knew she might be storing up for herself a great grief. And the war was an alibi, because at any moment everything might end and cancel out even the possibility of regret. As if to underline this, just as they were leaving the cafe the sirens went.

It probably wouldn't be anything much, and Kate disliked the public shelters, which always smelt like lavatories; so they evaded the whistle-blowing wardens who were bustling eagerly about the city centre and went down to the river. They heard the whine of planes in the distance, and two faint crumps like a piece of heavy timber breaking, but that was all: presently the All Clear sounded, while they walked beneath willows which caught the evening glow like a fine net.

He spoke of a man from his unit who had suffered a leg wound and whose one anxiety was that he might no longer be able to dance. 'They told him he would never be entirely free of pain, but he didn't care about that. His girl went off him because he was crippled, but he even shrugged that off. It was the thought of not being able to dance again that bothered him. He'd always been going to dances before the war. It was the one remnant of civilian life that he wanted. One day his sister came to visit him. I spoke with her while he was dressing. Turns out he was a terrible dancer: she said he could hardly get a partner because he couldn't keep the beat and trampled all over them.'

The story, and his wry expression as he told it, were typical of him: he did not mock at sadness, but he had a beady eye for its ironies too.

'It's a long time since I danced,' Kate said, recalling the schoolhouse, the village feast, Frankie Hope . . . how long ago it seemed!

'Do you dance?' he said. His tone was not all polite interest: there was surprise there too. 'Oh, not often,' Kate said, and felt discouraged. Remembering the summer of Helen and Richard and Stella, when she had bloomed into a person who did dance, she wanted to tell him of it: more than that, she wanted to summon that person again – but she wouldn't come. She remembered the drives with Richard in the truck, and how freely she had talked then, with no barriers between her heart and her lips. And yet she had not loved Richard. What conclusion she should draw from that she did not know.

Dried-up and spinstery, she thought. Spinstery and dried-up.

'It was rather hard of his girl,' she said. 'Giving him up because he was crippled. He's well rid of her by the sound of it.'

'Well, who knows what any of us would do in that situation? After all, the man she fell for wasn't a cripple. So probably she felt he wasn't the same man.'

'I think you'd argue the case for old Adolf himself!'

He laughed at that. 'I wouldn't go that far. But how can you be sure of anything nowadays? When we were over there a French woman spat at us and said the war was all our fault. And it's not just us soldiers. Suppose things turn around and we start capturing a lot of Jerries – you'd probably find yourself nursing them. You see?'

'I used to look at all the names on the war memorial in our village,' she said, 'and I swore if it happened again I would have nothing to do with it. I still feel like that in a way – the waste and suffering. But I suppose I am taking part in it now.'

'That's just it – what can you do otherwise except take the extreme conchie position? You know, where they refuse even to work on the farms because they're producing food for the war effort. There isn't any answer. That's what I mean. All you can do is look on, laugh where you can, and wait for it to be over.'

'The war, or life?' she said.

'Both, I suppose.' His face was shadowed and unreadable. 'It's nothing to get excited about, is it?'

And that was when it suddenly fell apart. The thought of young Private Evans appeared between them like a genie, and they spoke quietly about him, about the summoning of his family, and his youth. And then Jim began to say that he was better off out of it. Kate protested.

'Sorry, sound hard? I don't mean to be. I just mean . . . Well, no.' Like many not conventionally handsome people, he looked beautiful when thinking. 'I do mean that – he is well out of it.'

'I'm sure he wouldn't have chosen to be, if he'd been asked.'

He gave her a look, more inquisitive than surprised at her tone. Then he said lightly, 'Well, I'd have swapped places with him, anyway.'

She misunderstood this at first. 'Jim, he wouldn't have wanted that either, I shouldn't think.'

'No, but I would.'

She studied him, unhappily, and using an expression of his own said, 'Explain.'

'Oh, I've said the wrong thing. I don't want anyone to die and I don't want to die myself, but . . . I've found life disappointing, that's all. It's supposed to be wonderful, and it isn't, but it isn't a disaster either. It's just – disappointing, that's the only word for it.'

'So you don't want it?'

She saw him frown, but typically he stuck to his guns. 'Not particularly.'

'You should be ashamed.' She spoke vehemently. The violence of her response was due to love, but that very violence prevented her seeing it just then. 'A lot of people have taken a great deal of trouble over you. They've struggled and worked to make you better and when you did get better they were as pleased as could be and felt they'd really done something worthwhile. And now you tell me you'd rather they hadn't bothered and had let you die. Well, I think you should be ashamed.'

After a burning moment he said, 'I'm sorry,' though it was plain from his face that he did not mean it. They walked on in silence until he continued, with something of his old stubbornness, 'But surely that's not such a terrible thing to think. Your life's your own, after all, and if you don't particularly value it, then what does it matter?'

*It matters if someone else values it.* These were the words she did not say, but they stood between the two of them like a fence, while on either side of it misunderstanding deepened. If she had not been so hurt she might have seen that the death of Evans had affected Jim profoundly, perhaps more profoundly than he realized. He had adopted a stance as an amused observer whom nothing could touch or surprise; inevitably when something happened to knock him off that position he was confused and bewildered; perhaps also it made him see that that stance was false, and that he had adopted it out of pain, and fear of more pain.

But Kate was at that stage where love is mixed up with admiration. She did not suppose him vulnerable: she did not suppose that he said these things out of confusion; she thought he always knew what he was talking about. And all she could feel was the hurt that he did not care to live. They walked on in excruciating silence, which he broke at last by saying, 'I do say some stupid things sometimes. I wish I was like you.'

'Why?' This astonished her.

'Because you don't say stupid things. You've got a cool head. It's what I've always liked about you.' He smiled awkwardly. 'This is true, by the way, as well as being a way of trying to – well, get back in your good books.'

She could not speak. The things she longed to say to him were not at all cool-headed. And probably they were very stupid indeed. Aching, she wished she had never come: misreading her silence, he seemed to feel the same.

And then something came to their rescue. They ran into a soldier from the same hospital who was also on a pass, roaring drunk and under the impression that he was in Cambridge: he wanted to take out a punt and was roaming the river bank looking for one. Together they persuaded him to the bus station, laid him on a bus seat, and watched over him while they trundled out again to the country. When their eyes met over his loudly snoring form, they both laughed; and the distance between them closed up at once. By the time they reached the hospital they were chatting as before – though with that touch of over-eagerness, laughing greatly at weak jokes and agreeing with everything, that characterizes people who have said things they are sorry for.

'Here, are we still friends?' Jim said when they parted at the covered walkway leading to the nurses' huts.

'Silly – of course we are,' she said. He seemed enormously glad about that. If she could not be quite so glad, it was because of his choice of words. They fell on her ear like the diagnosis of a doctor confirming your worst fears.

## 3

It was absurd: they could only laugh when it happened. Both of them should have thought of it – Richard was a serviceman, Stella a serviceman's wife, and living in Norfolk they were close to what was expected to be the front line if the invasion came; but neither of them did. It merely seemed a splendid idea, when Richard at last got a couple of days' leave, to motor up to the coast around Hunstanton and have a look at the sea and sniff the ozone and forget about the war for a brief space.

Even when they were halted at the military roadblock several miles inland from the coast and the patrol sergeant was suspiciously questioning them, they shared a feeling that this was all some sort of mistake.

'Don't you know,' the sergeant said, 'that all this coast is a restricted area?'

'Well – but we're English,' Richard said. 'I mean, surely it's only restricted for the Germans,' and Stella suppressed a giggle.

'You might be anything for all I know, sir,' the sergeant said coolly. 'The fact is you can't come through here.'

'Isn't there any bit of coast we can get to?' Stella said.

'You might go to Wales,' the sergeant said: his dryness was not unappealing. 'Or Scotland. But you're not going to sunny Hunny, not today nor tomorrow. Now please turn your vehicle around.'

'We only wanted to *look* at the sea,' Stella said; but the

sergeant had had enough of them, and they had to do as they were told.

'I did know, I suppose,' Richard said as they drove inland again. 'It just seems so strange, not being able to visit your own seaside. Do we *look* like Nazi spies?'

'Well, I'm sure they wouldn't send spies who were up the spout,' Stella said, with a rueful glance down at her belly.

It was almost the first time she had been able to speak of her pregnancy so lightly, for it was a matter about which her feelings were complex. She did not see how it could be otherwise. Theirs was not a Hollywood marriage, in which a baby was the natural result of wedded bliss. Bliss there had been, certainly, and still was: there were even a few appropriate roses round the door of the cottage, or half-cottage that they were renting near Downham Market. But there were no escaping the fact that her husband was a bomber pilot in daily peril of his life, that both of them were estranged from their respective families, and that for Stella motherhood had never figured among the desirable things of this life.

And yet today she seemed to have arrived at a reconciliation with everything, including the mysterious development within her belly. For they had managed, after all: with everything and everyone from Lily of the Valleys to the Luftwaffe ranged against them, she and Richard had come through; and if the war would only allow them a few more days together like this, Stella felt that the two of them could set such an example of perfect love as the world would still be trying to match when Hitler and all his crew were so much forgotten dust.

The day, indeed, had something of the orchard summer about it, especially when after driving a few more miles inland they decided to set out their picnic in a meadow fringed by apple trees. It was not, however, a mere artificial reliving of lost memories. A deeper note had been added to that old tune; and when Richard lay beside her in the long grass and gently caressed the swelling that was stretching the thin material of her print frock, she felt for the first time that with the baby might come an even richer harmony.

She was not deceived: she did not suppose that this moment of exhilaration would transform her confused feelings about the child into glad simplicity. Stella was not made like that and she knew it. But she knew that moments had to be seized, and she seized this one with all its aspects: Richard's hand gently touching her, the dark crown of his head, the smiling landscape around her, the peace, the knowledge of love given and returned. Presently Richard would have to go back to his station at Marham and fly again, but not yet: presently they would have to face the cold fact of their families' enmity, but not yet: presently the child in her womb would become again a tough enigma for her, but not yet.

Stella stroked Richard's hair, because she loved him and he was hers and the world could not do anything about that, not yet.

# TWO

## 1

*A LAND GIRL SPEAKS*
*by Helen Harding*

*It is ten o'clock at night and I am writing by the light of a paraffin lamp in my room at Mr G's Huntingdonshire farm, with a cat called Mixie for company. Mixie is Mrs G's pet, but he comes up every evening to see me – as if he wants me to feel at home, and part of the family. And this typifies the welcome I have received since coming here as a member of the Women's Land Army three months ago.*

*Did I say three months? It seems much longer. Perhaps that is because one spends so much more time awake out here – and how much more alive one feels for it! Perhaps it's because I have learned so much in that time – everything from removing a sharp stone from a heifer's hoof to making a perfectly shaped hay-rick (almost perfectly shaped, at any rate). Perhaps it's because of that welcome I mentioned; for even Tom the cowman, who is very old, very wise, and very suspicious of newcomers, has given me the seal of approval. 'You're doing, gel,' he said the other day when watching me at work, 'you're doing.' And Tom, unlike a lot of people in our world today, never says a thing unless he means it.*

*I was brought up in the country. But it is only since*

*coming here that I have discovered how little that means, in terms of understanding what goes on there. To live near a factory is to receive a constant impression of thrumming industriousness: important things are surely going on within. But living in a village, as I did in a pleasant Rectory, one can easily fall prey to the delusion that nothing much is going on in those tawny fields beyond the garden gate: nothing urgent, that is, nothing complex, demanding – or vital. It all looks timeless and pastoral.*

*But these fields and barns are factories too; and the men and women who toil in them are engaged in war work just as intensively as those who labour to make munitions. If sometimes there seems to be a slowness and reflectiveness about life here, it is because the raw materials and the products of this vast open-air factory are natural things, growing things, that cannot be hurried.*

*Yet there is urgency – plenty of it. Here at Mr G's we are getting the harvest in, and slacking simply isn't a possibility. Of course war makes the task more pressing – but I've begun to see that in a way the folk who till the land have always been at war. To fall down on the job is not to miss a pay packet or take a wigging from the boss, not here; for they are dealing with the stuff of life itself. For some of us, perhaps, it has taken the experience of war to show us how precious life is. Out here I think they have always known it.*

*I have discovered something else too – that machines are quite as temperamental as animals. Mr G has two horses, pensioned off since the new tractor came; one has the most invitingly soft nose but Mr G has warned me against stroking it – 'he's an awkward one'. He cannot have been more awkward than the tractor. This machine does not like me one bit. Mr G has been giving me lessons in driving it. I watch how it responds to him, turning like a docile pony. I climb up and at once its character changes.*

*It becomes a mule. With great labour and persuasion I can get it to turn, but when I try to make it reverse, it decides it has had enough of me, and gives a great jolt that pitches me off the seat and into the mud.*

*But, 'You'll get it,' says Mr G; and I will too. There may be some Land Girls who have given up, but I've never heard of them. Our tutors are wonderfully patient with these strange creatures who have descended on them in their green jerseys, expecting to be turned into farmhands. 'It can't be done' was a phrase one used to hear a good deal, I think; but one doesn't seem to hear it nowadays. Certainly not out here. A little vignette occurred today in the harvest field that seemed to sum up this new spirit. Mr G was driving the tractor and I was on the binder – something I thought I wouldn't get the hang of, but it was done. Watching us were two cheery little boys from London who have been evacuated to a nearby farm – and I seem to remember there were voices saying that the evacuation couldn't be done either. And above us, a formation of our planes, wingtips glinting in the sun, were on their way home safely to base – and I don't think I need say any more about that.*

Helen stopped and rested her aching hand. She was tired and doubted she could do any more tonight; manuscript was all right for a draft but if she were to submit it to a magazine she would have to get it typed somehow; she wasn't sure about the reference to her own background, which might narrow the appeal; the chirpy tone was dictated by the needs of the moment and she was forced to be only selectively truthful . . . But none of this mattered. She was writing, and it felt wonderful.

The cat mewed at her bedroom door to be let out, having come to the end of his visit. As Helen opened the door for him she heard the sound of Mr Griggs slowly knocking out his pipe on the fender downstairs: he would go to bed soon. So should she, for she had to be up at dawn, but the writing had made her mind race and she was disinclined to sleep. She trimmed the lamp and sat down again on the oaken-framed, altar-like bed that filled most of the room, taking the writing pad back on to her lap. Her stomach made a contented gurgle as it reminisced about Mrs Griggs's suet pudding. Helen had once suffered from poor digestion, but not since coming here.

She knew she was lucky. She knew that there were other land girls who had been billeted in barrack-like hostels from which they were used as labour gangs, or who had been taken on by 'gentleman farmers' who treated them as skivvies, or who had ended up in squalid one-horse farms with cesspits and leering employers. Instead she had been billeted on a kindly couple who inhabited an old-fashioned, draughty but clean and comfortable farmhouse and whom she had already overheard referring to her as 'our Helen'. That her case was not universal was one of the things she had omitted to mention in the article.

There were other things, more personal, which had no place in the article. One, the fact that she was a married woman. No rule against it; but there had been raised eyebrows when she had been interviewed by the local WLA Secretary on first applying to join.

'You have no domestic duties that you feel are paramount?' said the Secretary, a fastidious county lady in tweeds.

'No.'

'Ah – your husband's away in the forces, perhaps?' the Secretary said, brightening.

'No, he isn't.' He might be eventually, as he was of military age: she didn't much care. 'I am legally separated from my husband.'

'Indeed.' The Secretary became more fastidious. Judging by the handshake at the end of the interview Helen might have had leprosy.

But the pressure of events was breaking down a lot of ancient prejudices: the Women's Land Army took Helen, and Helen took to the Women's Land Army. When she had first spoken of her intention to join, not long after the separation when she was staying with her parents, her father had been perplexed. With her education there must surely be a civil-service place for her, he said: perhaps even in something like Intelligence. But Helen knew what she wanted. She hadn't been fooled by the WLA recruiting posters with their apple-cheeked maidens caressing the necks of well-scrubbed cows: she had known the work would be fiercely hard, and perhaps lonely. This did not dismay her, because she wanted to feel alive again. She did not think office work would give her that feeling; and besides, in an office she suspected there would be Owens.

And she had not regretted her choice. The overwhelming feeling she had experienced in these past three months was one of liberation. This too she could not put down in the article, because it had to do with Owen, as did so much.

She was back in East Anglia: not in the fens proper, but only within a score of miles from a place that held significant memories for her. What part this played in her feeling of exultant rebirth she could not say: her mind still shrank from addressing the events of the orchard summer. But a beginning had been made in that direction – at least now she admitted to herself that those memories *were* significant. And more would surely follow, for after a period of numbness she was beginning to look clearly at her marriage, and to see that it followed on from the orchard summer and was not something separate from it. Indeed, she had begun to trace out a pattern of cause and effect that was alarming to behold. *For want of a nail the shoe was lost* . . . Hearing that rigmarole as a child, she had protested: things didn't happen that way. Now she knew better, but she still shied away from complete knowledge. Marriage to Owen had been a disastrous mistake: recognizing that was enough for now, but beyond it another recognition awaited her – the reason why she had made that mistake in the first place.

She wasn't ready to look that in the face – not yet. She was still convalescing from her marriage, which she considered as effectively over as if she had been widowed.

Divorce was a possibility that would have to wait on the war.

There was no doubting that Owen would like to be divorced from her: it was the idea of being a divorced person he did not like. Helen did not much care, as long as she was not with him. She had taken nothing with her when she walked out that day – it had been a beautiful spring morning and she had worn no hat and had left the garden gate open – and in a broader sense she had taken away nothing from the marriage that she had not brought to it. Owen paid her money for maintenance, in an arrangement brokered by his own law firm – he was typically good at keeping his dirty laundry private – but she tried not to touch it, putting it into war savings and living off her wages from the farmer. It was also characteristic of Owen that he had kept the house, something which had horrified Helen's mother, who had at first been all generous bewilderment at what had happened to her daughter and son-in-law. 'I really don't see how he can continue to live there,' Mrs Silverman kept saying – quite angrily for her. 'After what's happened – how could he?' Very easily, of course. It had been his house before his marriage, and remained so after it. Helen had merely passed through, making no more impact on that enclosed little world than a friend's pet looked after while they were away.

One thing she did take with her, of course, was regret. But it was a hard, clear sort of regret that had as its compensation knowledge gained. It did not include much self-pity: the unhappiness of the past couple of years mattered less to her than the sheer waste involved. But there had been learning as well as waste, and it was an indication of reviving self-esteem that Helen's appetite for learning was back – even such bitter learning as this.

What she had learnt was that she was the sort of person who made disastrous mistakes. It was a simple lesson but profound in its effect on her. She had always believed herself prone, like everyone else, to incidental misjudgements; but utter follies, like throwing yourself into a miserably doomed marriage, were for other people. And the marriage had indeed been miserable, and doomed from the moment she became truly aware of its misery, for Helen's capacity for self-destruction was, fortunately, limited. She could have gone on with it: it would have required only a subduing, a lowering of the flame of life to an eternal glimmer; she saw husbands and wives amongst Owen's set who had plainly done this. And Owen, she felt, would have tolerated such an arrangement. As long as he could have carried on with his life much as before, her presence in it would have merely been a minor irritation, like some unsightly modification that had been made to the house at great expense and now had to be put up with.

But Helen had not found it possible. There had been no single moment of awakening, no dramatic stroke that had opened her eyes. Her sense of self-worth, having receded to the furthest margins, gradually crept back like a tide; and when it was at the full, she saw the smallness of the man she had married, the dimness of his light. And fear fell away.

It was odd to think of fear in connection with Owen. He was a physically gentle man who never even raised his voice. Nor was he unpredictable: you knew that he would either be coolly pleasant or sunk in a bad mood – one of the two. Yet she lived with fear for a long time. It was the fear of his displeasure: as long as the tide of self-esteem was out, this mattered desperately to her. She recalled an occasion when she had accidentally broken one of his records. He was all restrained, delicate contempt, deliberately disposing of the broken pieces in the bin, making a note of the title to be replaced . . . whilst she flapped around him, apologizing, deploring her clumsiness.

'Let's not make a scene about it, my dear. It's only a record after all.'

It was not, of course, to him, and his face showed it. It also showed that he expected no better of her. By nature Helen was graceful rather than clumsy – she had coached herself in physical poise since growing very tall as a girl, knowing that her height would always be associated with gawkiness – but when she was around Owen she became a nervous, heavy-handed, rowdy hoyden. Naturally, the more she tried not to be the worse it became.

Inhumanly deft and noiseless himself, Owen made her feel a lumbering nuisance – without ever saying so, for then she could have at least replied. He specially disliked coughing, as he did most physical manifestations. He would make a barely audible humming noise of irritation in his throat when she coughed. The pitch of it would rise when she coughed again, as you inevitably did when trying not to, until it seemed he must surely cry out 'For goodness' sake!' But he never did. His patience was far too valuable a weapon to be thrown away.

Remembering herself sitting in her own home afraid to cough, Helen marvelled. How unreal it was now: how had she ever put up with it? But she knew that for a long time she had regarded her unhappiness as her just desserts. She had, to be crude about it, thrown herself at him; therefore she had no right to complain when things turned out badly. So she reasoned, and so she suffered until a voice spoke up in her that had been virtually silent since Cambridge, a voice that pointed out that the last thing men need in this world is special pleading, having enjoyed that privilege since time immemorial. Even supposing she had thrown herself at him, he had still been a free agent: no one had held him down and made him marry her. The realization had triggered no immediate change in her behaviour, but it was another milestone on the road that had led to that beautiful spring morning when she had walked hatless out of marriage, and ultimately to this Huntingdonshire farm where her transformation from bourgeois *hausfrau* to independent woman had been made complete.

Very nearly so, at any rate. Her parents still regarded her decision to enlist with the WLA as a drastic impulse born out of the trauma of the separation; they sent gifts and reminded her that a room at the Rectory awaited her, believing she would soon return to it. And out here she had met with more patronage and even disdain than she had chosen to mention in the article: Mr and Mrs Griggs were splendid, but some of her first efforts in the fields had been sneered at by mean red-faced countrymen who clearly thought her place was in the home, and on her occasional trips into Huntingdon, a dismal backward little town that seemed to have a permanent cover of cloud over its dingy streets, she felt herself regarded more as a freak than a war worker. The status of land girl was still dubious: she did a man's work, as the hardness of her hands and the stiffness of her back testified, but one felt it was on sufferance, and the travel warrants and NAAFI meals enjoyed by women in the forces were denied to her.

This was something else she omitted from her article – for she was writing unashamedly for publication. Whether it would be accepted was another matter, and not greatly relevant. The important thing was her decision to attempt it – to pick up the threads she had so abruptly severed when she married Owen. After living so long without aspiration, without intellectual stimulation beyond crossword puzzles and the political platitudes of Rotary Club bores, she almost trembled at her new freedom: could she really be that person again? Had the capability been drained out of her?

It might well be; but that too was an irrelevance, because she was going to try, and the rest was in the lap of the gods. Looking over what she had written, she pictured Owen reading it: he would smile thinly and find it glib and sentimental . . . Wondering what Owen would think was a mental reflex she had yet to get rid of; but *caring* what he would think was long gone.

She was too weary to go on with the article; but she was disinclined to relinquish the pen. Thinking of the person she had been brought back many memories, long banished to the edge of her consciousness. If she were truly to join the land of the living again, there was lost ground to be made up. The people with whom she had shared the orchard summer might not care that the old Helen they had known was back, but that too was an irrelevance. The doors must be opened, the hand extended: she wanted to bury the life of lies and reclaim her integrity, even though she still feared the full measure of self-knowledge.

She began to write.

*Dear Kate*

*I hope this reaches you. Please forgive the long silence.*

*Much has happened. I'll tell you my news presently – but let me ask for yours. Do tell me all. And Richard and Stella too – have you news of them? I don't have a recent address. I do want to hear of them – where they are and how they are. I'd love to see you, Kate. It's been so long. I feel as if I've been away, far away from everything, and have just come gratefully back . . .*

## 2

Stella had never had a garden before. The garden was the first thing that had impressed her when she and Richard had taken the house, or part of house, earlier that year. And in those warm early days of September, when the peace of the gentle Norfolk countryside coexisted with shattering violence up above in that pearly Anglian sky, she was more glad of the garden than ever – to the extent that she spent most of the daylight hours out there.

She dug and she weeded, she watered and pruned – inexpert blunderings, made even more hamfisted by the fact that she was heavily pregnant and every task had to be laboriously performed around the grotesque protruberance that used to be her belly. But in this case the means mattered more than the end. Exhausting herself in the garden was simply preferable to sitting indoors twiddling her thumbs and imagining Richard's plane plummeting out of a burning sky.

She had, besides, help of a sort for the heavier work. The rambling old brick-and-flint house which had become her first true marital home was divided into two dwellings, Richard and Stella renting one half, the owners living in the other. Mr and Mrs Musselwhite were an old couple who had been married, as they often mentioned, for over fifty years. Whether Mrs Musselwhite had always hated her husband, or whether the feeling had gradually mounted to its present pitch over the fifty years, was difficult to tell. Certainly everything he did – everything – seemed to infuriate her. She buzzed around him, a scrawny woman with a hard eye and a perennial cigarette clenched between her lips, finding agonized fault. '*No* – not there, for pity's sake.' 'Oh, for crying out loud! Here – give it to me.' 'Oh, you're useless, Edward. Absolutely useless.' Stella had even heard her once say to him, with a sharp motion of her hand, '*Leave*' exactly as if to a dog. Accordingly, it was no wonder that he too spent a lot of time out in the garden – though Mrs Musselwhite often pursued him out there, and made scathing remarks at him over the rose bushes. 'Well, you've ruined *that*, Edward. Dear God, don't you know *anything* . . .'

And yet Stella could see, in a way, why it was that Mr Musselwhite's wife lived in a continual state of suppressed murderousness. He genuinely was irritating. It was something about his purposeless dodder, his high quavering voice, his obtuseness – 'What is that, dear? Eh? I don't quite follow, dear. I don't quite follow' – and his habit of not simply trailing off his sentences but stopping them in mid-air. 'I remember a pal of mine from my old Navy days,' he would maunder to Stella as he tied back a rambler, breaking off all the flower heads in the process. 'Charlie Fairbrother his name was, and he came to me one day with a chit from the Captain, off the Azores this was, and with the funniest look on his face he asked me to . . .' And that was it. Trying to coax the rest of the anecdote from him was useless: all you got was a piercing, 'Eh? Eh, my dear?' Even her stepmother's talk, Stella thought, was gripping in comparison.

But today, the fifth of September, Stella had the garden to herself. Mr Musselwhite was off on Home Guard duty: presumably if the Germans landed he was going to exasperate them into surrender. Richard was at the station at Marham. As far as he knew he would be home later, but of course there was no counting on anything these days: she saw him when she saw him and murmured a prayer of thankfulness every time she did. Any secret relief she might have felt when he was assigned to Bomber Command instead of fighters was quite dispelled by now: though he had no part in the gladiatorial bouts with the Messerschmidts that she had grown accustomed to seeing screaming overhead, his peril was no less. For the past week his crew had been flying for hours that seemed superhuman, making raids on the French coast: their targets, as he had told her, the invasion barges moored there. 'It's now or never for Adolf, my darling,' he said in his casual way, 'and I'd say it's fifty-fifty.'

She was proud of him: she was afraid for him; and they were both under a strain so enormous that there was simply no talking about it.

Stella, straightening up with a groan, wiped sweat from her forehead and looked back at the borders to see the results of her weeding. As usual, they were undetectable to the naked eye, though she had been at it all morning. The garden was long, narrow and sloping – which was baffling enough, for all the country around was as flat as a tabletop. The village was a scrubby low-lying place on the banks of the oozy Ouse, and to both Stella and Richard it did not have quite the same feeling as old Monks Bridge, even though that was only ten miles away across the fen. Kate had written her that this was because they were just over the border into Norfolk, 'where they've all got chalk for brains.' Still, it had been wonderful when they had learned that Richard was to be posted to the fens, close to where they had met: you did not have to be as superstitious as Richard to see this as a good omen, a sign that fortune was on their side at last. And there had been happy times in this funny old place: especially when Richard, who had had to scrap his ancient Riley, had managed to buy an old Morris from a fellow airman and they were able to take the odd drive over to the orchard country. They had even called on Kate's parents, who seemed to have entered on a new lease of life with the fizzing presence of young evacuees in the house. Much was changed there, however. Walter Lutton was switching to vegetable growing on Ministry of Agriculture orders: most of the fruit had rotted on the branch: the hutted camp was empty, with rumours that the government were going to take it over for military purposes. It was a sad feeling: for Stella the orchard country was as much a place of the mind as a real location, and to find it touched by war was like finding your own memories altered. Still, it was peaceful there, and she could not help wishing that her own little brothers were among the evacuees whooping about the meadows. Auntie Bea and Uncle Will had packed their brood off as soon as the war broke out, and they were now in Wales, at a place which in Auntie Bea's erratic spelling and handwriting came out as Ethel's Willy; but Stella's father had kept the boys at home in spite of the threat to London. If the raids came to the city, Richard had said, they could have the boys up here – they could just call it a holiday; but though Stella had written to her father with the suggestion, his reply did not even take the trouble to decline. It was just another of his deadly, we-are-quite-well-hope-you're-the-same communications. Even the news of her pregnancy had got the same response. Jack Tranter had not forgiven her. She had made her choice. She was on her own.

As for the reaction of Richard's family to the news of her pregnancy, it was hard to tell: they were equally uncommunicative. Probably they saw it as no more than confirmation that the common trollop had got her claws into him good and proper; or maybe they were planning to whisk the child away as soon as it was born in case it grew up with Cockney vowels. Well, Stella thought, at least Richard was happy about the baby.

She sometimes felt he was the only person who was.

No, unfair. It was just that the arrival of a baby at this time seemed almost wrong-headed – like making a cup of tea when the house was on fire. Perhaps there was a faint sense of intrusion too: she and Richard had had a hard fight on all fronts in order to be together, and she so valued what they had that she resented the notion of its becoming a sudden threesome. But most of all, she had a less than glowing image of motherhood. She suspected that it either ground you down, as it had with her own poor mother, or turned you into a monstrous, mooing, drooling, baby's-bottom-kissing milch-cow like Lily of the Valleys.

Hearing a faint drone, her head instinctively went up; but after a moment she recognized the sound as farm machinery in the distance, and the sky was clear of contrails. It was still bizarre to think, when the raids came, that those silvery crosses up in the blue were machines operated by men who were trying openly to encompass her death. And, even more, her husband's death. Yet she found herself curiously without hate. Only when a German plane had come down quite nearby and they had driven over to look at the wreckage had something of the expected emotions risen in her: seeing it there, crushed and powerless, she had thought *There! Got you! You can't do any more damage, can you?*

As for Richard, his look had been enigmatic; but she had known what he was thinking about. A friend whom he had been on initial training with had died just the day before. A pilot operating from Duxford on his way back to base after a successful sortie, he had swooped to perform a victory roll, crashed into trees, and been burned up. It was one of the few stories he told her. Most of the time when he was home he kept quiet about what was going on. 'Shop-talk,' he said. 'Very dull.'

Stella went indoors to make herself some lunch. Her appetite had if anything diminished since the early days of craving (large black field mushrooms swimming in juice had been her favourite: luckily they grew in abundance in the paddock beyond the garden and Richard would go out in pyjamas in the mornings to gather them) but Richard was insistent that she eat during the day, so she picked at some bread and cheese and a bowl of soup. One compensation of the war, she thought, was that *all* meals were more or less horrible now: her awful cooking had become the norm. After eating she sat for a while with her feet up in the creaking wood-panelled sitting room – another insistence of Richard's – whilst Jimbo, the young collie they had got from one of the villagers, sat with his head where her lap used to be.

The quietness first soothed, then unnerved her. These were the times when she began to think, and awful images came unbidden to her mind. Turning on the wireless was no good: if it wasn't Freddie Grisewood on the Kitchen Front telling you what you could do with parsnips it was news, and news meant aircraft being shot down.

'Come on, Jimbo,' she said, levering herself up, 'back to the land.'

All afternoon she worked at digging over the vegetable patch, in a sort of fury of concentration; when at last she looked up, alerted by the sound of aircraft, the sun was low in the sky and her head was swimming. The aircraft were ours: Blenheims. Not Richard. She made herself go in and put supper on the stove and tidy round. This didn't take long: they didn't have much furniture – a couple of rocking chairs, rugs, upstairs an old box bed on bare waxed floorboards – but the ritual was important. While she was doing this the district nurse made her call. She was a youngish woman with an infectious laugh and a pretty face atop a body that was muscled like a footballer's from cycling round twenty fen villages. 'You're naughty. You should sit on your behind and knit,' she told Stella, spotting at once the gardening grime on her hands, 'but I don't suppose you will.' She was just cycling sturdily off when Richard came home.

It always seemed to happen like that. He would appear when her attention was momentarily distracted, rather in the way ghosts are supposed to. To sit and purposefully wait for him was no good: he wouldn't arrive.

'No, nothing much doing today,' he told her. 'Too much cloud over the Channel. Kicking our heels. This new sergeant over from Martlesham Heath cleaned me out at poker. What did the nurse have to say?'

'All quiet on the baby front,' she said. 'Want a drink?'

'Love one.'

Richard was friends with a Canadian pilot who had given them two bottles of exceptionally smooth whisky. It was his habit to drink two glasses of this when he came home. Everything revolved around habit, in fact, when he came home. There was a sort of unnatural, glassy casualness about him at these times. He wanted – and, Stella saw, needed – to do very normal, everyday things with painstaking thoroughness. He would go slowly through a routine of tapping the barometer on the wall, patting Jimbo, and glancing through the newspaper whilst drinking his two glasses of whisky, lighting a cigarette for each one. Only after that would he unbutton his tunic and loosen his tie – a small transformation for which Stella waited with a curious eagerness. The uniform made him look more conventionally handsome, but less like Richard.

She understood his need of these rituals. Only occasionally did she find them stifling, and ask herself what had happened to his old spontaneity; though the answer, of course, was that the war had bitten into it. She ought to be grateful that the war left her as much of him as it did; for usually the old Richard came through, once the empty-eyed stranger had performed his fastidious routine.

Tonight, though, Richard seemed unable to wind down. It was as if he had to keep forcibly reminding himself that he was home. Practically living at the station as he did now, it must all have looked very strange to him; but perceiving this was no comfort to Stella, who felt herself to be among the things he gazed blankly at but did not see. Over supper he began to talk, ramblingly, of a fellow pilot who had not come back yesterday.

'Larry Martin it was – I think you met him, didn't you? At that do for Ted Thorpe's wedding? Maybe not. Just got engaged to a WAAF at Feltwell anyway – Scottish girl, black hair . . . Anyway, his kite didn't come back. Larry and Jenkins and Murdoch and they had this new wireless man, can't remember his name, anyway it was over the ports last anybody saw of them – nobody saw them go down. Might have bailed out. There's always that possibility, you see. In all that confusion – you can't trust your eyes really. There was old Chalky White, remember I told you, someone swore they'd seen him go down and he came back . . .'

Stella let him talk on, surprised but also a little relieved. She did not believe in bottling things up, and in his reticence about flying she often discerned the gnawing of an inner wound. She had met his crew and the rear-gunner, a cheerful Ulsterman called McCulloch with hair as red as her own, had told her that the skip, as they called him, had the safest pair of hands he had ever flown with. But it was this aspect of his duty which most haunted Richard and made him look at times ten or fifteen years older than the man she had married: it was because of this, and not because he longed to be one of the glory boys, that he sometimes spoke with quiet ferocity of his regret that he hadn't made fighters instead of bombers. 'It's just your own neck then,' as he put it.

She understood this, but a part of her felt bitter when he said it. Because even if he were flying solo, it wasn't just his own neck. Whatever happened to him happened to her too.

'. . . Well, they're still trying to knock us out, anyhow. The runways at Duxford took a pounding again, they say. One thing's for sure, it can't go on much longer. Something's got to give . . .'

Stella felt a sharp nudge down below: his lordship was restless today. This was a sensation she felt she would never get used to. She stood up and started gathering the plates.

'Leave that, darling, I'll do it. You look all in.' As he said this he took a closer look at her: saw the heavy way she leaned her hands on the table. 'Hey. Come and sit down.'

'I'll just clear away—'

'No. God, you're exhausted – and here am I wittering on . . .'

He took her by the hand and led her to the oak settle by the hearth. As she sat down he turned her palm up and examined it.

'I thought as much. You've been working yourself to a frazzle in that garden again, haven't you?'

'Only a bit of weeding. Mr Musselwhite does most of it.'

'You do most of it. I know you. Sweetheart, there's no need. You ought to be resting instead of wearing yourself out like that.'

'I like doing it,' she said feebly.

'Well, it sounds savage amusement to me. Honestly, if the garden needs a lot of work we could get some old chap from the village to do it . . .'

This was the last thing she wanted, but it was difficult to explain it to him. She could not tell him that she needed to keep herself fanatically occupied because otherwise she would go mad sitting and picturing the day when he didn't come back. His own superstitious habits had been intensified by flying, and she knew that there was a strict taboo on mentioning such a day. To speak of it was to invite it to come. Nonsense perhaps, but she understood the feeling and indeed shared in it.

Still, it was difficult to restrain herself when he was insistent, as he was now. 'You should rest up,' he kept saying. 'Gardening's too heavy in your condition . . .' She felt it as a failure in him, his inability to understand why she did it: he was normally so sensitive to unspoken things. 'I don't know what the nurse would say if she knew . . . I know you're strong, but it's not just yourself you've got to think about, there's the baby too . . .'

'Oh, I don't care about that!' All the impossible tension of this life suddenly burst within her. 'I don't care – I don't want the bloody baby anyhow!'

She had shocked herself, so she could only guess at how much she had shocked him. She attempted a recovery.

'I mean, of course I do, but it's – it's us I care about – it's *you* I care about. I mean babies are tough little beggars, and anyway he's safe in here, he doesn't have to . . .' She couldn't go on.

'I didn't know,' he said. His face showed no more than perplexity: but there was a great stillness. 'I didn't know you felt like that.'

'I don't,' she said, holding his hand. 'I don't, I'm just tired, and – and sick of it all.'

He looked unseeingly at her: then seemed to haul himself up out of some deep well of thought, and smiled kindly. 'It's no wonder. Look, you sit there. I'll do the dishes and make us a cup of tea.'

They went to bed early that night, after an evening of carefully talking about nothing in the intervals of listening to the wireless. They were quiet, even gentle with each other; but tension teemed beneath the quietness, and when she lay down Stella seemed to feel a great suffocating weight pressing down on her. In the darkness, with Richard lying still beside her, memories of their past and visions of their future came vividly to her; but she felt herself unequal to bridging the gap between them, a weak link in the chain. *I can't bear it any more,* she thought, and again cursed the baby, or rather the fact of the baby. It was the fact of the baby that had brought them close to quarrelling: it was the fact of the baby that intervened between herself and Richard at a time when the world was doing quite enough to separate them. All she wanted was Richard: that simple truth was what she wished to convey to him, and it was that simple truth that the fact of the baby distorted.

And now she really was tired, so tired that she couldn't stop herself drifting away, let alone piece together some reasoned account of her feelings. All she could do was murmur, 'I do love you, Richard,' and then let the tide take her. But she did come to herself, some time later, to find that Richard was giving her one of his special strokes – an inimitably gentle fingertip caressing from her hair down over her shoulder and along her arms to her thighs and then back again. He did this wonderfully well and often when she was uptight and bad-tempered it was the only thing that could calm her down. Now it had the effect of dispelling all the niggling complexity that surrounded them and easing her further into a sleep that was like another world, a world without war, separation or trouble, a world that it seemed to her dreaming mind she had once possessed and foolishly lost.

She woke from it all too soon. He had to report back at the station very early. While he hastily breakfasted she sat blinking in her dressing gown at the table, feeling the world was very cruel. Even the birds sounded only half-awake. The morning chill had the first true note of autumn in it.

She saw something sticking out of the breast pocket of his tunic.

'Richard – what's that?'

'Hm? Oh—' He brought it out. 'Rabbit's foot. Supposed to bring you luck. Oh, I don't suppose it's a real one. Horsehair and stuffing, that's all. I take it with me – you know.'

'How long have you been doing that?'

'Well . . . it was Ginger Bailey's originally. He happened to leave it behind.'

'What happened to Ginger Bailey?'

Richard tucked the rabbit's foot away in his pocket. 'He didn't come back.'

She gazed at him silently.

'Didn't bring him much luck, did it?' she said, and then bent to pat Jimbo.

'Maybe the luck wasn't meant for him. I don't know. I feel I owe it to Ginger, somehow, so I take it with me. To throw it away seems like washing your hands of him . . . Make sense?'

She looked at him. Everything he said made sense, even – or perhaps especially – the things that shouldn't; and although she could not say this in words, her face probably expressed it, for her love for him welled up like a surge of physical pain.

'You'll always be careful, Richard, won't you?' she said with difficulty.

'Always,' he said; and then, patting his breast pocket, 'Don't need this, you know. Got another.'

'Yes?'

'Yes. I don't need any luck. You're my luck, Stella. I got my ration – more than my ration – when I met you. That's as much luck as anybody can expect in one lifetime.'

She lowered her eyes, which were stinging.

'You daft beggar,' she said faintly.

'Sorry.' His voice was at once amused, troubled, and tender. 'I suppose it's a bit early in the day for hearts and flowers. Mean it though.'

She reached out blindly and squeezed his hand. When a few uncountable moments later she looked up to see him putting on his jacket it was like a second waking.

'Here – it can't be time for you to go yet.'

''Fraid so.' He bent to kiss her: she clutched at him. 'You won't tire yourself out in that garden, will you?'

'No – all right.'

'And if you feel anything, any twinges, any uneasiness, you'll knock for the Musselwhites, won't you?'

'Promise.'

Just as she was coming to herself, remembering the stroking last night, seeing how handsome he was, it was time for him to go. She went outside with him, kissed him again, and then had to relinquish him.

'Richard . . .'

'Take care, love. See you soon. Don't . . . don't worry about anything.'

'All right.'

She waved and waved as the old Morris sputtered off down the village street, then felt like both cursing and crying. She hadn't said what she'd intended to say this morning. She'd wanted to say: ignore what I said about the baby last night. I didn't mean it, of course I want our baby, of course I do . . .

Did she, though? She certainly couldn't answer an unequivocal, clear-cut 'Yes' to that. No doubt that made her an unnatural ogre in the eyes of someone like Lily of the Valleys, but she couldn't help it. Her feelings about his lordship, who seemed to have put on another few pounds in the night by the feel of him, were decidedly mixed, and that was the truth.

But never mind: she still should have undone what she had said last night to Richard – of that she was absolutely sure. To Stella truth didn't matter when it was put in the balance with people's feelings. And besides, truth changed. When his lordship finally made his appearance she might well think he was the most wonderful thing the world had ever seen. Or her ladyship, of course: though she had a strange conviction that it was going to be a boy.

Yes, she should have said something but it wasn't too late. After all, Richard wasn't one to sit on his hurts like a broody old hen: his nature was fluid; it was one of the things she loved about him. When he came home, she wouldn't go all round the houses: she would say it straight out.

And she would tell him too that she hadn't so much as touched the garden all day. Which would be another white lie, because as soon as she had cleared the breakfast things she was out there with trowel and fork. There was no help for it: she just couldn't sit indoors today of all days. But she made herself go slowly. Ladylike gardening, she thought, the sort Ma Marwood would do: nip a sprig here, sprinkle a little there.

She had dug over practically the whole garden and had made a start on clipping the long box hedge when it occurred to her that the sun had passed its zenith and she ought to eat something. She had been so absorbed that only now did she register the fact that the sky had been raucous with planes all morning. Looking up, she saw the faded scribbles of contrails in the blue. 'Blimey,' she said to herself, 'Goering could have dropped a bomb on me head and I wouldn't have known anything about it.'

She went indoors, and found to her pleased surprise that she had an appetite. The green ration book that was issued to pregnant women entitled her to extras, and for the first time she was grateful for it. She was just cooking herself a fry-up on the old kitchen range, watched by hopeful doggy eyes, when she heard a sound that set her heart leaping: a car engine.

She hurried to the front door, and flung it open to see two men walking slowly up the garden path towards her. One she knew, only by sight, as Richard's squadron leader; and that drove a dreadful coldness into her. But the other was McCulloch, the rear-gunner with Richard's crew, and at the sight of his carroty head the coldness evaporated and she felt only relief. If he was all right, then Richard was all right: of course.

Then McCulloch did a curious thing: he took hold of her hand as if he were going to shake it. Haltingly, he began to tell her something about enemy attacks on the aerodromes early this morning. She listened, but didn't understand. Why tell her this? She could hear such things on the wireless.

'I'm sorry, Mrs Marwood – I'm so sorry,' McCulloch said; then broke off with a grunt, letting go her hand, and it was the Squadron Leader who told her, calmly and gently, that Pilot Officer Richard Marwood had been among the casualties of an enemy bombing raid on the station at RAF Marham. A Sergeant Pilot and a WAAF had also been killed, he said . . . and it was only with that *also* that Stella understood at last, and turned, stumbling, to go into the house. The movement was instinctive. She wanted to run into somebody's arms. But of course, no one was there.

# Part Five

## *October 1940*

# [illegible]

To her great [illegible] she jumped down from the train and lifted a hand in the air when she saw Kate in her [illegible] cloak at the other end of the platform. She did not wave, and neither did Kate: it was as if all that had happened since they last met had made them shy or uncertain of something.

'I'm late, I'm afraid,' Helen said, as they came together.

'The trains are [illegible] up this [illegible].' After a moment's hesitation, Kate [illegible] her [illegible] [illegible]. They stood [illegible] and for the first time they both smiled. 'You look very well.'

'Country living. Up with the lark, and [illegible] of [illegible]. I shall be like some [illegible] [illegible] [illegible]. You look well too.'

[illegible] we have [illegible].'

In the station buffet they [illegible] tea [illegible] while [illegible] taking turns to stir it with the solitary spoon that was tied to the counter with a piece of string. A few [illegible] rock cakes lay [illegible] under glass. Two soldiers were sharing a single cigarette; Helen took out a packet and passed them a couple.

'Funny,' she said, offering the packet to Kate. 'Wouldn't have dreamt of this not so long ago. Smoking in public, [illegible]! These trousers too. I practically live in them now.'

'Did you have any trouble getting away?'

# ONE

## 1

In her green land girl jersey Helen stepped down from the train and lifted a hand in the air when she saw Kate in her nurse's cloak at the other end of the platform. But she did not wave, and neither did Kate: it was as if all that had happened since they last met had made them shy or uncertain of something.

'I'm late, I'm afraid,' Helen said, as they came together.

'The trains are never on time nowadays.' After a moment's hesitation, Kate brought her hand out from beneath the cloak. They shook hands, and for the first time they both smiled. 'You look very well.'

'Country living. Up with the lark, and lashings of home-cured. I shall be like some strapping German maiden soon. You look good too.'

Kate acknowledged this with a faint smile and a half-shake of the head. 'We've got a little while before the Wisbech train. Shall we have some tea?'

In the station buffet they had tea in chipped white mugs, taking turns to stir it with the solitary spoon that was tied to the counter with a piece of string. A few dismal rock cakes lurked under glass. Two soldiers were sharing a single cigarette. Helen took out a packet and passed them a couple.

'Funny,' she said, offering the packet to Kate. 'Wouldn't have dreamt of this not so long ago. Smoking in public, good heavens! These trousers too. I practically live in them now.'

'Did you have any trouble getting away?'

'No, the farmer I work for's an absolute pet. I was very lucky. Some land girls get billeted on the most awful brutes.' She stretched, wincing. 'You know, I was never really aware of my back till now. It was just the thing you hung your coat on. Now it's taken over my life. I could keep a diary of the pains . . . Sorry. You must see much worse.'

'Not now. It was pretty rough when they first came in, after Dunkirk. A lot are being discharged now.' Kate drew inexpertly on her cigarette. 'Anyway, I wanted to work in an E.M.S.hospital. The Sisters aren't quite so vinegary, for one thing.'

'I suppose nobody can afford to be squeamish nowadays. I hate it when Mr Griggs shoots rabbits, but I eat the pie all the same. Which reminds me.' Opening her bag, Helen unwrapped a handkerchief and furtively displayed four eggs. 'I thought . . . you know, in her condition . . .'

Kate nodded. 'That's kind.'

'Well . . .' Helen hid the eggs away. 'How do you suppose she's managing?'

'It can't be easy. No matter how tough you are.'

Helen, drinking the last of her tea, did not raise her eyes as she said, 'His family?'

Kate shook her head.

'No . . .' Helen stubbed out her cigarette. 'Some might say it was doomed from the start.'

Kate hesitated, then seemed to abandon the question that had been on her lips. 'That's a nice thought,' she said. 'The eggs.'

'Well, living on a farm does have its advantages. But I'd give anything for a really nice bar of soap. Or a proper hot bath for that matter . . . She does know that I'm coming too?'

'I wrote her.'

Helen examined herself in a compact mirror and, as if asking the question of her reflection, said, 'I wonder if she's changed?'

'I suppose we all have.'

'Not you.' Helen rested her chin on her hand a moment, her eyes frank. 'It brings back a lot, seeing you again. What made you choose nursing?'

'You, I think,' said Kate, after a moment's thought. 'Partly you.'

'Me?' She was surprised. 'How so?'

Kate did not answer. She said, 'We'd better get the train.'

They went out to the platform. The murky day was made darker by coal-smoke and smuts. A train had just pulled in at the platform opposite and a woman porter was walking along beside it, calling 'Peterborough, Peterborough.' All the signs had been taken down, and a rail traveller unfamiliar with the route could easily get lost.

'I suppose,' Helen said as the Wisbech train slowly approached round the turn, 'we'll pass through the orchards on the way, will we?' She turned to look at Kate with a face that contained a sort of pained suppression of excitement. 'The orchards, and the strawberry fields?'

'What's left of them.'

Helen nodded. '"Time flieth away".'

'What's that?'

'It was carved on the old sundial. Owen and I . . . had a sundial in the garden. I never liked it somehow. "Time flieth away".' All of a sudden she smiled brightly. 'As if we needed telling!'

They had a compartment to themselves, though it was cold and unswept and smelt of fusty blackout material. The train had barely rumbled out of the station when it came to a halt again, hissing and creaking.

'What is it?' Helen asked, as Kate peered out of the window and down the line. 'Not a raid?'

'I don't think so. I think we've got to let something go first, a goods train maybe. I got held up for two hours like this once.'

'As long as it's not a raid. I hate the idea of being caught in a raid on a train, I don't know why.'

'We had a plane come down near the hospital last week. One of ours. The pilot bailed out without a scratch. That got a few comments from the men in the ward.'

'They're all army, of course.'

Kate nodded. 'There's still a bit of resentment there. Not so bad as it was. They grouse a lot, but you can't blame them. I know you're not supposed to say it, but they've been treated pretty shabbily. Some of them still haven't been issued with hospital blue, and hardly any have got warm clothes for their passes. They . . .'

All at once, she was weeping. She made no sound: the tears simply flowed down her cheeks, and her shoulders shook violently. For a moment Helen looked dreadfully embarrassed, and cast a glance towards the carriage door as if for help. Then she leaned forward and took Kate's hand and held it.

'Sorry, sorry.' Kate mopped at her face with a handkerchief, and then made a scrubbing motion in the air as if to wipe out what had just happened. 'Sorry, sorry, all gone now. Stupid.'

'You're only human,' Helen said. 'You can't be expected to look on unmoved all the time.'

'I do though. Most of the time. You're so busy that you don't have time for . . . It isn't that. Or in a way it is. Oh, damn.' She bit her lips and drew in a deep breath. 'Matron would have me shot if she knew.'

'Ah.'

'Sorry about this.'

'Hush.' Helen took out her cigarettes, lit one and passed it over. 'There's . . . someone at the hospital?'

A nod.

'A patient?'

'Yes. A soldier. Copped a packet at Dunkirk. He's had several operations.'

'Is he . . . all right?'

'He'll probably never be entirely free of pain, but yes, he'll – he'll have his life.' The embarrassment of her lapse had made Kate brusque now. 'So that's all right. One of the lucky ones really.'

'It isn't all right,' Helen said flatly. 'Is it?'

'No.' Kate could only whisper it.

'He's not . . . married?'

'It's not that. It's just . . . he doesn't know.'

'Doesn't know . . . ? Oh. Oh, I see.'

'He doesn't know.' Kate gave a quick shaky smile. 'To him I'm just one of the nurses in Ward B. Madness, isn't it?' she concluded lightly, looking out of the window.

'I see. Yes, of course, I see . . . Oh, but surely he—'

'I'm exaggerating when I say I'm just one of the nurses, I mean I – we . . .'

'Friends?'

Kate sighed. 'Of course, you can't help but make friends with some of them – most of them. It's a curious sort of friendship, I suppose, because of what you've had to do for them—'

'To say the least,' Helen said dryly.

Kate smiled at her, then dropped her eyes. 'We've met outside the hospital once or twice. When he has a pass. Tea in a cafe and such. He hasn't got any family and so I suppose he's a bit, you know, at a loose end.'

'My God, what absolute hell for you.'

Kate looked surprised at the vehemence of Helen's tone.

'Hell,' Helen repeated. 'And does he tell you all about his girl and how sweet she is and all the rest of it?'

'No, no. Not that at all. In a way that would be easier, if you see what I mean. At least then there wouldn't be the . . . I'm sorry. I feel a fool for carrying on like this.'

Helen barely shook her head, serious and attentive. 'Go on.'

'Well . . . that's all there is, really. Except that it isn't hell. Not when I'm with him. Then it's . . .' She dropped her voice so low it was almost inaudible. 'Then it's the opposite.'

'That's what makes it hell.'

Helen spoke with such firm though gentle authority that the words seemed to rule a line under what had been said; and they were silent for some moments, while the train began to clank and jerk into movement again.

'Do you know, I think Mr Griggs is a bit of a conchie in a way,' Helen said at length. 'When we were harvesting, and there were the most tremendous battles going on in the sky, he never once stopped to look up. And when we cheered at one of theirs going down he said, "It's some mother's son," and went on with his work. And yet he gets quite fierce about Hitler when he listens to the wireless.'

Kate had scarcely had time to look grateful for the change of subject before Helen said abruptly, 'Of course you know what you've got to do.'

'What about?'

'There's only one thing to do and it isn't easy, but there it is,' Helen said, ignoring this. 'You've got to tell him. Tell him straight out.'

'I can't.'

'Can't, or daren't?'

'Oh, I don't know . . .' Kate laughed weakly. 'Look at us. I haven't seen you for ages and right away I'm pouring my heart out to you. No, really, it's not on. Don't think any more about it.'

Helen regarded her steadily. 'If you don't tell him, you're going to regret it for years to come. It's better to receive one good downright knockback and then pick yourself up than be eaten away by regrets.'

'Is it?'

'Believe me,' Helen said. 'Believe me.'

'You see, I'm not good at these things,' Kate said in a tone of simple confession. 'It's supposed to come naturally, isn't it? Like breathing or eating.'

'That's the general idea.'

'Was that how it was for you?'

'It . . . simply happened,' Helen said slowly. 'There he was, and before I knew it I was married. So – yes, I suppose so.'

'I always envied you.'

'Envied me? Good heavens.' Helen laughed softly, leaning forward and gazing out of the window. 'Good heavens.'

The country through which they had been passing was fen farmland, bleak and stripped after harvest and colourless under the cold sky; but now scattered plantings of low trees began to appear clustered around dwellings and outhouses of brick and clapboard. There were glasshouses too, and little market-garden plots like neatly hemmed handkerchiefs: suddenly, after the unfenced vastness, here was a landscape in miniature.

'This is the place,' Helen said. She pressed her face to the window. 'It looks so grey now, and yet the way I remember it . . . It's the season, I suppose.'

'A lot of the strawberry fields have gone. And the rosebeds. Everything has to go under the plough now.'

'Ministry directives, I know. Mr Griggs had to plough up his meadow . . . Such a pity. They can't cut down the orchards too, can they?'

'I don't know. Apparently this year most of the fruit rotted on the trees because there wasn't the labour to pick it.'

'"Time flieth away". . . What's his name?'

Kate had hoped the subject had been dropped, and discomfort made her sharp. 'It doesn't matter. Forget about it.'

'There wouldn't be much point in our meeting up again after all this time,' Helen said calmly, 'if I'm just to forget about a thing like that. We're not strangers. Are we?'

'His name's Corporal Benham,' Kate said after a moment's tight silence.

'Well. Military hospitals must be *very* formal.'

Kate laughed crossly. 'Jim,' she said, giving the word scarcely any articulation.

'Names are powerful, aren't they? Magic in them . . . It sounds as if he had a rough time. Is he bitter?'

'I don't know. Perhaps.'

'Bitterness is an evil thing. It's the worst thing in the world because it's death inside.' Helen, her eyes on the window, spoke casually, as if she were talking of some disagreeable food. 'Don't let it happen to you. It will, if you don't act.'

'You sound as if you speak from experience.'

Helen seemed to hesitate between two replies. 'I'm speaking as a friend,' she said at length. 'We were friends back then – weren't we? – and I think we're friends now. Call me a busybody if you like, but I'm not going to drop it, you know. And after all, it does seem as if you've let me influence you before. If it was really me who made you go into nursing – though I can't think how.'

'It was something to do with making a life for myself, instead of having it made for me. Having an aim. It was a new idea for me. I've certainly never regretted that – the nursing, I mean.'

Helen raised an ironical eyebrow. 'Until now?'

Kate thought. 'No. Not even now. I've found something there. I won't let that go whatever . . . whatever happens.'

They had come to the outskirts of Wisbech, but there was another delay while the train gave place to a vital shipment, and it was afternoon, dim and lowering, when they got out at the station. The town, an inland port of Georgian terraces and ancient river warehouses, still carried its quiet distinction beneath the accoutrements of war: the sandbags and the grimly cheerful posters and the drab concrete of the public shelters. It was possible to see it, indeed, as fundamentally untouched. But the country bus they boarded was an old wheezing affair, past its allotted span, and the seats were wooden slats bare of upholstery.

'And so they came back to live here,' Helen said, as the bus ground its way out into the Marshland hamlets, amongst more apple trees and smallholdings. Here and there a church of cathedral-like dimensions rose above the low roofs, sublimely and bafflingly. 'Where it all began.'

'I think it was happy accident as much as anything. He was posted near here. But then I suppose there were the associations too.'

'Yes.' Helen fell silent, watching the countryside as if she were reading a book.

The tiny village that was their destination was a backwater among backwaters, just on the Norfolk border: a silent place of hobbled willows and houses so mellowed with age there was scarcely a straight line amongst them. Few of them had numbers and after the bus had set them down and gone shuddering on its way Helen and Kate spent some time wandering round the deserted street before they found the one they sought.

'Good God, what a mausoleum,' Helen said, as they paused

before the gate. 'I simply can't imagine her here. And isn't it rather large for her?'

'Apparently it's divided into two dwellings. They rented it from the old people who live in the other half. I suppose when he was posted over here they had to take what they could get. Pretty safe from raids, at any rate.'

'I think I'd rather face the bombs than get bored to death,' Helen said. Almost immediately she blushed a dark congested red, from the roots of her hair to the collar of her jersey. Kate, pretending not to notice, stepped forward to the gate; but Helen did not follow. It was as if the blush had immobilized her as effectively as a cramp.

'Oh God,' she said, 'I don't think I can do this.'

'Why ever not? She's expecting us.'

'I am not a nice person,' Helen said, looking up at the tiny warped windows of the old house. 'No, I am not a nice person.'

Kate put her hand on her arm. 'Come on.'

The door was answered to their knock at once, as if they had been eagerly, almost desperately awaited. A smell of boiling cabbage wafted out as the door was opened, and a collie dog came frisking out to greet the visitors.

'Hello.' Kate spoke first. 'Sorry we're late.'

Standing in the doorway with her pinafore stretched over the bulge of her late pregnancy, Stella still seemed to look ethereal and fragile with the marks of her grief obvious in the hollows etched below her cheekbones. With the same eagerness, almost desperation, she looked from one to another, searching their faces. Kate smiled, but Helen was occupied with patting the dog, and did not look up to meet Stella's eyes for some moments.

'That's all right,' Stella said, and she stood aside and held the door open wide with a broad wholehearted gesture that again had something of desperation about it. 'You've had a long way to come.'

'Well, not really,' Kate said. 'Isn't it strange that we should all end up in the fens again? I—'

'No, you're right,' Helen said, cutting across her. She stepped across the threshold with a conscious look, as if she were crossing a border. 'We've come a long way. At any rate, it seemed it – the train absolutely crawled along. You look – you look well.' Then she glanced at Kate. 'Of course, I bow to professional opinion on that.'

'Gawd, I don't feel it. I feel like I'm carrying a ruddy ten-ton weight around with me,' Stella said. 'Come in, come in. Take your coats off – get near the fire. Jimbo, go down.'

'How long have you got to go now?' Kate said, slipping off her nurse's cloak.

'A week, they say. But I don't think he's ever going to come out. He's staying in there to spite me. Sit down, sit down – I'll just go and check the dinner.'

'Oh, my dear, you shouldn't have gone to that trouble,' Helen said, 'not in your condition—'

'Now listen,' Stella said, 'the pair of you. I don't want any more talk about me condition. It's been nothing but me condition since – well, it seems like donkey's years – and I'm fed up with it. I know it's hard, but don't take any notice of this great lump here. And anyway – ' there was great poignancy in the smile that broke out on Stella's face, a face that was plainly marked with grief – 'once you've tasted *my* cooking, you'll *really* wish I hadn't taken the trouble.'

She disappeared into the kitchen. Helen and Kate, sitting on either side of the fire, looked around them at the dark-beamed room. Both were noticing the same things about it – little tokens of Richard. There was a cigarette-case of his on the mantelshelf, a photograph of him from his college days, even a pair of slippers by the hearth. They saw, but neither of them spoke.

'Now what about a drink?' Stella said returning. 'Oh, just a drop to take the chill off. We might as well finish this. It's good stuff. Richard got it from a Canadian mate of his. Poor bloke bought it just last week over Holland.'

Helen looked puzzled. 'How did he . . . ? Oh – I see . . .'

Stella nodded, then shrugged, sipping the whisky. 'You pick the RAF slang up pretty quick.' A ghost was in the room with them now; but none of them was prepared to face it. 'Now then, nurse,' she said, holding up a warning finger at Kate, 'don't tick me off. This is just a nip to keep you company. I ain't turning his lordship here into a toper before his time, don't you worry. Well! This is a treat, seeing you both. I never dreamt – I mean, when Kate wrote me you'd be coming along too, you could have knocked me down with a feather. And you're on the land! You look damn well on it too!'

Helen was a little abashed. 'Thank you. I – I'm sorry I haven't been in touch for such a long time. It was just – well, so many things happened. And then I ended up in the fens again and I thought, well, it's high time I picked up the old threads. I only had an address for Kate, so I wrote and asked for news and . . .'

'And you got it,' Stella said, with an unreadable twist of the mouth; and drank her whisky.

'Yes.' Helen took a deep breath. 'When Kate told me, I . . . Oh, Stella, I'm so sorry.' Her eyes darted around the room, and for a moment she looked almost frightened, ready to flee. 'I don't know how you can bear it.'

'You have to,' Stella said dully.

'You're very brave,' Helen whispered, her eyes downcast.

'No, I ain't. I haven't done anything. I just . . .' Stella cleared her throat. 'I just went to his funeral and then I carried on living. That's all.'

'That's a great deal,' Kate said.

Stella shook her head almost desperately. 'No. Nothing. He was the one who . . . Anyhow, look at you two – all in uniform and official-looking! Proper war workers. You're the ones who should be proud. All I am is this ruddy bloated whale sitting around no good to anyone.' She laughed painfully.

'Oh, Stella, that's not true,' Helen said.

'Isn't it?'

'No . . . after all, you're carrying life.'

Stella shrugged again, and seemed about to say something that was as desolate as her look; but just then there was a knock at the front door. Stella got up with a grunt and went to open it.

'Hello there – just checking to see that your visitors arrived.' It was an old man's voice, high and quavering. 'Oh, they did? Good, good – delayed, eh? Oh, nothing's on time nowadays. It's this beastly war. In the last lot, you know, the trains ran on time, not that we had such raids of course, but I remember an old pal of mine who got leave from Flanders and he travelled all the way to . . . So, you're all right then? Jolly good – jolly good. Give us a knock if you want anything.'

'The old fella who lives in the other half,' Stella said coming back. 'Gawd, he goes on. They're kind, though. Come and see me every day since it happened.'

Frowning, Kate said, 'Stella, are you completely on your own here?'

'No. I've got Jimbo,' Stella said, ruffling the collie's head. 'And the old sticks next door are just on the other side of that panelling – see there? – I've only got to give a rap on there and they can hear me. And then there's the district nurse. She stops by every day. And there's Richard's squadron leader and a WAAF officer from the station, they come and see me whenever they can, they've been ever so good . . .'

'So you are on your own,' Kate said, in her quiet downright way.

'Suppose I am.' There was a sort of brittle shell around Stella, but her real self began to show through it as she went on, 'I know it ain't exactly ideal. But there you are – if you're a service wife you have to expect something like this. And I know what you're going to say – you expect to have some help from your family. Or your husband's family. Well, it ain't like that in my case. There's Dad down in London, but he can't leave his work. I suppose at a pinch I could go down there and stay with him till the baby's born – he said as much in a letter – but I don't want the upheaval and London's hardly the safest place in the world just now and to tell you the truth, I don't want to be there. Not with that bitch he married, excuse my language.'

'What about Richard's family?' Kate said.

'Talking of bitches, you mean?' Stella said with a weary laugh.

'Well, they didn't like me from the start. No surprises there. But they like me even less now. They were up here for the funeral. Richard's dad was all right but he's half dotty anyway and just does what his wife says. And she had a few very choice words for me. Said if he hadn't married me he'd be alive now and she'd hate me for the rest of her life.'

Kate made a scornful noise. Helen, very pale, said, 'Oh, but Stella, she can't . . . I mean, surely, her grief—'

'You ever meet the charming Mrs Marwood?' Stella said, sharply.

'Once – just briefly, at Cambridge.'

'You were lucky you had it brief. She means what she says, Helen, believe me. I took Richard away from her and she hates my guts for it.'

Helen looked away.

'But you are carrying her grandchild,' Kate said. 'Doesn't that mean anything to her?'

Stella seemed to catch herself up on the brink of another outburst of bitterness, and sighed. 'Gawd knows. The sprog's half me, so I suppose that puts the mockers on it as far as the old bat's concerned. She did say something about "we shall of course wish for a say in our grandchild's future, blah blah", but I don't think that means a lot. I asked Richard's squadron leader about that and he said they couldn't do anything with regard to the child that I don't want 'em to do, so that's all right. Oh, and there was a cheque. Not from them – from Richard's brother Maurice. He was always a bit more human. He's just joined up. I think he was properly cut up about Richard . . . But I don't know. I've just put it in the bank. I've got me entitlements as a forces widow, so I can pay the rent on this place, and . . . Well, this was our home.' Stella's voice grew soft. 'We were happy here. So I shall stay put and see how things go.'

There was a silence. Helen stirred, seeming to come out of a deep abstraction. 'I think,' she said looking at her hands, 'that that was a terrible thing for Richard's mother to say. I think it was – unforgivable.'

Stella looked her surprise at the feeling in her tone. 'Oh well,' she said with a short laugh, 'I never heard her say a nice thing, to be honest. I dunno. Perhaps it's a rule of life that you just don't get on with your in-laws.' Rather shyly she said to Helen, 'What about you? I heard from Kate that you – you weren't with your husband any more. What were your in-laws like?'

'I didn't have any,' Helen said. 'Owen's parents are dead. No, I never had that problem. It was my husband I couldn't abide.'

The introduction of this cool, acerbic, Helen-like note into the conversation had an effect like the lifting of a cloud. For the first time all three laughed together; at the sound of it the collie dog set up a long howl that made them laugh again.

'Well,' Stella said, brushing her eyes, 'it's funny how things turn out. Here we are again, the three of us, after all this time, and . . .' Impulsively she leaned forward and seized their hands. 'I didn't think anything could make me feel glad again, but seeing you two is – well, like I say, it's a treat. Now, what about some dinner?'

The cabbage was soggy, the potatoes burnt. 'I can't cook – never could, never will,' Stella moaned, her despair at least partly real. But there was also that rarity – real butcher's meat, in the shape of chops. 'An old chap in the village gave 'em to me,' Stella said. 'And where he got 'em from I don't know. But he said as I was eating for two I ought to have proper meat once in a way.' Helen, living on a farm, was used to certain off-the-ration perks, but Kate was agog. 'There's nothing like this at the hospital canteen,' she kept saying, 'absolutely nothing,' and her relish was so great that it made the others smile. And it was Stella herself who said, 'It reminds me of that time in Cambridge – do you remember? When Richard took us all out to dinner. And there was that funny old girl in the lounge with the wobbly head . . . That was a good time.'

'Sometimes it seems you don't know the good times until they're gone,' Kate said.

'Not all of 'em,' Stella said gently. 'Some of 'em you know while they're happening. They're the ones you don't forget.'

There was the throbbing of an aeroplane engine overhead. Everyone paused, listening.

'Do you get many raids out here?' Helen said.

'Not really,' Stella said. 'Just – well, on the airfields and that.'

Helen put down her fork. 'What a stupid question. What an unutterably stupid thing to say . . .'

'Here, shush,' Stella said. 'It doesn't matter. What *can* we talk about, if we have to watch everything we say? After all, Richard's here with us now, isn't he? The last time we all met was with him. It was always the four of us. So it'd be a lie pretending he never existed. And that he never got killed.' She put down her dinner, hardly touched, for the dog. 'Do you nurse pilots at that hospital, Kate?'

'No. It's all casualties from the BEF.'

'Only you see how some of these pilots end up – when they survive. Richard once said he hoped that would never happen to him and I was wild with him about it – because didn't he realize I just wanted him, no matter what . . . But I've thought about that since, and well, at least it was the way he wanted it. I mean it was quick – instantaneous, they reckoned.' She gave Kate a straight look. 'Do they fib about that sometimes, Kate? To spare the relatives?'

'No,' Kate said promptly. 'It was a thing they used to do, I know, in the last war. Not any more.'

'Good. You know, one of his mates from the service said something to me at the funeral, about how rotten it was to go like that instead of in combat, and I thought no . . . you're wrong . . .' For the first time Stella began to cry, quietly. 'He was worried about his crew, you see. If his kite got shot down they all copped it, that's the thought he couldn't stand, that it wouldn't just be him, so . . . God, I'm no good without him. It's all gone, everything. I used to be so snotty about these women who put their whole lives into a fella, but it's come home to me because – because I'm like that now. I miss him and I want him all the time, y'see, and he ain't here – he ain't here any more, and it's more than I can bear, I swear to God it is . . .'

Each patting a hand, they let her carry on.

'Well . . . that's my lot,' Stella said at last, wiping her face. 'All done now. Sorry, you must have been wondering when I'd do that.'

'The suspense was terrible,' Kate said, and they all laughed excessively at the weak joke, with a sort of shaky relief.

'So what about where you are, Helen? Get many raids?' Stella said.

'It's very quiet. It's an awful thing to say, but I think Huntingdon town is the one place I know that would be improved by a few bombs. But it seems to be London that's catching it now. That must be worrying for you – with your family there.'

'I wish Dad would send the kids away like Auntie Bea did. Corbett Street hasn't copped it yet but he says the next street's half flattened already. What a world, eh? D'you suppose it'd be any different if the women ran it?'

'Perhaps we will, after this lot's over,' Kate said.

'Coh!' Stella laughed. 'You taking bets on that?'

Overriding Stella's protests, Kate and Helen washed up. 'You should go and put your feet up,' Kate said, when she hung around the kitchen with them.

'Now, now – none of that stuff about me condition, remember.'

'Well, I know you won't think about yourself,' Kate said, 'so I'll be stern and nursey and say think about the baby.'

'Oh, him!' Stella said. 'Yes, I think about him all right.'

Helen made tea. They swapped bits of news while they drank it, the afternoon darkening at the windows. When Kate looked at her watch, a look of almost panicked alarm came over Stella's face.

'I'm sorry, Stella,' Kate said. 'I've got to be on duty tonight.'

'I shall have to go too,' Helen said. 'The trains don't run late.'

'Oh, I know,' Stella said with a sigh, 'I know you've got to go . . . Gawd, hark at me. Giving you all that stuff about how well I can manage on me own and now I get the miseries because you've got to go home. It's just . . . well, it's just that it's been like old times and I don't want it to end.'

'Well, it won't,' Kate said. 'We're going to come again. Aren't we, Helen?'

'. . . If you can put up with us.'

'You don't have to do that,' Stella said, looking sadly hopeful.

'What, just say ta-ta and leave you here expecting a baby?' Kate said. 'No, no. I wish I could come and look after you continually, but I don't think Matron would think much of that. But I get my day off on Saturday. I could come then.'

'I could swing it with Mr Griggs,' Helen said. 'He owes me a day.'

'No,' Stella said, 'no, you two are busy, you're doing important things – and anyway I don't need looking after—'

'You need friends, though,' Kate said.

'Oh . . .' Stella smiled, half-tearful. 'You'll set me off again!'

'Come on then, slim,' Kate said, offering a hand to help her up, 'you can wave us off.'

'Oh, to look like you two,' Stella groaned, and added with a look of admiration at Helen, willowy in Land Army breeches and jersey, 'and to be able to wear that!'

'Me? I look like a long green bean.'

Stella shook her head. 'No. You've got it, you have. Always did have, but now . . . you look like you know where you're going.'

'Do I? Well . . . I took a couple of wrong turnings, perhaps.'

## 2

Dusk had come down when Kate and Helen caught the Peterborough train. The blackout was already up at the carriage windows, and the only illumination was a dim blue bulb, just enough to see each other's faces and, supposedly, to deter pickpockets and molesters. Reading on the train was one of the minor comforts of life that the war had already done away with.

'Strange meetings,' Helen said. 'Did she look well, do you think? Really?'

'I think so. We did a little basic obstetrics in training, and it's a healthy pregnancy as far as I can see.'

'A posthumous child. Like David Copperfield. One doesn't think of it happening in real life . . . I don't think I could live there alone like that.'

'Well, like she said, she's not really alone. Richard's with her.'

Kate could not be sure, but she thought she saw Helen shudder as she said, 'That's what I mean.'

'Helen – you said something to me earlier – on the way up. About regrets. And how there's nothing worse.'

'Yes, my dear.'

'Were you thinking of your own regrets? About – your marriage, I mean?'

Helen smiled a little thinly. 'Probably. I – I'll tell you about it some time. Or perhaps not. It's not an edifying story.'

'Do you suppose Stella has any regrets?'

'Oh, dear,' Helen said, taking out a cigarette and lighting it, 'ask me one I can answer.' Then, as if regretting this briskness, 'Are you thinking about your soldier? At the hospital?'

'Partly . . . Other things too. Do you remember George Maxey? Our neighbour at Monks Bridge?'

'I do. A hero out of Jane Austen.'

'After that summer . . . he asked me to marry him. I said yes, but then I couldn't go through with it.'

'Why?'

'I suppose because I thought it was wrong to marry a man just because you were flattered that he'd picked you.'

'And you regret that?'

'No. No, I don't. But he said something to me – when we parted. He said that I was afraid. Afraid of committing myself, afraid of life I think . . . Of course, you say things you don't mean at times like that. But now I look at you and I look at Stella and I wonder if he was right after all. I feel like I – I missed out somewhere.'

'But my dear, that's sheer nonsense. Thank you for the implied compliment, but believe me – you were the brave one. I mean that entirely. My regret is that I have been a coward.' The tip of her cigarette sent an upward glow across Helen's fine-boned face, giving it a look of sudden, helpless nakedness. 'Funny, isn't it? When I'm working in the fields and our planes go over I think: what courage to be up there, what unthinkable courage. And yet I always believed Richard to be – rather weak.'

'Did you? You were such good friends.'

'Yes, we were.' Helen extinguished the cigarette, and it was as if a mask dropped over her face. 'What you think of a person doesn't necessarily alter your feelings about him. Your soldier, my dear – Jim, isn't it? What do you think of him? Do you think he's perfect?'

Kate hesitated. 'He can be very awkward.'

'Love him any less for it?'

'I never said I loved him.'

'Oh, my dear Kate.' Helen laughed softly, and took her hand in the dimness. 'You know, you may be quite wrong about missing out. It might be that for you things are only just beginning.'

Kate bit her lip. 'I do love him. But—'

'Ah, ah, ah. Never add *but* to those words. Now, about Jim: you know what I think you should do, don't you?'

'Yes . . . but you see, I don't want to lose his friendship.'

'You might do anyway,' Helen said; in such a strange distant voice that Kate felt she must be tiring her.

She said quickly, 'Anyway – I shouldn't keep going on about it. Sorry. We meet up after all this time and straight away I'm confiding in you.'

'I'm honoured. As I think I once said to you before, a long while ago.'

Kate had not meant to confide; yet somehow she felt that it had not been all on one side, and that, without direct words, she had taken Helen's confession too.

## 3

Kate got back to the hospital at six. In the hut she shared with five other nurses she was about to sit down and try to occupy herself with mending when Nurse Wallis, whose moaning voice had been unfavourably compared with the air-raid siren, came in complaining.

'. . . just look at that time, I've only just got off duty and Sister would have kept me there even longer if Matron hadn't turned up because of course she started sucking up straight away then and sent me away with that flick of her hand, you know, as if I was the one who wanted to be hanging around there. She's such a pig, I know she's always a pig but today she's been the absolute limit and you're jolly lucky you've been out of it. First there was the fuss over Davidson's injections and then that business about the mackintoshes on Lambton's pillows which was the orderly's fault and not mine, and then she got into a tizzy simply because Benham's bed wasn't stripped straight after he'd gone. I mean it's not as if there was a new man needing it—'

'Gone?' Kate sat bolt upright. 'What did you say? Where's Corporal Benham?'

'He's been transferred. The Major had him in this morning. They've finished with him here, I think they were sending him for intensive physiotherapy—'

'Where?'

Nurse Wallis looked surprised at Kate's tone, but she was too self-absorbed to be curious. 'The city hospital at Peterborough, I think. They've better facilities there – and I don't suppose for one moment the nurses have to put up with the conditions that we have to, I mean I haven't managed a proper hot bath since . . .'

She was due on duty at nine, which gave her rather less than three hours; there were the buses in to Peterborough for the men on passes, but they were slow, and if she was so much as two minutes late back Sister would have her hide . . . Kate was already on her way out of the hospital gates as she thought these things.

She did not have to wait long for the bus, but it seemed a good hour; and she was so distracted that she unthinkingly hopped on ahead of a patient who was on crutches, and who called out, without malice, 'Where's bloody Florence Nightingale now?'

'Oh – oh, I'm so sorry,' she said, helping him on. He sat next to her and chaffed with her all through the slow juddering journey. She was afraid she was very absent in her replies, but it helped to pass the time; and when she had to say no to his invitation to the cinema, he only smiled and said, 'Well, I hope he's worth it, Nurse.'

As she walked through the blacked-out city up to the Memorial Hospital she remembered Helen bringing her here to visit her injured father, and how she had trembled to enter. She was trembling again now, and again with a sort of fear: yet now she wore a nurse's uniform and faced down sickness every day. Life seemed strange and unpredictable almost beyond bearing, a series of abrupt conundrums.

Her uniform was of the Emergency Services, and stood out here in a civilian hospital; she had just decided to brazen it out by presenting the Ward Sister with some tale of bringing a message to Corporal Benham from the EMS authorities when she noticed the comings and goings, and realized it was still visiting time. There was nothing against her being a visitor. She found the ward, which seemed vast compared with the prefabs she was now used to. The Sister, with a sour look at her new-fangled white overall, directed her to a bed on the left, in the centre. For a moment Kate's mind could not accommodate this simple fact: somehow she expected his bed to be in exactly the same position as at the EMS.

He was sitting up, reading: he had, of course, no visitors.

'Hullo,' she said. 'I tracked you down.'

His face lit up; but of course, it would. He was alone, and here was company.

'You . . . what a surprise!' He gave her his hand: he must have been completely taken off guard, because the hand he gave her was his weak one, and she realized now – she hadn't been conscious of it before – that he usually contrived to keep that one away from her. 'But I never imagined . . . It was all so quick, you know what the army's like – I wondered whether I could get a message to you before I left this morning, but I didn't know who to trust with it – what with frat rules and everything . . .'

He stopped, or rather ran down, and looked at her. She returned his look; then glanced about the ward. It was a forbidding place, with many screens: none of that easiness of having your comrades about you. So it was no wonder he gave her that welcoming look. Helen's words had carried her here, thrust her indeed to the edge of decision; but as she sat holding Jim Benham's hand, she realized that they were only words. They could not create something out of nothing.

'So how are they treating you?' she said.

'Well, so far it's been business as usual. I get my first physio tomorrow – it's to try and get the old wing working, you know. The Major said he didn't think it would be a long course and I can expect my discharge pretty soon. It's . . . well, I liked the old place better.'

Despite the hospital bed, the change in his surroundings seemed to have altered him: he looked indeed as if he had practically got his discharge already, moved out into the world, left her behind. All at once Kate felt she couldn't stand this.

'So how was your day?' he said. He still had hold of her hand, and his thumb was weakly stroking it. When she did not answer he said, 'It was today, wasn't it? You were going to see your friend who'd been widowed. I remember you telling me about it.'

'Oh yes! It – it was good to see her again.'

'Bearing up?'

'Pretty well. I don't know whether having a baby makes it easier or harder for her.'

'He was a pilot, wasn't he?'

'Yes. They bombed his station and he was killed.'

Jim licked his lips, his eyes searching her face. 'God . . . I seem to remember saying some ruddy stupid things on that subject the other week. Too much staring up my own ar . . . backside.' He glanced towards the Sister. 'Have to watch yourself in here. No barrack language. Kate . . . are you all right? Was it very upsetting?'

'No, but this is.'

She couldn't look at him; but she seemed to feel his gaze

travelling over her face, like the touch of soft fingertips.

'I don't think it is,' he said at last. 'When I saw you – when I looked up and you were there, it was just . . .'

She pulled her hand away from him. 'This is very unfair on you,' she said. 'I shouldn't do it. It's wrong of me, I'm sorry.'

'Why – what?'

'Well, of course you're going to – feel something. You're alone and at a loss and this girl comes looking for you and – and as good as tells you how she feels about you – so you're hardly going to tell her to get lost, it wouldn't be natural or even kind . . .'

'No,' he said slowly, 'it wouldn't.'

'But I don't want you to be kind, Jim – don't you see?'

'I don't think I am as a rule – am I? An awkward beggar, you called me the other day.'

'Oh, it isn't a joke.'

'I know it isn't. Here, Kate, you're crying – don't, please. I didn't know. . . I didn't think that you . . .'

'It doesn't matter. I'm sorry, sorry about this – I can't stay. Goodbye, I hope they look after you all right . . .'

*You were the brave one.* Well, that was wrong, because she was running now, running from the field of disaster. The ward seemed a hundred yards long: there were such fierce prohibitions on nurses running that patients and visitors stared open-mouthed. She heard Jim calling her name, then she was out in a cold beige-painted corridor. She found the stairs, took them three or four at a time, very nearly tumbling in a heap. Downstairs she got herself lost, and for some crazy moments experienced all the old dread at the sight of wheelchairs and gurneys and white coats. By the time she burst out into the hospital forecourt the sob that she had been holding in burnt her chest like a live coal, and she gasped it out, staggering.

*Well, at least the worst is over now.* The words passed through her mind to such mockingly ghastly effect that she began to laugh through her tears. Then she recollected that she was a nurse and a responsible war worker and not supposed to behave like a madwoman. Dried-up and spinstery: spinstery and dried-up. She scrubbed at her face with her hand and took some deep breaths, preparing to begin her life again: she did not like the look of it at all, but it was all she had. An ambulance came through the gateway, its headlights blacked out to narrow slits, and she stepped smartly aside to let it past. Then she began walking towards the gateway, until she was stopped by a hand on her shoulder.

'Kate. Kate, please.'

It was Jim: he had put on his hospital blue uniform, hurriedly by the look of it, and one bootlace was flapping loose. He looked beautiful to her, but she didn't want that; didn't want, either, his kindness pressing like a tight bandage on her embarrassed pain.

'I'm sorry,' she said, with a sort of blind weariness. 'I'm sorry for that awful scene in there. That was rather rough on you, visiting hours are supposed to be nice. Now please go back in – you're not supposed to be walking out, are you? – the Matron'll have you shot—'

'Stop it, for God's sake.' He thrust something at her, made her take it in her hand: an envelope. 'Read that. No, don't say anything. Just read it.'

She could not, of course, with the blackout; but in her pocket she had the torch that she used on her rounds, so, hardly knowing what she was doing, she shone it down on the envelope. It was stamped, and addressed to her at the EMS hospital.

'Open it,' he said.

The writing was shaky and childlike: he had had to train himself to use his left hand, lacking control in his right. *Dear Kate,* it read, *You'll know by now that they've transferred me here. It all happened so fast. I couldn't believe it. I couldn't say goodbye to you. But the thing is I don't want to say goodbye to you. Probably this isn't the right way to say it but I've got to. If you don't want to see me again after reading this then that'll be easy enough. Only when you love someone I think you've got to tell them or else something goes rotten inside. So even if this is something you don't care to know, never mind: I'd like to think we could still be friends anyway. I know people always say that but I think we could, if you wanted to, I mean. I shall never forget you in any case . . .*

She couldn't read on, because she couldn't see any more, but she stayed there blinking down at it, feeling his breathing on her hair, until he snatched it from her fingers.

'Anyway, that's the damn letter – I was writing it this afternoon, and then you came and it was like – oh, God, Kate, come here . . .'

The strength of his embrace was all in the one arm, but still it was ample; and her own was no less. The texture of his hair in her fingers was exactly as she had imagined it so many times, and this correspondence added the crowning touch to a moment that in its intensity left her entirely wordless, as if the power of speech in her had simply finished.

'One thing,' he said at last, 'one thing I didn't write – chickened out. Should have told you. When I had my physio today – well, I asked them straight out, and the fact is the back's always going to give me gyp and this bloody arm of mine is never going to be much good. Not as arms go, anyway,' he added, with a stiff laugh.

'You don't have to tell me that. It doesn't matter to me.'

'I know. I know. That's the damn trouble . . .' He lifted his chin above her head, his face out of her sight. 'You're a nurse, you see. You don't mind – looking at cripples – because you have to. And so all the time I kept thinking – well, that I shouldn't get ideas. Just because you didn't seem put off – it was unfair of me to think that that meant anything, it was like taking advantage of your job . . . Make sense?'

It made sense: much made sense to her now – the enigmatic carelessness, the refusal to accept half-truths. The EMS hospital had had no brief for an injured mind, least of all one that declined to take the easy way of self-pity. She saw struggles ahead, a battle with self not yet won; but she would not be a bystander. And this warmed her. She did not want to hide in a lover's shadow: she wanted them to walk together under the open sky, with all its dangers.

'Jim, to me you're perfect. That's all.'

'Perfect?' He brought his face down to hers. 'Blimey.'

'Well, apart from being an awkward beggar.'

They had just begun kissing when they were startled by a piercing whistle of prurient surprise. A small scruffy boy had just come out of the hospital, running ahead of his parents, and was now standing a few feet from them pointing a grubby finger.

'Now you've done it,' he shrilled delightedly. 'I saw yer. Now you'll *have* to marry 'er.'

# *TWO*

## 1

Saturday was breezy and bright and quite mild, and so when Kate and Helen arrived at Stella's house for their second visit it seemed quite reasonable that they should have tea in the garden.

'After the baby's born and I'm on me feet again,' Stella said, 'I shall get all this garden into shape. It was starting to look reasonable this summer, but now it's a mess again.'

'It looks far from a mess to me,' Helen said appreciatively. 'Did you do it all yourself?'

'Mr Musselwhite does a bit, but I'd rather he kept out of the way to be honest. He doesn't understand plants. Well, *I* don't, but I understand enough not to kill 'em.'

'You ought to go in for it,' Kate said. 'You could make a bob or two.'

'Get out of it!'

'No, really. I was thinking that when I got a letter from Dad this week. With the fruit-growers having to stick to basics because of the Min of Ag, there's a lot of market gardens and such like going begging. He was telling me that all Ernie Delph's cherries and plums went to the wasps this year: he was concentrating on veg and there wasn't the labour to pick them. He wanted to sell the picking outright but there was nobody to buy. I thought that might be an idea for you.'

'What, buy an orchard?' Stella cried. 'You're joking.'

'Well, you don't buy the land. What you buy is the produce on the stem, say for fifteen pound down. For that it's all yours for the season. You do the picking and the marketing, or employ whoever you need to help. You're near the Marshland here: I saw some stands of apple on the bus in. The Min of Ag can't plough it all up. And I know Dad'd help you. It's just a thought.'

'It's a good one,' Helen said. 'Just think – it would be like old times.'

'It would an' all,' Stella mused. 'There is that money that Richard's brother sent me . . .' Then she threw up her hands and cast a despairing glance down at herself. 'Oh, but what's the use of me thinking of anything like that when I can hardly waddle from one place to another . . .'

'Well, the baby'll come soon,' Kate said, amused. 'And then you'll be slim again.'

'Will he come? Will he ever?' wailed Stella. 'I'm beginning to think he's decided to stay in there for the duration.' She flapped irritably at the tablecloth, which kept blowing up into her face in the strong wind.

'What does the district nurse have to say?' Kate said, removing a dead leaf from her teacup.

'She says everything's fine and it'll be another three days, four at most. She'll be here today around half-three. All cheerful. It's all right for her, she don't feel pain.'

'Stella!' laughed Kate.

'It's true – she's one of these strapping types who jumps into cold baths and comes up smiling,' Stella said, laughing crossly. 'And come to think of it, Kate Lutton, *you're* very chipper today. You're not allowed to be happy, you know, when I ain't. What's it all about?'

'Just happy to see you, Stella dear,' Kate said, smiling over her cup.

'Hm. I'll get it out of you, don't you worry—' Just then the milk bottle on the tray blew over and in the same moment the tablecloth clouted Stella's face again. 'Oh! that's it. Sod this for a lark, we're getting blown all over the shop – come on, let's go in . . .'

She got up and made a grab at the tea tray, then stood in a

curious arrested posture, with a look that was startled and almost affronted, as if she had been pinched.

'Kicking?' Kate said.

'I don't think so,' Stella said. 'I don't think that's what it was . . . Oh Gawd . . . I dunno.'

They helped her into the house. Once there she subsided in a gingerly way on to the settle and, puffing and perspiring, gazed beseechingly at the two of them as if they had the answer to a crucial question.

'What does it feel like?' Kate said. 'Is it—'

'Whoa!' Stella shouted, jerking up in her seat.

'Is it contractions, I was going to say.'

'I dunno . . . it feels . . . ooer.' Stella gripped fiercely at the arms of the settle. 'What else can it be? Oh! Christ . . . !'

'It isn't, is it?' said Helen, standing by with elegant helplessness. 'Kate, can it be? It isn't due for another three days.'

'Helen, it's not the bloody *Picture Post*, it's a baby, they come when they want,' moaned Stella.

'When did you say the district nurse comes?' Kate said.

'Half-three. Ow.'

'Only eleven now,' Helen said. 'Well, thank heaven you're here, Kate, anyhow.'

'Me? But I'm not a midwife, I mean they trained us mainly in medical and surgical and then the war came and—'

'Listen, folks,' Stella cried, 'if anybody should be panicking it should be me. But it's all right. Mr Musselwhite's got an old banger and – ow – he's been saving his petrol coupons and he said he'd take me to the maternity wing at Lynn whenever – whenever I was ready. So it's all right.'

'Thank heaven,' said Helen. 'I'll knock, shall I? On the panelling – just here?'

'That's it. Give it a good old hammering, they're a bit cheesy in the ears.'

The knocking brought the old lady, Mrs Musselwhite, who took one look at Stella and then gave a shriek.

'Blast that man! Oh, blast him to hell! He's so *stupid*.' The old lady turned to Helen in trembling, vituperative appeal. 'Would you believe it? Would you believe what he's done? He's only gone and driven the Wolseley all the way over to Wisbech today of *all* days.'

'When will he be back?' Stella cried.

'Lord knows. Hours, knowing him. He's gone with one of his stupid cronies to pick up some canvas or something for some stupid Home Guard exercise. It's all rubbish. Imagine *him* fighting the Germans . . . I hope they machine-gun him,' she added with a final writhe of supreme contempt, and then, more calmly, 'I'm sorry, dear. He's let you down. You'd be used to it if you'd been married to him for fifty years. Lucky you've got the nurse here—' with a nod at Kate. 'I'd better go back, my kettle's on the stove. I'll knock you when he comes back. I'll knock *him* when he comes back.' She went off muttering.

'There must be someone else in the village with a car,' Helen said.

'Mr Ashford's got a truck,' Stella groaned, 'but he goes to market Saturdays . . . Miss Tewkes has put her car up on bricks in case the Jerries get it or something . . . Oh! bleedin' hell, what am I going to do, I hate pain . . .'

'Breathe slow,' Kate said. 'Time your breathing between the contractions – slow like you're going to sleep. That's it. Now put your feet up here. It's going to be all right. The district nurse, she must be on the telephone?'

'Yes . . . Stowbridge 259. You'll be lucky to find her in – ow – but her sister takes messages. There's a telephone at the Oxcart, down at the other end of the village.'

'Right.'

'Oh, shouldn't I go?' Helen said in some agitation as Kate put on her cloak. 'I mean – if anything happens . . .'

'I won't be a minute,' Kate said. She smiled at Stella. 'Anyway, it's going to be a long haul yet.'

'Oh, Gawd, all you nurses have got that ruddy cheerful tone,' Stella moaned. 'Go on, clever clogs. I'll just sit here and suffer . . .'

'Shall I make you a cup of tea?' Helen said when Kate had hurried off. 'Or how about a nip of that whisky? Is that allowed?'

'I dunno. I'm new to this meself. Phoo. It is a bit better if you – breathe like that.'

'Tea with a nip in it,' Helen said. 'How about that?'

'Oh – Helen, could you just stay here with me? I shall be all right as long as – as long as I'm not on me own.'

'Of course, my dear.' Helen sat down by her. 'I wish I could be of more use.'

'Oh, you are . . . just to have you here – to know you've got friends. It's a shame we were out of touch so long.'

'Yes. These things happen.'

'Here – that husband of yours – is he mad or what?'

'I don't think he's mad, my dear,' Helen said with a short laugh. 'Why?'

'A stunner like you – he ought to be begging you to come back.'

'Good heavens. I'm no stunner.'

'Pull the other one. I always – wished I was like you.'

'Very flattering, but nonsense. Anyhow, one thing I can say is that no amount of begging on his part would be any use.'

'No? Good for you – it's his loss.'

'Not really. It was all a mistake. I never should have married him, that's all. I did him a wrong, in fact. Never mind.'

'How did you do him a wrong?'

'Marrying him when I didn't love him. I've tried to excuse myself by saying I didn't know what I was doing, but I think I did.'

'Richard always said you were the one person who always knew what they were doing. He thought the world of you.'

'Oh, don't talk rubbish, Stella, it was you he thought the world of,' Helen snapped. 'If you think I don't know that . . .'

'Helen?'

Helen shook her head, her hand clenched tight over her mouth.

'Oh . . .' Stella swallowed, her eyes widening. 'Oh . . . I never thought . . .'

'Sorry, sorry.' Helen drew herself up. 'I'll just make that tea now.'

'No, don't.' Stella tried to take her hand, but could not reach, and Helen did not move. 'Oh, Lord, Helen . . . you must have hated me.'

'Nonsense. Really, my dear, it's nothing, it's all in the past. I wonder where Kate can have got to . . .'

She got up quickly and went to the window, stood for some moments looking out. When at last she turned round Stella was watching her, white-faced, with a large tear running down her cheek.

'My dear – really I won't have you upset yourself like this. Come – sit back. Put this cushion behind your head—'

As Helen leaned over her Stella reached up and grabbed her hand convulsively.

'What a bloody awful thing life is! What a bloody – ow – stinking mess – I wish I'd never been born, the whole thing stinks . . .'

'Hush. Don't you dare say that. You're going to be all right and you're going to have a beautiful baby and I . . . I . . .'

'You're going to be his godmother,' Stella said, 'ain't you?'

For a moment Helen was open-mouthed; then said, her voice wavering, 'Oh, my dear, that's the nicest thing . . . I'm afraid I haven't got much of the fairy about me.'

Stella laughed; then gave a yell of pain, almost crushing Helen's fingers.

'Oh, Lord – is it getting worse?'

'It's bloody murder!'

'Hell, I don't know what to do – should you lie in bed? Could you get up the stairs if I helped you?'

'I dunno . . . Oh, Helen, I'm such a coward – I can't do this, not without him. I don't know what I'm going to do – he's gone, he's gone, and I can't – I can't bear it . . .'

Helen knelt beside her. 'I can't help you, dear. I can't do anything except tell you to – to hold the memory. Think of what you had – and never mind that it's past because if you can just hold it good and fast in your mind then it's always with you and never dies. I'll be truthful with you now, Stella. I did hate you, I think: resented you, certainly; because I loved Richard too and he wanted you. And all I could do was feed my resentment by telling myself that you wouldn't be happy, that it would never work. Even when my marriage, the marriage I rushed into out of spite, turned out to be pretty well as miserable as a marriage can be, I still tried to console myself with that. Charming of me, wasn't it? But it doesn't matter because now I know – I've seen – that I was wholly wrong. You and Richard did have happiness together – wonderful happiness: it's plain to anyone with eyes to see. And it wasn't a bad thing that you ever met, as I tried to convince myself and as that vicious mother of his said – it was a good thing, one of the fine and good things that happens in the world every now and then. And it's not over, because there's this baby to carry it on.'

'I know,' Stella sobbed, 'I know – but oh Helen, I told him I didn't want it. The day before he was killed – I got mad and told him I didn't want the baby. I should burn in hell for that, shouldn't I?'

'I don't believe in hell. And Richard didn't either. And I'll tell you something else he didn't believe. He didn't believe that people had to be consistent – all the same, through and through like the letters in a stick of Blackpool rock, never changing. He didn't believe that they always had to say exactly what they meant, or that they always had to be perfectly brave or perfectly truthful. He didn't see people that way. He saw what mattered about them. And what mattered about you was that you loved him. Do you think he ever doubted that?'

'No . . .'

'Then don't think about anything else. Oh dear – ' as Stella gave another yell – 'is it very bad?'

'Bloody hell! Bloody hell fire . . . !'

'Have a proper swear, my dear. Let it out. Don't mind me. After all – ' she squeezed Stella's hand – 'it's not as if we've any secrets from each other, is it?'

The door burst open to a windblown Kate. 'Bit of luck,' she

panted. 'The district nurse was in – she's on her way.' As she spoke a distant wailing could be heard carried on the buffeting wind: the siren.

'That's all I need,' Stella groaned. 'Goering for a ruddy midwife.'

## 2

The wind had dropped at last, and the All Clear had sounded some time ago, and the October afternoon was mellow in its dying. Stella lay in the big box bed, feeling as if she had just been through a free-for-all with a gang of six-foot bruisers. And, somehow, had won it.

The prize, her daughter, lay in the crook of her arm, exhausted too. It was no wonder, with all the screaming fuss she had kicked up when the nurse had coaxed her out into the world. Tremendous voice she had. Easy to tell who she took after in that. But she had taken her feed well and was now as good-natured as you pleased: she even seemed to have a sort of lazy smile on her face.

Easy to tell who she took after in that, too.

Stretching her legs down in the bed, Stella remembered something about that last night of Richard's life. The stroking. She had forgotten that till now: the way he had stroked her in this bed when she was on the verge of sleep, that wonderful soothing, warming caress of his. She had thought often of that night, but only of the words that had been spoken, the stupid, reckless words. Words, though, were not everything.

Drowsily she listened to the voices downstairs: Kate and Helen, seeing the district nurse out. They had been so good to her: she was wonderfully lucky to have such friends. If she hadn't decided to go with Uncle Will and Auntie Bea to the orchards, she would never have met them.

'And I wouldn't have met your dad,' she whispered to her daughter, 'and I wouldn't have had you.'

At the window the sky was ripe with evening. Stella shifted her baby gently and pointed at the glowing bars of soft cloud. 'That's where your dad is,' she said. 'And I'm here – and your aunties are downstairs; so everything's all right. Oh, I know it sounds daft saying your dad's up there. But – well, he could fly, you know. Yes, he could. Your dad could fly even before they taught him. And he took me up with him . . . I was very lucky. And I still am. So you see, my duck. Everything's all right.'